THE GOLDEN HILLS OF WESTRIA

DIANA L. PAXSON

A TOM DOHERTY ASSOCIATES BOOK
NEW YORK

This is a work of fiction. All the characters and events portrayed in this novel are either fictitious or are used fictitiously.

THE GOLDEN HILLS OF WESTRIA

Edited by David G. Hartwell

A Tor Book
Published by Tom Doherty Associates, LLC
175 Fifth Avenue
New York, NY 10010

www.tor.com

Tor® is a registered trademark of Tom Doherty Associates, LLC.

ISBN-13: 978-0-765-34784-8
ISBN-10: 0-765-34784-9

First Edition: February 2006
First Mass Market Edition: February 2007

Printed in the United States of America

0 9 8 7 6 5 4 3 2 1

✦ TO LOPPIE ✦

companion on my wanderings

CONTENTS

Prologue   1

1   Initiation   5
2   Grandfathers   24
3   Prey   42
4   The Lady of Pain and Roses   58
5   Guardians   74
6   Serpent of Fire   92
7   Sun and Wind   108
8   The Furnace   126
9   The Road to Elaya   143
10   Condor's Victory   159
11   Two of Swords   179
12   The Way to Westria   195
13   The Falling Tower   212
14   The Defender   229
15   Resistance   246
16   Point of Balance   264
17   Shadow Play   283
18   The Fortress Falls   300
19   Spring Storms   316
20   Veils of Light   335
21   Night Battles   352
22   The Song of the Spear   368
23   Test of Fire   388
24   Midsummer   406

The Covenant of Westria   421
People and Places   423
Afterword   431

NORMONTAINE

BARREN
LANDS

DESERET

○ Arena

Laurelynn

WESTRIA

ELAYA

AZTLAN

Los Leones ○

City of
Firebird ○

PROLOGUE

There is a land I know—with shining gold,
Its gentle hillsides glow. Now as of old,
It lies in dreaming peace.
There will I find release,
And all my sorrows cease when there I go. . . .

The singer's light tenor soared above the confusion of tongues in the dusty little town like a lark in the morning sky, ceased, and was replaced by the pure piping of a flute. It carried the melody to even higher spheres of sound so sweet that even men fresh off the Plains paused a moment to hear.

Everyone in town, it seemed, had turned out to greet the caravan. There were buckskin-clad tribesmen from the high plains who had come to trade buffalo robes, and farmers in faded cotton who scratched a living from the fields beside the river. They would have few coins with which to buy the luxuries the caravan had brought from the Iron Kingdom. It had been a dry year on the Plains. And roistering among them were the drovers from the caravan, drunk with the sights and smells of human habitation after the windy silences of the Sea of Grass.

A man paused to listen, and others, seeing the broad shoulders, the sword in its well-worn scabbard, and the grim, dark-skinned face, swallowed their curses and moved carefully around him. He scarcely noticed, although if he had thought about it, he would have been amused to realize that men still gave him a clear path. For a moment he was a boy again, listening to the birds that played above the rich fields by the great muddy river that was the lifeblood of the Empire of the Sun.

Then he shook his head and moved on. Beyond the wooden façades of the sod buildings he could see only the immensity of sun-bleached sky, as if the world ended at the outskirts of the town. In a way, he supposed, that was true. Except for the shallow meanderings of the Plateau River, edged with willow and the occasional cottonwood tree, there was an awful lot of nothing out there.

He licked dry lips and fingered the pouch at his belt, counting through the coins with which he had been paid off when the caravan arrived. Then he shook his head and continued his circuit of the square. That money had to last him until he found work again, and from the looks of Cottonwood, it might be awhile.

A wind-borne breath of sagebrush off the prairie brought momentary relief from the mingled scents of unswept refuse and unwashed humanity. It would be quiet out there, but no cooler, and at least they did not yet charge for a drink of water in the town.

His steps were already bringing him back toward the singer, who had started a new verse—

> *There is a land I know, where mountains high,*
> *Forever crowned with snow, against the sky,*
> *Keep watch above the land,*
> *Where trees immortal stand,*
> *And waves kiss golden sand, and soft winds blow.*

The singer's clothes were dusty too, but his brown hair curled vigorously, and there was a light in his eyes. Maybe his song refreshed him. As he lifted the flute again, the images the song had evoked blossomed in the minds of those who heard. The singer was surrounded by a circle of quiet, where men and women for a moment closed their eyes and dared to dream of a better place than this.

"He sings of paradise." The speaker was a woman, strongly built with a broad face reddened by the sun and a mane of golden hair going silver-gilt as she passed middle age. She wore a long robe that had once been white, and leaned on a staff—some kind of visionary preacher, no doubt. Strange new religions were always coming out of the Sea of Grass. It must be the way the land lay open to the sky, with nothing between a man and the Eye of God.

"Nay," said one of the townsmen. "He comes from somewhere to the west of here and sings of his home. But maybe when one is far away, everyone's home seems a paradise."

> *There is a land I know, by Guardians blessed,*
> *Where the sun dips low, and seeks her rest;*
> *Where man and beast are free,*
> *To live in harmony,*
> *Beside the peaceful sea, there I would go.*

"There I would go . . . ," repeated the woman. "Thus, all men dream."

"Sometimes we need dreams," the dark man said bitterly. "The caravaners promised me a way home, but they've paid me off with never an apology and left me stranded here. If I knew the way to such a place, I'd seek it. I have nowhere else to go."

"You have the bearing of a soldier. . . ." The woman's eyes fixed on his face and he suppressed an impulse to flinch. They were pale hazel, and curiously clear, as if only a lens for a light that burned within. When her gaze was fixed elsewhere, she was only a stout, aging woman, but there was something very compelling about those eyes.

"My name is Tadeo Marsh, and I was a general of the armies in the Empire of the Sun," he answered with a remnant of pride.

The woman nodded in understanding. Even here, men had heard about the terms the armored legions of the Iron

Kingdom had imposed on the Empire. Defeated commanders made convenient scapegoats, and the general had been lucky to escape with his hide.

"You are a man of courage and honor." Her gaze kindled. "I am called Mother Mahaliel, and there is a place for you among the Children of the Sun. Come and worship with us. We are humble folk, but you are welcome to share our meal. You will find us camped beneath the banner of the sun and serpent at the edge of town. . . ."

"If you take my advice, you'll stay away from the Suns, stranger," muttered the townsman. "They're a rabble of beggars and thieves who dance with rattlesnakes, and the sooner they're run out of town the better!"

"Thus do sinners always revile the Faithful!" Mother Mahaliel's eyes flashed. "The righteous man takes up the Serpent and is not harmed! Who among you will dare do the same? My followers have been wanderers since the Sun first filled me with His light and bade me proclaim His will, but I tell you, we will dwell in our paradise on this earth while you are still eating dust here!"

Her voice had a peculiar resonance that penetrated the babble of the marketplace, and men were turning to listen, beginning to mutter as they saw who it was. Someone spat, and another bent to pick up a stone, but the scorn in the woman's glance kept them at bay. A dozen white-clad men hurried into the square, the panic in their eyes turning to relief as they saw her, yet it was not their presence but something in the woman herself that kept her foes from following.

Not courage, Tadeo thought as the priestess stalked away, but rather a sublime conviction of invulnerability. He had known men like that in the army. Most of them were crazy, but some were heroes.

Was Mother Mahaliel a madwoman or a mystic? Perhaps he would go out to the camp of the Children of the Sun and see. For certain he would get no better offer here.

INITIATION

"Seeker, why have you come here?"

Sunlight blazed suddenly through the moving leaves, overwhelming sight, but the voice of the priest who guarded the Gate carried clearly. Sombra strained to hear the response of the red-headed boy who stood before it.

The late-summer sun released the sweet smell of ripe grass from the golden hills, though there was a brisk bite to the wind. The blue summit of the Lady Mountain rose above the trees, watching over the province of Seagate as she watched over the young people who had come here to seek initiation into Westria's mysteries.

Sombra repeated the words she knew he must be saying now—

"I come to seal myself to the Covenant of Westria."

They had drilled each other on the responses all the way from Seahold to the initiation grounds, using their anxiety to mask deeper fears.

"What is your name?" The voice of the warden came once more. Wind rustled the leaves of the live oaks and firs that grew among the laurel trees as if to whisper an answer.

Since his birth the boy had been called Phoenix, but here they all must leave their milk-names behind them. *Beyond those gates*, Sombra thought, *Phoenix will not be the son of*

*the king of Westria, and I will not be the granddaughter of
the sorcerer who tried to destroy him.*

But Sombra's *other* grandfather was Eric of Haven, Lord
Commander of Seagate, and her father was King Julian's
seneschal.

We carry our histories with us, she thought, *even here.*
She shivered, and told herself her chill came from the fog
bank that was rolling in from the sea.

Phoenix leaned forward to warm his hands at the campfire.
They had scarcely had time to stow their bedrolls in the
shelters and put on the anonymous tunics of undyed cotton
everyone wore here before the teaching began. It would
continue for the full month of the Retreat, except for the
hours each afternoon that were given over to exercise. For
those brought up on outlying holdings, who knew only the
rites by which their parents honored the spirits of their own
woods and fields, this intensive education might be necessary, but the story of how the sorcerer Caolin stole the Four
Jewels of Westria, and King Julian won them back again,
was part of his own family history.

"Take up a handful of earth. Hold it, feel its texture,
reach out to its energy . . . ," said the priestess. Her name
was Mistress Larissa, and her stocky body had the solid
strength of the earth she held.

Obediently he scooped up a little dust, then sat back,
shifting in a vain search for comfort. A folded cloak was
not much protection from the hard ground, but he had already overheard a few comments about spoiled princes. He
was surrounded by girls and boys with whom he had
played every summer on the docks of Seahold when Queen
Rana brought him to visit her kinfolk there.

They should have sent him to some remote gathering in
the Ramparts where no one knew him—but no, his father
had been kidnapped by slavers on *his* Retreat in those hills.
Julian would never have risked his only child there. Perhaps the southern part of Las Costas? But that was no good
either. King Julian took a personal interest in every corner

of his kingdom, and his family had accompanied him on too many of his journeys for his red-headed son to be anonymous in any part of the land. As it was, Phoenix had put off facing this test until he was nearly eighteen, when he could do it the same year as Sombra, who was a year younger than he.

"Live in this moment," said Mistress Larissa. "This earth you hold is the ground of being, just as the radiance beyond all understanding is manifest in the simple light of day. There is no need to turn from the world to search for meaning. The Creator is not separate from her Creation. Look for Spirit *here,* in the fire, in the wind and water, in a single grain of sand—" She opened her hand and a little wind set the dust swirling to mingle with the smoke from the fire. "Here, with the holy earth of Westria, is where it all begins."

"Do you mean that there is no life beyond this one?" asked a fisherman's son.

"I mean that the Otherworld is *in* this one, as our spirits are in our bodies, for those who have eyes to see."

"But we die, and our bodies decay," said the boy.

"The tide recedes, but it always returns," said the priestess. "Everything changes, but nothing is lost. When you leave this gathering your names will be changed, though your bodies seem the same. As you grow older, both body and spirit will grow and change, and yet there is something that endures through all the transformations. That is the paradox and the mystery."

Phoenix sighed. Sometimes he felt as if his body were the only thing that *did* stay the same, while his spirit hid behind the masks that others expected to see.

"Words cannot convey this meaning," she said sharply as someone giggled in the shadows. "It is something you must *know.* Look into the fire!" The sudden note of command compelled attention. There was no sound but the crackling of the flames.

"Look into the light. . . ." The voice of the priestess modulated to a hypnotic murmur. "Listen to the voice of the fire and the wind in the trees. . . . Feel your weight supported by the earth. . . . Live in this moment, this point of time that is all time. This, *this* is reality. . . ."

For a moment, then, the light surrounded and consumed him. He was all things; he was nothing; he knew eternity. And then someone gasped and laughed, and he was jerked back to ordinary reality. Heart thudding, he gazed around the circle. Some were stirring and looking about, while others appeared to have gone to sleep. But as the flames flared, he saw Sombra sitting at the edge of the circle, her soft hair a cloud of shadow around a face smoothed to an incandescent purity by trance. Her dark eyes, half concealed by thick lashes, looked at—no, *through*—the fire.

She is there, he thought. *Only a few words were enough for her to reach the place of vision . . . and stay. I am going to fail my testing and shame my father. She should have been heir to the Jewels of Westria, not me.*

Mistress Larissa had resumed her lecture, but Phoenix did not hear her. He gazed across the fire at Sombra, his spirit straining to get free.

———————

"Sombra! There you are!" Phoenix sounded as if he had been running.

Sombra was already turning. She had felt his presence even before he called. The girls with whom she was sitting giggled, but Sombra frowned. Didn't he know how quickly gossip could grow? Already she had heard her own name linked with his—just because they had been childhood friends. To single her out this way would only add fuel to the fire.

To be sure, he looked like a flame himself in the white tunic the boys wore on this night when they all claimed their status as men and women. As she greeted him, she straightened the folds of her own black gown. *We are Fire and Smoke,* she thought, *Sunlight and Shadow . . . but after my vigil I will have another name!*

"Maidens, my apologies for taking this fair flower from among you—" Phoenix swept a bow that would have suited his father's court, and Sombra rolled her eyes.

"Fix, be serious!" Deliberately she called him by the nickname that was all she had been able to manage as a child.

"I am serious—" Now she could see the worry in his blue eyes. "I have to talk to you!"

Still scowling, she let him lead her away from the campfire and past the dancers who circled it. Behind her, she could hear the other girls whispering, and then laughter. Drums throbbed like a heartbeat, vibrating through the soil.

"What's wrong?"

"It's what will be wrong if you don't help. Sombra, come with me up onto the hill!"

For a moment she simply stared at him. It was inevitable, when this many young people were thrown so closely together, that some would pair off. The night of the dance was the traditional time for them to consummate their bonding. Some couples had left already, hand in hand.

"Are you mad? It would be like sleeping with my brother!"

"I doubt that." Phoenix grinned. "I'm pretty sure that Lenart likes boys. But I didn't mean that we should actually *do* anything. That girl from Seahold is after me, and there's one from across the Bay right behind her, and my father will kill me if I get involved."

"I had no idea you were such a stallion!" Sombra said scornfully, but in fact she believed him, having seen how girls fluttered when they realized he was the son of the king.

"They want my seed, not me." He looked over his shoulder at the blond girl who was pushing through the dancers, and seized Sombra's hand. "Come *on*!"

"Would it be such a chore to make her happy?" she said breathlessly as they halted in the shadow of a fir tree. "You wouldn't have to—you know. . . ." The lessons they had just received had included some very explicit instruction on how to achieve pleasure without pregnancy.

"I suppose not—" He tried to hide behind her, not entirely successfully, as his last growth spurt had left him four inches taller than she. "If you must know, I don't want my first time to be with someone who looks at me as if I were a side of beef in the market square!"

Sombra's eyes widened. She had assumed that with all his opportunities, Phoenix would have found someone to initiate him into those other mysteries of adulthood before now; but as she opened her awareness to touch his, she sensed that what he was saying was true.

"Unless—oh, I'm sorry, Sombra—was there someone *you* were waiting for?"

"No, Fix," she said gently. "Come on, little virgin, you'll be safe with me. . . ."

———

Sombra leaned back against the rock and felt her heartbeat slow. Above them rose the peak of the mountain; to the west, the young moon was sinking toward the sea. The sky was a field full of stars.

"I suppose I should thank you," she said finally. "This is certainly better than listening to gossip by the fire."

Phoenix snorted. In the starlight his bright hair was a banked flame. "Aside from gossip, has this month taught you what you wanted to know?"

"My father was an adept before he was seneschal, and yours is the Jewel-Lord. I doubt that there was much in the teaching that we have not heard debated over the breakfast table since we were infants. But if we are going to serve ordinary people, we will have to understand what they hope, and fear, and know."

"So you still mean to go to the College of the Wise?"

"Of course. But you'll be there too, won't you, at least for a while?" It was usual for princes to take an ordinary priest's training, to prepare them to bear the Jewels.

"By the time they send me, you will probably be halfway to Awahna. At least you have a goal! What is there for me but to wait for a day I hope will never come?"

"You love your father. . . ."

"Of course!" he exclaimed, and then, "I don't know. Do you love this mountain, or the moon? They are there, and you cannot imagine life without them. To imagine trying to *be* them is even harder. When the king looks at me, we are both wondering if I will ever be fit to fill his shoes. I don't think we *can* see each other simply as father and son. At least you—"

"On those intervals when she is not running Westria's navy, my mother looks at all her children as if she is not quite sure where we came from," Sombra said abruptly. "My father is kind to me, but Westria has eaten his life too. I have always known that I will have to find my own path, and so will you!"

Phoenix sighed. "No, you don't. You think that going to the College will solve your problems. But some things that don't get talked about over your breakfast table may get discussed at mine. The College was fine when the Master of the Junipers was running it, but they have had two Heads since he went away, and this new man, Master Granite, seems more concerned with codifying rules than nurturing souls."

"If I don't learn from them, I will learn despite them, but I *will* learn!"

"I envy your certainty. . . ."

She glared at him. "Look, Phoenix, nobody gets to choose the life she's born to, but we do choose how we live!"

"Yes, mistress—" He grinned with the swift change of mood she remembered. "So tell me, wise one, what mysteries did they reveal to you girls while we were being taught separately these past few days?"

Sombra laughed. Most Westrians grew up on farms and were well aware of the mechanics of sex by the time they came for initiation. The teaching had focused on the more esoteric means by which man and wife might act as priest and priestess to each other and to their land. But a few of the details had been . . . surprising. . . . She could not help wondering if what they told the boys about women was the same.

Comparing notes was enough to set both of them to giggling, but presently the conversation slowed. The moon had disappeared into the fog bank that lay over the ocean. It was very still. Rousing, Sombra was about to suggest that they might safely make their way back to the shelters when she realized that Phoenix was asleep, leaning awkwardly against the stone.

"It's time we got you to bed. . . ." As she touched him he fell over into her lap, and when she tried to move him he only burrowed more comfortably against her, mumbling incoherently. As children they had joked that once Fix was properly asleep, not even a second Cataclysm would awaken him.

Her own position was not too uncomfortable, even with his weight across her thighs. *I suppose I might treat this as the first night of my vigil,* she told herself, *even though I am not exactly alone.* She looked down at him with a smile. Leached of color by the starlight, and with all the swift changes of expression smoothed away, the strong bones of his face showed clearly, and for the first time she could see a resemblance to the king. Was his father's strength hidden there as well?

When they were children she had been able to reach out and touch his dreams. Carefully she stroked a tumbled curl back from his broad brow. At the touch, he stirred a little, and still sleeping, smiled with a piercing sweetness that was entirely his own.

For a moment her heart stilled.

Abruptly she was a child once more. Her brother had been teasing her, and Phoenix had come to her defense like the rising sun chasing the clouds away. At the age of three, her heart had been won by that smile, and now, as it began to beat again, she realized with an intensity that bordered on pain that she loved him still. Her entire body trembled with awareness of his. Instinctively she sought to stifle her emotion, for if he woke, her mind would be open to his, and he would know.

Sleep, my beloved, Sombra thought as the strong curls sprang back beneath her trembling fingers. *Be still.* Her destiny waited in the sacred valley of Awahna, and though the Masters of the College were free to form liaisons, any relationship must always take second place to the work to which they were called. She had seen her father torn between the demands of the College, his family, and Westria, but her mother had the comfort of a vocation of her own. The king of Westria needed a queen who would be his partner and support in all things. And Phoenix, beloved, brilliant, and vulnerable as she knew him to be, deserved a wife who could love him heart-whole.

But if she never held him again, at least she had been given this moment in which he was all her own. For this one night, she could hold him, memorizing the shape of each limb, the scent of his skin, the warm weight of him in her arms, as the stars wheeled overhead and the land of Westria turned toward dawn.

Even before they took off the blindfold, Phoenix recognized the powdery scent of redwood. He took a careful breath, trying to hide his fear. The initiates were not supposed to know where they were being taken for their vigils, but as soon as he felt the horse begin to go downhill, Phoenix had suspected that they were carrying him to the Sacred Grove.

It was not fair! he thought, fighting a sneeze. If he ever became king the Trees would have him in the end, as they had received the bones of all the rulers of Westria. Why must he endure the little death of initiation here as well?

Your father was buried in the Wood, and came back to his body again . . . , said a voice within. It sounded like his mother, who had told him how they had buried Julian after Caolin struck him down. She had found him walking in the Sacred Wood with the earth of the grave still on his shoulders, eyes dazzled by the first light of Midwinter Day. The boy's mind-voice often sounded like someone else—one of his parents or the many other teachers with whom they had burdened him. Those who called him heedless had no idea how hard it was to ignore them. Sometimes Phoenix got into trouble because it was the only way he could claim a separate existence at all.

The forest floor here was deeply covered by fallen needles, and as his escort left him, the sound of hooves faded quickly. They had brought him all the way down to the narrow valley where the stream sang a soft accompaniment to the whispering of the trees. Ruddy, soft-barked trunks strained toward the forest canopy, their foliage filtering the sunlight in tones of gold and green. There were trees in this wood that had sprouted before the Cataclysm. Their patience spanned centuries. Phoenix had only to endure three days.

He was not imprisoned here. He could hike uphill to the encampment, or follow the stream to reach the edge of the wood. But the only thing he feared more than the ghosts of his family was facing its living members if he ran away.

For some, to be left in the wilderness, alone and fasting, was ordeal enough. But their teachers had spoken truth—the worst dangers were the demons they brought with them. The Initiation Retreat was supposed to be a time of spiritual transformation, but there were always stories, whispered at night in the tents when the teachers had left them, about people who had gone mad on their vision quests, or killed themselves, or simply disappeared.

I will survive this . . . , he promised himself as he picked up his water bottle and his bedroll. *I will not give in to my fear. . . .*

When Sombra pulled the blindfold from her own eyes, she found herself in a small meadow on the western shoulder of the mountain. Below, a tangle of fir and spruce and cedar fell away in waves of dark green to the wrinkled blue of the sea. The fog bank had drawn back enough for her to see the Far Alone Islands. Above, a pair of small hawks sported with the wind, half-closing their wings to let the breeze tumble them, feathers suddenly blazing red as they tipped back toward the sun. They called, four cheerful chirps repeating as they chased each other in circles up the sky. The flash of their wings reminded her of Phoenix, and she tried to thrust the memory away.

She had left him at dawn, while he still lay sleeping. Their ways must now lie apart, and whatever challenge this vigil might bring would be faced alone. Setting down her bedroll and water bottle, she began to pace around the meadow, consecrating it to her purpose here.

From his bedroll, Phoenix glimpsed parts of constellations winking in and out as branches stirred in the wind. *Like my life,* he thought, gazing upward, *a confusion of fragments.* For a moment he entertained an image of the consternation if he should declare himself nameless, unworthy not only of the Jewels, but of citizenship in Westria.

But he knew he would not do it. Initiates were never asked to describe their visions. Most had decided on their adult names years ago. Many took a name that had been handed down in the family, or called themselves after some figure of legend. Julian, still ignorant of his true parentage, had yet dared to claim the name of the first king to wield the four elemental Jewels of Westria, the founder of House Starbairn.

Phoenix would just have to think of something. After all, they could not call him "Hey, you—" in the unlikely event he ever got a chance to reign.

That prospect was even more terrifying. He told himself that his father was going to live forever, and if Phoenix was lucky, no one would ever know that no vision had come to the heir of Westria.

He had arranged his gear within the shelter of a redwood whose center had been blasted by some ancient storm. The outer bark had survived, and green branches flourished above. On the side where the trunk was gone, saplings rose from the ashes. It was all very inspirational, he supposed, but he sympathized with the young shoots, fighting for light and space in the shadow of a mighty sire.

His eyelids grew heavy, and he turned onto his side. Here among the dry needles, there was nothing to attract a night-prowling raccoon or bobcat; aside from a few spiders, even insects took little interest in the trees. The rustle of wind-stirred branches was a lullaby that merged gradually into whispered words.

"So this is the sapling—" The voice was deep, as if it came from something almost too huge for words.

"He is not much like his father." The other speaker sounded female, her tones sweet and low.

"He has his grandfather's eyes," the first voice replied. *"It remains to be seen whether he has his soul."*

Phoenix struggled to open his eyes. There seemed to be more trees around than he remembered, and surely there had been no madrones in the redwood grove. He blinked, sure for a moment that he saw the form of a woman outlined in light instead of a tree. His vision grew clearer; he made out graceful, ruddy-skinned limbs and a garment of leaves. Her head was covered with curls of bark instead of hair. Her eyes were green; deep as forest pools. For a moment they met his; then he sank into their depths, sliding back toward sleep.

"The seed does not fall far from the tree," said the deeper voice as oblivion took the boy once more, *"but each sapling must endure different seasons. We cannot yet see how this one will grow. . . ."*

———◆———

Sombra slept deeply, wearied by her vigil the night before. When she opened her eyes, the meadow was filled with golden light. Throughout that day, it was the light that dominated her awareness, glowing through the leaves and in the grass, filling the great bowl of the sky.

The preparation for their initiation had focused on the four elements, the powers on whose interaction depended the life of the land. By means of the Four Jewels, the rulers of Westria maintained the balance between them. The lore taught at the Retreat was all that most people needed to know to live in harmony with the spirits with whom they shared the land. But from her father, Sombra knew that the realms ruled by Earth, Water, Air, and Fire were only the foundation of a greater structure, the trunk and first branches of a Tree that stretched toward infinity.

And the realm above them was ruled by the sun, the life-giving light of the world who represented both sacrifice and sovereignty. Sombra demanded more than a mere balancing of the elements. If she could, in this vigil, banish the shadows from her soul, she might become a vessel for that light, and traverse the realms of the spirit as her mother sailed the trackless seas.

When she was an infant they had called her Sombra—Shadow—because of the cloud of dark hair she had inherited from her Elayan grandmother along with her golden skin. She had always wondered whether they had been thinking of her grandfather as well—whether Caolin's evil might give another meaning to her name. Perhaps, Sombra told herself, she was foolish to worry. Perhaps everyone found it difficult to believe in their own goodness. But it was not evil that she feared, or at least not evil intent. What haunted her was a fear of her own power.

Light . . . and dark . . . were they truly twinned?

She found herself humming and realized it was a song her father had taught her, from one of the rituals at the College of the Wise.

> *By wandering ways we seek to gaze,*
> *Upon the Light,*
> *Though shadows fall, still comes the call,*
> *And hope burns bright.*
> *The pilgrim path seems endless,*
> *Yet we walk the way,*
> *And know the darkness deepens,*
> *Just before the day.*

I am following the Pilgrim Path . . . , she thought then. *This vigil is its beginning. I will prove myself worthy to face the Light.* She stripped off her robe and lay down in the meadow, seeing the red glow of the sun through her closed eyelids, absorbing that radiance through every pore.

By day, the Sacred Wood was a pleasant place. The great trees shielded Phoenix from the sun. He could wade in the clear stream where the fingerling trout and salmon darted

away from his shadow, and watch the deer step delicately
from the shadows of the trees. Ravens called higher up on
the mountain, and from time to time a buzzard slid across
the fragment of blue that was all he could see of the sky.
Where sunlight shafted through the forest, at times he
thought he saw something more; around the most vigorous
plants shimmered a luminous shadow. Was it lack of food
or his vision of the night before that made him think he was
seeing another reality?

When night fell, he was sure of it, as trees that had
drowsed through the long summer day, woke, whispering.
To his parents, the Guardians of Westria were old familiar
friends. He wished he could be as certain of their blessings. Still, if what he had glimpsed the first night had been
truth, the Lord of the Trees had now inspected him and
might be expected to leave him in peace hereafter.

For what seemed a long time he lay wakeful, while the
waxing moon crossed his circle of sky and disappeared.
That day he had gone looking for the graves of his ancestors, but the lords of Westria, who in life were honored by
all, in death were wrapped in cotton shrouds and laid in un-
marked graves. Even now he might be resting above his
grandfather's bones.

He was still wondering when the whisper of wind
worked its magic and he moved from musing to dream. At
first he saw only a confusion of images—he was marching
through a dry land, endlessly, it seemed, until another sequence replaced that vision with one in which he fought a
succession of faceless enemies. People and places flickered by. He recognized none of them, but he knew he was
searching endlessly for something infinitely precious that
he had forgotten or lost.

It was almost with relief that he recognized the confused
roar in which the clangor of metal on metal mingled with
cries of pain as the clamor of a battlefield. The fighting was
fiercest in the center, where foes who fought beneath the
banner of a serpent-circled sun threatened a man whose
shield bore the star of the royal house on a field of blue.

"Westria, to me!" came the cry.

"Father!" Phoenix cried, desperate to go to his aid. And even as he spoke, he realized that he had somehow acquired armor and a sword. But as he battered his way through the enemy, he saw that this man lacked the heavy shoulders that marked King Julian. But his small frame was all muscle, and his sword darted in and out like a silver flame.

With a last effort Phoenix reached his side.

"Now that we are together, who can stand against us?" laughed the king. At the sound, Phoenix felt his spirit ignite with the joy of battle, all his fears consumed by that flame.

And presently their foes retreated and they stood victorious upon the field. As the king sighed and pulled off his helm, Phoenix saw that his hair was dark like Julian's, but his eyes were as deeply blue as the boy's own.

"You are King Jehan—" Phoenix recognized the doomed ruler he had seen in a portrait in Laurelynn, the grandfather who had died before his own son was born, leaving his pregnant wife alone. "What are you doing here?"

Some of the laughter left the king's eyes. "Defending Westria, as in life I failed to do—"

"But why have you come to me?" said Phoenix as the figure of the king began to fade.

"Son of Julian," came the king's reply, "redeem my name!"

⟞⟝

For Sombra, the third night was the hardest. Her enthusiasm—or perhaps her pride—had betrayed her, and her skin was still hot and tender enough to make the touch of her robe an agony, though her sunburn did not keep her from shivering once the temperature began to fall.

Kept wakeful by her discomfort, she started at every night noise. The deer that drifted across the meadow were quiet, but from among the trees came the sound of snarling—raccoons, perhaps, or the gray foxes that haunted the higher slopes. There were other shapes, too, more sensed than seen—the spirits that lived on the peak, moving through their domain.

She listened to her stomach growl and consoled herself with the thought of the many others who had kept vigil here. Queen Faris herself had slept out on this mountain before her wedding to King Jehan and initiation to the Jewels. What must she have felt? What would Phoenix feel when his turn came at last?

The night held clear, and she saw that she had been wrong to worship the sunlight so completely, for the heavens were like a bowl full of stars. Old tales held that each of those twinkling lights was another sun, though how anyone knew for sure she could not tell. And yet it was from the stars, they said, that a spirit had come and lain with the priestess who became the first Mistress of the Jewels. His morning gift to her was the Wind Crystal, and by its power she created the other three. His other gift had been a son, who became the first King Julian and used those Jewels to defeat the sorcerers whose wars threatened to bring a second Cataclysm.

Perhaps she should seek her name from the stars that shone so sweetly against the darkness. Wavering between sleep and waking, it seemed to her that they were pulsing in time to her heartbeat. Whatever her Name might be, it should hold light. Above the trees she glimpsed the ruddy flicker of the red planet who brings war. Overhead, Jupiter reigned like an orb of gold. But all of them shone. She lay upon the cool grass and gazed up at the white road that crossed the heavens, trying out different words for that radiance until her eyes closed at last.

She was awakened by the damp kiss of the wind. The great slow-motion wave of the fog was rolling in from the sea. Shivering, she watched as it broke against the slope of the mountain and divided, covering everything below the peak with a pale shroud. She huddled into her blankets, and this time, as sleep took her, she dreamed of burning houses, weeping children, and a horde of white-clad warriors who swept across the land. She reached deeper, and suddenly the power within her blazed forth and she found herself riding a dragon of crystal that surged through the skies. At the sight, the battling hosts, both friend and foe, reeled back, overwhelmed by her light.

Luz—your name is Luz! a clear voice cried.

———

Phoenix tried to spend most of the last day of his vigil sleeping. If he could watch through the night, perhaps he could avoid more dreams. A little past midnight he glimpsed the first tendrils of the incoming fog as a blurring of the stars. But as the temperature dropped, the mist thickened, settling like a thick gray blanket across the trees. Phoenix fought the temptation to take out the flint and steel they had left him to make an emergency signal and light a fire.

It had always been dark beneath the branches, but now the blackness was absolute, denying even the possibility of light. Fire, sun, stars—all were delusions. Even thought became difficult, deadened by that featureless pall. It was said that his father had learned to see through the dark when he was trapped underground, but his father had had the Earthstone.

I have nothing! he gibbered. *You left me alone in the dark!* A fragment of awareness wondered where and when he had been so abandoned, but he could only remember the scent of dank earth, cold and slippery beneath his small fingers, and the total lack of light. *I am not me . . . I am not here . . .* , his spirit cried, but there was nowhere to go.

Phoenix gripped the leafmold on which he lay until the small needles bit into his skin, seeking in touch to compensate for the lost sense of sight as he had done so long ago, retreating until at last he sensed that someone was with him, and recognized it as the spirit he had encountered the night before.

"Is it you, Grandfather? Why are you haunting me?"

"Because you need me, and I need you . . . to redeem my name. . . ."

With a sigh of relief, Phoenix retreated into the dream.

Growing up in the shadow of Julian's victories, he had never thought much about the father Julian himself had never known. It was a comfort to realize that not all of Westria's kings had lived up to that impossible standard.

"If I tell you to leave me, will you go?"

"I cannot help you against your will," the other answered patiently. "You must choose your own allies, but to rule them you need me."

This was crazy. Other people had visions of animal spirits or the Guardians during their vigils, not dead grandfathers. He could hide this haunting from his parents, but he winced at the thought of the act he would have to put on to keep it from Sombra. He would not trouble her bright spirit with his darkness. And yet, perhaps just because King Jehan had not been perfect, his presence brought comfort.

"Very well—" Phoenix said at last. "It is a bargain. Watch over me, and I will take your name. . . ."

The sense of approval grew stronger. Was the shadow passing from his spirit? Awareness of his body was returning, and with it his senses. He opened his eyes and saw the mists beginning to brighten with the approach of day.

———◆———

Sombra was no more. Luz stood blinking in the sunlight, her spirit still resonating with the words of the Covenant of Westria to which she had just sworn and the single syllable that was now her name. All around her, those who had gone through the gate of the Retreat as children were being welcomed back by their families as citizens of Westria. From somewhere in the tumult she heard her father calling her new name, but she was looking for the flash of copper hair that would lead her to Johan, or had the priest meant to say "Jehan"? It had not been clear.

Why had he chosen that name? What visions had come to him? She had tried to speak with him when they were brought back from their vigils, but boys and girls had been hustled off to their separate tents to bathe and dress in new tunics of green. And then they were being taken one by one to the sanctuary to be blessed by each element in turn. It was as close as most of them would ever come to direct experience of the powers focused in the four elemental Jewels that were wielded by the king. Was that what had put the cloud in Johan's blue eyes?

"Luz! Where are you?"

That bellow surely belonged to her brother Lenart. She turned and saw his fair head bobbing above the crowd—oh, Guardians, the whole family was here! Behind Lenart she could see her sister Bera, her frizzy hair sparking with garnet highlights in the sun. And there were her grandparents and her father. Master Frederic's arm was around a tall woman with skin tanned to a deep brown and hair bleached silver as it always was when the Lady Ardra came home from the sea.

"Mother! I didn't think you would be back in time!" Luz smiled through sudden tears as her family surrounded her.

"You must thank Sea Mother, who sent us kind winds—" Ardra gave her a quick hug and drew back to let the rest of the family in. After three days alone on the mountain, the babble of congratulation did not seem quite real.

"Where is—the prince?" It would take time to get used to his new name.

Lenart pointed, and she saw another cluster of people, not so numerous as her own, but more richly dressed. There was Queen Rana's red head, and next to her that of her son.

"Wait for me a moment. I wanted to say goodbye—"

Ignoring her sister's raised eyebrow, Luz started toward them, her relations trailing behind her. The queen smiled a welcome, and the royal family and her own melded into a single chattering mob.

"I see you survived—" Luz felt her smile fade as she realized that the prince was the only one who was silent. She pushed her way to his side. "Are you all right?"

"What could hurt me, protected as I was by my ancestors' bones?" Johan gave her the same armored smile she had seen him wear at Court functions when he had endured to the point of boredom and beyond.

Was something wrong, or was it just that he had finally

begun to accept his destiny? Luz told herself that she should have expected it. He was the heir of Westria, and she was going to the College of the Wise.

"What indeed, my lord," she answered, summoning up the pride to mirror that smile. Only four days ago he had been as close as her own heartbeat. It was bewildering to recognize the pain of loss at a moment when she had expected to feel only joy.

✤ 2 ✤

GRANDFATHERS

"I summon Johan Starbairn to the mark—" The herald who was announcing the archery competition pitched his voice to carry over the babble of the crowd.

Laurelynn was overflowing with people who had come in for the Autumn Sessions of the Council of Westria. During King Julian's reign, this twice-yearly conclave of those who ruled the country had become an excuse for a festival, with entertainments and a fair to amuse their families while the landholders were in council, and athletic competitions for their offspring.

Jo picked up his bow and quiver and made his way past the other contestants toward the mark below the banner pole. A murmur of interest followed his progress. Even if his red hair had not been known throughout the kingdom, folk would have recognized the blue tunic with the silver star of his house on the shoulder. Automatically he held his head high. Since babyhood he had been taught to walk like a prince even when he did not feel like one, but today it was easy. He had always liked archery and expected to do well. Even the awareness that his father was one of the people observing him so closely could not disturb him now.

But he did wonder if the king had deliberately scheduled the archery competition for the day before the actual opening of the Council so that he could be here. Since Jo returned from his initiation, his father had been making opportunities for them to be together. It was a little unnerving, really, to be the focus of Julian's attention, as if he had looked up to find that the Red Mountain had eyes and was watching him. His father had that same quality of assured and uncompromising identity.

The butts were set up in the old archery range beside the orchard, at the end of a long lawn that sloped down to the small lake in the center of the island on which the city was built, where any arrows that missed both the targets and the wall behind them would fall among the reeds rather than the crowd. Jo took a deep breath, his narrowing awareness noting and releasing the blue water, the rose brick walls of the palace beyond it, the line of geese arrowing across the pale autumn sky. Above him flapped a banner with the arms of the city, a red castle wreathed in laurels upon a white ground, its blazon repeated on the tabard of the girl who was fixing a fresh target to the straw.

He nocked his first arrow loosely, waiting until she had gotten back to the shelter of the stands. His breathing slowed as he focused on the bull's-eye eighty paces away. Then, in a single smooth movement, he brought up the bow with his left arm as his right bent to draw back the string. He *was* the bow, as he was the arrow's swift flight, singing through the air to its goal. He knew before it struck that it would hit the center, and turned, smiling, to acknowledge the applause.

Jo's next four shots were almost as good, and he had reason to grin as he strode back to the table where the contestants could refresh themselves with cheese tarts and lemonade. He was not the only lord's heir to reach the final stage of this competition. Alaric of the Corona, a big, cheerful young man with his family's yellow hair, was shooting now, complaining that he was more accustomed to aiming at a deer's smooth hide than this bright target, every time one of his arrows went awry.

Lord Alexander of Las Costas was waiting with his daughter Carola, who at thirty was the oldest of those entered in this division. People said she took after her grandfather Brian, both in size and in pride. Her young son Badger, who was running along the shore and waving his arms to scare the geese, was merely a brat.

"Good shooting!" One of the boys Jo practiced with clapped him on the arm, and the prince grinned. "We'll show those country folk how it's done!" A girl and two other lads joined him, critiquing the form of the archer who followed Alaric in tones that earned them disapproving glances from those who stood near.

Certainly Lady Carola heard. Jo saw her speak to her father, who turned to see. As Alexander's glance fell on the prince, his usual hauteur sharpened into something more personal. Jo felt the polite mask he wore at official functions slide into place. Though the Lord Commander of Las Costas always treated the king with wary courtesy, Jo knew there was some kind of history between this man and his father. *But he feels safe in showing his resentment to me,* thought the prince. *I'll have to watch those two if I come to the throne. . . .*

He thrust the possibility that he would ever have to take his father's place into the darkness where he kept everything that was too painful to contemplate and turned his attention to the shooting again. There was such beauty in the smooth, focused movement, the harmonic lift and flex of the bow. He wondered what it would be like to feel so—*singular*—always. He had thought that after his vigil he would be certain of his own identity, but when he announced his chosen name at the initiation ceremony, the royal "Jehan" had come out "Johan," and what seemed to be left as people started using it was this diminished "Jo." *But Prince Johan is real, and I will prove it today!*

And then it was his turn once more. Jo was rather touched by the enthusiasm with which his friends cheered him. They could be a rowdy bunch, but all they asked of him was his company. As he stepped up to the mark, he glanced back to the shaded stand where his parents were watching. His mother's smile was always warming; his father's—unexpectedly proud. *I'll win this for you!* Jo responded with his most brilliant grin.

A sudden gust off the lake spoiled his first shot, despite his resolution, but the next three were in or close to the gold. He walked away not too displeased with his performance. He was still in the top third, anyhow, and that would qualify him for the final round.

Jo was not given long to get nervous. Alaric of the Corona was out, but Lady Carola was still a contender, along with a girl from Rivered and two young men who were in the king's guard. *So my father has three chances to come out a winner.* He clapped loudly when one of the guardsmen scored. But he had to admit that Carola had also done well. He approached his own final turn with a tempered determination, inspecting his arrows minutely, and wetting a finger to test the wind.

He set his feet with particular care, taking a moment to send his awareness down through the soil. He had been blessed by the Four Jewels of Westria when he received his milk-name, and even without the initiation of a Master of the Jewels, his connection to the elements was strong enough for him to feel a moment of union with the earth on which he stood, the waters that surrounded it, the wind that lifted his bright hair, and the fire of life within. The target before him was part of that whole. He drew and released, knowing that the arrow would speed to its goal, and a second time, a third, and again.

When he came to himself once more, everyone was cheering. The heart of the target was a blur of blue; all four arrows had hit the bull's-eye and only the feathers could be seen. Glowing with the certainty of victory, he stood aside for Carola to take her turn.

The prizes would be given at the evening's feasting, but everyone knew that the prince had won. The king pushed through the crowd toward him. In all that babble of congratulation, the only sour note came from the Las Costas contingent, but it fixed Jo's attention.

"Oh, yes, it was a pretty performance!" Carola was

sneering now. Her tone sharpened when she realized he was listening. "But what challenge is it to pink a target whose distance is known that will not run away? For *real* shooting, you need a battle, or the hunting field."

"Do you think I cannot do it?" Stung, Jo snatched an arrow and fitted it to his bow. Badger had startled another flock of geese; Jo's eye followed the flock's explosion into the air. He fixed on a fine gander and in the same moment loosed the arrow, watching its singing arc intersect with the bird's soaring flight. Harmony broken, the goose fell.

Steely fingers closed on Jo's arm. He turned around, his triumph abruptly extinguished as his father tore the bow from his grasp.

"What were you thinking, or was that just the impulse of a child?" Everyone was looking at them, even though the king kept his voice low. "Have you so quickly forgotten the Covenant you swore? 'I will take no life without need!' We already had meat enough for the festival."

"The Lady Carola—" Jo began, but his father's dark eyes were cold.

"—is not the heir of Westria! Lucas Buzzardmoon has just sent me proof of a gang who are trapping wildcats to export their pelts. I will have to exile them. What should I do with you? You should be setting the example here!" At that, Julian mastered himself, let go, and turned his back on his son.

Jo picked up the bow, aware that he could not hide his own sudden pallor. As others came up with questions or sympathy, he tried to smile.

They served up the goose at that evening's feast—once the bird had been slain, to have wasted the meat would have added to the sin. But Jo could not force any of it down.

The tea gleamed amber in the morning sunlight as Rana filled a cup and handed it to Lady Rosemary. She had taken a pot to Jo before joining Lord Eric, his wife, and Julian on the terrace that overlooked the lake, but to judge by the reek of spilled wine, it would be stone cold before he

was capable of drinking any. A wall blocked her sight of
the archery range, but not, alas, her memory of Jo's flawed
victory.

"Both my granddaughter and your son came safely home
from their vigils," said the older woman with a smile. "I
told you there was no need to be anxious, but mothers always worry so."

Rana managed an answering smile. It had become a
family tradition to invite the Lord Commander of Seagate
and his wife to breakfast when they were in town for the
Council, but it was a strain to keep the conversation going
when what she really wanted was to talk to Julian.

"And no surprises," said Eric. "Not like *your* initiation,
Julian! You got the best of the slavers who carried you off,
but the trade still flourishes in Arena."

"What do you expect?" snapped Rosemary. "They know
themselves safe beyond our borders. The only way to stop
those vermin is to burn out their nest."

Julian shook his head. "A return raid in force is one
thing, but we cannot support the army we'd need to keep
the peace in the Barren Lands as well as Westria! Elaya is
too preoccupied with her own dynastic struggles to make
any trouble, and Normontaine has always been our friend.
I would rather spend my energy making Westria a prosper-
ous, peaceful land than fighting our neighbors. Caolin gave
us enough of that to last me a lifetime!"

"Of course," Eric sighed. "Folk are right to call this the
Golden Age of the Golden Land. I suppose that is why I
am worrying. We have had it too easy, for too long. Perhaps I am feeling unbalanced because I have just realized
that my youngest grandchild is almost grown."

He reached for another scone and his wife snatched the
basket away. The Lord Commander of Seagate was now a
vigorous sixty-seven, but he had developed what might
be charitably described as a noble belly, and his wife
fought a perpetual battle to keep him healthy. Rana
frowned thoughtfully at Julian, who was also somewhat
more solid around the middle than he used to be. Well,
and so was she. Only Rosemary's comfortable shape had

been much the same for as long as Rana could remember.

They're getting older, and so are we. The morning light picked out glints of silver in her husband's dark hair.

"Your girl has a head on her shoulders. I wish I could say as much for my son," said the king.

"Now Julian—Johan is a good lad!" Rosemary exclaimed. "You are too hard on the boy."

"I have to be! For all that I complained at not having a royal upbringing, between them, my foster father and Caolin taught me to survive. Where will Johan get the strength to rule if I coddle him?"

The air still held a hint of summer's warmth, but overnight the lake had filled again with migrating waterfowl. Now and again a group would spiral upward and circle the lake, testing their wings. Soon those practice flights would become departures, and the lake would be quiet once more.

If only I could hold this moment forever, thought the queen. But the birds would fly, and despite debacles such as yesterday's, her little boy would become a man.

"From now on, life will teach him—," Rosemary echoed her thought. "It will teach Luz as well. We have to learn how to let our children go."

"It was a bit of a surprise, though, about the names . . . ," Eric said then.

Julian set down his cup with a click. "He meant to say 'Jehan' but the priest misheard and he let it stand. Just as well—to call the boy Johan will avoid confusion."

"Yes . . . I don't think that anyone who knew your father has ever forgotten him. It would wring my heart to hear that name again . . . ," Eric sighed.

"Will *Johan* be joining us for breakfast?" asked Rosemary briskly.

Julian grimaced. "Not very likely, when he only went to bed, I am informed, just before dawn. Having taken his grandfather's name, he seems determined to imitate his dissipation."

"Now, now—" Eric looked rather shocked. "Jehan was

no roisterer. If he had a fault, it was in wishing too greatly to please."

"Oh, he was a great lover, from what I have heard," said the king. "At least with my son there's been no trouble of that kind."

"Well," said Rosemary, "the boy has certainly inherited his grandfather's smile, but I hope he has more confidence. For all his charm, Jehan never truly believed he deserved the love we gave him, and so was too easily wounded when men failed him. He came young and untried to the throne—"

"So did I," muttered Julian.

"But you did not grow up in his shadow," answered Rosemary.

Rana frowned. Johan was also greatly loved, though his parents had not always had the time to show it. If she had been able to give him a brother or a sister, his childhood might have been less lonely. The constraint between husband and son tore at her heart, but Jo was past the age where a mother's arms could shelter him from the world.

"Perhaps you should have sent him to the College of the Wise with Luz," said Eric. "There's not much trouble he could get into there."

Rana was beginning to agree, and perhaps the boy would have preferred it. She recognized now that it was her own unwillingness to let him go as much as Julian's plan to give him some tasks in the government that had kept him in Laurelynn. If Luz sometimes seemed older than her years, it had been easy to think of Phoenix as younger.

"He did not ask it, and there seemed to be no hurry. Your granddaughter's choice of name concerns me more," she said to distract them. Jo's behavior worried her too, but she did not wish to offer Eric and Rosemary an opportunity to criticize. "Just how 'gifted' is she?"

"What do you mean, dear?" Rosemary frowned.

Rana hesitated, caught Julian's eye, and saw him nod permission. "You remember when Caolin died . . . ," she said with some difficulty, knowing that Julian still could not speak of that day. "His mind was gone when we found him, and we had to . . . search for his soul. He had forgotten everything except his childhood. The name his mother called him—his milk-name, was *Luz*."

Eric let out his breath in a soft whistle.

"I've watched that girl from infancy, and I'd swear there's no harm in her," Rosemary said stoutly. "The letters she writes from the College of the Wise don't say much, but she seems to be all right. I don't know what evils warped Caolin's soul, but—Luz—has been loved all her life. It's only chance that she decided on that name."

"Still, she chose to go to the College, and Frederic is not the only one from whom she might have inherited power," said Julian. "Perhaps they should be warned to keep an eye on her."

"Well, so did her sister, and no one can accuse Bera, Mistress of Beasts, of emulating Caolin. Perhaps we should ask Luz to keep an eye on *them*!" Rosemary responded tartly. "There seems to be rather more . . . structure . . . in the program than I remember Frederic describing. This Master Granite who is head of the College now seems determined to live up to his name."

"I wonder if he was at the College when our son was there. Frederic might know something about the man that would help us to understand him," observed Eric.

"Discipline is necessary," said Julian. "I could have avoided a lot of grief if I had not had to blunder into my power."

"True, but the Jewels themselves taught you—us—how to use them. Even the Master of the Junipers could only advise . . . ," Rana answered him.

"It is Johan, not Luz, who will have to learn to master the Jewels," said Julian.

"And both of them have time for whatever they need to learn," Eric said comfortably. "Not like you, or your poor mother, for that matter."

"True enough," agreed Rosemary. "We are not likely to see another Caolin!"

A tumult from the lake brought both men half out of

their seats, feeling at their sides for swords; but it was only the birds, startled into flight by some children running down to the shore. Beating wings cast a flicker of light and shadow across the breakfast table as they wheeled, settled into formation, and soared southward. Rana's gaze followed them. *The only thing certain is change,* she told herself, but suddenly the wind seemed cold.

"Time for us to go as well," said Eric, "if I'm to finish my report before the Council." He shoved himself upright and offered his arm to Rosemary. They were a fine-looking couple, thought Rana as they made their way along the ruddy stone of the walk. She envied their nearly fifty years of marriage.

Julian was still standing, watching the arrowhead of birds disappear.

"Do you wish you could go with them?" Rana asked softly.

"South with the birds instead of to the Council Hall with Eric? I suppose I do."

To some southern holding where you might find another young priestess to lie with? wondered Rana bitterly. A merchant from Tamiston had mentioned the king's participation in the Beltane ritual, not intending to make trouble, assuming she already knew. The town was grateful, for the crops had been good that year.

The old rites have power in them, she thought sadly, *especially when performed by princes.* Had not she herself lain down with Julian's cousin Robert as proxy for the king that terrible spring when Caolin's tortures had left Julian incapable and the sorcerer's armies laid siege to Laurelynn? She had no right to reproach him, but why had he not told her?

No—she recognized sadly—that was not the cause of her pain. She should have been the one to act as his priestess for the land, but she had become a barren branch, of little use to Westria or her king.

"At least Piper is seeing the country!" Julian turned back, pulling a folded paper from his pouch. "Another letter has come—"

"What does he say?" Rana made herself smile as he handed it to her. The king's uncle had had no son, but in Farin Piper he had an heir to carry on his name and his songs, who was now retracing his teacher's wanderings. In the bright morning light she could see the writing clearly, and waved away the reading glass Julian offered her.

"I have been for some weeks in a place they call Cottonwood, one of the free cities that cling to the rare rivers that flow through the plains. It is hot here, and dusty—for several seasons they have had little rain, and there is an ugly mood in the town. I was intending to push eastward, but I'm told that the war between the Iron Kingdom and the Empire of the Sun has left the land full of refugees. In comparison, Westria seems like a paradise.

"Perhaps that is why these people like my songs, even those who have turned for comfort to the new sun cult that has set up its tents at the edge of town. Do you remember how the people in Awhai danced with rattlesnakes at the Autumn Festival? These Children of the Sun do that too, on their great holy days. Their leader is called Mother Mahaliel. I don't know where she got her training, but she has magic, and now she's recruited a refugee general from the Iron Kingdom who is organizing some muscle for her as well. They'll need it—the townsfolk are talking of running them out. I'm going to stay awhile to see what will happen here—"

"He had better stay out of trouble," muttered Rana, "or I'll wring his neck when he does get home." They had rescued the boy, mute survivor of a reiver raid, when they were searching for the Earthstone, and she still considered him in the light of a little brother.

"That's what I'm telling him," said Julian, "but if you like you can add a few well-chosen words of your own."

She handed the letter back to him, and her smile this time was genuine. With no other woman could the king relax in the comradeship of shared experience. Rana was still the guardian of his memories, but the memory of the love that had faded was like a sword to the heart.

Blade against blade meet and part in the dance,
Man against man pitting courage 'gainst chance—

Earthenware mugs pounded out the beat on the scarred wood of the tables, and a dozen drunken voices joined in. It was just another night in the Phoenix Tavern. The prince had thought that name a good omen, several hours ago.

How the crowd roars as the dust rises high,
They're at the arena to see someone die—

A breath of cool air stirred the sawdust on the floor as the door swung open.

Man against catamount, man against bear,
Claws against dagger or fangs against spear—

A broad hand closed on his shoulder. He turned, swiping clumsily. Lenart's brown face and tightly curled fair hair swam in and out of focus.

"Come on, Phe—Johan—it's time to go. . . ."

"Jo, Phoenix, I don' care . . . ," the prince giggled softly. "Who am I, really? Nobody knows. . . ." He made a grab for the wine cup, which tipped over, and Lenart hauled him out of the way as red liquid spread like spilled blood across the table and began to drip onto the floor.

Still holding up the prince with one hand, Lenart fumbled a few coins from his pouch and handed them to the barmaid. "Sorry for the mess. We'll be going now."

Jo protested, but Lenart had inherited Lord Eric's inches. *"How the crowd roars,"* roared the singers as he was hauled toward the door.

"What are we coming to," said Lenart in disgust, "when the only thing our tavern louts can find to sing is trash from the Barren Lands?"

The cool air outside was beginning to drive some of the

wine fumes from Jo's brain, and he shrugged off Lenart's grip.

"Did my father send you, or has the Office of the Seneschal made you my keeper?" he asked bitterly. Lenart was the oldest of Frederic's children and the only one to follow him into royal service.

"Neither . . . ," Lenart said evenly, reaching out to draw Jo aside as the door of another taverna opened and a sodden body was ejected. "This is in the nature of preventive custody."

"Guardians, Lenart, don't you ever get tired of being right?" Even when they were children, Luz's brother had been the one who always tried to extract them from scrapes before their parents could find out about them. "Where are we going?" Jo added as his friend steered him down an alleyway. A damp wind from the river ruffled his hair.

"To sit by the wharves until you are fit to go home again, unless you prefer to be dunked in the river and sober up suddenly."

"I worked hard to get this soused," muttered Jo. "Why waste the wine?" But even as he spoke, he felt his stomach lurch and realized that he was about to waste some more.

He had to admit, though, that the cool breeze that blew upriver was welcome. Lenart had brought him to a small jetty behind the palace, where a few rowboats were kept moored. The river lapped softly around the pilings and a few nightbirds called. It was peaceful here.

"I suppose I ought to thank you, though I don't know why you should care," he said at last.

"Well, for one thing, you are the closest thing to a brother I have. . . . What's wrong, Johan?" Lenart went on. "Initiation is supposed to settle one down, but you've been acting like—like you did after you got lost in the woods that time when you were seven years old. I could understand getting drunk if you took any joy in it, but you don't, do you?"

Jo shook his head. He'd been told about that episode, but he didn't remember it.

"Do you *like* operating on half a brain?"

Jo shrugged, testing his awareness, as a man with a

toothache will explore the spot with his tongue. He was still alone in his head.

"If that half is my own!" Jo saw Lenart's frown and sighed. "Some people acquire spirit animals on their vigils. I got King Jehan," he said sourly, and jumped as his friend began to laugh. "It's not funny!"

"I'm not laughing at *you*—" Lenart took a shuddering breath and stilled. "I'd rather you were haunted by *your* grandfather than that I should start hearing from mine!"

Jo stared at him. These days few remembered or cared that Caolin, in the days when he had served the Prince of Elaya, had begotten a daughter upon Palomon's sister. Until Caolin had ensorceled her into leading a band of reivers against Westria, Ardra herself had not known her parentage. But Frederic had freed her from her father's domination and made her his lady.

"Has he . . . um . . . tried to talk to you?"

"Not in words. I would recognize that, I think, and fight it. It's the taint of his blood that frightens me. That's why I wouldn't go to the College of the Wise."

"But Caolin was a seneschal before he was a sorcerer," Jo blurted, and then wished he had kept silent. As his head cleared, he was beginning to pick up his friend's pain.

"I tell myself I am following in my father's footsteps there, not *his*," Lenart said tensely, "but whenever they give me a new responsibility, I wonder whether this will be the thing that wakens the lust for power. . . ."

Jo felt a sudden shame at his own self-pity. At least Jehan had not been *evil*. But according to rumor, he had been the lover of the seneschal who betrayed him. Were he and Lenart destined to repeat that relationship? *Not likely,* he told himself, *since I'm not inclined that way, and in any case, we will both be too ancient to be capable by the time I become king.*

"It won't be, so long as my father keeps a firm hand on the reins," Jo said aloud, "if I understand what King Jehan has told me. It is hard to know sometimes which thoughts are his and which my own—he died before my father was born, so we never talked about him at home."

"That sounds about right," Lenart said thoughtfully.

"My grandfather—Lord Eric, that is—was knighted by him on one of the Elayan campaigns, so we *did* hear all the old tales. But even Granda, who idolized his king, has admitted that Jehan should not have let his seneschal run the kingdom while he . . . played."

"Maybe that's why he sounds so guilt-wracked in my dreams . . . ," murmured Jo.

"And why your father is so angered by your drinking," agreed Lenart.

"He thinks I'm going to turn into Jehan? If he only knew. . . . I've been hoping wine would shut him *out*, but it isn't working, anyway. . . ." Jo pulled himself together and stuck out his hand. "All right—let's make a pact! Since you seem determined to watch over me, allow me to keep an eye on *you*. I promise that if I see you breaking out in spots or in sorcery, I'll let you know!"

"You have been brought up to believe that the gifts of the spirit come from the Guardians, that those who receive them are holy and deserve to be honored by lesser men." Master Granite surveyed the neophytes with a gaze as impassive as the stone for which he was named.

Gray eyes, gray hair, and gray robe—if you set him down on the granite scree above the treeline of the Father of Mountains, thought Luz, he would disappear. As it was, she had the odd impression that his figure had been carved from the stone of the wall behind him. She blinked and shifted her gaze to the open door. Beyond the trees she could see the snow-dappled slope of the peak shining in the morning sun.

"If you came to the College with that in mind," the master went on, "leave now, and waste no more of our time or your own, for you will get neither power nor holiness here."

"Whew!" whispered little Radha, who had become Luz's first friend when she arrived. "That's put us in our pla—" She fell silent as that gray gaze swept their way.

Luz had thought it an honor that their meditation class should be taught by the head of the College, but she was beginning to wonder. He seemed to be doing his best to scare them away. She put up her hand.

"What *will* we get?"

For a long moment Master Granite considered her, rather, thought Luz, as if she were an insect he was deciding whether to squash outright or sweep out the door. "Discipline . . . ," he said finally. "Just as if you were training for music, or for war. Most people have some potential for magic, just as most can fight or sing. Some find it easier than others, that is all.

"You are all here because you have talent, or think you do. That remains to be seen. But be very sure of this—there is nothing *special* about you. Some of you have come here intending to become priests or priestesses in some village or great lord's holding, and some are more ambitious, and would take the Pilgrim's Road to Awahna and return as masters. But do not be deceived. A goatherd who follows his flocks across the hills may be holier than the chief priest in Laurelynn."

But is he more powerful? she wondered, and then, *Do I want holiness or power?*

⊷

That was only one of the questions Luz found herself considering during her first month at the College of the Wise. Having grown up on tales of the masters, she had thought she knew what to expect. She wondered now if there were things her father had not mentioned, or whether the College had changed since he was a student here.

But she found the work absorbing. The training cycle was based on the four elements so basic to the spirituality of Westria. In the first year, the focus on the element of Earth introduced the foundations of the rest of the curriculum. As Master Granite had promised, the basis for most things seemed to be discipline. Each day began and ended with a sequence of movements and postures that flexed the limbs and centered the mind.

Appropriately enough, the study of Earth included helping the cooks, and tending the gardens and animals that provided the College with food. The older students called the first-years "muddies," but the teasing was not allowed to go too far. In the hours that remained, the newcomers studied history and theology and the basics of meditation.

Surprisingly, it was this last that Luz found hardest, not from lack of talent, but because she had found her own way to that path a long time ago. To be told she must crawl where she was used to fly was a constant frustration; it was perhaps inevitable that she should rebel against Master Granite's instructions.

———

The muddies sat cross-legged in the great hall of the College, its high, whitewashed walls unadorned except for the tapestry of the Tree of Life that hung at one end. The lamp that always burned before it was the only illumination. Luz preferred the lessons they had outdoors, where she could breathe in the scent of the trees instead of damp stone, but she knew that most of the others found it easier to concentrate here.

Master Granite was taking them through the all-too-familiar sequence, in which one sent awareness downward to root itself in the mountain, tensed and relaxed each limb, and *breathed* in and out in a slow, steady rhythm, which is where Luz always lost awareness of what that cool, precise voice was telling them. This time was no exception. Between one breath and the next she soared free of the flesh, spiraling upward toward the light.

Senses, time, even thought were consumed in that radiance. Luz rushed toward a Knowledge that transcended them all—

—and slammed back into her body, pain lancing along every unshielded nerve.

She curled into a shuddering ball, throwing up her hands in a futile attempt to protect herself from the force that had struck her down. Instinctively she hit back with her mind, and reeled as the energy rebounded. For a few moments longer, the intolerable pressure held her, then eased.

Carefully, Luz opened her eyes. Master Granite was

standing over her, his face impassive, as secure behind his sealed aura as any warrior armed and covered by his shield. She drew a shuddering breath and tried to sit up, aching as if she had been beaten, though she was beginning to realize that he had not touched her with his hands.

"What did you do to me?" She spoke mind-to-mind, not yet able to trust her voice with words.

"I demonstrated the consequences of inattention," the master said aloud. "The doors of your spirit were open for anyone, or anything, to walk through, and as for your pitiful attempt to fight me—a plowboy from Elder could have done better; at least he would have known I was there!"

"I tried—," she protested.

"You did not. You ran off to play and I brought you back to earth again."

"Isn't the purpose of meditation to reach the Light?" Luz exclaimed. With her barriers still down, she could feel the emotions of the others, appalled or avid, with a painful clarity. "I was almost—"

His eyes became, if possible, colder, and her protests died.

"The Light? Any fool can reach it. Jump off a cliff and be done with it if that is your only goal. You will save us all a great deal of time and free your bed for someone who actually wants to *learn*. What use will you be to anyone who must live in this world if all you know how to do is escape it?

"Or do you think that because your father is an adept that you have inherited some special status?" he went on. "If he *is* a master—it does not seem to have stuck well enough for him to keep the name. Why do you think adepts are not allowed to marry? If *Frederic* had to breed, he should have fostered out his children where no one would know them." Master Granite's accusations rolled on, all the more scarifying because there seemed to be no passion in them.

But his words about her father had aroused Luz where his attack on her had not.

"How much do *you* know about living in the world, up here on your mountaintop? My father *does* live in it! And if he has had to make compromises, at least he still knows how to love, not this—bloodless—" She sputtered to a halt, her fury exhausting itself against his impassivity.

"Discipline?" he suggested softly. "But it is discipline that will save you when passion fails. Your *grandfather* knew that well. . . ."

Her eyes flew to his, terrified he was about to say Caolin's name. If the other students knew who her mother's father was, none of them had had the gall to say so. But the master's words suggested an appalling possibility. Caolin had been famous for the power of his will. Was *that* why she had feared to learn control?

"No one forced you to come here, Luz Fredericsdaughter, and you are always free to go," that cold voice ground on. "But while you stay here, you will learn what I tell you to learn. You *will* obey!"

⊷ 3 ⊶

PREY

"The report from Elaya is here—"

Recognizing Frederic's voice, Julian looked up from his desk and nodded a welcome, then grabbed for his papers as a wind off the river gusted through the open window.

"Leave the door open—we can use the draft," he added as the other man came in. The heart of Westria lay baking in the heat of Indian summer. In such weather the breeze from the river was the only thing that made living in Laurelynn tolerable. He supposed that was why the survivors of the Cataclysm had chosen to make a city here, building an island where the sluggish waters of the Darkwater percolated through many channels to join with the Dorada and crowning it with a city of rose-colored brick.

It was fire weather, and knowing that wildfires were the

Guardians' tool to clear excess undergrowth from the land did not lift the instinctive anxiety Julian felt when he smelled smoke in the air. He would be glad when the first of the winter rains rolled in; he only wished the wind could cool his anger as well.

Frederic set down his papers and opened the window still wider, taking in the breeze with an appreciative sigh. He was wearing a sleeveless linen robe of pale gray, with only the Seneschal's golden key on its chain to mark his office. Julian himself had put on a loose yellow cotton caftan from Elaya, with no mark of rank at all.

In the clear light, Julian could see the sheen of perspiration below Frederic's fair hair. That brow was higher than it used to be, he observed, but then so was his own. Memory overlaid his vision with the image of the eager boy Frederic had been when they met. Lord Eric's son had been eighteen years old and he himself a bare year older. *Jo's age . . .* , he thought bitterly. *But we were ready to sacrifice ourselves to save our world.*

"And you did—and Westria was saved. Would you wish another such war upon our sons?"

Julian realized that his emotion had carried his thought as Frederic's mind touched his. Instinct snapped up his mental barriers, and in the next moment he wondered when he had developed the need to hide his soul from his most trusted friend. But Frederic had no need to be ashamed of *his* son. How could Julian trust Jo with responsibility when— The image of an old woman weeping over the bloodstained body of her daughter rose in Julian's memory and with an effort, the king clamped down on his fury once more.

For a moment Frederic considered him thoughtfully. Then, accepting the king's withdrawal, he pulled out a chair.

"You were wise to choose this room to work in. The seneschals' offices are like an oven today."

Julian smiled. This tower, with shaded windows that looked out in each direction, had been his own contribution to the plans for rebuilding the palace after Caolin's War. Set at the western point of the island, it received the full force of the river wind. The overhang kept the sun from shining in directly, but it caught the light refracted from the river and sent a pale glimmer across the oak floor. Westward, the river was a gleam of silver twining toward the Great Bay. Across the river the hills ran away to the north in lines of blue. Eastward the view faded into the haze above the Great Valley. And in the south—there rose the Red Mountain, the heart of Westria, where a granite tomb held the bones of the sorcerer who had been Julian's greatest teacher as well as his greatest enemy.

But that war lay twenty-five years in the past. He turned his gaze back to Frederic, who was extracting a folded paper from its leather case.

"So what is the word from Al-Kaid?" he asked.

"Another palace coup." Frederic grimaced. "Prince Martom is dead and the Condé de las Palisadas has taken charge."

"Ardra's cousin!" Julian exclaimed. "Well, at least Harun descends from the old Tambaran line. I daresay the people there remember Prince Palomon's reign as a golden age!"

Frederic sighed. "My father used to complain about Palomon when I was a boy, but his nephew Prince Ali was worse. This man is a younger son of his other sister, I believe, who inherited Las Palisadas when it became clear that Ardra was going to stay in Westria. The Palisadas seem to have prospered under Harun's rule, so perhaps Elaya will do so as well."

"He'll need more than kindness to survive." Elaya was smaller than Westria, but after the Cataclysm its peoples had separated into six counties that co-existed in an uneasy confederation. Julian did not envy the man who had to make them all get along.

"It is a pity Prince Palomon had no child to inherit," said Frederic.

"Maybe," growled the king, his anger rekindling. "Or maybe he was the lucky one!" Last night a girl had been trampled during a midnight horse race through the streets of Laurelynn, in which one of the riders had been his son. He had paid the honor-price for the dead, but gold would not bring the girl back again.

"Julian, it was not all Jo's doing—"

"But he—" There was a soft knock on the doorframe and he turned, glaring, and saw the prince himself hesitating there. There had been a time, thought Julian, when the sight of his son brought an instant rush of joy. But now, to see the grace in that leanly muscled frame and the fine modeling of the boy's features only increased his anger, as if he had found a flawed jewel in an exquisite frame.

"I'll go," murmured Frederic.

"No," muttered the king. "I'll keep a better hold on my temper if you are here. . . ."

The seneschal raised one eyebrow, then eased back into his seat, his expression changing to pity as Jo came into the room.

I'm glad someone *can pity him,* thought the king, noting the pallor beneath Jo's freckles and the shadows beneath his blue eyes. Even the flaming hair he had inherited from his mother seemed dull.

"Father—," the boy said suddenly. "It was only a race— we didn't think anyone would be about at that hour!"

"Johan, this is a city of ten thousand people." With an effort, Julian kept his voice under control. "Surely it is more likely to find one of them on the streets, even at midnight, than half a dozen drunken riders careening down the main avenue!"

"I wasn't drinking! I promised you, and I kept my word!"

"The more shame to you," Julian answered bitterly, "if you were sober when you lent yourself to that madness! Nor does it matter that it wasn't your idea! You have sat at this very table and heard the magistrates of Laurelynn urge that horses be banned entirely inside the town. You *knew* the danger, and you are the prince. Do you think those other louts would have held to the plan if you had refused to go along?"

From pale, Johan had gone crimson. His lips tightened as if he were biting back a retort, and Julian nodded grimly. "At least you have the sense not to argue with me! I did not summon you to hear your explanations but to pronounce my judgment. If you cannot act like an adult here in Laurelynn, I will send you where you will not be faced with so many temptations. In the morning you will be escorted to your great-aunt Jessica. Perhaps a few weeks in the Ramparts will cool your blood!"

"It must be like an oven in the valley right now," said little Radha, gazing at the hazy blue ridges that bounded their southward view. Atop the Father of Mountains the elevation moderated the heat, but in the thin air the sunlight had a peculiar intensity. At times Luz felt as if it were shining through her bones. It filtered now through the boughs of the spruce trees that sheltered the terrace, sending dizzying dapplings of light across the semi-circle of benches carved into the hillside.

She shut her eyes, took a deep breath, and concentrated on the solid support of the stone until her vertigo passed. That was one useful thing, she thought sourly, that she had learned here.

She felt her companions stir and opened her eyes to see Master Badger seating himself on the bench before them. Behind him, the massive granite buildings of the College of the Wise edged the mountain meadow. Dark masses of conifers swathed the lower slopes of the Father of Mountains beyond.

"Some of you will have found animal helpers when you went out seeking visions at your initiation," he began, "and you already know how useful they can be. Others will encounter their helpers during their time here at the College. But most of those who walk the spirit paths find that they need more than one, for the folk of the inner worlds have specialties and preferences, just like those who live in our own."

His large white teeth gleamed as he laughed. He was rather like a badger himself, short, stout, and muscular, with a shock of brindled dark hair, a welcome change from Master Granite's grim intensity.

"Do they choose us, then, or do we choose them?" asked Vefara, who came from the Danehold on the southern border of Westria.

"It works both ways," the master answered her. "Sometimes your helper comes because he is the mirror of your spirit, and sometimes his purpose is to bring balance to your soul."

Luz raised her hand. "My sister Bera speaks to all animals, but I think at heart she *is* a bear."

Master Badger grinned again. "Indeed, I remember Mistress Bera very well. If we had been able to persuade her, she would be teaching this class instead of me. But I can tell you that the attraction of opposites can be just as powerful. I was a flighty, flimsy sort of lad until Badger came to me, and look at me now!"

"Does that mean that if I get a jackrabbit I'll win all the footraces?" said a lanky boy from Las Costas called Joffrey.

"If that is what you are meant to do," came the reply. "But to go seeking an ally because you covet his power or beauty will get you nowhere."

"Oh, dear, and I was hoping to get a unicorn!" Vefara shook her head mournfully.

"But unicorns are not real!" objected a stolid boy from Seagate who had not yet learned to appreciate Vefara's sense of humor.

"Does that matter?" asked Radha. "I've heard of people who got griffins or dragons."

"It can happen," said Master Badger, "but don't hope for a dragon."

"Are such allies so rare?" asked Luz.

"Fortunately for all of us, they are," the master answered a little grimly. "They are very powerful elemental powers. If you try to ride the dragon, he may end up riding you."

No doubt that was true, thought Luz, but a rush of joy dizzied her anew as she remembered her vision of the Dragon of Light.

Firelight sparked from the shards of ancient glass set among the stones of the fireplace, sending flickers of light across the oak planks of the floor. Everything at Great-aunt Jessica's house was well-worn but precise and polished. Rather like the old lady herself, thought Jo, as he took the mug of tea she had poured for him.

"Would you like some honey with it, my dear? Chamomile will relax you after your long ride, but some find it needs a little sweetening—"

"No thank you. This is fine," Jo replied, and saw her eyes sparkle as he smiled.

The house was an old one, built of round river stones and shaded by a noble stand of black oak trees, set on a hill above the canyon where the Amata River flowed down from the Snowy Mountains. Lady Jessica, who had been King Jehan's older sister and wife to the lord of the Ramparts, had retired here when her husband died. She was the only one to be delighted by her great-nephew's choice of a name, and she had done her best to make him welcome.

Jo was still not quite sure how Lord Robert felt about him. The king had laid the task of conveying his son into exile upon his cousin, who was overdue for a visit to his mother anyway. Robert sat now with his feet to the fire, the warm glow highlighting the graceful curve of cheek and brow. "As beautiful as Robert of the Ramparts," they said in Laurelynn, and Robert was still a handsome man, though Jo suspected that these days the rich brown of his hair owed something to walnut dye.

"And Robert, here is some for you—"

Marcos rose with his usual silent grace to hand the cup to Robert, then resumed his seat just behind him. As devoted as an old married couple, they were, and though Jo felt no attraction to men, he envied them.

"My child, you must not look so sad—" Great-aunt Jessica shook her head. "Your father will forgive you. He got into his share of trouble when he and Robert were in the Border Guard—even I heard some tales, and I daresay there were other stories you lads thought unfit for a mother's ears!"

"I have heard something about the Elayan envoy's horse . . . ," Marcos said slyly.

For a moment there was more red in Robert's face than could be blamed on the fire. "Guardians! I had nearly forgotten!" He laughed. "We'd spent the summer in the mountains chasing raiders, and when Philip asked us to escort him to the Autumn Sessions you'd think we'd never seen a town before! That year we had to play host to an embassy from Elaya—you never saw so many plumes and ribbons. So one night, when we had dipped a little too deep into the wine casks, we decided that the envoy's white horse really ought to match his master's attire. I think your father was the one who persuaded the dye merchant to sell us a selection of his wares." Robert grinned.

"So what happened?"

"Well, the poor beast was quite colorful by the time we got through with him. So was my brother's face when he saw what we'd done," he added reminiscently. "We had to spend a week cleaning the stables after that one. And then there was the brawl in the Dancing Owl that ended with the lot of us scrubbing the steps of the Council Hall. . . ."

Jo appreciated the attempt to cheer him, but none of those escapades had killed anyone. He supposed that some of the punishments Robert's older brother had imposed might have been more painful than this exile, but at least they had soon been over. He felt like a child who had been sent to his room. Or perhaps he felt so resentful because he suspected that his father, after that memorable outburst, simply could not be troubled to deal with him. And what was new about that, after all?

The next morning Jo persuaded Robert to let him ride out in search of game. But as he cantered across the golden hills, his thoughts cycled round and round. He had meant no harm—it was not his fault that others could not hold their wine. He had promised Lenart to stay sober himself;

he had neither the right nor the power to enforce sobriety on other people. It might have been different if the king had given him anything to *do*. . . . It was his *father* who needed to cool down. It was already winter in Jo's soul.

At least his cousin had let him go alone. Jo reined in to let his pony breathe and shaded his eyes. To his left, the land fell away in a series of broad steps covered with sun-cured grass. Indian summer was over and the night would be cold, but the autumn sun retained at least the illusion of kindness. On such a day, when a crisp wind had scoured the sky, every leaf seemed etched with preternatural clarity against the pale blue of the sky. Far across the valley, the Red Mountain was a pointed cone set before the gray silhouettes of the coastal hills. The prince took a deep breath, seeking to fill himself with that light, then turned away and set his mount up the slope once more.

He had promised his great-aunt venison for her table. Though he had the natural coordination to handle all weapons well, his real love was for the bow. But so far he had seen no deer.

He reined the dun pony around one of the granite boulders that dotted the hillside as if some giant child had left his jack stones there and urged it into a canter. With a good horse between his knees and the wind in his hair, he could imagine for a moment that he was free.

The rich hues of golden grass and the occasional splash of tawny color from turning leaves were reminders that this was only summer's last smile. On such a day, one might ride forever. Or at least far enough from the house and pastures to have hopes of bagging a deer. His great-aunt expected him back in time for dinner, whether or not he provided part of it; but Jo had tied his cloak to the saddle, and if he must spend a night under the stars it would be no hardship. What harm could come to him in this gracious land?

The horse slowed as the slope grew steeper, and Jo let him walk for a while. Beyond the pines that fringed the ridge, he could see long swales of forest rising one behind another in blue-veiled majesty. Surely there would be deer in those green shadows. He turned the pony's head and urged it up the hill.

Darkness found him happily settled by a small fire beneath the pines, with a brace of rabbits, the only game he had found thus far, roasting over the lovely flames of the long pine cones he had found beneath the trees. A few pine nuts that the squirrels had missed enriched his evening fare. With dry grass for a bed and a cloak for cover, he would stave off the worst of the night's chill. And the crickets were making enough noise to keep him from getting lonely.

He suppressed a slight guilt at the thought that his great-aunt might be anxious. He was a man now, and he ought to be his own master. It would do them all good to worry, and he would enjoy their embarrassment when he returned safe and sound with a fat buck tied to the saddle. Early morning, when the deer came out to feed, was a good time for hunting, and if the night was cold, it would be that much easier to wake early. A tassel of wild oats from his bedding tickled his nose as he turned, and he smiled.

"Why are you planting seeds now, with winter on the way?" asked Radha, who was town-bred and full of questions. Luz suppressed a smile and sank her own shovel into the soil. It was the turn of the muddies to work on the College farm at Strawberry Valley at the foot of the mountain.

"Ah, but the rains will be coming soon." Mistress Melissa smiled. With a brown apron tied on over her ochre-colored healer's robe, she looked as round and busy as one of her own bees. "We do but seek to persuade the seeds that they have been here since summer's beginning, as they would have been, in the wild. There's some that propagate better from cuttings, but bloodwort, now, 'tis best grown from seed." She scooped a handful from the pouch at her waist and scattered it over the ground the two girls had been turning.

"There now, little sisters—settle into your new bed. Sun warms you, earth will cradle you, rain will feed you.

Grow and be strong!" Light seemed to follow the old woman's hands as she moved them above the soil in blessing.

While the mistress brought the other students back for the lesson, the two girls took their shovels back to the shed and sat down to wait in the shade beside the cairn where they made offerings to the spirit of the field.

"Why is it called bloodwort?" asked Radha when the class had gathered again.

"Because the extracted oil is crimson," said Joffrey, who came from a holding on the Darkwater. "It is good for the blood, too, isn't it?"

"If you make the blossoms into a tea, yes," Mistress Melissa replied. "You use the oil externally for conditions of the skin. I add a little to the olive oil and aloe when I make the sun salve we use at the College."

Luz, who had been helping her grandmother in the stillroom since she was old enough to hold a basket, nodded, but kept silent. It had become quite clear that not only the masters but many of the other students expected her to be stuck-up or proud. She would have a word with her sister when next they met for not warning her; but perhaps Bera, who had always cared more about animals than people, had paid no attention. Bera was assigned to a community of priests in the foothills of the Ramparts now, exercising the healer's skills she had learned at the College on the animals that were brought for treatment there.

Mistress Melissa was still speaking of the ways that bloodwort could be used in healing. Luz listened with half an ear. The air here felt heavy after the transparent atmosphere of the peak, but even at the end of the dry season the ripe grass seemed luxuriant compared to that spare world of spruce and stone. With her eyes half-lidded, all the world seemed made of gold. She stared until she lost focus and the brightness became a shimmer of motion and she realized that everything she could see was made of light.

"Luz—"

It took a moment before she realized that it was not the radiance they were calling, but her own name. *Is that what I am? Is that what the world is?* she wondered as her vision contracted and she found herself gazing at the surfaces of things once more.

Jo crouched behind a screen of manzanita, bow strung and arrow ready, watching as the brightening day revealed the deer trail he had marked the afternoon before. He had seen recent droppings—soon the animals would be coming down to drink at the nearby stream. He wet a finger and held it up, waiting for the chill that would assure him he was still upwind. Then he settled back again, breathing slowly, becoming one with the expectant stillness of the dawn.

Now he could see a gleam of light on the water. He fixed his gaze on the path beyond it. Were those antlers or branches? Jo straightened as a dark shape emerged from the shadows, and reached for his bow. *"Come now, my brother . . . ,"* he thought, *"we are all part of the pattern, and as you feed me, I will feed the earth one day."* The thought bore with it a fleeting image of the Sacred Wood, but he thrust it away. He must allow nothing to disturb the unity between hunter and hunted now.

The bow lifted like a branch moved by the breeze. He glimpsed the gleam of a dark eye, and then the line of neck and shoulder, waiting for the animal to bend its head to drink, when the shifting foreleg would reveal the paler patch of hide above the heart. . . .

The wide ears swiveled and the deer's head came up, nostrils flaring. In the next moment Jo heard the sound that had alarmed the animal—hoofbeats too loud to be those of other deer. The stag exploded into movement, leaped the stream in a single bound, crashed past him through the undergrowth and away.

The prince ducked back behind the manzanita. Had Robert and Marcos come out to search for him? If they had not frightened the buck, he would have had his shot and been happy to leave, but it might well take another day for him to get his deer now.

More than one horse was coming. Jo hunkered down, cloak draped to give him the shape of a stone. Four others followed the first man, and after them, a dozen more. As they crossed the stream, one mount stumbled and his rider pulled him up with an oath that was not in the accent of Westria.

Raiders! What were they doing so far from the border? Jo had to warn the holding! He waited for an endless moment as the men passed, then began to worm his way backward through the brush.

When he reached his campsite, his pony's head was up, ears pricking. The other horses must be entirely too near. Swearing softly, Jo slipped the bridle on and leaped to the pony's bare back, squeezing its sides gently as he reined the animal through the trees. If only he knew where the raiders were heading! He calculated furiously, weighing the speed he could make in the open against the danger of being seen.

The slope beyond the oakwood was still half in shadow. Jo eased the pony onto the grass and shook the reins as he dug his heels into the animal's sides. The pony's hoofbeats drummed in his ears, so loud that by the time he realized he was hearing other horses as well, precious time had been lost. Casting a desperate look over his shoulder, Jo saw riders behind him. But his mount was fresh—surely he could outrun them!

The thunder behind him lessened, but his grin faded as he realized it was because his pursuers were angling out to either side. The only escape was forward—he whipped the reins against the pony's neck, grimacing as drops from the sweated neck flew back to splatter him.

Straight ahead was the shortest way, but not the safest. Jo saw the drop just before they reached it and wrenched the horse's head around. The pony's haunches clenched beneath him as hooves scrabbled on rock. Then they were clear, but he had lost too much time. As he straightened, he saw his enemies ahead. He wrenched his dagger from its sheath, swearing, as they came at him, slashed outward, and heard a cry. Then a blade caught the rising sun. He looked up, light flared in his head as the flat of the sword hit him, and he knew no more.

———◆———

Luz sat bolt upright in her bed, gasping as pain blasted through her mind, and clapped her hand to her head. Had she hit it somehow while sleeping? She massaged her temple gently as the echoes of agony faded away. There was no tenderness—she began to wonder if the pain had been physical at all. She extended her awareness and felt only the minds of the other girls in the dormitory, slowly beginning to rouse as the light that shafted through the eastern window grew stronger. The pain she had picked up had not come from anyone close by.

It might be someone in her family. Once more she reached out, but found nothing. It was just a bad dream, then, unless—frowning, she summoned up the image of a faintly freckled, strong-boned face topped by flaming red hair, and winced as she felt another twinge of pain.

It was Phoenix—Johan—who was hurting. He was not dead. She thought she would have sensed his spirit more clearly if that had been so. The dull confusion she was picking up suggested he was half-conscious. But Johan was the heir of Westria. If there had been an accident, he would have the best of care.

She was settling back beneath her covers when another thought brought her upright again. She knew how the prince chafed at the restrictions that surrounded him. What if he had escaped them and been hurt while he was alone? And if that was so, then what could she do?

Only this—send out a warning with all her power. But she would have all the other girls in hysterics if she did it here. Frowning, she slipped her feet into sandals, grabbed her cloak against the early chill, and crept out of the dormitory.

A few minutes brought her to the slope above the school. The forested ridges below were still in shadow, but the peak of the Father of Mountains shimmered in the light of the rising sun. Southward, mists glowed above the Great Valley. Somewhere beneath that luminous veil were others who loved Johan, their sleeping minds as yet undistracted by the demands of the day.

Luz sat down with her back against a spruce trunk, and tucked her cloak tightly around her. Against her closed eyelids the sunlight was a red glow. She took a deep breath and then another, counting as she felt awareness focus within. Though Master Granite might not believe it, she was learning control. But he did not matter now. It was the king and the queen she must reach—she summoned their faces in memory. She sank deeper still, and then, between one breath and the next, poured forth all of her power in one desperate call.

"Johan is hurt! Find him. Find him!"

A surge of heat brought Rana to consciousness. She threw off the covers and waited as the chill air cooled her skin. More often than not, these days, she would wake thus in the dawning, soaked in sweat, while Julian, still cocooned in his blankets, slept on. Rosemary said that the flashes of heat were a natural part of her body's maturing. Rana's opinion was less charitable; though why, considering her poor success in breeding, she should resent this evidence that her body was losing its fertility she did not know.

Beneath her lashes she could see a haze of light from the eastern window, bringing into soft focus the murals that King Jehan had painted for his mother long ago. Was she uncomfortable enough to get up and put on a dry nightgown, or could she slide back into sleep again?

And in that moment of indecision, she heard the mental call. For a moment she thought it a remnant of dream, but she had been dreaming about rowing a boat on the Great Bay. That was not the touch of Johan's mind—when he was small she had always known when he was in pain. Yet the message had been clear.

As she sat up, the bed heaved and Julian fought his way

free of the blankets, reaching for the knife that hung from the bedpost. In the next moment he was on his feet, the blade bared in his hand. She had a moment to admire the responses trained into him by his years as a warrior before awareness came into his eyes and he straightened, scanning the room with a frown.

"What woke me?"

"Something's happened to our son. I don't know who called, but I heard it too."

She could see him evaluating the information, felt the moment when the separation brought by recent years fell away and his mind opened to hers as it had long ago. The message was still resonating in her memory, resonating between them now. Lines deepened in his face and he reached for his breeches.

When the door opened, they were almost fully clothed. Frederic, his hair all on end and his gray robe unbelted, took a step into the room. Seeing them both dressed, his face grew grim.

"The call woke you, too?"

"Yes," answered Rana, "but who?"

"It was Luz. I know the feel of her mind. She and Johan have always been close," Frederic answered her. "I didn't realize she was so sensitive, but she must have picked up something from him."

"One way to find out," said the king, pulling on his boots. "I'll ride to Aunt Jessica's, and if this is some child's scrape, he'll *wish* he was only in pain!"

"You're not going alone," Rana and Frederic replied as one.

For a moment Julian looked at them, his lips quirking in a rueful smile. Then he nodded.

It was just like old times, she thought, remembering some of the desperate deeds to which they had followed him. He had never succeeded in stopping her in the past, and now he knew better than to try. But anxiety was coiling like a serpent in Rana's belly, and she had no room for any emotion but fear.

4

ThE LADY OF PAIN AND ROSES

This is not Westria. . . . Jo coughed, tasting dust in the air.

It was a lack, rather than a presence, that had roused him from his stupor of despair. The lands in the southern part of the Great Valley were as bleak as the flats they were crossing, but the difference was not only in the desiccated air. Something was missing—a connection to the land that he had never really noticed until now, when it was gone.

He remembered endless trees, and rock that gleamed beneath an immensity of sky. But now everything he could see was brown. The sun was warm, but the beads of sweat beneath his hatband dried instantly on his skin. The angle of the sun told him that they were moving northward. Beyond the bobbing line of men and packhorses, the land stretched away in a dim haze. To his left the brown slope was studded with clumps of sagebrush. Bleached grasses waved beside the dry streambed in the valley. The hills on its far side seemed to be entirely bare.

"So ye're awake, eh, Red?" One of the raiders moved his horse up alongside as he saw Johan stir. "Welcome t' Barren Lands!"

The Barren Lands. . . . His father had escaped from the reivers who would have carried him into slavery here. His father had not been drugged, and he'd had companions, but Jo was sure the great Julian would have found a way to free himself even with no help at all.

"Ready t' tell us yer name, boy?"

"Red," Jo muttered sourly. He knew he ought to be screaming his name and rank, but this scum would not have the authority to arrange for ransom. Better to put off the shame of admitting who he was until they reached some town.

"Red!" Stained teeth showed through the man's dark beard as he laughed. "An' a ruddy Westrian rose ye be! None such grow 'n Arena, for sure! Ye'll fetch a good price there!"

Not so great a price as the one my father will pay for me. . . . Jo shuddered, though he was not sure if it was at the prospect of Julian's wrath or the thought of slavery. Everyone in Westria had heard tales of Arena, the city where anything could be bought or sold.

At least, he thought even more grimly, *I'm worth* something *here!*

"Hey, muddie, think you're somebody! All you are is muddy now!"

Luz sank her shovel into the floor of the stall without looking up. They only kept a few horses at the College, but she had been assigned to muck out the stalls for all of them. The nickname for the first-year students was supposed to be affectionate, but too many of the older students had been awakened by her mental shout. By now, her undyed cotton gown was almost as brown as the cord that belted it.

She had not anticipated that for the other students, their own developing sensitivities still unshielded, her shout would cause real pain. Several students had ended up in the healer's rooms. Luz had grown up with the assumption that few outside her family had the full inner hearing required for such communication. After almost three months at the College, she was beginning to understand that the gifts of which she had been so proud carried their own vulnerabilities. She felt the other students' resentment like a dull ache in her heart, but at least she now understood why she must develop the skill to ward her soul.

She slid the shovel under another pile of manure. At this season it was only the night's output that needed to be dealt with. The smell was not so bad, really, not like the acrid, stinking mess a stall could get into when bad weather kept the horses in night and day.

Luz admitted the Master of the College was justified in disciplining her. She should have waited to send her warning until he could help. Yet she had been right too, and her father's reply proved that she had gotten through. They might disapprove of her judgment, but they should at least recognize her power!

But if mucking out the stables was hard work, at least the horses appreciated it. Luz was in a mood to be grateful for any approval she could get just now. And if she worked her body hard enough, she could slow her mind's ceaseless questioning, for after that first, anguished cry she had felt nothing from Johan, and no news had come.

Jo stood on tiptoe, peering out through the single window. Arena lay in an oval bowl surrounded by sculptured dun-colored hills. But the same sun shone here as in Westria. At sunset its golden light coaxed the rough slopes into shifting folds of ochre velvet, and for that single hour, Arena was beautiful.

There was nothing else here he could take pleasure in. Slaves brought him food and lotions for his sunburnt skin, but Jo had seen their master, Alondro, only once. No one could refuse the reward that a kingdom would offer for the return of its heir. Alondro had given him paper and pen to write a letter to his father—surely the man had sent for ransom! He thought sometimes that the waiting would drive him mad before any news could come. The most menial job in Westria would have been a privilege. Mucking out stables or digging ditches would at least have left him too tired to think. With a sigh, he moved to the middle of the room and resumed the flowing sequence of exercises with which he attempted to fill his days.

Bend and stretch, reach and twist, balance strength against strength . . . once more, the familiar moves brought a measure of peace to his soul. He had learned the moving meditation from Master Frederic, who had learned it at the College of the Wise.

I should have gone this summer with Luz, he thought, and for a moment he could almost see her cloud of dark hair and her skin golden above the pale gown. *Luz! Don't forget me!* his spirit cried, but his call sank into the darkness like water into desert sand.

———————

Luz sat with the other muddies in a circle in the great meeting hall, but close as they were in body, in a sense she had not known since she had first learned to distinguish the other thoughts that passed through her mind from her own, she was separate. It was part of the penance that the Master of the College had imposed upon her, to lock up her spirit, neither sending thoughts nor receiving them except when he gave her leave. Originally their group had been larger, but the disciplines of the College had taken their toll. Luz was determined to stay. And so she listened to Mistress Iris lecture on the Guardians of Westria with her ears alone.

"Mistress, I have never understood why only Westria honors the Guardians—are there none in the other lands?"

Luz turned and saw that Kamil, a dark-skinned boy from the south, was asking the question. The fact that she must look in order to recognize him told her how much she had come to depend on the mental flavor of communication.

"Indeed there are, as they were here in Westria before the Cataclysm, for without them how would the elements of life put forth their powers? Even in ancient times there were some who understood how to hear them, and it is so even now in other lands, though the Guardians may be known by different names."

"I think I understand . . . ," Kamil said slowly. "At home there are many people from Elaya, and they call the Lady of the Ocean 'Yemayá.'" His gaze turned to the west, where the element of water was pictured. A female figure with long dark hair and a gown like sea-foam rose from the waves, but where rain fell in the gray distance the form of the Lord of the Waters could be seen, and in the depths the fringed cloak of Sea-Mother, who guards all the sea peoples in the form of a giant octopus, swirled.

"Where I come from, we hail the Lord of Thunder as 'Thor'!" put in her friend Vefara, a sturdy, brown-haired girl whose home was the Danehold in Las Costas.

"But surely to do so is rather . . . primitive . . . ," said Joffrey. "The great powers are forces, not *people*."

"Sometimes . . . ," Luz said softly. "But the Lady Madrone traveled with King Julian when he was looking for the Earthstone, and my father says she seemed very much a person to them."

Their teacher sighed. "The great truths are never simple. I have seen the spirits in an iris bed dancing as swirls of light, and I have seen those lights join all together and become the form of a woman cloaked in folds of purple over a gown of green. . . ." Her gaze softened, and it did not need a mental touch to know that she was seeing once more the vision in which she had been given her Name. She was rather like an iris herself, thought Luz, one of the petite ones, a small round woman with smooth dark hair and violet eyes.

"Is Iris many, or one?" the priestess went on. "And is the Lady of Fire the flame on the hearth or the flame of love in the heart, or the Lady of Love who has been called by so many names?"

Now it was the southern wall they were looking at, where warm-blooded beasts leaped joyfully and a radiant female form with fiery hair rose from the flames. Coyote was there as well, bringing the gift of fire to humankind with the flaming torch tied to his tail. In the east it was all clouds and birds, the mighty figure of the Lord of Storms and the enigmatic smile of the Windlord, and in the north the beasts that burrow into the earth and the great trees of the Sacred Wood, the Lady of Earth and the Lord of the Trees.

"They are the Shining Ones, the Mighty Powers." Vefara nodded. "When they speak to us they seem to be people, because that is all we can understand."

"Just so. In our highest moments we may apprehend something of what they truly are, but so long as our own spirits are clothed in bodies, those are the forms in which we perceive the Guardians," Mistress Iris went on. "Though men may call Him by different names, the Sun shines everywhere, but the spirit of each land is different, and that difference affects the way its people view the world. And there are Powers whose concern is primarily with humankind, who may appear anywhere."

"So there is a Guardian for the Barren Lands," said Radha, as if she found it hard to imagine, "but only here do we honor the Lady of Westria."

The city of Arena existed because of its river. From the storm-scoured heights of the Snowy Mountains it flowed eastward, losing itself in the wastes without ever coming to the sea. But where it ran, life flourished, and if this place seemed a desert in comparison to Westria, to those who followed the trade trails, Arena was an oasis of luck and light that men had made to fight the dreary memory of existence in the Barren Lands. To Jo, the spirit of this place was a whore bedecked in red and black with a pair of dice in one hand and in the other a bag of gold. In his dreams, ripe breasts surged from the low neck of her gown as she sang—

> I am the Mistress of pain and roses,
> Choose how you will, I am she who disposes,
> I am the queen of hearts and fires,
> I am the Lady of dark desires,
>   Who comes to me must take his chances,
> In lust or luck, so that he dances—
> Come to me and roll the dice—
> Win my love and pay my price!

By night the city's tawdry glitter masked its squalor. The brilliance of the stars was mimicked by the myriad points of light below. Torches burned outside the doorway to each gaming hall, where women or boys with painted smiles called out to the passer-by. Flames glowed behind mosaics of colored glass mined from the ruined cities of ancient times.

Jo was seeing it now from between the curtains of a palanquin, part of the parade of merchandise that Alondro was marching through the main street of the town. The slave-master had said that Jo was to be taken to the prince of the city, and because of that he had consented to be bathed and to put on the white silk tunic they brought to him.

Jo flexed his wrists against the silken ropes. If they meant to treat him with honor, why was he bound? Still, his legs were free. He leaned forward as they passed a promising alleyway, and felt the prick of a dagger beneath his shoulderblade.

"Ye'd not be thinkin' o' leavin' us, would ye?" said the guard who sat beside him. "Th' prince wouldna take it kindly an' ye refused his hospitality!"

"Not if hospitality is what he's offering," muttered Jo, but he eased back against the cushions. Best not risk a try for escape until he knew for sure.

The center of the city was dominated by a great hall, three stories high and built in the shape of an octagon. This must be the arena from which the place took its name, the home of the gladiatorial combats on which some of the city's largest wagers were laid. But he had heard that when there were no fights scheduled, they used the arena to auction slaves.

The procession halted and another guard pulled open the curtains. Jo braced himself against his grip. "This is no palace to which you're taking me!"

"Even so," said his guard, "but this night 'tis where the prince will be."

The steel pricked again and Jo let them pull him out of the palanquin, but the griping in his belly intensified into pain.

"So you are the heir to Westria?" Prince Roderi leaned back in his chair. "They say that Julian's queen is a red-headed woman. Is her temper as fiery as her hair?"

"As fiery as mine, anyway!" Jo thrust out his hands. "Is this the courtesy of princes, to leave a guest bound?"

The walls of the room to which they had brought him were covered by a somewhat faded stamped velvet, but the figured rugs that covered the planked floor were good Elayan weave—an odd mix of luxury and shoddiness, like the town. Behind the heavy curtain that hid one wall, he could hear the murmur of a gathering crowd.

Roderi was a tall man, one side of his face disfigured by a livid scar. Jo guessed that it was no peaceful succession that had brought him to this throne.

"But you are a rather unusual . . . guest," the prince said then. "Sit. Will you drink with me?"

One of the bodyguards cut his ropes, and still massaging his wrists, Jo sat down. A soft-footed servant came forward with a tray. The wine was sweeter than he preferred, but he was in no position to quibble over taste.

"Have you heard from my father?" he asked abruptly. "How much are you asking for me?"

"Those questions may have different answers. You must be patient while I try to explain. Arena runs on profit. It makes things so much simpler when people understand that. You must not take what is truly a matter of business personally. . . ." Roderi paused, watching Jo as if waiting for some response.

Jo stared back at him. The wine had been stronger than he expected. Best wait until his head cleared before he tried trading words with the fox who ruled Arena. From outside he heard shouting, punctuated by cheers. He could not make out the words.

"I sent my agents to Westria. As you might expect, the place was humming like an overturned hive. The raiders who captured you took the precaution of tidying up your campsite so no clues would remain. Your people have no idea what has happened to you." The prince smiled. "And do you know, after consulting with my counselors, I think it may be better to leave it that way. . . ."

Jo tried to speak, but all that emerged was a croak. The servant needed only one hand to keep him pressed down into the chair. He was thinking clearly, but the connection between his brain and his body seemed to have been broken somehow.

"You see, if the Westrians know we have taken you, they will feel vulnerable, and then they will feel compelled to do something about it, and that would be bad for business. We have co-existed well enough in the past because our raids were never—quite—damaging enough to require retaliation. It would be better, I think, to leave the situation as it is, and make our profit in some other way."

"Wha' . . . ll you do . . . wi' me?"

Roderi lifted one eyebrow, as if surprised Johan could talk, and took another sip of his wine. The wine—that's where the drug had been. When Jo saw Roderi choose first, he should have refused to drink at all.

"There may be no one with the wealth of the king of Westria among the bidders, but there are some who would pay well for a boy with your beauty—for a prince among slaves." He rose and moved to the curtain, drawing the heavy velvet aside.

Struggling to focus, Jo saw behind it a balcony that hung above the arena. The bleachers were full, all eyes fixed on a central stage where four women were standing, clad in nothing but their flowing hair and their chains.

"And what will ye give for these beauties?" The shout of the little auctioneer drifted up to them. "Untouched maidens from Deseret, trained to please a man. 'Twould be a pity to break up the team! The starting price is four hundred gold tokens. What am I bid, eh? What am I bid?"

"You would have made a fine show, Prince of Westria," Roderi said softly. "But to display you before the whole city would hardly serve when we wish to conceal the fact that you have been here at all. For you, I have arranged something more private. I warrant you'll bring a royal price, either way. It is known that Alondro has a prime piece of beef for sale, and the wagering has already begun over who will win you. I'll get a cut of each bet, and all of the sale-price, for Alondro works for me. So I'll not lose much by not sending for ransom. It's all business, you see."

There were masters at the College of the Wise who could kill with a word, but even if Jo's head had been clear, that gift was not his. No gift was his, he realized as they hauled him into the next room, except his looks, which had now betrayed him. If he had been ugly, they might have tried for the ransom—or killed him. He tried to fight as they stripped off the silk tunic and the clout, which was all he wore beneath it, but he had no more coordination than a babe. Someone whistled in appreciation as they pushed him up onto a small dais.

The room was full of lamps and mirrors that reflected light across his body and dazzled his eyes. Shadows moved beyond them. There were men there—he smelled tobacco and wine. His flesh crawled beneath the pressure of their devouring eyes.

"And here's the item you've all been waiting for!" said Prince Roderi in silken mockery of the auctioneer. "What will ye give for this beauty? High-born and healthy—ye've never seen his like upon these boards. The bidding starts at a thousand gold tokens. What am I bid, eh? What am I bid?"

"You know, the chances are the lad just took off on his own. If we haven't seen a trace of him it's because he doesn't want to be found."

As they rode, the men behind the king were talking softly. Now and again, when fallen leaves muffled the hoofbeats, some of the words were clear.

"He's the age to think that changing places will change your life. . . ."

"That's so, and wasn't the king's uncle just that old when he disappeared? Maybe there's something in the lost queen's blood that sets them wandering. . . ."

They do not mention our quarrel, thought the king, reining back as an involuntary dig of the spur set his mount surging forward. *They have all very carefully avoided suggesting that my own harshness drove my son away. . . .* The black horse plunged, protesting the conflicting messages of spur and rein.

Julian had never appreciated just how vast and complex a territory his cousin Philip ruled until these past weeks, when it seemed to him that he and Robert had searched every fold in the hills. Rana had ridden with them for a time, but one of them had to be in Laurelynn in case information should come there. They had even sent to Luz at the College, but whatever connection she had had with Jo was broken now.

The Snowy Mountains bred trees and stone, not men. Anything could lie hidden among them. They had found bones of deer and other beasts, but the only human remains they had come across were too old to be those of his son. He had abandoned the center of his kingdom for too long, but how could he return to Rana with nothing to report but the fact that they had found no clues?

In his distraction he had loosened the rein, and Shadow grabbed the bit and broke into a rocking run. Julian tried to regain control, but the furious motion was as much a relief to him as it was to the animal. A part of his mind gibbered warnings about speed on such a path, but in that moment it seemed to him that if only he could go fast enough he would catch the one who eluded him.

The path curved; Julian clutched at the mane to keep his seat as Shadow scrabbled for footing. Hooves clattered on rock; the beast lurched again. Julian slammed into a branch and parted company with the saddle as the black horse went down.

When he came to, he was lying on the ground and Robert was bending over him, swearing. As his breath came back, he felt the first sharp twinges of pain.

"No, don't try to move him," Robert said to someone behind him, then turned. "Julian, where does it hurt?"

"Everywhere," grunted the king as his limbs began to report in. "But nothing critical . . . unless—" His breath caught as he tried to sit. "I may have cracked a rib. How is Shadow?"

"Not much better than you, from the looks of him. But at least he can set all four feet to the ground. What happened? You're no raw recruit, to let your horse stampede that way!"

"I don't know—" Julian gestured helplessly. Above him the black silhouettes of treetops etched a wavering line against the evening's translucent blue.

"Were you trying to kill yourself? It's my job to die for you if there's danger, and yours to stay alive, at least so long as I'm your heir!" Robert exclaimed, voluble with relief. "There are whispers already because the boy disappeared while in my charge!"

"Who?" Julian gripped Robert's arm.

"No, no, it's foolishness. I pay it no mind and neither should you! Marcos!" He turned and called again. "Find us a campsite near water! We'll go no farther today!"

"Then I'd best not get myself killed while in your company . . . ," muttered the king. "Help me up, Robert." He bit back a groan as his cousin hauled him to his feet.

"Damnation, Jul, you know what I meant!"

Julian squeezed Robert's arm in reply.

By the time they had gotten everyone settled into camp, the king was almost too stiff to move. Robert comandeered extra blankets from the other men to pad his bedding, but as the night drew on, Julian began to shiver. Robert crawled in beside him, cradling him spoon-fashion.

"Thank you," the king whispered as the other man's warmth began to ease him. "But what about Marcos?"

"Marcos radiates heat like a furnace," murmured Robert. "He won't even notice I'm gone. And if he did, do you think he would resent it, even if you were in any condition to do more than sleep with me?"

For twenty-five years Robert and Marcos had been a pair, but there had been a time when the lover with whom his cousin shared his bedroll had been Julian.

"Thank you," Julian said again. "I don't deserve your love."

Robert made a small sound of disgust against his hair. "If you thought you did, maybe you wouldn't, but you have always been too hard on yourself, Julian."

"And on my son. . . . I've heard *those* whispers too."

"Who?" said Robert. Then he laughed softly. "Never mind. Folk will talk, and by now we should be used to it."

"Even when it's true? I failed him, Robert. I never learned how to be both a father and a king. . . . At least I have not yet failed Westria—"

"No, my lord." Robert's grip tightened.

"But what should I have done for my boy?" There was a silence as he waited for Robert's reply.

"That's a question my nature has saved me from having to answer. I never had to choose whether to father a child. . . ."

"Then what can I do?"

"We can only do our best, my dear. All we can do is try."

"We have searched," muttered the king. "I have even sent men to Arena—but surely if they had him they would have asked for ransom by now." Remembering their own captivity, the thought of slavers had leapt to both men's minds. "I've kept half a province searching. Lucas Buzzardmoon could track a butterfly on the breeze, and he's found nothing. Soon the men's own families will need them, and I will be needed back in Laurelynn. For the sake of Westria, I will have to give up soon."

Robert sighed. "We have done all that men can, but you are the Master of the Jewels, and it is the heir to the Jewels who is missing. Call on the Guardians, Julian. They know every rock and tree in Westria. I can't think why you haven't done it before!"

"Can't you?" whispered Julian. "And what if they tell me he's dead? Then I will have no hope at all."

Robert's arms tightened around him, but he kept silent. And why had Julian expected it to be otherwise? No one else could do this for him. All that Robert had to offer him was love.

"Help me to get free of these blankets . . . ," Julian said after a little while.

"Can you walk? Do you want me to come with you?"

Julian shook his head. Rana had also borne the Jewels. For a moment he wished she was beside him, her bright energy complementing his own. But the sin, if there had been one, was his. It was better that he face the Guardians alone.

Jo is walking across a golden hillside, beneath live-oak trees. The scent of the air and the gentle warmth of the sun tell him it is Westria, and the relief is so great he finds himself weeping. His dreams have been evil, but now he is safe at last! He reaches out to touch the tree, but something is preventing him. Why won't his arms move? He struggles, and feels the shock of cold water—

And he woke into the nightmare once more. He was lying on a bed with his wrists and ankles locked together by padded cuffs joined by a chain. The servant who had doused him stood back, grinning as if he were hoping for an excuse to do it again. Aware of those mocking eyes upon him, Jo stifled a groan. His mouth tasted like a privy and his head throbbed.

"Welcome to your new home," said the man—*my fellow-slave,* Jo thought bitterly. "There be water for a bath, if you will be gentle. Master has ordered it."

"I'll cooperate," muttered Jo, "if you will tell me where I am and this kind master's name. . . ."

"Supervisor Lake," the man said proudly. "The richest man in Arena, richer even than Roderi, even after buying you. Aye, the prince had best be watchful. Another throw of the dice and he may lose that high chamber from which he has watched so much pain."

"Did Roderi buy his throne?"

"In a manner of speaking. There are many kinds of coin. But up with you now. You've slept the clock around. 'Tis late already, and Master does not like to be kept waiting." He bent to unlock Jo's bonds but left the cuffs in place.

Jo sat up, shivering. His captors had made it pretty clear what they thought he was good for. In theory, he knew what men did together in bed. Even his father—but everyone knew that Julian and Robert had loved each other. He wished now that he had lain with that blond girl at his initiation, or that there was someone—the image of Luz flickered into his awareness and he shut it away. He dared not even think of her in conjunction with what was going to happen to him now.

———————

Jo had expected to be taken to a bedroom, but though there was a bed, the chamber in which Supervisor Lake was waiting for him seemed designed for more active games. He had an impression of gross flesh and bright, porcine eyes, but his gaze kept sliding away from the man. *I will endure this,* he told himself, *whatever he does to me. . . .*

"You are awake now? Yes, yes, I see. Beautiful. Worth every token I paid!"

Jo stood upright as the man padded around him, wondering how much his price had finally been.

"And you understand that you belong to me now, and you will cooperate?"

"That depends," said Jo through stiff lips, "on what you want of me." Given the man's size, his worst danger might be suffocation.

"Ah—still a fighter? Well, it may be more enjoyable that way."

Lake gestured suddenly, and two men who had been standing so still Jo had not noticed them made a grab for his arms. Instinctively he struggled as they hooked the cuffs to ropes attached to the ceiling and the floor.

"That's better." Supervisor Lake's features were not improved by a smile. "Now perhaps we can make you a little more . . . interested . . . in our games."

Jo had thought the sexual instruction at his initiation was comprehensive, but his new master had toys never covered in the Westrian curriculum. Who would have thought that clips on his nipples would bring pleasure mingled with the pain, or that the ring around his member would stiffen him despite his disgust at the hands that put it there? Lake was watching him like a glutton at a feast. He had stripped down to a sarong, and there were beads of sweat on his brow.

"Go—" He gestured to the other men. "Leave us alone."

With hearing that seemed unnaturally sharpened, Jo

heard the door click shut, and then, from the other side, a laugh.

"Ah, my beauty, my beauty—"

Jo's flesh twitched as Supervisor Lake stroked his arm, his side, his back, as if he were a horse to be gentled. It was not working. *Did you do this, grandfather, with Caolin?* he thought desperately, but there was no reply. As his tension increased, the large veins stood out upon his arms. Those damp, pudgy hands were moving all over him; he could feel the man's sweat like the slime of a snail upon his skin. And now the man had moved behind him.

I will endure this . . . , Jo told himself, but he started shaking as his captor began to do things he could not see. Insidious fingers slid oil between his buttocks, pushing them apart, and then he felt the man's flesh pressed against him as Lake reached around to grasp his manhood in one cold hand.

And at that, all his rage and shame exploded and awareness fled. Roaring, he bucked, and the rope that held his right arm tore free. He twisted, and with an instinct beyond thought caught the flailing end, flicked it around Lake's pudgy neck, and pulled. The man's weight plus his own broke the other rope, and Lake fell with his foe on top of him. Now Jo could twist the rope with both hands, riding the shaking belly as the man thrashed, not even feeling the fingers that clawed at his sides for a little while and then fell still.

He stared uncomprehending at the purpled features that had once been those of a man. Then Lake's servants broke through the door.

Nameless, he fought them, too, though they had clubs and swords. He could not defeat them, but that no longer mattered. He continued to battle until blood loss bore him down into the dark. As he fell, he thought he heard a woman's mocking laugh.

5

GUARDIANS

The Master of the Jewels set his back against the trunk of a great pine tree. Life thrummed beneath the bark as the tree drew up nourishment and brought down energy. Gratefully he merged awareness with that balanced strength, focusing inward until he was as centered as the tree. His body's pangs ceased to matter as he took a deep breath and then another, extending his awareness from the roots of the tree through the earth itself to touch everything that grew, seeking the identity that burned within.

"Lady of Earth!" his spirit cried, *"Do my son's feet rest upon you?"* He reached out to the wind that rustled the branches—*"Windlord, does he breathe your air? Can Water or Fire give me news of him? You spirits of tree and bush, has my boy touched you? Lady of Westria, where is the one who will serve you when I am gone?"* The appeal burst forth in a mighty, voiceless cry.

Julian fell back into an expectant silence that deepened as if the whole world were waiting.

"He does not rest upon me. . . . He does not breathe me. . . . He does not swim in the Water or burn in the Fire. . . ." The answer built like the chorus of a sorrowful song. *"Leaf and Tree see him no more. . . ."*

Now Julian recognized the presence, like seeing a scent, or touching a sound, of the Lady who had come to offer him a destiny when he was no older than his son was now. Her answer came all too clearly.

"Johan of Westria is nowhere in this land. . . ."

On the last day of October, the queen of Westria ordered her sorrel mare to be saddled and rode out alone from Laurelynn. She took with her a pack with food and water, and gave out that her intention was to stay a few days with the Lady of Heronhall in the Royal Domain. But that was not her plan, or at least not yet. Her goal was the Red Mountain. Julian's last letter was a burr against her breast whose pricking could not be denied.

"If the Guardians are speaking truth to me, they know nothing. Even the Lady of Westria can give me no word. Our son is gone. . . ."

Once, the peak of the Red Mountain had been crowned by the sorcerer's fortress. Now it bore Caolin's tomb. But below the summit there was another path, overgrown now and little used, that led to a hilltop covered by bay laurel trees. Julian might still be the beloved of the Lady of Westria, but when he lay captive in Caolin's dungeon, Rana had been guided to that hill by a different Power, a Guardian on whom she suspected her husband had never thought to call.

In the light of the setting sun, the lower slopes of the mountain lay still and golden, waiting for the first rainfall to awaken them to vibrant green. Even the leaves of the laurels were dusty. Rana smiled reminiscently as she pushed through them to the sheltered space within—she would have to be careful with fire. . . .

By the time darkness had fallen, the little flame was crackling merrily. She held her drum above it to tighten the skin. She could hear the rhythmic tearing of ripe grass as her horse, hobbled securely, grazed on the slope below. Otherwise the hilltop was still. In Laurelynn, the gates stood open on this night and torches were lit to welcome the spirits home. Families laid an extra place at the table for their dead, and groups of children dressed as ancestors or Guardians trooped from house to house, begging further offerings.

Some whispered that a plate should be set out for Johan this Samaine Eve. That was one reason Rana had come here. The Guardian she sought walked in both worlds.

Surely it was better to seek certainty, even if she must follow him to the land of the dead to find it, than to give up hope without having tried.

She gave the drum an experimental tap, held it to the heat a few moments longer, and beat it again. When she was younger, she would have planned a more elaborate ritual, but she knew now that humans needed such ceremonies more than the Powers on which they called. On such a night as this, Coyote would already be abroad, perhaps tailing the children in the shape of one of the city's dogs in hopes that some food might fall.

"Here's something better, Greedy One—" Rana tossed a string of sausages on the fire, then poured whiskey over it until the flames leaped high. Softly she began to tap on the drum. "Coyote Old Man, are you listening? Wanderer, Shape-shifter, Trickster, by the fire we shared here, I call you now!"

If only out of curiosity, she thought, he would come. Rana beat the drum, eyes half-closing as the rhythm took her, awareness deepening until the fire rose up in a shower of golden sparks that took the shape of pointed ears and glowing eyes.

"Hullo, Old Man, it's been awhile. . . ." She stared into those bright eyes. "I have more meat. Will you sit and talk with me?"

"Is that all yer offerin'?" Wind swirled the sparks sideways, and suddenly it was a man sitting there, wrapped in a gray blanket, with a battered hat pulled over his grizzled hair.

"You flatter me—" Once he had seemed old to her, but he looked to be about her own age now. Her pulse quickened at the appreciation in his eye.

"Always did sell yerself short—" Coyote shrugged and plucked another sausage from the fire.

"I need your help, Old Man," she said briskly. "I need to find my son!"

"Yer menfolk do need lookin' after, an' that's a fact," he said, still munching the sausage. "What makes ye think I'll tell ye what the Lady o' Westria would not say t' Julian?"

"He said she did not *know* what had happened to Johan!

But you could track a sparrow on the wind, or a spirit through the shadow. Must I seek my boy in the land of the dead?"

"I knew a queen who made all creatures swear t' spare her son, but the Lady of the Dark Lands had him even so. There he bides, 'til this age ends and the world's reborn."

"Is that what happened to Johan?" Rana's voice cracked. "My friend at Heronhall has told me that story, but we're not talking about the world here, only Westria!"

In the silence that fell between them, the burning coals hissed and hummed.

"Yet the phoenix must bide in darkness yet awhile, and your world will change before he arises. . . ."

The flames sank low, veiling his face in shadow. His accent had shifted. Even the shape on the other side of the fire looked different now.

"Who are you?" she whispered.

"Coyote, or Wolf, as you please. An old dog, anyway, who has wandered through many lands. . . ." Wind whispered suddenly among the laurel leaves and the fire leaped. Beneath the brim of the hat, she glimpsed the gleam of a bright eye.

"Many lands—," she repeated, "not just Westria . . . and in one of them my son is living. Is that what you mean?"

"That is all I will say," the Wanderer replied. "Hope, and prepare for the storm that will come." The leaves rustled to a new gust. Her companion's outlines blurred like smoke in the wind.

"What do you mean? Where will I see you again?"

"On the wings of the storm!" The voice was the wind that swirled around her. Then it passed, and Rana was alone with the fire.

Jo wandered through dreams of fire and shadow. Presently he realized that he was lying in a wagon, and the wagon was part of a caravan. To their left, the land stretched away in rolling hills of gray and brown. To the right rose the barren eastern slopes of the Snowy Mountains, a rampart against any who might trouble the peace of Westria. Jo did not look at them. Damaged and defiled, he no longer even dreamed about going home. Even the voice of King Jehan had fallen silent. But though the trauma to his body had been great, it seemed determined to heal. As November darkened, awareness returned, and with it memory.

His wounds closed, and the pain of a broken nose, cracked ribs, a strained shoulder, and an impressive array of bruises began to recede. Why was he still alive? He seemed to remember hearing Prince Roderi arguing with several other men as he lay bleeding on the floor. Some had called for a public execution, but that, said Roderi, would be bad for discipline, as well as leaving a trail of evidence for agents from Westria.

"Best to get rid of the boy with whatever profit we may. His looks are spoiled, but he's no use as a bed-slave anyway. There's a man from Marvel's Circus in town, buying fighters for the ring. Sell the lad cheap and get him out of Arena. I owe him that much—" and Roderi had laughed. "He solved a problem for me. . . ."

Jo was still captive, but he could feel the siren song of the Painted Lady receding. Before him stretched the gray distances of the Barren Lands, where the only singing was that of the wind.

A day came when they boosted him onto a horse where he clung, sweating and cursing his weakness. By evening he could scarcely move, but from then on he regained strength rapidly. His fellow-captives acquired names and faces. There were nine men and three women, most of them enslaved for debt. They were not chained, for where in this land could they go? To all of them, the arena seemed a welcome alternative to certain doom in the mines.

They called Jo by his slave-name of "Red," and he did not correct them. The last thing he wanted now was to go back to Westria. Better his people should mourn him as dead than to be saddled with a prince who was useless even as a catamite. The life of a gladiator was usually short, but that hardly mattered. After all, wasn't he a murderer? Only at night did he sometimes dream of sunlight on golden hills. But he did his best to banish those memories, and presently found that if he still had such dreams, he no longer remembered them.

The agent who had come from Aztlan to buy slaves for the circus was a scarred old warrior called Garr. If from time to time his cold gaze fixed on Jo, it held not lust, but a grim speculation. That was all right, thought Jo. He was beginning to view his future with—if not hope—at least a flicker of curiosity.

The heights to the west grew white with snow, and the rivers woke with the first of the winter rains. If the wind's bite was chill, at least they had water, and as they traveled southward, the sky grew wider and the air more free.

Two weeks' travel brought them to the ruins of a city that had been even more splendid and more decadent than Arena. But in the Cataclysm the dam that gave it water had burst, and the city died. Now all that remained were a few humps in the sand, though some said that when the wind blew, you could hear the ghosts of dead gamblers praying for one last lucky throw.

That evening Garr gripped Jo's shoulder and drew him aside. The afterglow of the sunset softened the rough face of the desert and the rugged features of the old armsmaster alike. For a moment, as Jo looked from one to the other, he had the fancy that the light was coming from within, as if only at this magic hour was the reality beneath those harsh surfaces revealed.

"Feeling better, are you, Red?"

"Yes, sir." It seemed natural to respect this man.

"Good," rumbled the armsmaster. "From tomorrow, I wish you to walk with the others. 'Tis not a punishment— you must be in condition if you wish to train for the ring."

"If I *wish*?" Jo exclaimed. "Why else did you buy me?" He looked up swiftly, trying to read those scarred features.

The mule-drivers whispered that Garr had once been a gladiator himself, taken captive in someone's war. Where he had come from originally, no one knew. In the morn-ings, when everyone was stiff and cold, Garr limped, and some lucky stroke had split one eyebrow and left the lid drooping over a damaged eye. One was never quite sure how much the old man saw.

"We will get our money's worth out of you. If you cannot fight, we always need strong arms to load gear and muck out stalls. But in the arena you can earn your freedom in a year."

"If I survive . . . ," observed Johan.

"In the circus, we don't ask men about their past, but those who sold you say you fought as if you did not care to live. My job is to give men like you something to fight for. I gather heroes. . . ." The man's voice deepened. Jo tried to read his expression in the fading light.

Jo felt the rage coiled deep within him stir. "I am no hero . . . ," he whispered. "But there's a dragon inside me. Give him teeth and he will fight for you."

"Yes. He will. . . ." The armsmaster laughed, and for a moment Jo saw in his damaged eye the glitter of stars. Then the last color left the sky. "Ach—'tis growing cold." Garr coughed, and he was only a battered old man once more. "Maybe by now those fools have got the tea boiling. Time we went back to the fire."

At the beginning of December, the air of Aztlan was like crystal. The caravan had made a difficult passage through the mountains, following what was left of an ancient road, but once it reached the lower hills the weather grew more mild.

Now, when they stopped for the night, Garr set his charges to sparring against each other. Any impulse Jo might have had toward friendship with his fellow-captives faded quickly. He had avoided intimacy in any case, lest someone learn his history, but now they all began to withdraw from one another, aware of the dangers in friendship with someone you might one day face in the ring. And soon the others had reason to be wary, for Jo's training as a squire gave him a head start when it came to handling a sword. Once this became apparent, Garr himself took over his training. Then Jo was humbled, for the old man had learned his swordcraft in a sterner school, and knew tricks of the blade that made Jo feel like the rawest recruit from the hills. Even wooden swords could draw blood, and they certainly left bruises, but the body's pain could deaden that of the mind, and Jo welcomed it.

Aztlan was a land of tribal territories, where families lived in small groups or on scattered holdings, or followed sheep or cattle from the high summer pastures to the lower winter feeding grounds in a yearly round. Some spoke Anglo or the tongues of the First Peoples, but for most, the favored language was Spanyol. It was not until the first days of December that their road led them into a broad valley where formations of red rock stood like fortresses upon the plain and the smoke of many fires smudged the turquoise sky.

"'Tis the City of the Firebird," said one of the mule-handlers when Jo asked. "Didn' ya know that's where we're goin'? The circus lies in winter quarters there!"

———————

"I hope that this letter will reach you before winter puts an end to travel." The crabbed writing danced across the page, and Julian moved the lamp and held the paper a little farther off so that he could see. *"I hope to be with you before Sunreturn, but if I should be delayed, there are things you must know."*

The king glanced back at the top of the page. It was dated the twenty-eighth of August, and the Guardians knew how many hands it had passed through to reach him here. The caravaners ran an informal mail service, funded by donations. A pouch full of letters was worth the extra trouble for what it earned in good will. Nonetheless, such missives rarely came by the shortest road.

Rana would be pleased to hear that Piper was on his way home. Julian sighed. Folk said that grief brought people together, but the loss of their son seemed to have raised a wall between himself and Rana. Or perhaps it was his failure to find any trace of the boy. He might have borne it better if she had reproached him. She seemed detached, waiting, but as time passed with no word, Julian became more dismally certain that no news would come.

What fate is on my House that it should so easily lose its princes? he wondered then. But at least the Master of the Junipers had known where *he* was during those years the kingdom thought him lost. The king sighed, remembering how the master's smile had made that little, ugly old man so suddenly beautiful. The adept had been chaplain to Julian's father and confidant to his mother until the sorcerer Caolin's treachery killed them. And during the years when Julian was growing up in the Ramparts, ignorant himself of his true parentage, the old man had come each year to teach him. It was the master's wisdom that had supported them through Caolin's War. . . .

Twitching shoulders still strongly muscled even after all these years, Julian picked up Piper's letter once more.

"Shortly after I met them, the Children of the Sun were run out of Cottonwood. At that time they numbered no more than a few hundred. But they were interesting, and they liked my music.

"That is why I am writing to you now.

"For two months I have traveled with them down the upper branch of the great Middle River that divides the Sea of Grass from the more fertile eastern lands. They stop in each town they come to, from river crossings to city-states, and hold camp meetings. Mother Mahaliel preaches, and when she is talking, she is the mother you always longed for and never knew. They sing and drum. People go out of their heads and dance with snakes, and the sick get healed.

"A curious cult, you will say. At first, I thought so too. But now they number a thousand, and they are no longer a rabble. The black general from the Empire of the Sun has taken charge and rules these 'children' with an iron hand. They are seeking a place to settle, and the folk along the river fear them. But perhaps they are not the ones who should be worrying.

"The Children of the Sun like my music, especially my songs of Westria. They are making their own songs now about the fabled land to the west—to them it seems an

earthly paradise. If it were just that Mother Mahaliel preached about the Golden Land, I would not fear that dreaming, though she has a power to seize the mind that a Master of the College would envy. But the Iron General puts men's bodies at the service of her dream. If the river cities join forces to repel them, where will they go?

"I will try to leave before winter comes. A man alone can travel swiftly, while the leagues between the Sea of Grass and Westria are too many, and the road too hard for such a multitude as the Children. But still I fear. What if they should see no choice but to follow the setting sun?"

The orange winter sun was sinking toward the jagged silhouette of the western hills. Long rays of light glowed in the dust raised by the feet of the fighters so that they seemed to move through fire. The circus called it the Training Hall, but in truth it was no more than a long shed, whose flat roof was needed more for protection against sun than rain in this desert land. Somewhere nearby a woman was singing, and the wind brought scents of hay and horse dung that reminded Jo of home. But the groaning of the camels that came with it was nothing he had ever heard in Westria. Everyone assured him that the gawky beasts would do good service when the circus began its summer progress through the land. Jo hoped so—the one time he had tried to help feed the camels, one of them had bitten him. He preferred to curry the horses, sleek beasts who appeared to enjoy their work as much as did the riders they bore.

At home, thought Jo, folk would be going about in cloaks and woolen caps by now, but in the City of the Firebird, a light poncho gave enough warmth even when the evenings grew cool. The gladiators practiced stripped down to loin-cloths—the better to show off their muscles, said some, or their bruises, said others, and certainly a splendid dappling of purple and green marred Jo's fair skin.

But he was developing the muscles too, he thought with pride, and he had not acquired any new bruises for several days. Contemplating his father's solid strength had always made him feel spindly. He lifted his arm, watching muscle flex as he tightened his grip on the wooden sword. He need fear comparison with no one now, and in the ring, a mask would hide any beauty the broken nose had left him.

The dummy on which he had been practicing swung slowly from the roof beam, lines of white showing on the leather where he had struck it with his chalked blade. He saw that they were grouped closely in the target sectors, grinned in satisfaction, and started toward the bench to get more chalk for the wooden sword.

He stopped short as Garr moved past him to inspect the lines.

"You are doing well. You'll continue to practice, but training the muscles is only part of the job. We need to train your mind, and for that, we must work with steel."

Jo shrugged, and Garr gave him a wolfish smile. "Your speech marks you a gentleman," the armsmaster said. "You've no doubt worn a sword since you were tall enough not to trip over it. But I'll warrant you've never drawn it when you meant to kill."

Jo swallowed. During these days when his whole purpose had been to test his body's limits and go beyond them, he had not allowed himself to think about the purpose of this search for perfection.

"I have killed . . . ," he muttered, twitching as he remembered the sudden terror in Supervisor Lake's face when his captive burst his bonds.

"In a rage," Garr agreed. "Now you must learn to fight with intent and control."

Jo's nod hid a sudden qualm. In all these weeks of training, the dragon within him had been still. Perhaps, he thought hopefully, he was not really a killer. He had slain Supervisor Lake in a berserk fit brought on by unendurable shame. Could he bring himself to strike another human being who had never done him harm? For a moment he considered telling Garr he'd rather serve the circus as a laborer after all. He had made friends with some of the bareback riders, who had no need to fear him as a potential foe and were always glad of an extra hand.

But the other slaves would think that fear had driven him from the ring, and what if some chance taunt brought on the rage once more? At least in the arena, his opponent would have a weapon in his hand. *And if I can't fight back, he'll use it to kill* me, Jo thought as he followed Garr toward the end of the shed.

The end of the shed was enclosed. Pieces of armor hung on the wall and helmets were stacked on the floor.

Garr cast a critical eye over Jo's long frame and tossed him a breastplate and vambraces of hardened leather and a pair of greaves.

"What about you?" Jo asked.

The old armsmaster laughed. "What, do you think you can take me?"

"No, but I might get lucky. You said yourself that you know where a good fighter will aim if he's trying to hurt you, but an untrained swordsman may land a blow anywhere."

Garr raised one eyebrow. "So I did." At the end of the row of hooks hung a battered set of armor whose color had once been black. The armsmaster strapped it on, then unlocked the big chest and drew out two swords.

As they went back to the shed, Jo realized that people were gathering around the training ring.

"Garr's fighting the red head," said one of the women.

"The old man's put on his armor—never saw him do that with one of the new ones before," Manofuerte replied. He was a lithe, dark man, who rumor said would win his freedom this year. Jo had been matched with him in practice and admired his speed, but gladiators made no friends of other gladiators.

Murmurs eddied around him, and the sword felt cold and heavy in his hand. *What am I afraid of? He doesn't want to kill me.* But there was something unexpectedly chilling about the dark figure that faced him. Through the slit in the helm he caught the glint of a bright eye. Yet when Garr spoke, the voice was the same.

"Guard yourself, boy. We'll begin with the sequence you know."

"Aren't we going to use shields?"

The armsmaster laughed. "Think you're a knight? Might give you a buckler to play with later on, but first we work with the blade. The audience wants to see blood flow."

Jo winced as his blade came up to block Garr's first cut and the force of the blow shocked down his arm. It was time he forgot his grandfather's lessons in chivalry. He would never be a knight of Westria now.

Steel clanged as the blades kissed and parted in a sequence that the past weeks of practice had made instinctive. Then he blinked at a red flicker as Garr's sword caught the light. He'd not trained against this move! Jo leaped backward, getting his blade up at an awkward angle. The force of Garr's riposte nearly knocked it from his hand.

"You can do better than that—" Garr laughed and came in again. Those first cuts had been no more than a warm-up. The armsmaster was pressing him now. He heard laughter from beyond the barrier as Garr hunted him around the ring.

I was a fool . . . no good at this . . . after all. . . . Jo's thoughts were as disjointed as his defense, but somehow he kept his feet, and the sword was still in his hand.

"Fight me!" hissed his foe. "Where's that rage you boasted of? Or was your master right, and you're naught but a pretty catamite after all?"

The ring disappeared; Jo glimpsed silk-hung walls and felt the invading pressure of pudgy hands. Then the pain in his belly uncoiled like a snake bursting from its old skin and he screamed.

It was red, all red around him. He knew only the need to slay, and then he knew no more.

When he could think again, Jo found himself lying on his back in a pool of cold water. A man with an empty bucket stepped back, watching him with wary eyes. Jo sat up, shaking his head, and saw Garr removing the shattered shoulderpiece from his armor. Beneath, a smear of red stained the armsmaster's skin.

"Did I do that? I didn't mean—" Jo's voice failed. Garr

had said—something—but his head throbbed a warning when he tried to remember what it was.

"You did what I asked you to do," Garr sighed. "I had to know. . . ."

"It was like a . . . dragon . . . inside me, raging. . . ."

"I know." The old man knelt beside him. Jo blinked, dizzied, as Garr's voice deepened. "Listen to me, warrior. I would spare you the fury—but things are rarely so easy, for you or for me. Need drives us, and one way or another you will become what you must be."

Jo shook his head. "I . . . don't want . . . to kill. . . ."

"It won't be you who does it," the old man said gently. "Only the Dragon. And if you cannot chain him, then I will—" Jo felt himself pierced by that single gaze. "The Dragon needs teeth. He will only come out when you are holding steel."

———◦◦◦———

The cold cut like a knife as Luz sat down, and she drew her cloak tightly around her. Swathed in layers of wool, she had climbed to her favorite perch on the hill above the College to see the setting of the sun. At noon, reflection from the snow intensified its radiance until it was like living in a crystal; but night came early, and the light was dying fast.

The first storms of December had sheeted the western ranges in white and wrapped the Father of Mountains in a snowy mantle. From now until March the only travel would be by snowshoe or sleigh. Already the drifts were growing around the thick walls of dormitories and meeting halls, and from the eaves of the peaked roofs icicles hung. For those students who remained through the midwinter holiday, the College held this to be a season of retreat and contemplation, relieved only by the solemn celebration of the rebirth of the sun.

Luz was one of those who had chosen to stay. At Bongarde, they would be talking about the disappearance of Prince Johan, or worse still, carefully *not* discussing it. To most of Westria he was as good as dead, but those who had the skill to walk in the Otherworld had not found him there. Luz would not have admitted it to Master Granite, but the disciplines he had imposed upon her made it easier to endure the lack of news. At the thought, she felt herself beginning to shiver, and with a firm mental shake returned her focus to the spark within. Like the setting sun, her inner fire was hidden, but it continued to burn. Silently she repeated the words of the solstice invocation—

> *Fire of Life in Power descend,*
> *From the perfection of the One,*
> *Through spheres of splendor without end,*
> *To blaze in Beauty in the Sun.*
> *Holy healer of the heart,*
> *Thy birth redeems each dawn again;*
> *Golden glory, Child of Light,*
> *Sacrifice and Sovereign!*

The sun deepened in color, flaring crimson in the last moment before it disappeared. *Bright as Jo's hair. . . .* He had been born to be a sovereign. Had he, somehow, become a sacrifice? That did not make sense, but then nothing about what had happened did.

Luz slowed her breathing, following that bright orb into the darkness. They had been told to contemplate the inner meaning of the waning days, the reasons to keep trusting that when the world seemed darkest, the sun's course would turn northward once more. She observed the thoughts that floated into her mind, then let them drift away. Smaller and smaller the point of light became, until finally only one thought remained. . . . The Phoenix, like the sun, must die in order to be reborn.

> *A Guardian sings; on mighty wings,*
> *The power descends.*
> *His shining spear destroys all fear,*
> *All life defends.*

Fifty young voices joined in the hymn. Luz watched her breath puff in clouds of mist as she sang. To the east, the gray pallor of the sky was beginning to warm to a delicate pink, but it was bitterly cold on the Father of Mountains in these last moments before the sun rose. At home, she thought rebelliously, they put out the fires at midnight, but everyone stayed cozily in bed until the sun was well up, and they did not venture outdoors to light the solstice fire until noon.

The exaltation of the previous evening had departed. Luz had been at the College long enough by now to realize that dawn rituals were always going to be an ordeal, but even in her current groggy state, she could sing, and the beauty of the music was—almost—enough to reconcile her to the early hour.

> *The harmony that rules the spheres,*
> *And heals the soul,*
> *In beauty balances the world,*
> *And makes it whole.*

The music deepened as other voices joined the song. Robed in yellow, the Masters of the College were processing into the courtyard and making a circle around the square stone altar. Around their necks, large medallions hung. The Master of the College led them, leaning on a staff, and Luz blinked at the splendor of his cope of gold. As the light grew stronger, light glinted from the beads that formed the image of the sun on his breast, and threw the strong planes of his face into relief.

This was the first time she had seen him conduct a major ceremony. For a moment his features seemed without emotion—his nickname in the College was "the Great Stone Face," but she would have expected to see some response to the ritual. Then he turned, and she realized that what she had taken for impassivity was an intensity of focus that made her a little afraid. Blinded by her resentment, she had forgotten that he was a man of power.

The master came to a halt before the altar, waiting as they sang the last verse of the song.

> *It is no chance the planets' dance*
> *Surrounds the sun.*
> *The pivot of our lives is love;*
> *The Holy One,*
> *Restores the world in radiance,*
> *With each new morn—*
> *Redeemer, ruler of the heart,*
> *The sun reborn.*

The last vibrations of the music faded. In the east, the sky was brightening to a radiant salmon pink, barred now with bands of gold.

"This is the uncertain hour," Master Granite said softly, "the hour when we tremble with winter's chill, wondering whether the sun will rise. But there in the sky, you can already see the promise that all will be well. In the four years of your studies here, you will become initiates of Earth and Water, Air and Fire, the elements that are the foundation of our world. In the time of the Cataclysm they rioted in madness and nearly destroyed the land. Yet throughout those years, the sun rose and set at his appointed hour, and moved north and south with the changing seasons in undisturbed harmony."

This altar was for offerings, not devotion. As the master spoke, the other priests and priestesses came forward, carefully laying in its recessed center the dry kindling and firewood they bore. One of the fourth-year students, whose gown was cinctured in the red of fire, knelt to slide out the loose stones in the base that would create a draft upward through the hollow core. At least the clouds in the eastern sky were scattered. Luz had heard of years when Midwinter morning brought a storm and they had to wait for several days to relight the fires.

"And so our ritual year is built around the sun's movements," Master Granite went on, "and each festival has a lesson for our lives. At Midsummer he is sovereign, but that triumph begins his decline. In the spring and fall we celebrate a moment of balance and equality. But in the winter he goes down into darkness that he may be reborn."

That is the thought that came to me last night, Luz remembered. *But what does it mean? Is this a lesson for me alone, or is there some significance for Westria?*

"This dawn is a time for hope, not fear. It is during the midnight vigil, at the hour of earth's deepest darkness, that the miracle occurs and the sun begins to return. It is always so in times of uncertainty. The real moment of change is hidden. We must align ourselves with the forces of Light with only faith to assure us that our efforts will be rewarded. Doubt not that in a few moments the sun will lift over the borders of our land. He needs no help to do so. But will we be able to manifest that holy light here below? Be still, and make of your spirits a mirror that can kindle the sunfire once more. . . ."

He faced the east, where long golden rays were piercing the clouds. The waiting silence hummed with an anticipation that beat against the awareness more loudly than sound. Then brightness flared suddenly in the notch between two mountains, and between one breath and the next the sun appeared. Luz slitted her eyes against the radiance as it began its swift climb up the sky. Then Master Granite lifted his staff, and Luz saw that what she had taken for a crystal was a disc. It swung round, and suddenly it was a spear tipped with a lens of light.

"*Now,* oh ye who serve the Light! Call down the fire!"

Mistress Iris sounded the note, and softly the assembly began to intone the syllables of power. A point of brilliance blazed in the heart of the lens as Master Granite turned it, shafting downward into the kindling laid ready below. The other priests and priestesses were moving forward, uncovering the discs at their breasts to reveal mirrors that they also angled to catch the sun.

Would it be enough? Luz took a deep breath, releasing it in a steady stream of sound. A little white smoke was rising from within the altar, glowing in bands of brightness as the priests shifted position to catch the light. Then came a moment when all joined in a blinding flare.

Luz recoiled, her gaze flickering upward to the sun from which that radiance had come. Transfixed, she stared, then squeezed shut her eyes, whimpering as the afterimage imprinted on her retina burned in an orb of light. From all around her came cries of triumph as the kindling burst into flame. But there was something wrong. To her inner vision, a dark band was twisting around the brightness—a serpent, strangling the sun.

✦ 6 ✦

SERPENT OF FIRE

Six red horses danced around the ring. Beneath the stretched canvas of the great tent, torchlight made their shining coats shine like the chili peppers hanging on the walls of the village whose people cheered them on. Marvel's Circus had begun its yearly migration through the lands of Aztlan, and the Tohono O'odham tribesmen of Estrella had given them an enthusiastic welcome. Even Jo, watching from behind a screen as he waited for the combats that were the climax of the show, felt his tension overwhelmed by wonder as the horses lifted their hooves with exaggerated grace, swaying and curvetting to the touch of Señor Chigaio's wand.

Their names had been announced as they pranced in: Serrano and Salsa, Rocotillo, Jalapeño, little Tepin, and Habañero, the great stallion who ruled them all. Jo grinned. These days, helping Chigaio and his sister Chiquita with the horses was almost the only human contact he had, and he had learned to call the horses by their stable-names. To him they were Sara and Sally, Rocky and Penny, Tip and Baby—great, curious creatures with hearts as warm as their sorrel hides, quite unaware of their power.

Chiquita opened the flimsy barrier and four of the horses trotted out of the circle, ears pricked and tails swishing as the crowd applauded them, russet coats dimming suddenly as they passed into the shadows outside. Within the ring, Sara and Baby stood and stamped as the two riders cinched their saddles. Now, as the horses trotted around the circle, the performers vaulted to their backs, riding with crossed arms, directing their movements by shifts in weight and pressure of leg and heel almost imperceptible to the eye.

Aztlan bred fine horsemen, and the audience was accustomed to see men swing down from the saddle to snatch up a dropped handkerchief, to shoot the bow or throw the lasso while the reins flapped loose on a pony's neck. But all those were extensions of a horse's natural inclination to run, to herd, to play. Sara and Baby moved in perfect unison, stallion and mare mirroring each other's movements without apparent direction from their riders, their powerful bodies extensions of the humans' will.

Jo's breath caught at the harmony of motion, the animal's natural agility transmuted by the human mind into poetry, human imagination brought into manifestion by the horse's willing offering of power. *It should be that way when I'm fighting,* he thought with unexpected pain. *I should be riding the Dragon. But when I take up the sword, it is Jo who is the horse and the Dragon who rides. . . .*

The sand of the ring absorbed the horses' hoofbeats so that they seemed to float across the ground. Jo's heart drummed in his breast; in a few minutes it would be his turn to perform in that ring. Light blinked outside, whitening the canvas; then he heard a roll of thunder. The horses threw up their heads, ears flattening, and Jo sighed, recognizing the galloping beat of spring rain.

Rain drummed on the roof of the great hall of Hightower, but Lady Elen and her maidens had garlanded the beams and decked the tables with April flowers. From its position on the heights above Rivered, Lord Philip's fortress offered a fine view over the Great Valley, whose marshes and pastures were blooming beneath the veils of rain. Behind it the foothills rose in folds of green, with the mountains no more than a brooding presence beyond. Snow still lay in the high passes, but the season had advanced sufficiently for a few pack trains to get through, and one of them had brought with it Farin Piper, finally home from his wanderings.

Philip's message had said that Piper was well, but the last push across the Snowy Mountains had been exhausting. It seemed foolish to make the bard travel any farther before they welcomed him home. And Julian had other reasons for visiting his cousin now. The kingdom needed to know that he did not blame the Ramparts for Johan's loss, and the Council wanted to know which of Philip's children might be the best choice to take his place as heir.

They sat now with their own families just below the high table. William, the eldest, was a short, stocky young man whose hair was already beginning to thin though he was only thirty years old. He had two little boys of his own, now tucking enthusiastically into the tarts that had been served at the end of the meal. His sister Jeanne was only two years older than Johan. She had taken Elinor of the Corona as her model and was a regular winner in the tournaments. William was more mature, but he had grown up expecting to rule the province one day, and had close ties to his land. Jeanne, being younger, might find it easier to adjust to the idea of ruling Westria. Best, Julian supposed, to begin working with both of them. That was assuming that either was willing to take the job. At the moment, he could not see why anyone would want to.

He closed his eyes, memory summoning the image of the Lady of Westria who had come to claim him so long ago. *"Lady, you chose me. Choose now a new Champion!"* For a moment the murmur of conversation around him faded, and he seemed to hear a reply—*"When Westria is in need, one of your line will always hear her call. But first must come the testing."*

Julian sighed, and reached for his goblet. At the movement, Osleif leaped forward to refill it with the rosy wine that had been served with the meal, blushing the same color as the wine as he splashed the tablecloth. Wiry and enthusiastic, with a mop of brown curls, he was the fifteen-year-old son of a former guardsman from the holding of Greyhaven in the Royal Domain. The king had recently taken him as a page. He hoped he could do better by this boy than he had by his own.

"Piper looks older," said Rana, her gaze on the table just below theirs, where the bard sat with Frederic and Lenart, his faded purple bard's cloak dulled by the rich red of their seneschal's robes. "Or perhaps it's because he is so thin."

We all *look older,* thought Julian. His own hair had grown perceptibly more grizzled since last fall. But Farin's cheekbones stood out above the short brown beard, and there was something haunted about his eyes.

"I had hoped he would play for us. Do you think he is too tired?" Julian said aloud.

Philip shook his head. "He would be disappointed if you did not ask." And indeed, with a bard's instinct for timing, Piper was already swinging his legs over the bench and reaching for the battered harpcase that leaned against the wall behind him.

"Your Majesties, and ye Lords and Ladies of the Ramparts—" He bowed to the high table and to the hall. With an audience before him, his weariness seemed to have fallen away. "The snows of your high country were too chill for my voice, but my fingers have recovered, and if you wish it, I will play for you—"

"Please, Master Farin—we have missed your music!" Rana used his formal title, and held out her hand in greeting as someone brought a stool and set it on the dais before them.

The bard smiled, and for a moment Julian was reminded of the shy boy Piper had been so long ago. Then he began to play, and the king remembered that he had won the cloak of a master bard on his own merits, not in memory of Silverhair, even though it was with Silverhair's "Wander-song" that he began. Perhaps he would never have his mentor's magic, but he had been well taught from the beginning, and his technique was seamless.

That tune seemed fitting, since Piper had set out to retrace Silverhair's wanderings, but the music that followed was new to them—a bouncy, brash piece that Piper had heard in a gaming hall in Arena, slow sad tunes that caravaners sang on the long miles on the trail, and ballads from towns with names they had never heard before. Sometimes he would put down the harp and take one of his flutes from its case; the pure, sweet notes floated through the hall with an aching intensity. But presently the melodies took on a more formal character, the chords building compellingly. It seemed to Julian that the bard frowned as he played them, his expression easing only as he finished with a rendition of "The Black Swan Rising," a song of the Ramparts by a legendary bard called Mistress Siobhann, who had lived before the Cataclysm.

> We came, strangers to this land,
> With nothing but our will.
> Our hands were open and deeds were put therein.
> Stone surrendered to our will,
> Sweat made barrens yield our fill,
> We wrought in ice and fire, a home to win.
> Blood and spirit bind us to the hills,
> And to the soil,
> Our hands were open to do and not just try.
> Faint hearts never won the spoil,
> Boldness makes the cauldron boil,
> We'll feast with Fate and dare her to reply!
> Welcome, stranger, to our home;
> The feasting board is laid.
> Our hands are open to all who come as friends.
> Share our pride in what we've made,
> But come not with a foeman's blade,
> For what the Swan has built, the Swan defends!"

When the feast was over, the boards were cleared for dancing, and Philip led his more notable guests to the privacy of a smaller chamber in the tower. From time to time they could hear the music of the consort drifting up from below.

As the others found seats, Julian paused by the western window, looking down over the walls to the tangle of lanes and dwellings in the town. Rivered had been built in that liminal zone where the plain gave way to the foothills, clinging to the high ground south of the river. Long ago the Ancients had built a great city downstream where the Silvershine flowed into the Dorada. But when the dams were destroyed in the Cataclysm, all that was swept away. In a wet year, the spring floods could still be dangerous. But everyone knew there was another reason that the meadows by the river were only used for pasture. Once, it had been the site of a prison, and the place was still haunted ground.

"Well, Master Farin," said Frederic. "You have lost none of your skill. After such a concert, we hardly need to hear your report. Your music has painted us a picture of those distant lands."

He sat down—his son, like a taller, solider shadow, standing behind him. Philip's offspring were there as well, their grave faces suggesting that they knew very well why they had been invited to join this select company.

"Not entirely," said the bard. He coughed, and Lady Elen handed him a mug of mulled wine. "Sorry—this rheum is my own fault, really. I smelled the storm coming, but I thought I could outrun it."

"Well, you should have known better!" Rana observed tartly. "After almost two years away, surely you could have waited another two days. . . ."

"Perhaps, but at the time—" He shook his head. "Well, I am glad you liked the music."

"What were those last pieces you played?" asked Frederic. "I could not decide whether they were meant as marches or hymns."

"Perhaps they were both," Julian answered, coming away from the window and sitting down beside Rana.

"They made me think of your reports, Piper. Was that the music of the Children of the Sun?"

Some of the tension went out of the bard's face as he nodded. "I would have been home sooner, but they put me under guard. It was not until November that I escaped them. The Suns had split into six camps by then, each with its own commander, settled in for the winter along one of the rivers that runs through the Sea of Grass."

"Their numbers have grown, then?" asked Rana, beginning to understand.

"Beyond all imagining—" Piper ran his fingers distractedly through his thick brown hair. "They are too strong now for the cities to destroy them. They descend like locusts, and they strip the countryside of more than food. They open their meetings to all who will come—every Sunday a festival! Rana, do you remember that story you told me about a piper who lured all of a town's children away? After listening to Mother Mahaliel, I begin to think I do not deserve my name. When she preaches, young and old leave their hearths to follow her."

"That cannot be good for their lands," observed Frederic thoughtfully.

"It's not. The Sea of Grass cannot support so many all together, but if Mahaliel's Children separate, they will be at the mercy of whatever forces the city-states can raise. They might move east, where the country is richer, but the Iron Kingdom would see that as a threat, and its army is strong."

"Do you really think they will come here?" asked Robert. "They would have to cross both desert and mountains. Could so many make the journey?"

"If spring comes early," answered Piper. "If they moved fast, by now they could be nearing the borders of Aztlan." In the silence that followed, the patter of rain on the roof sounded like distant hoofbeats. "There are words to those songs I played for you," he added then. "They sing of the golden road, the sun road their god has shown to them. They sing of a promised land where the sun sets into the sea."

The faces of the others showed the beginnings of anxiety,

but Robert's gaze met Julian's. He did not need to speak aloud. *What army could we raise if they should come? Our swords are rusty and our bows cracked with age. It has been twenty-five years since we had to think of war.*

"There are many leagues between us, and Aztlan breeds fierce warriors," Philip said bracingly. "Any enemies the desert spares will fall to their spears."

No doubt he was right, thought Julian as conversation started once more around him. But he made a mental note to sit down with Robert one day soon and arrange for an inventory of the weapons in the armories of Westria.

Down stabs the trident and down stabs the spear,
Thumbs stab the air for the man who shows fear!
How the crowd roars as the dust rises high,
In the arena, who'll be first to die?

Jo stepped aside as Chigaio and Chiquita trotted out of the ring, still standing on Baby and Sara's backs. The stallion snorted and flicked an ear at Jo as he went by.

But he dared not think about the horses now. As he turned back to the arena, the music grew louder and his lips curled in a feral smile. The first time he heard that tune he had faltered, remembering Lenart and a tavern in Westria; but in adobe towns all the way across Aztlan the song had acquired a new meaning, coming from throats already hoarse with cheering. From the City of the Firebird the circus had moved south to the lands of the People of the Desert, and then to the east, playing for the Chiricahua and the Mescaleros before moving northward up the Grand River into territories shared by Chicano and Pueblo tribes. In the south, the brief desert spring was almost done, but with each mile north they had moved higher, and the wind that blew beneath the canvas sides of the tent was cold.

Jo scarcely noticed. The song was his now, a call to battle more certain than any clarion. In war, a man *might* die, but death was certain when the Red Dragon strode into the ring.

Remote though the town of Ogaponge that nestled

against the Blood Mountains might be, its people understood. The combats were always the final attraction, after
the performing animals and the acrobats and the clowns.
The animals grew dangerous and unpredictable when they
smelled blood on the sand.

In Jo's first fight in the City of the Firebird, the distraction of so many eyes upon him had nearly made that blood
his. A pink scar across one cheek bore witness to his initiation as a gladiator. Only the responses Garr had trained
into him had enabled him to kill his man. They said you remembered your first kill as you remembered your first
lover. His arm still quivered to the instant of resistance before the force of his blow carried his blade through the
man's neck and a crimson fountain sprayed across the
sand, as his skin still twitched from the clammy pressure
of Supervisor Lake's hands.

The memory summoned the familiar red haze to color
his vision. Tomorrow, when he saw who was missing at
breakfast, he might feel sorrow, but for now, the net-and-
trident fighter who had appeared at the opposite gate was a
faceless embodiment of all Jo had learned to hate and fear.
As Garr had promised, it was growing easier to unleash the
fury. The weight of the sword in his hand had become a
key to release the Dragon within.

The singing turned to cheers as Jo stepped out from behind the screen. Liza the clown held out the red leather
sheath, skittering back with a panic that was only partly
feigned as Jo jerked out the blade and stepped forward.
The other performers treated their star attraction with a
wary care. But they were accustomed to dealing with dangerous animals. The Dragon, Jo thought grimly, was only
one more.

He could feel Garr's gaze upon him and did not know
whether to welcome or resent it. He shook his head, feeling
a rush of heat despite the lingering winter chill as the monster began to wake.

Not yet. He tried to rein it in. *Let me remain myself for
just a little while.*

The two combatants halted in the middle of the ring,

bowing to the alcalde of the town, who sat with his wife and daughters in the gilded box next to Master Marvel, then turning back to salute each other. Jo settled into a fighter's crouch, the small buckler on his right fist angled forward, longsword poised in his left. A red dragon had been painted on the buckler. From his helmet fluttered a red plume. Beyond a harness of red leather and his clout, no clothing hampered him, and he exulted in the free flex of muscle beneath his skin.

He could see the moment of uncertainty as his foe realized he was fighting a left-hander, and his grin broadened. Sand squeaked beneath his bare feet as he dug in, drawing up strength from the soil, and the burning knot in his belly flared through every limb as the Dragon uncoiled.

The net was a blur, sweeping toward him. He ducked, whipping the buckler up and across to deflect it, catching the trident as the motion continued, whirling, and bringing his sword down and around toward the man's knees. But his opponent was already leaping backward, pivoting to ready the net for another throw. Some part of Jo's mind recognized the move as one he had trained against, though he did not remember the man's name. Next he would leap sideways—the Dragon slid aside to meet him, sword rising to beat the plunging trident aside.

Another flurry of action left a stinging line of red on Jo's thigh. In the next, the net whipped around his sword arm, but he slipped free and responded with an upward cut that slashed his opponent's arm. As the warriors circled, cheering erupted from the bleachers in waves of sound.

Jo saw an opening but ignored it. They did not like these fights to end too soon. The other man drew breath in harsh gasps as he settled into a crouch, waiting. Sweat glistened, defining the swelling muscles beneath his tan skin. Between the slits of the helmet, eyes gleamed. *Take position and outwait him,* thought Jo, but the Dragon had other ideas. Straightening, he began to pace around his enemy, arms extended, sword and buckler held high. *Preening . . . ,* thought that part of the mind that was still Jo's. His enemy turned uneasily in place to face him.

"Red Dragon! Red Dragon!" The earth quivered as the audience shouted his name. And at that call, the Dragon expanded fully, and Jo's awareness was lost in a haze of flame.

To the watchers, the moment when the prowl became a strike passed too swiftly to see. The net flew high and settled over both men, heaving as they struggled. Dust rose in veiling clouds. And then one fighter stood, flinging the net aside. It was the pale man. His helmet had come off and they could see his flame of red hair. His opponent lay shuddering, blood seeping from a wound in his belly. The point of the Dragon's sword hovered, then settled to the throat of his foe, and he looked up at the gilded box. The crowd stilled, recognizing something unhuman in his eyes. Throughout the bleachers, thumbs were turning down.

For a moment the alcalde conferred with Master Marvel. Then he rose, extended his arm, and slowly turned his fist so that his thumb pointed toward the sand. The Dragon twisted, his blade whirling back and around once more to slice through the throat of his prey. Then he stepped back, sword raised high, and red ribbons of blood twined down the shining steel as the people of the Pueblo cheered.

Ogaponge was an old town. According to the locals, even at the time of the Cataclysm it had been ancient. From all accounts, it had not changed much in all those years. In the beginning it had been a gathering of flat-roofed adobe buildings grouped around a central square, and that is what it was still, the crossbeams of its shaded walkways festooned with strings of red chilis and hung with bunches of Indian corn.

The rancho of the alcalde sprawled across the rolling piñon-studded grasslands to the south of the town. To celebrate the arrival of the circus, he had arranged for a fiesta at which performers from the circus were the featured guests, and Jo found himself the star. But really it was the Red

Dragon they were welcoming, he told himself, adjusting the cape of crimson wool over his sleeveless burgundy tunic and breeches sashed with red, and remembering to walk with the swagger they expected. In Westria, this night was also a festival. He thrust aside the memories of Beltane dancing around the fire.

"Ah, Señor Dragón, that was a fine fight!" The alcalde himself took a glass of some cloudy liquor from the tray the servant was holding and offered it. "I have seen all the great fighters, and indeed you have the gift, young man. That final feint and thrust—beautiful!"

"You are gracious, Señor." Jo had learned to deal with such questions in ways that would not reveal how little he actually remembered of what happened on the arena's sands. The drink had a sharp, fruity flavor. He sipped, then coughed as the initial sweetness kindled explosively in his gullet.

"It is *torbellino*—" the alcalde explained, smiling. "Worthy of the dragon, no?"

Jo blinked back tears and resolved to drink no more of it as he struggled to hold back a sudden surge of agreement from the Dragon within. *You do not want him at your party, trust me!*

Jo's lips twisted wryly. "Its fire is worthy of this land—"

"Then drink, my young friend! I won a nice stack of *reales* on you!" Still smiling, the alcalde passed on to his other guests.

Jo eased toward the door and passed his drink to the armsman who guarded him, wondering how much he had won or lost for others in the room. Wagers were taken by those who sold the tickets for the circus. Each time Jo was the victor, a percentage went into the account that was building to buy his freedom. He never asked how much was in the fund, and his guard's presence was only a formality. What use had he for liberty?

A servant came by with a platter of meats rolled in bits of tortilla. Jo took one, thinking the food might absorb the fire in his belly, and looked around desperately as the chili sauce in which the pork had been soaked filled his mouth with new flame. He had thought himself accustomed to Aztlan's cooking, but the chilis of Ogaponge were of a strength to make even the Dragon quail.

Where were the ubiquitous servants now, when he needed one? Ancient alcaldes glowered at him from old paintings in tarnished gold frames. The *sala*'s massive beams, dark with age, continued on to shade a balcony that ran the length of the room. Beneath a painting of a large flower, two local merchants were arguing about why the spring caravan from the Sea of Grass had been delayed. Near the door, several of the acrobats chattered to a man in the fringed buckskin garb of a trader. Jo started toward them in hopes one might have some water. He sometimes helped them with their chores, and they had taught him a few tricks in return. He had found that he could not live without human contact entirely, and at least he would not be asked to face the tumblers in the ring.

A soft hand grasped his arm and he whirled. The woman who had touched him gasped, then laughed and slid her fingers back across the hard muscle of his forearm.

"I should have expected," she said a little shakily, "that you would be fast, as well as strong. . . . I am Milagra de Mirabal y Begay, daughter to the alcalde here."

Jo bowed, willing his pumping heart to slow. After the manner of this country she was beautiful, with dark eyes and sleek black hair coiled and held by filigreed silver pins.

"My apologies, Señora. I was intent upon finding a drink—your chilis—" He fanned his face and she laughed.

"Come," she said then, signaling to a servant. "It is hot here and crowded. We will find you something cool to drink and then go out to the balcony. From there you can see the snow on the mountaintops. In the moonlight it is very beautiful."

His skin tingled as her nails moved lightly across it, and he felt a tightening at his groin, followed almost immediately by a roiling in his belly. Gently he pulled away. One of the first bits of folklore he had learned at the winter quarters of the circus was that some women were attracted to gladiators. There were fighters who had made more profit from their exploits in the bedchamber than in the ring. But the evening after his first victory, Jo had discovered that he would not be one of them.

"You are very beautiful, but the vows on which my power depends require me to abstain from women . . . ," he said quietly, wishing it were true. "But if you still wish it, I will come and look at the moonlight with you." He took the fine blackware mug the servant brought in response to the lady's order and swallowed the tart-sweet liquid gratefully.

The sickness that prevented him from making love to a woman was not dispelled by recognizing its origin in his initiation in Supervisor Lake's playroom. Knowing that the experience had been even more traumatic for the supervisor did not help. Killing was the only release he had.

Milagra looked at him from under her lashes. She was older than he had at first thought her, old enough, anyway, not to be flustered by his response. "Then we will look at the moon," she said, smiling, and led him into the cool night air.

To the north, the town lay quiet, leached of color by the moonlight except where a fire showed sometimes through an open door. To the south and west, the land fell away in a patchwork of plowed fields and range land studded with small piñon pines. To the east rose the Blood Mountains, their lower slopes clad in groves of aspen and their tops rich in fir and spruce and pine. The snow that still clung to the highest peaks glowed in the moonwashed sky.

"There is the trail that leads over the pass and east to the Sea of Grass—" Milagra turned him a little to the right, where a pale ribbon of road ran toward the hills.

"Who lives up there?" Jo asked.

"A few hunters—why do you ask?"

"I see lights, like Beltane fires."

As she turned to see, they both heard a rider approaching at full speed. In the distance behind him, points of brightness pricked against the dark mass of the hills, more and more of them, winding down the road like a serpent of fire.

Luz slapped the taut skin of her drum and felt the vibration in her bones. Light pulsed across her flickering fingers as the dancers stamped around the Beltane fire. At her side, half a dozen hands rose and fell on drums of all sizes in swift syncopation, and the earth quivered in sympathy. At such celebrations the first-year students were the drummers, just as it was the privilege of the third-years, who were studying the element of Air, to complete the music with flute and viol. Other "muddies" were responsible for the feast, while the second-year students, working with Water, had brewed the mead and ale.

Those who were not busy otherwise were free to join in the dancing, but for the senior students it was an obligation. Part of their training had included kindling the fire of life through ritual dance, and the bonfire did seem to blaze more brightly when one of the crimson-clad dancers passed. Some of them had stripped off their festival robes—their eyes were dilated in trance already, and now and again two bodies would twine together before the dance whirled them apart once more.

Luz found herself staring at the dancers' tossing hair, the smooth slide and play of trained muscles beneath sweat-sheened skin, lost the beat and forced herself to focus again. Her breath was coming a little faster, and the heat that coursed beneath her own skin was not entirely from the fire. The dancing at her initiation had not aroused her, but this was both more intense and more focused, an ecstatic response to the season's burgeoning energy.

Some of the masters had joined in the dancing as well, though they all still had their clothes on. Gray robes blurred into the shadow beneath the oak tree. Luz had heard Master Granite say that to allow such license at the College was not immoral, but unworthy. Rutting in the fields was all very well for farmers, but priests and priestesses should be able to sublimate the sexual energies into power.

"Look at Ginevra," whispered Radha. "She's always seemed so quiet, but now she's beautiful!"

The tall blond girl was spinning in place, her shining hair raying out like beams of light. Firelight flickered on the smooth curves of breast and thigh. As she turned, Ginevra's eyes fixed on Luz and she smiled. A pulse of heat surged through Luz's body, and she fought the compulsion to leap up and join in the dance.

"That's not Ginevra . . . ," she muttered. "It's the Lady of Fire. . . ."

"Well, whoever it is, she's looking at you—"

"I don't want to do anything we'd both regret in the morning when she's herself again. Ginevra has never said two words to me!"

"What makes you think she'd be sorry?" asked Radha. "A lot of people think you're pretty, boys and girls too." She set down her drum and slipped one arm around Luz's waist.

For a few moments Luz allowed herself to lean into that soft embrace. Then, with a sigh, she pulled away. "If I lay down with anyone at this festival, it would be you, but—"

"But what?" said Radha crossly. "It's Beltane—that's what we're supposed to do." Clearly she had not heard Master Granite's views on the festival.

As if the thought had summoned him, Luz looked up to see the Master of the College watching her from across the fire, but she could not read the expression in his eyes.

"I don't know what's stopping me." She turned to her friend with a defiant smile. "Maybe I'm afraid I would be too distracted from my work if I let myself fall in love with you. Or maybe I am just afraid to lose control."

"Sweet-talker!" Radha shook her head. "Give me a kiss, then, because I absolutely cannot sit still anymore."

Radha's lips tasted of cinnamon. Luz was still smiling as she watched her friend leap into the dance. Why, she wondered, had she refused? Did some part of her agree with Master Granite? It seemed unlikely, when Radha's kiss had set a sweet pulse throbbing between her thighs. She stilled as another thought came to her—would she still be sitting here if it had been Johan, with the firelight gleaming on his naked limbs, summoning her to dance?

I would go to him, she thought bitterly. *I should have done it last summer—at least I would have had that memory!* And what use had she now for the passion she would have offered him? Perhaps Master Granite was right. If memory barred her from any other lover, she had better take the Way of Renunciation and transmute her love for one man into love for the world.

Phoenix! her heart called. *Where are you? Arise and come to me!* She got to her feet, staring into the fire. If Master Granite was still watching, she did not see him. The face that appeared before her was Jo's, his features distorted by the surging flames.

⇥ 7 ⇤

SUN AND WIND

On the festival grounds outside Ogaponge, the Children of the Sun had stretched enough red and yellow canvas to shade the hundreds gathered there. Over a week had passed since their arrival, and today the more prominent members of the community had received an invitation they could not refuse. As Jo followed the other circus folk into the shadow, the murmur of voices rose around him like the wind in the treetops, or perhaps it was the distant whisper of an approaching forest fire. He twitched nervously as that energy pulsed around him.

The invaders had arrived with the inevitable power of some force of nature, though the lack of news from anyone to the north should have warned them of the oncoming storm. By the time most people woke up on Beltane morning, their fields and pastures were filling with tents and wagons and livestock and people—hundreds of them, marching beneath the banner of the serpent and the sun.

The militia had fought a short, bloody engagement at the foot of the pass, and the alcalde had sent warning south to the governor of Cibola. But if the invaders were trail-worn and hungry, they were also well armed and well organized. The best guess put their numbers now at three thousand, more than doubling the population of the town. At the height of spring, there was ample forage for the animals, but the fields and gardens had been newly planted, and people were living on what was left in their storerooms. In this land, the most valuable gold was corn.

On a wagon in the middle of the pavilion stood a single sturdy chair. Behind it hung a white banner with the device of a crimson serpent coiling through the rays of a radiant golden sun.

"Simple, but effective," muttered Master Marvel, surveying the setting with a professional eye. His purple coat seemed garish against the undyed homespun worn by the crowds who were seating themselves on the grass. Jo had tried to be unobtrusive in a tunic and breeches of pale tan, but nothing could dim his hair. Ahead of them, Milagra and her father were being herded into place. The old man looked ill, but his daughter's face was set and proud.

Their escort pushed the circus folk toward the worn carpets that covered the ground before the wagon. Jo put out a hand to help the circus-master sit, then sank down cross-legged beside him with a grace that made the older man sigh.

"There was a time I could of done that, lad. I was a tumbler once, did ye know? 'Twas a fall did for me—hazard of the trade. Just as well my tongue was more nimble than my legs. Old man Marvel adopted me, and here we be—" He looked around him with wry resignation.

There was a stir at the edge of the tent, and drums began a slow, steady beat. Down the aisle that had been left through the crowd a procession was approaching, led by men in white tunics belted in red who bore unsheathed swords. No mere honor guard this, thought Jo, noting the scarred faces and muscled shoulders. These were warriors.

Behind them came young men and women in white with gold sashes, singing. Soon he was able to make out the words.

> *A mighty sovereign is the Sun,*
> *A never-failing power—*
> *Above all gods the Mighty One—*
> *This is His holy hour.*
> *His Chosen Ones are we,*
> *His triumph we shall see,*
> *Led onward by His grace,*
> *To claim our promised place,*
> *Where we shall dwell forever. . . .*

Their smooth faces intent and exalted, the singers split off to left and to right as the warriors took their places before the wagon. Behind them, people bent like corn beneath the sickle. Jo blinked, trying to focus, and realized that they were bowing to a woman, clad in a gown so purely white it seemed to glow. Her escort was a big man, his skin shockingly dark against his own white robes. Around his neck was a golden gorget; from his crimson baldric hung a great sword.

I would not like to face him *in the ring,* thought Jo. He forced his gaze back to the woman. His first thought was that she was not so young as she had seemed. Then she looked at him, and he knew he had never seen anyone so radiantly beautiful, although in the next moment he could not have said in what feature that beauty lay.

"Mother Mahaliel," went the whispers, and Jo realized this must be the invaders' mysterious leader. The black man would be her general, Tadeo Marsh. Then she had passed, and Marsh was assisting her to ascend the steps to the wagon. A dozen female guards continued around to its other side.

The last murmurs stilled as Mother Mahaliel lifted her hands.

"My beloved children! What joy it is to see you here! For surely you are the Faithful, the Chosen Ones, who have survived the *jornada de la muerte*—the journey of death, as they call it in this land. Rejoice in your suffering, for thus you are purified!"

A sigh went through the gathering. Jo lost the next few phrases as he tried to understand what it was about the voice that was so compelling. Perhaps it was warmth—to listen was like coming into the sunlight on a dark day.

"And so I tell you once more—" Mother Mahaliel was saying now. "Love is the answer to all your questioning. You have nothing to fear, for nothing can separate you from my love for you.

"What do you love, my children?"

"We love the Light!" a thousand voices answered her.

"Who do you love?" her words rang out.

"We love our brothers and our sisters in the faith!"

"What do you love?"

"We love all that is pure!" The litany gained intensity.

"And who loves you?"

"Our Mother loves us!" shouted the crowd. Some of them leaped to their feet, stretching out their hands to the woman who stood with her own arms outspread as if to embrace them all.

"Indeed I love you, and like a good mother, I will ease your pain, for the power of the Sun shines through me and I work His will. Who among you is suffering? Bring him to me!" She lowered her arms and stood waiting with flushed cheeks and shining eyes.

The people began to sing again, clapping their hands as they swayed, and they came—men with fevered wounds and women coughing from illness, old and young, they came to her. Some, from their dress, were natives of Ogaponge and not her people at all. And she knelt at the edge of the wagon and embraced them, and they went away eased. When a man was brought to her moaning in his litter, she laid her hands upon his chest, eyes closed and lips moving in prayer. Jo blinked and looked up for some gap in the canvas, seeing her bathed in a golden light that spread gradually from her body to envelop that of the sick man.

And it was not Mother Mahaliel only. Here and there among the crowd he saw others who were also glowing, their faces rapt. People formed circles around them, singing. Instinctively Jo tried to block the energy that pulsed around him. It reminded him too much of the Dragon's ecstasy.

At last she sat back, and the light faded. For the first time since her entrance, Mother Mahaliel looked old. But the man on the stretcher was sitting up, his face shining with joy.

The crowd buzzed as the procession made its exit, the chorus singing once more—

> *And though a thousand foes should stand,*
> *Their spearpoints sharp and ready,*
> *To bar us from the promised land,*
> *Our purpose shall hold steady.*
> *The Sun's pure power rules all;*
> *The evil ones must fall;*
> *Their strength will not avail,*
> *Our faith will yet prevail,*
> *His Light will shine forever. . . .*

The people of Ogaponge honored the sun as Tewa; for Westrians, the sun was the sacrificed sovereign. How could the same power generate such different theologies? Jo was still trying to understand when their guards returned for them.

Mother Mahaliel and her general received them in the long meeting room that looked out onto the courtyard of the old Palace of the Governors. The previous week had been stormy, but the invaders seemed to have brought the sun with them. The sweet scent of the lilac bushes planted by the entry filled the air.

With a bitter smile the alcalde looked at the table over

which he had once presided. "What do you want with us? Is it not enough that you have taken all we had?"

"Except your lives . . . ," Tadeo Marsh observed dryly. The alcalde shrugged.

"Except your souls," Mother Mahaliel corrected. She looked up, her eyes soft with sorrow. "It is not bloodlust that drove us here but the need to find my people a home—and to bring light to all people who still walk in superstition and darkness."

"As you did for those you killed at the pass?" Milagra exclaimed.

"I grieve for the necessity, but the will of my god must be done," Mother Mahaliel said simply. "For the crowd I must make the message simple, and compel those who cannot understand. But you are people of culture, and so I appeal to your reason. Does your faith teach you how to banish sickness, whether of soul or of body? Ours does. Does your faith give men clear precepts to follow? Does your faith join all men and women in loving community? Ours does. . . ."

Does your faith teach men how to live in harmony with their land? wondered Jo, his Westrian upbringing surfacing, but he knew better than to ask. The teachings of the Covenant seemed hard compared to all this love and joy.

"They tell me that your territory here is called Tiwa, after the Sun. It makes sense for you to join us—" She held out one hand, her face growing luminous as she smiled.

"The governor of Cibola has rejected our ultimatum," said the general. "We will leave a garrison here and march on the city, and we will need men who know how to govern those of your people who convert to our cause."

"We would be foolish to let you remain here, but we can give you another place to rule . . . ," Mother Mahaliel said then.

"And if I refuse?"

"Then you will have nothing," rumbled Tadeo Marsh. He gestured toward the door. "You are free to go. But the Children do not share their food with unbelievers, and there is not much left. Mahaliel has a hungry family. . . ."

"I . . . understand. . . ." The alcalde gazed around him as if to memorize the room. "What must I do?"

"Come to me—" Mother Mahaliel moved around the table and took him in her arms. For a moment he stood stiffly. Then he seemed to relax, and when she released him his face was wet with tears. Still weeping, he stumbled toward the door, and the Mother's gaze shifted to Master Marvel.

"My lady," the circus-master said swiftly, bowing, "I cannot imagine what ye might want with a band of mountebanks, but can we be of any use, Master Marvel's circus is at your service!"

Jo eyed him with mingled admiration and annoyance. The man owned his body, but not his soul, and except for the fighters, the performers were free men. What right had Marvel to make such promises? *No right but necessity . . .* a bitter inner voice observed. *We "people of culture" know how to cooperate with the inevitable.* But he wished that Garr had not somehow managed to make himself invisible when the Sun guards came. Surely *he* could have found some other way.

"And is this the will of all your performers?"

"These are the stars of my show. They will speak for the others—" The tumblers nodded nervously as Master Marvel introduced them. One by one, the others made their bows—Chigaio the horsemaster and scarred old Tam who trained the cats and wolves, Ezequial the sinuous juggler, and Liza and Bon, the two principal clowns.

"And the red-haired lad?" asked Tadeo Marsh. Jo grimaced, knowing that the general had recognized him as a fighting man.

"They call me the Red Dragon," he said in a low voice. "I am a gladiator."

"No—" Mother Mahaliel's voice overrode his, and he flinched, subjected for the first time to the full intensity of her gaze. "You have passed through the fire of combat and emerged reborn, is it not so?"

Transfixed, he felt himself nod.

"You are the serpent of the sun." She smiled radiantly. "You shall be our talisman."

———⟐———

The banner of the sun and the serpent flew from a pole in the courtyard of what had once been the Cibola residence of the governor, who ruled the eastern territories for the king of Aztlan. Through the wide doors that led out to the veranda, Tadeo Marsh could see it clearly. Scarlet bougainvillea hung from the eaves and twined down the posts of the porch, a frame for the white banner and the blue sky. The picture gave him considerable satisfaction, tangible proof that their gamble in leading so many people through the *jornada de la muerte* had paid off. He stretched, grimacing as he saw how lean his arms looked now. Their supplies had been running very low, at the last, but with the resources of Aztlan to draw on, he would fill out again fast.

The people of this land held to the wise practice of maintaining a two-year supply of food in their storehouses in case the crops should fail. As they moved south, the Suns had stripped Ogaponge and the Tiwa and Keresan pueblos that lay along the Great River, and his men were ransacking the town of Cibola for more. The small garrison King Bartolomé maintained here to deal with inter-tribal squabbles had fled when they saw the size of the Suns' migration. The king himself was wintering at the City of the Firebird. No doubt, riders were pounding along the trail to bring him news of the invasion even now, but they had a long way to go.

In the dry warmth, Tadeo felt muscles he had not known were tensed begin to ease at last. Cibola lay where an ancient road crossed the Great River. There was grace in the rugged contours of the mountains beyond the garden wall, and the river, edged with groves of oak and cottonwood and the new green of irrigated fields, drew a strip of verdure through the land. He thought he could grow to like it here. But did he truly want to stop now? The trek through the wilderness had winnowed out the weak and tempered the strong among the Children of the Sun. What remained was the material from which he could shape an army unmatched by any force in this part of the world. In any case, for the majority of the warriors, settling was not an option. Even if this land could support them, it was not the golden land of Mother Mahaliel's dreams.

As if the thought had summoned her, the door opened and the priestess entered, attended by old Hortensia and Bett, a raw-boned, brown-haired woman who was the child of a clan-father who had died on the march. Tadeo rose to his feet and bowed.

"Blessed be the Light, Lady," he murmured, assisting her into one of the heavy chairs.

"Destroy the darkness," Mother Mahaliel replied.

If he had begun to relax, thought Tadeo, *she* was positively radiant, as if she had absorbed some of the sunlight blazing outside.

"The men are ready to march?" she asked.

"By tomorrow morning they will be. Some of the new horses need shoes, and we are still loading supplies."

"What exactly are our resources?" Mahaliel asked then, with the clear grasp of essentials that had first persuaded him to put his skills at the service of her dream.

Tadeo picked up the papers he had brought to this meeting and began to list the wagons that carried the clan-fathers and their families, and those filled with supplies for the marching men, one wagon for each two files of ten. They were loading now with corn and beans, and more oxen and mules were being gathered, along with flocks of sheep and goats to supply them with meat on the way.

"So your counsel is to move on now?" she asked when he had done.

"Yes, if we are going to go. The men I've talked to say that there will be more grass for the stock if we take the northern way. The tribes there are fierce, but unlikely to unite against us. We can raid for more supplies, and in any case, men are better at marching on empty bellies than beasts who do not understand the need," he replied.

"The need . . . ," Mahaliel echoed. "There have been times when you doubted it—do not trouble to deny that, my son. If my Father's Light did not burn within me I would have doubted myself sometimes. That assurance is the gift He has given me. Your gifts are of the flesh, not the spirit, Tadeo, as they need to be. Together—" She laughed, stretching out her hands. "See what we have accomplished! We crossed the desolation where our foes predicted we would die, and we have taken these towns almost without losing a man. We surprised them, to be sure, but the victory has put heart into our soldiers. I think you need not fear to pit your men against whatever forces the king of Aztlan eventually leads against you. My god does not lie, Tadeo Marsh—" She leaned forward, and he found himself transfixed by that lambent gaze. "He has promised to lead me to the Golden Land, and He will open the way!"

She sat back and poured cool herb tea for both of them from the earthenware pitcher the alcalde's daughter had brought in while they were talking. They were leaving the alcalde himself to rule here in the Suns' name, with a garrison and those families who for one reason or another could not continue the march, nearly a thousand in all. But the numbers they lost had been made up by new converts, men whose knowledge of this land would guide them on the next part of their way.

Tadeo blinked, a little surprised that he could still be caught by her spell. "To victory!" He lifted his cup in salute and drank, savoring the aromatic flavor.

"To the triumph of the Light!" she echoed him. "Go on now, my son, and see to your horses."

* * *

Jo surged to his feet, dropping the carrybag he had been mending, as a stallion's scream split the air. Men ran toward the horselines and a woman's keening shrilled through the warm air. When Jo got there he saw Chigaio lying sprawled in Chiquita's arms, while Sun guards in white tunics backed away from the horses, who were plunging in terror as the scent of blood filled the air.

"They came for Chiquita," whispered one of the grooms, "to make her a whore for their soldiers."

Jo's eyes widened. He had been aware of the Suns' peculiar custom of assigning a captured woman to each file of ten soldiers, to cook and mend for them and meet their other needs, but they had all assumed that the circus women would be exempt. He dodged between two soldiers and knelt at Chigaio's side.

"He tried to defend me," whispered Chiquita, gazing down at her brother. The curved knife with which he had been paring the horses' hooves was still gripped in his hand, but his bronzed skin was growing gray as the last blood drained from a great hole in his side.

"I'll speak to the priestess," said Jo. "She's adopted me as some kind of mascot."

"No," said the woman with grim finality. "They kill you, too. . . ." She took the knife and crossed her brother's hands on his breast, murmuring to the Lady Guadalupe to receive his soul. A boot crunched on sand and she looked up, eyes flashing as one of the soldiers came toward her. "Take care of the horses, Red. Don' let them 'ave Baby— he's always been loved—they try t' force him, he'll fight crazy."

Like me . . . , thought Jo, then realized that Chiquita was rising, the hoof-knife in her hand.

"You want me?" she taunted, the little blade flashing. "I geld you, outland dog, if you try!"

"I've a weapon that will tame you, infidel mare," the man replied, lowering the lance with which he had brought Chigaio down. Blood was darkening on the tip of the spear. He jerked it suggestively and his companions laughed.

There was no humor in Chiquita's answering smile. She gazed around the circle of white-clad men. "You beat your horses an' your women, I know. You will not beat me—" Her hand flashed up, but the curved blade was angled inward. Before any of them realized what she intended, she tore it through her own throat. Blood sprayed as she fell.

The Sun soldiers started forward, and Jo snatched the weapon from her limp hand. Its steel was tooth enough for the Dragon, awakened by the iron tang of new blood on the sand.

"Let her die untouched by your dirty paws," he snarled. The Suns stopped short. They had not seen him in the ring, but apparently they had heard tales.

"Watch out!" cried someone behind him as the red stallion neighed, and before Jo's fear for the horse, the Dragon fled.

"Ezequial—," he called out to the juggler, who stood staring in horror at the two bodies on the sand. "Take care of them! And you—" He motioned to the grooms. "Help me get the horses out of here." Scornfully he tossed the knife aside.

The red stallion flung up his head as Jo approached him. He stopped, murmuring, hands open at his sides, and as the horse stilled, ears pricking, eased forward again. The first time he heard the stallion's name he had laughed at the idea of giving the name of the smallest of the chili peppers to the largest of the horses. But Chigaio had explained that habañeros, though tiny, were the hottest, and Baby had been undersized as a colt, though spirited from the day he was born.

"Habañero, my proud one, be easy . . . your master and mistress are gone." He fought to keep his voice even. "But I'll take care of you. . . . Come now, Baby—" He stroked the taut muscle of the stallion's neck and braced himself as the horse butted its nose against his side. "Come on, lad—" He reached out to loosen the picket rope with one hand and with his other grasped the halter, feeling a rush of relief as the great head came down and the stallion turned to follow him. "We'll take care of each other. Come away with me. . . ."

———◦◦◦———

"Your ally will lead you, protect you, carry you," said Master Badger. Light flickering through the interlace of branches barred his face with shadow like his ally's mask. "He may even lend you his shape. He is, you see, not your servant but your friend."

The month of May was coming to an end, and the alpine meadow beyond the buildings was starred with pink and white flowers and veined with sparkling rivulets where the seep of snowmelt pushed through the thin soil. Once more, the students who had gathered to work with their animal allies found the trees that shaded the amphitheater a welcome protection from the sun. But almost everything else, thought Luz, had changed. Her Earth Year at the College of the Wise was almost over. Her fellow-students had forgiven her for that psychic shout once they learned that the prince was gone. Her relationship with the Master of the College remained uneasy, but the man had ceased to persecute her.

I should be proud of what I have accomplished, she thought sourly. But though the shift into trance was easy, none of the animals she saw in her journeys seemed willing to stay with her.

"Friends, ha!" muttered Kamil, who had been working with an astral red-tailed hawk since before he took his name. "Do allies always talk to you as if you were an idiot child?"

The master shrugged his powerful shoulders and laughed. "Most of the time. Makes you wonder why they bother with us, doesn't it?"

"It makes me wonder whether they are really animals or our own spirits, finding a way to speak to our minds that we can hear," Radha said then.

"Ah now, there's a question that has puzzled the masters," the adept replied. "But if working in this way gets results and does no harm, does it matter what our allies *really* are? If Badger helps me to dig into a problem, I will not question him."

"Mistress Iris says that there are many parts to the soul, and at the highest levels our spirits are connected to the spirit in everything," observed Luz. "So maybe in the end it doesn't matter how the soul-stuff divides."

"So that by becoming separate selves, Spirit may become self-known?" Master Badger asked. "That is a question for your Air Year, and each person must find his or her own answer. Just now, however, we need to act as if our allies were real. Settle yourselves for a journey, my friends, and let us seek them."

As the master took out his drum, Luz crossed her legs and straightened her back, rooting her own energy to that of the earth in the way that had become habit. She closed her eyes, riding the drumbeat into a vision of the meadow atop the Lady Mountain, where since her initiation her journeys had always begun. She had enjoyed her explorations, but the creatures of earth remained strangers. Would the heavens be more helpful? She allowed her awareness to surge upward.

As a child she had often lain on the hill above Bongarde, seeking creatures in the sky. Now she did so once more, searching for shapes in the clouds. Was that a horse or a camel, or perhaps a whale? Even in trance she knew that she was smiling. *If I could call for an ally,* she wondered, *what would I choose?* Even as she was aware of the thought, she recognized the serpentine elongation of the cloud above her—a white dragon, a cloud dragon, soaring the skies.

Enthralled by that pure beauty, her spirit arrowed after it. The shining shape looped and spiraled, interlacing the clouds. She laughed, trying to imitate the sinuous motion, and the long, elegant form of the dragon flowed toward her.

"Will you be my friend?" she called. *"Will you carry me through the spirit world?"*

Glowing eyes transfixed her soul. *"If you will carry me in the world of men,"* came the answer. *"Give yourself to me—"*

Luz recoiled as the eyes expanded, their beauty suddenly too great to bear. The dragon was too powerful—frantically she drew in her awareness, fighting for control. For a long, desperate moment, the dragon was a tumult of energy around her. Then it passed, and she was left gasping in the wind.

On the third week out from Cibola, a cold wind began to blow, rattling the canvas covers of the wagons. The Children of the Sun were passing across an arid plain, broken in places by canyons where sage and greasewood held down the red soil. On the horizon, fantastically sculpted peaks and mesas banded in red and white rose from the sand.

To Jo, the journey had passed like a dream punctuated by moments of explosive action. The Pueblo of the Lake, just off the old road where sandstone bluffs tried to bar the way, was easily overcome, and Jo discovered that the maneuvers that made the red stallion's performance in the ring so impressive could be used in battle as well. However Acoma, where they had headed for the sake of the springs at the foot of the mesa, proved impregnable. While the warriors of the Pueblo shot down at them from the shelter of adobe houses that seemed to grow out of the rock, they watered their stock and then went on.

At this season, the washes and streambeds were dry, but by those who knew where to look for seeps and springs, water could be found. The general had divided the migration into three groups, traveling a day apart to allow the waterholes time to refill. A surprising number of plants grew here, though most were of little use to man or beast as food. From a distance, they turned the land a pale silvery green. As they plodded onward, the patient oxen grazed on tufts of grass that grew in the spaces between the clumps of sage. In the distance they sometimes saw pronghorn antelope, which bounded away as the wagon train drew near. The land stretched before them in broad swathes, broken by rock formations in every shade of red and gold. Where it rose, scattered clumps of piñon replaced the sage. Climbing higher still, they passed through mountain meadows surrounded by great long-needled pines.

By the time they came in sight of the noble mesas that guarded the lands of the Ashiwi, the general had seen the wisdom of sending messengers ahead with gifts to buy safe passage, water and grazing rights, and to hire guides for the next part of the journey. And still they went on. To Jo, each day became part of an endless present in which he was suspended between worlds.

But just now, the dream was becoming a little too exciting. Habañero shied as a gust sent dust-devils spinning across the rutted track that was their road. In the west, gray clouds were gathering. It would be a good day to spend indoors, but for the travelers that was not an option. The grass here was sparse, and the water from the spring where they had camped the night before had been exhausted by their company. They could only hope it would have recovered by the next day, when the group that was behind them in the line of march came along.

Only the ravens seemed to be enjoying the weather, calling back and forth as the wind flung them across the sky. They made Jo think of a song he had learned from Piper, who had gotten it from the bard Silverhair, who might once have traveled this very road. Softly he began to sing.

Over the prairie, the wild wind is blowing—
Is it a flute song I hear, or the wind?
Where have you come from, and where are you going?
The ravens are dancing, high in the wind.

Over the desert, a trackway we follow.
The footprints that lead us are blurred by the wind.
But still from ahead sings the flute, sweet and hollow,
And ravens are dancing, high in the wind.

Whose are the footprints, and whose is the playing,
That sounds through the wild lands, borne by the wind?
Look, through the sagebrush a humped shadow's straying,
As ravens go dancing, high in the wind.

"Don't you let the soldiers hear you singin' that song," said the driver of the wagon beside which Jo was riding, a man who had been drafted in Ogaponge along with the oxen he drove. Some of the other circus folk had drifted back to ride with him. They had all drawn together since being absorbed by the Suns. Despite the uncertainty of their situation, Jo found himself less lonely than before.

"Why not?" he asked.

"It's a song 'bout the little flute-player who led the Ancient Ones a-wanderin'. Long before the Cataclysm that was, but folk hereabouts say he shows up sometimes still."

"Seems to me we can use all the guidance we can get," said Jo.

The drover laughed. "Not from Kokopelli. The Suns say that's all superstition. Don't want no guide but the sun."

Jo peered at the sky, which was turning a dirty grayish brown as the wind swirled more dust into the air. The gusts were stronger now, rocking the heavy wagon on its wooden wheels. The only one who did not seem worried was Garr, who set his gray horse to chasing the tumbleweeds, and laughed when the ravens swooped low, and croaked an answer to their calls.

"What sun?" he asked grimly. The clouds building on the horizon trailed gray veils of rain. Even the brilliant colors of the mesas were muted beneath such a sky.

The drover laughed, but Jo had not been joking. He could feel powers abroad that owed no allegiance to the deity the Suns adored. The Diné tribesmen had a spirit they called Nílch'i, Holy Wind. The Suns were passing through that tribe's territory now—it seemed to Jo that the Guardians of this land might not be pleased at this invasion of folk who honored no gods but their own.

As the day drew onward he began to be sure of it. The wind blew harder, lifting veils of red dust and flinging them across the road so that men must tie their scarves across their faces and trust to the beasts to find the way. Sometimes the dust gave way to a spattering of rain, and once, for several uncomfortable minutes, the two were mixed and they were pelted by blobs of mud.

It was enough to daunt even the Suns' resolution. Presently a rider came cantering down the line with orders to halt and form the wagons into squares with the animals inside. It would be a dry camp and a hungry one, but at least they would not be blown away. Jo unsaddled Baby and turned him loose in the square, then climbed onto the wagon box with Garr and the driver while the rest of the circus folk and some of the Sun soldiers took refuge within the wagon or beneath it.

The wind no longer reminded him of flute-song. As he huddled into his blanket, he felt anger in the gusts that plucked with hungry fingers at its folds. The spirits of this land did not know, much less welcome, him; but he could feel them on the wind. Here, even before the Cataclysm, the tribes had never ceased to show the Holy People honor—no wonder, he thought, shivering, their guardian spirits had such power.

Wind whirled stinging dust around him. He glimpsed a square head crowned with thrashing plumes spitting lightning bolts, and recoiled with a cry. Then he felt Garr's firm grip on his shoulder.

"What is it?" said the older man when the tumult subsided.

"A face—," he said hoarsely. "A face in the clouds."

"The Wind People and the Cloud People are playing. You never seen them before?"

"The storms are gentler in—in my land," Jo replied.

"No sense in fearing the wind." Garr sighed. When he spoke again his voice had changed, as it did sometimes. "What you saw was only a mask. Holy Wind is everywhere. The same breath of life that flows through you flows through the world. Without it," he added with a smile, "nothing could live. So there is no reason to be afraid." But in the next moment he stiffened. Something thunked into the side of the wagon, and he thrust Jo down.

Jo stared at the black-feathered arrow quivering in the wood, his first thought amazement that anyone could shoot in this wind. He heard a woman scream. The desert erupted in a cacophony of cries, and they all scrambled to get behind the wagon, fumbling for knives and swords. The Diné were the largest of the tribes, but by now their clans should have separated to follow their sheep to the upland pastures. The Suns had thought they would be unable to muster a large enough warparty to dare an attack.

Then the Diné rushed the wagons, and there was no time to point out anyone's mistakes, only to react, grappling furiously with enemies who struck with the ferocity of the wind. This was not the ritualized butchery of the ring, but a scrambling, breathless struggle for survival in which there were no rules. Jo was not aware of the Dragon's arrival, but when he came to himself once more, a sword was in his hand and most of the blood that covered him was not his own. For once, he found himself grateful for the berserk fury that had carried him through the fray.

The wind was fading, and with it the Diné tribesmen, carrying their dead and wounded with them, so that if it had not been for the blood on his sword and the body of the drover next to him, Jo might have thought the whole affair an evil dream. Even the clouds seemed bloodied, dyed a dirty rose by the setting sun. The butte behind them glowed an even deeper red. Jo picked up a handful of sand and began to scrub at his bloody hands. From the other wagons came calls of greeting as men hailed the light, but when the sun appeared for a last moment between the horizon and the skeins of cloud, he saw not the serpent-wreathed golden disc of the Suns, but the face of the tribesmen's Tewa, framed by raven feathers and painted in red, turquoise, and gold.

✦ 8 ✦

THE FURNACE

"Baby! Stand still, you red demon! Those hobbles will rub your fetlocks raw!" Jo cursed as Habañero plunged awkwardly across the mountain meadow. "The Yavapai hunters will get you, boy. . . . Look, I have something for you—" Fighting the temptation to run after the stallion, Jo shook the loose corn in his hat suggestively.

He had learned the hard way that even hobbled, the horses could outrun him. He had inherited his mother's gift with them, and when this journey began he had thought he understood them fairly well. But the past six weeks had taught him many things. In Westria he had ridden constantly, but his mounts had been brought to him groomed and saddled, and pack horses were only beasts that brought up the rear of a royal cavalcade. He could now treat everything from a sprain to a saddle gall, and hitch a pack that would stay put through stampede or sandstorm.

"If you don't come now, I'll give it to Sally—" He turned toward the red mare who was already tethered to a pine tree and shook the corn in his hat again. He had been riding the two sorrels, changing mounts each day, and it was the stallion's turn. In truth, Baby would be lucky to get a few kernels. After nearly two months on the road, the Suns had no grain to spare for horses. The contents of Jo's hat had come out of his own share.

Instinctively he ducked as a shadow passed overhead, and looking up, saw the raven's wings flare momentarily bright in the sunlight as a long glide carried it between the pines. The road had brought them to the mountains through high desert drier than anything they had faced before, a barren land of red earth on which little but sagebrush grew. Mesas and escarpments of sculptured stone stood like monuments set by the gods to guard the land, and the snowcapped peak that hung on the horizon seemed a mirage. The mountains belonged to the Flags, an Anglo tribe whose town nestled below the peaks. After a brief and bloody clash, the Suns had stripped the town of supplies, but scouts told them that to the west water was scarce and human habitation even scarcer. It was now June, one of the driest months even in an unusually wet year. They needed a place to re-stock and rest until the summer monsoon rains arrived.

So now they were moving southward through Yavapai territory, a land of mountains whose pine-clad slopes reminded Jo achingly of the Ramparts. It was hard country, but the Ancients had carved stone like butter, and though eight centuries had healed many of the land's scars, the road they had cut through the mountains still led to the Valley of the Sun, where even now the first harvest would be ripening in the irrigated fields.

Something brown moved among the trees and Jo stilled, eyes narrowing. There were elk and mule deer in these mountains, either one of which could provide a feast. But right now, even one of the wary wild turkeys would be a welcome addition to the menu. Carefully Jo set down his hat, eased his strung bow over his head, and slid an arrow from his quiver. A pine branch moved, and he saw the finely shaped head of a deer. Scarcely breathing, he raised and drew the bow, sighting more carefully than ever he had done to win a prize. *"Not without need,"* he thought, remembering the words of the Westrian Covenant. His bow creaked as it took the strain.

As Jo released the arrow, a large red shape shouldered up against him—Habañero, whuffling gently as he stretched his head to lip up the corn. The clearing echoed with the sound of Jo's curses, the thwack as the arrow hit a branch, and the crashing of greenery as the buck bounced off through the trees. But even as he dropped the bow, Jo was grabbing for the stallion's halter.

"You pig," he muttered. "If I didn't know I'll need you when King Bartolomé finds us, I'd shoot *you*." And the warriors of Aztlan must be waiting for them. There was no way to hide the approach of so great a company.

Jo caught a whiff of woodsmoke and his stomach growled. At least someone had found breakfast. Then he realized the scent was coming from the wrong direction, and a yellow haze was veiling the sun.

Fire . . . his nerves twitched. He wondered if King Bartolomé had some equivalent of the Four Jewels of Westria with which to maintain the balance of elements in his kingdom. Could he invoke the powers of his land against his foes?

As he led Habañero back to camp, he saw that the column of smoke was rising from a distant ridge. The fire would not catch them this time.

But it is waiting, he thought then. *The spark that will ignite the fury is always there, waiting within.*

The City of the Firebird was burning. Fingers of smoke groped at the pure blue of the sky. Jo had last seen the Valley of the Sun in the early spring, when the desert was starred with flowers. Now it baked in the furnace of July. It seemed redundant for the Children of the Sun to add fire.

In Aztlan the sun was a constant presence. The people called him Tewa, and called on the other Guardians—whom they knew as the santos or the kachinas or the yeibichai—to moderate his power. But there was no moderation here. Heat beat down upon Jo's helmet and Habañero stamped nervously beneath him as King Bartolomé led his warriors around the humped red rocks they called the Camel and across the flat. The red stallion had learned to face yelling tribesmen without flinching, but the sustained tension of oncoming battle was new to both horse and rider.

Starkly sculpted hills framed the valley like the benches in the circus, and outcrops of stone rose from its floor. It was an arena, thought Jo, where men would die. In the two months since they had left Cibola he had fought in many skirmishes, but this was his first formal battle. The night before, he had dreamed that he stood with his grandfather upon the field, the first time in months that King Jehan had come to him. He wondered if the dream presaged death or victory.

In this land, towns of any size were few. Isolated forts might have palisades, but there were no walls around the cities—nothing to stop a hungry horde like the Children of the Sun. Bartolomé's approach had forced a rapid withdrawal, but the city still burned. Jo caught the sound of distant screaming and swallowed bile. There were women and children in the town. Many of them had cheered for him the first time he walked out onto the arena's sands. *I should be with them,* he thought grimly, *not here. . . .*

In theory, the invaders outnumbered the Aztlan forces, but two companies were still behind them on the road.

More of their fighting men had been delegated to guard the slow-moving herds of sheep and goats on which they lived. Still, between the challenges of the march and the general's discipline, in the two months since they had arrived in Aztlan, the eight hundred men who faced Aztlan's thousand had become an army.

But the warriors of Aztlan were accustomed to fighting in the dry heat of the desert. They rode like centaurs, and they were defending their homes. During their trek through the mountains, the Suns and their captured mounts had received some seasoning, but few had formal training in cavalry tactics. For most, horses were still no more than a means to transport soldiers to the battlefield. The untrained mounts waited now in the rear.

Habañero's nostrils flared as he scented other stallions among the foe. It tore at Jo's heart to see the gentle training with which Chigaio had redirected the stallion's natural aggression eroded by the stresses of combat. The horse trainer must be cursing him from whatever afterlife he had come to, but his mount's swift responses and agility had saved Jo's life several times.

He could make out faces in the approaching army now. If the Sun infantry squares broke, the enemy's massed cavalry would be very dangerous. The men of Aztlan rode in tribal groups—he recognized the broad brown faces of the Tohono O'odham and the rougher features of the Chiricahua. Silver flashed from the bridles of the Spanyol horsemen. Beneath their steel caps, the faces of the Anglo foot soldiers were red with sun. The circus had taken the southern route on its way eastward to Ogaponge, passing through their lands. They would know that the Red Dragon on whom they had wagered now rode, however unwillingly, with their foes.

The sour summons of a cow-horn bellowed from the enemy side, and from the Suns, a ram's horn trumpet replied. A spotted pony was emerging from among the ranks of the Aztlan warriors. Its rider carried a white flag.

"What do ye think, Red—are they going to ask for terms?" muttered Manofuerte. Most of the gladiators had been absorbed into the fighting companies, but Manofuerte had once been a hunter, and the general found him useful as a scout. At least, thought Jo, he now dared to make friends with his former rivals in the ring.

The herald drew close enough for them to catch the scornful flash of dark eyes beneath his helmet brim. His torso was protected by a cuirass of boiled leather painted in tribal designs. Jo, who was sweating profusely beneath a red leather brigandine stiffened with plates of iron, wondered if the garment allowed more air to circulate than his own. Habañero stamped and switched his tail, then stilled. He was more patient than his rider, thought Jo, as well as being marvelously sensitive to his every move. Would that sweet responsiveness survive the blood and tumult of the battlefield? Jo had asked for a different mount for the battle, but the Suns had few horses swift and agile enough for mounted combat, and Mother Mahaliel liked the picture the circus horses made with their red pelts shining in the sun.

The herald reined in before them. "My king says, 'Why do you come to my country and burn my cities? Why do you kill my people with the sword?'"

"We did not come here to conquer." The screen of Sun soldiers moved aside as General Marsh moved his big brown horse forward. "We are on our way to the land that has been promised us. But our people must have food, and if it is not given freely, we will fight for what we need." That sounded like conciliation, and there was a sullen murmur from among the Sun troops who could hear. After weeks of being picked off by arrows from ambush, they were eager to come to grips with a tangible enemy.

"You are bandits and murderers, and you follow a false god! Tewa watches over us and will punish you."

"Perhaps." Marsh gestured at the infantry companies he had arrayed in a series of blocks to face the enemy. Their armor consisted mostly of hardened leather, but each block was protected by overlapping shields and bristled with spears. "But I have eight hundred soldiers who say differently—"

"Eight hundred and one more, who carries our luck in his fangs," a new voice put in.

The general glanced back, frowning, as Mother Mahaliel urged her white mule through the line. "Lady," he muttered, "you should not be—"

"Your people have called the Sun by many names. I bring you the new revelation that supersedes all," she interrupted him. "By His light will we conquer. But it is true that there has been too much killing." As she lifted her veil, the enemy herald flinched, unwilling to meet her eyes. Jo wondered what tales of her the people of Aztlan had heard, and whether they came anywhere near what he knew to be true. "If these armies meet, more will die, no matter who prevails. I challenge your king to a duel of champions, the army of the loser to retire from the field."

"And who would your champion be—him?" The herald gestured toward Tadeo Marsh.

"Your king is a young man." Mother Mahaliel's voice was like honey. "I would send a young man, if Bartolomé is brave enough to face him. I will offer you the warrior whom vision emblazoned on my banner before ever he came to my hand. I will send the Red Dragon out to face your king!"

Sweat prickled beneath the padding underneath Jo's helm. Before she had finished, he had known what she would say, and understood why she had furnished him with the knight's lance and armor. But from the tension in Marsh's lips he guessed that this plan had not been discussed with the general.

"What if the boy loses? Will we run like scairt hens?" came a whisper from behind him.

"These be unbelievers, lad," came the answer. "If the gladiator dies, we'll avenge him an' have our fight jest the same."

By now Jo had seen enough of General Marsh to know that no considerations of sportsmanship would prevent him from seizing any advantage he might find. Had it been different in the days when King Jehan fought Elaya, or was war always this bitter testing in which men both transcended and abandoned their humanity? For certain, it was nothing like the ceremonial combat of the arena—except for the red veil that hazed his vision when he drew his sword. But today the sword would stay in its sheath. The Dragon was not stirred by the weight of the spearshaft in his hand. Jo's objections faded. He too wished to end the killing, and there was at least a chance that the men of Aztlan would retreat if he went out there and won.

The herald frowned. "I will tell my king." He reined his pony away.

Watching the flurry of activity on the other side, Jo could imagine what King Bartolomé's advisors were saying. But by all accounts, the high king of the tribes of Aztlan was both young and proud, and he was not surprised when a figure on a golden palomino emerged from among the ranks of the enemy. King Bartolomé had been born to the Mescalero tribe, but his gear was Spanyol. His polished steel cuirass and cocked helmet glittered as brightly as the plates of silver adorning his saddle, and the pennons that fluttered from the tips of his light throwing spears were as as deeply turquoise as the sky. He rode as if he and the horse were one being.

He will kill me . . . , thought Jo as Habañero, obeying a command his rider had not been aware of giving, trotted forward, his springy gait as easy as a rocking chair. Automatically Jo settled his lance beneath his arm. To his surprise, he felt relief. He had come to admire the Children of the Sun even as he hated their deeds. Death would free him from that conflict as well as from his captivity. *I am sorry, Chiquita,* he thought then, *but the Suns know Baby's value now. They will be kind to him.* A final glance burned the flat gold of the plain and the shape of the sculptured red rock that overlooked it upon his vision.

Behind him, the war drums began their steady thunder. The palomino broke into a canter. Instinctively Jo leaned aside as King Bartolomé's first spear flashed by. *I'll lower my shield and it will be over quickly,* he told himself, but his will could not so easily overcome his training, and as the next spear flew he found himself raising the shield so that the missile glanced off and rattled across the ground. The third blurred toward him, and he rocked in the saddle as it struck. A shift in weight brought his mount wheeling to the right, the stuck spear flying free, and as his foe reined around to meet him, Jo felt a warmth spreading through him that banished fear. It came from behind him. Continuing to turn, he glimpsed the white figure of Mother Mahaliel.

It was *her* power he was feeling . . . her will that drove him as he braced his spear and urged the red horse toward the enemy king. Habañero was heavier, but the palomino proved more agile, spinning as its rider slid down to hang by one leg and hand so that Jo's lance sliced harmlessly through empty air. As he thundered past, his foe righted himself once more and he saw white teeth flash. Bartolomé was laughing.

Once more they circled. The king had loosened the reata tied at his saddle horn and was whirling it about his head as the trident fighter had whirled his net in the ring. The Children of the Sun shouted—"Red Dragon! Dragon!" Across his vision the red haze rose. Jo fought it, but once more instinct brought his spear up to bat the rope away. A clever flip settled the loop around the weapon and jerked it from Jo's hand. A cheer went up from the Aztlan men. But now the heavy spear was the king's problem. It was Jo's turn to laugh as Bartolomé continued his swing and sent spear and rope flying across the field.

Unwilled, Jo's sword seemed to leap into his hand. The horses hurtled together. King Bartolomé had his own blade out as well. Steel clanged and scraped as the swords met. Jo lost a stirrup, but half of a turquoise plume fluttered to the ground. He had time for a moment of admiration as the palomino whirled on its haunches and charged. The response of his own mount was slower. Habañero started to rear, but Jo lost his seat and his shield as the Aztlan horse shocked into them, jerked his other foot from the stirrup, and rolled free as they went down.

The breath left Jo's lungs in a whoosh as he hit the ground. *Now he will kill me,* said his mind, but as if freed by contact with the earth, it was the Red Dragon that uncoiled, roaring, as Habañero scrambled to his feet, neighing defiance as his foe thundered back toward them. The palomino shied as the Dragon leaped, grabbed Bartolomé's leg, and pulled him to the ground. The earth shook beneath them as the front ranks of the Sun infantry opened to let the rear guard, who had reclaimed their horses, go thundering toward the men of Aztlan.

Then thought fled entirely as the Dragon stooped to savage its foe.

<hr/>

"You were right, grandson. That is not how Westrians make war." Jehan looks down at the bloody wreck that was once a man. Jo holds out his own hands and sees them red. On the ground beside the body lies a turquoise plume.

"No! He was supposed to kill me!"

"No." Jo repeated, and with that, came fully to consciousness. His eyes focused on a white curtain that fluttered in the wind. A ruddy light filtered through the cloth, but he did not smell smoke. Instead, he felt a hint of moisture in the air that touched his brow, and recognized the scent of hot, wet earth. He was in the City of the Firebird, and they were letting the water into the ditches that irrigated the fields as they always did when evening came. He tested his limbs, felt scrapes and bruises and a throbbing head, but he seemed to be intact. He had gotten worse in the ring. And with that, he remembered everything. He sat up, clutching at the back of his skull.

"Lie down, my son. That was a mighty blow! You have lain unconscious for a night and most of today." The voice was soft, but Jo jerked around, heart pounding. Mother Mahaliel was sitting beside him, smiling. He had no will to resist as she pushed him back against the pillow. "I am afraid it was one of our own men who hit you. You were standing above the unbeliever's body, and you would not stop fighting."

The unbeliever . . . , thought Jo. Then it was true. He had killed Aztlan's king.

"You made me fight him," he muttered. "I felt you. . . ." To be so close to her set alarm screaming throughout his body, but she was the snake now, and he the bird transfixed by its spell. He had never realized that her eyes were golden too, like her hair. The hair owed something to the dye-pot, but no artifice could have created those eyes.

"You could sense that?" Her gaze sharpened.

He shrugged and managed to look away. "You had no right," he mumbled. "You people don't belong here. I should be fighting *you*. . . ."

Beyond the curtain that separated the bed from the rest of the chamber women were talking softly. He caught a breath of some spicy scent, as if Mother Mahaliel had packed incense with her robes. Imperceptibly his tension eased.

"You cannot. We do the will of the most high god."

"I have not sworn to serve him."

"Do you think He waits for your love in order to love you? Do you think that I have waited, my young dragon?" Her face shone. "I loved you before ever I saw you, for He showed me your face in a vision. This is your destiny!"

Jo shook his head. "The Dragon fights because that is *his* nature, but *I* hate your god," he said bluntly. Even her anger would be better than this appalling certainty.

"You cannot—" She took his hand and he stiffened, but there was nothing sexual in her touch. "You are the only one I have found who is pure enough to be His champion!"

"Pure!" Jo shuddered, remembering Arena.

"Knowing the weakness of men, I do not require celibacy from my warriors, but my god does desire it. You have never lain with a woman, is it not so?"

Unwillingly he nodded, understanding now the unusual arrangement that assigned to each file of ten men and their leader one camp follower, called a spear-wife, to cook and wash their clothes and serve their lust. For an unmarried man to lie with any other woman, or with another man, would earn him ten lashes. Rape, whether of their own women or enemies, was punished by death. There was a girl who served the scouts with whom Jo was quartered, but he had never touched her.

"My child—" Her voice softened. "What is it that so torments you?"

She held him still and he had no strength to pull away, no will to wrest his gaze from hers.

"I am a murderer. . . ."

For a long moment Mother Mahaliel looked at him. "Not by your will, or by your fault . . . ," she said finally, as if she had indeed seen into his soul. "You are forgiven. Let me take the pain away. . . ."

You can't . . . , he thought, but her eyes were very bright, and from the palms of her hands a warmth was flowing, easing the pain of his body and dulling the ache in his soul. It was like the red haze of the Dragon, but this light was golden. Her radiance kept at bay the shadows that gathered in the corners of the room. He had not realized how much pain he carried until now, when he felt it flowing away. He gazed into Mother Mahaliel's face, and what he saw there was beauty.

"I want only your good, my son," she whispered. "Will you not rest in my love?"

"Stay with me," he whispered. "I am afraid of the dark."

That lovely warmth was filling his body. From anything sexual he would have recoiled, but what Mother Mahaliel offered was a pure and undemanding affection he had never known. *My name is Fix,* he thought, and all that had happened to him fell away as he wept like a little child in her arms.

———◦———

Jo sat in the courtyard, watching a band of sunlight move across the tiles. He could feel the heat soaking into his uncovered head and shoulders, but he did not move. It was not the best house in the city—that had burned—but it was spacious enough for Mother Mahaliel's household, into which, since the battle, he seemed to have been absorbed. There were roses in the courtyard, and a fountain that plashed softly. The sun kindled the droplets into a shower of rainbows as they fell back into the pool. Presently the light reached a gecko crouched next to the big water jar. For a long moment the little reptile remained still. Then it began to stir, as if absorbing energy from the sun.

The Dragon is like that lizard. . . . The thoughts came slowly. *But the sun who gives him life is Mother Mahaliel.*

All around him Jo could hear the sounds of preparation for the next stage of their journey. Corn and beans were being poured into sacks, strips of squash dried, and waterskins, many waterskins, sewn and caulked. Only he was allowed to sit idle—healing, Mother Mahaliel called it, but to Jo it felt more like estivation, and he was content to have it so.

Inside the house someone was singing in Spanyol— "*Corre, corre caballito. . . .*" It made Jo think of his horses. He supposed he should go see them, but there seemed to be no hurry—he had been assured that Habañero had not been hurt in the fight.

A shadow fell across the tiles and the gecko, now fully charged, darted away. Jo looked up and instinctively straightened as he saw Garr standing there.

"They told me ye were sick," the armsmaster growled. "Ye look sound enough, lad, so why're ye dawdling here?"

"Our Mother has not given me anything to do. . . ."

"*Our* Mother!" Garr exclaimed, but cut short whatever else he might have been about to say as Bett, Mother Mahaliel's younger handmaiden, came through a door on one side of the courtyard and took a shortcut across it to the other, carrying a pile of the brightly striped blankets they wove here. "Well, the lady is a busy woman," he said more quietly. "But surely she won't want ye to be gettin' weak from lack of exercise."

Jo considered this for a few moments in silence. Then he pulled himself to his feet. "Where shall we go?"

Garr frowned, and a part of Jo's mind observed that his response had sounded rather . . . young. But that was all right. Mother Mahaliel had rebirthed him after—the time he did not want to remember. One of the times. He figured he had about reached the age of six. That was old enough, he supposed, to go outside.

"Ye need to keep in training, my boy," Garr said gently. "Ye don't want to fergit what ye know."

Oh, but I do . . . , thought Jo. He frowned at the arms-master. *What do you want? Why do you keep pushing me?* He felt like a child indeed, caught between a protective mother and a harsh father. Of the two, Mother Mahaliel was certainly more comfortable. His own parents, he thought resentfully, had managed to be overprotective and distant at the same time.

"We will practice with the lance and the bow."

Jo relaxed a little. "Good—the Dragon uses the sword."

"If Mother Mahaliel had not appointed you the Suns' champion, he would not have had to use it," Garr observed quietly. "You are *her* gladiator now. . . ."

Jo glared at him, but now that he was in motion, it seemed easier to continue walking. Resisting the armsmaster was futile anyway—the man seemed as inevitable as the wind or the rain.

As they passed out into the street, Garr stopped, sniffing the air. "Storm's coming—" He pointed toward the southwest horizon, where white cumulus clouds were beginning to pile. "The monsoons are on their way. We'll be pulling out o' here soon. . . ."

※

To Jo, accustomed to the rainless summers of Westria, a climate in which the hottest time of the year got the most rain seemed strange. Men had called the high plateau between Cibola and the country of the Flags a desert, but the road they followed now passed through a region that was both hotter and far more dry. Here, sage and piñon gave way to creosote and brittlebush and the deceptive green of Palo Verde trees. Dust-devils led the way between lines of gray peaks whose serrated summits scored the blazing sky. Each afternoon they would wait for the storms to roll in from the distant Elayan sea, watching in frustration as distant clumps of cloud wafted over the desert, trailing veils of rain. They looked like the cloud-symbols in a Diné sand-painting, and were about as useful.

"Do you think that storm will come close enough to do us any good?" asked Bett, pointing from her seat beside Mother Mahaliel on the box of the wagon. They had left the patient oxen in the City of the Firebird. Now, a team of six mules drew the wagon. For this journey they would need speed.

"It's moving fast," observed Jo, reining the red mare, Salsa, into the shade of the big canvas cover. "I think it will pass to the north of here." From the long rise the trail was cresting, they could see for miles. A few saguaros took advantage of the added elevation, standing on the slope like spiky sentinels.

"Then we should drink something now—" Bette held out a waterskin to Mother Mahaliel.

"I am not thirsty," said the priestess. "The sun is meat and drink to me." Loose white draperies fell back as she spread her arms to embrace the desolation around them.

Mother Mahaliel liked the desert because it was bright and uncluttered, thought Jo, seared clean of the debris of humankind. That light had scorched his fair skin to the color of brick, but he liked it here too. The endless vistas put his own problems in proportion, and the alien landscape assured him that he was still a long way from home.

Jo took the waterskin and sipped carefully, holding the tepid liquid in his mouth to let it soak into his parched tissues before swallowing. His lips were cracking again. He wondered if the salve he had brought with him would last. A big brown bird launched itself from the nearest saguaro and he turned to watch. It was a wolf hawk, arrowing toward the others that circled in the sky. Most raptors were solitary hunters, but the wolf hawks worked in extended family groups. He wondered what they were after now.

From the distant cloud came a grumble of thunder. As if that had been a signal, the first bird struck like brown lightning, then lifted, screeching, as the next one followed. In another moment they were all in action, attacking and retreating in turn. Jo nudged the red mare in their direction just in time to see the biggest bird bear a convulsing rattlesnake upward and drop it onto the spikes of the saguaro. The cactus became the center of a synchronized flurry of talons and wings as the rest of the pack tore at the dying prey.

He glanced quickly back toward the wagons, eyebrow lifting. Would the Suns consider that an omen? The rattler was deadly, but by working together, weaker beings could overcome it. If the tribes of Aztlan had combined their fighting strength, they could have overwhelmed the Suns. But their muster had been too little and it had come too late.

General Marsh had left another garrison to rebuild and hold the City of the Firebird, along with most of the clan-fathers and their families. Loris Stef and Vincent Chiel led the families who rode with them now. Only the strongest had dared this trek across the desert. The others could follow later, in the winter, when the weather moderated and the way was secure. Would the surviving warriors of Aztlan unite to attack them? Their federation had never been a strong one. Perhaps the tribes would prefer to fight each other, and leave the Suns alone.

They hit the downslope and began to gather speed. A distant mutter of thunder echoed the rumbling of the wheels. Ahead, the dull expanse of the desert was broken by the pale slash of a dry wash. Jo turned his head to follow the progress of a dust-devil across the sand and sighed at the touch of a cooler breath of wind. The mare seemed to appreciate it as well, and danced ahead eagerly.

Now the first of the wagons was lurching down into the wash. Jo trotted back to Mother Mahaliel's wagon and moved up beside the lead pair of mules. If the descent was rough, they might need some steadying. Mule-skinning was another skill he had had to learn. The fact that the beasts were stronger and smarter than most horses was not always an advantage.

The wash was a sandy gash in the desert about two wagon-lengths wide, its floor littered with small boulders and studded with clumps of sage and a few tufts of dry grass. As Mother Mahaliel's wagon lumbered down, one of the lead mules tried to snatch a mouthful. The driver swore, and Jo urged Sally forward, reaching for the rein. In the next moment he was clutching at his own reins as the mare shied.

"Sally, you idiot, what's the matter with you?" He turned her in a tight circle and she danced sideways. Now the mules were plunging in their harness. He wondered what had spooked them.

"Santos! El agua! El agua—corde!" cried the driver behind them, whose wagon was just tipping over the edge to follow Mother Mahaliel's. His mules squealed as he hauled back on the reins, but momentum carried them into the wash on the other wagon's heels.

"Flash flood, Sun save us!" men were crying. A woman screamed.

Jo felt the mare lurch under him and threw himself free of the saddle as she went down. The earth was trembling. The red mare scrambled to her feet and took off down the wash, and the mules ripped the reins from their driver's hands and tried to follow her. Jo made a desperate grab, caught the lead mule's rein, and dug in his heels, swearing. The mule pulled harder, dragging him through the sand. A blast of moist air heralded the approach of the water; now he could hear it, feel its mindless compulsion to sweep away all in its path.

Jo threw his arms around the mule's neck, projecting the simple image of the far bank and the high ground beyond with all his soul. An ox would not have understood, could not have changed course in time if it had, but the mules surged forward. He found his feet again and glanced over his shoulder. The waters were stampeding toward them in a twenty-foot-high brown froth, but the bank was nearer. He shouted at the mules and they leaped for it. He was jerked off his feet; the rein whipped through his hands and he fell.

Wheels churned past his head as he tried to stand. Then the waters were upon him, bowling him under and tossing him high in frantic glee. He struggled, swallowed muddy water as the flood closed over his head once more.

Be it so . . . , he thought, abandoning himself to its power. *Better this way than by the sword.* But oddly, the image that flashed through his mind was of the Sacred Wood. *I'm sorry, Grandfather—I failed your name.*

From the forces around him he felt surprise, amusement, and suddenly, a rejection that broke the mental contact as they tossed his body upward and flung him hard against the bank. He landed on a Palo Verde bush and grabbed at the springy branches, drawing air in sobbing gasps.

The flood was already beginning to subside. People were hauling Mother Mahaliel's wagon up the bank. The remains of the wagon that had followed it bobbed on the muddy flow. Soldiers jumped in with open waterskins, filling them frantically as the level sank. The red mare was nowhere to be seen.

You didn't want me, he thought at the departing waters. *Don't worry—we're leaving your land as fast as we can!* He pulled himself farther up the bank.

His clothes were steaming, his skin already dry. The flood had passed, leaving the savaged wagon-train to endure the furnace of the sun.

⊱ 9 ⊰

THE ROAD TO EŁAYA

"Behold, the god Himself shows us our road," said Mother Mahaliel, pointing ahead. The track they were following ran straight toward a notch in the hills that framed the setting sun.

Jo stood in his stirrups and shaded his eyes to see. A murmur of appreciation rose from the aides who had ridden up with the general. Red light sparked from the metal fittings of weapons and harness and lit faces and canvas with a ruddy glow.

"We look as if we are riding through fire," Jo said softly.

"We have already done so," she answered. "We are the Sun's children, and we have passed through His furnace. By our sufferings we are purified."

Jo took a deep breath as a light wind stroked across the hills, carrying with it the aromatic scents of sagebrush and sun-cured grass, and wondered if that were true. The air was dry, but this was not the desiccating desert heat that sucked the moisture from the lungs. The soil beneath the stallion's hooves, as ruddy as his hide, was earth, not sand. Compared to the lands through which they had passed, the hills of Elaya, covered with chaparral and thick golden grass, seemed lush indeed. There was even an occasional palm tree.

"Look, sir—" One of the aides pointed to a hilltop, where for a moment the silhouette of a horseman showed against the sky. "Is that one of our scouts?"

"If he's not, letting himself be seen was his last mistake," someone replied in an undertone. Four riders were already arrowing away from the column toward the hill.

"And if he is one of ours, he'll wish he wasn't when the general gets through with him," said one of his companions with a short laugh.

Jo nodded. Riding beside Mother Mahaliel's wagon had offered him ample opportunity to listen to the general's theories on the value of surprise. His orders to the screen of scouts that constantly ranged ahead of the migration were quite explicit. They were moving through territory that was certainly unfamiliar and must be counted hostile, and their only hope lay in seeing any enemy and neutralizing *his* observers before their presence was known.

The riders had spread out now, two angling up the slope and the others keeping low. Jo tensed in the saddle. Did that mean they had identified the horseman as an enemy? General Marsh was frowning, his dark gaze flicking back along the line of horses and wagons in a quick evaluation as if he were wondering the same thing.

That line was shorter than it had been when they left the City of the Firebird. If it had not been for the monsoon rains, they would not have made it through at all. But the

rains had brought danger as well. Jo still shuddered to remember the gleeful greed of the flash flood. His red mare
had been swept away and her body had never been found.
But most of the people had made it to the Painted River
alive.

It was the eastern desert of Elaya that had nearly finished
them, a land whose desiccation made Aztlan seem verdant.
This was a country of stony mountains, hard earth, and only
the most enduring of plants, and it stretched for miles. When
Jo reached out to its spirits, as he had learned to do in any
new land, he found only wind. This desert might belong to
Elaya, but it reminded him of the Barren Lands. The Suns
had filled their waterskins and barrels to bursting at the
Painted River, but by the time they reached the first springs
at the base of the mountains, they were almost out of water,
and almost every team had lost at least one mule.

They sucked the springs dry of water, and the small
band of tribesmen who lived there dry of information. After that they were able to move from oasis to oasis and
from one canyon water hole to the next. There was no
grass.

The few inhabitants they encountered offered little opposition. The closest thing to a real battle had come when a
contingent of crossbowmen marched down from the Drylands mines. Jo had enjoyed shooting back at them, having
been brought up on tales of how Prince Palomon's crossbowmen had killed Lord Brian of Las Costas almost fifty
years before. Indeed, he contemplated the advance of the
Children of the Sun into Elaya with a grim satisfaction, for
this was Westria's ancient enemy.

But they were certainly in a new land now.

Jo remembered the moment when he had first known
that, coming through another rocky pass and looking up to
see the peak of the high mountain to their left still dappled
with snow. At its foot there were wells. When they reached
the valley on the other side, the horses jerked at the reins,
reaching for clumps of wispy grass, and that night a whisper of coolness in the western wind hinted at the distant
sea. After that, it grew easier. Compared to the hills of

Westria, these slopes were harsh and dry; but after the desert, they seemed a paradise.

The sun had disappeared, but the western sky was still emblazoned with banners of scarlet and gold. From the north to the east, the harsh contours of the mountains were veiled now by purple haze. Before them the road led through a gap in a line of low hills. From somewhere among them a coyote called, and Jo wondered if their Guardian was honored here as he was in Westria. The mules moved more slowly up the rising road, tired at the end of a long day. Soon the riders who had been sent ahead would be returning with directions to the evening's campsite. Perhaps beyond the next rise they would see a new valley, quiet beneath the emerging stars.

Habañero's ears twitched as two of the scouts appeared on the hillside, coming fast. The escort drew in more closely.

"Your Holiness, get back in the wagon-bed and stay down!" the general said tersely.

As Mother Mahaliel started to move, the air thrummed. Bett choked off a startled scream and cast herself in front of her mistress. Instinctively Jo ducked as arrows thunked into the side of the wagon and the brush-covered slopes ahead of them bristled suddenly with archers. He grabbed for the helmet that hung from his saddle and snatched up his shield as more arrows came. The drivers of the two wagons behind them whipped their beasts to bring the wagons alongside, where they could offer some protection. A horn call brought a troop of lancers thundering past.

A Sun rider cried out and slid from the saddle, but in the next moment the yells were coming from the hillside as his companions fell upon the archers like hawks on a chicken-yard, lances stabbing as the enemy scattered. Behind them, wagons were being dragged into defensive squares, foot soldiers forming up around them.

Jo strained to see in the dimming light. Now only a few arrows still flickered by. The rest of the enemy were drawing the riders up the hill, where they were met by another volley from the mounted archers who guarded the attackers' horses and held the pursuers long enough for the fugitives to mount and flee.

The horn blatted again and another troop of Suns swept forward, this time, the harriers—an elite force, on the fastest horses the Suns had. The troop leader, a convert from Aztlan called Manuelo, paused beside General Marsh.

"Stop them!" the general growled. "Prince Harun will be waiting for their report. We want to keep him wondering where we are as long as we can."

"Aye, sir, and we'll find the enemy for you as well. Live in Light!"

"Destroy the Darkness," the general replied. Tadeo Marsh rewarded talent regardless of origin, and nearly a quarter of the army had joined it since the Children of the Sun entered Aztlan. The newcomers' knowledge of the land was the other reason the migration had survived.

Then the harriers were gone, and the remainder of the army and the wagons it guarded were left to hold their defensive positions and watch the stars kindle in the darkening sky.

Several hours passed before the harriers returned. In all that time, not so much as a candle had been lit in the wagon train. From the wagons Jo could hear the voices of soldiers and sometimes a woman's laugh. In one of the family wagons Loris Stef was telling a story to comfort his grandchildren. Only the clan-fathers lived with their families, and many of those had been left in Aztlan. The men of the armies marched and camped with their files, and those who had wives among the migrants visited their women only on Sundays.

It always amazed Jo that a people who worshiped the sun could endure the lack of light, but the faint glow that surrounded Mother Mahaliel as she walked among the wagons was all the more apparent in the gloom. And it was at night that he could feel most clearly the presence, like a pillar of fire in the darkness, of the god she served.

Jo had been brought up to honor the Guardians of Westria, but he had been taught that the gods had different names in other lands. He had always assumed that those forms grew out of the relationship between land and culture. He had lost his connection to his own Guardians when he passed beyond the domain of the Lady of Westria. The Red Dragon that possessed him when he fought was no god, though certainly a Power. But the Sun, at least as Mother Mahaliel proclaimed Him, was unchanged and unchanging no matter where His worshipers might roam, superseding all other allegiance. Again and again, in the past months, Jo had seen men succumb to the appeal of that shining singularity.

At times like this, and when he attended Mother Mahaliel at the ceremonies, he felt its power himself, like sunlight seen through closed eyelids. At first it had seemed a force of nature like any other, but increasingly he was beginning to perceive it as a Person, watching, *wanting* him. Mother Mahaliel's pure and undemanding love eased his pain, but if he gave up his will to Father Sun, that uncompromising light would burn that pain away.

It ought to have been easy. Was it his own sinful nature or the Westrian grandfather who spoke in his dreams that prevented him from making the final surrender? He did not know, but for now, Mother Mahaliel was sufficient focus for his devotion. He would leave it to others to argue with the gods.

The general had returned to the lead wagon and they were sharing a cold supper with the Mother's women when they heard hoofbeats and the soft, repeated hooting of an owl.

"Sir, Holy One—" The scout nodded briefly toward Mother Mahaliel as he drew rein. "The archers are destroyed, and we have found the main force of the Elayan army."

"Did they see you?" snapped the general.

"I am sure they did not. We left the horses and crawled through the chaparral to observe. They're making camp for the night. We counted more than a hundred fires."

"How far?"

"An hour's ride from here," chimed in a second man. "There are ten cohorts of horsemen armed like the Spanyol riders of Aztlan and twelve companies of infantry, dark men with cowhide shields and short spears. The banner above the command tent is blue and silver."

"The prince is with them then. What's the land like?" asked Marsh.

"Just beyond the rise is a valley. Fields and pasture down to the river, mostly dry at this time of year, but there are wells. Good feed and enough room. The river continues on through some little hills, and the enemy is camped beyond them."

The general looked up at Mother Mahaliel. "Take the wagons and make camp by the river. No fires. I will move the fighting men forward. Surprise is a powerful weapon. Let us make it ours." He turned back to the scouts. "Get fresh horses and ten more riders. Spread out in a screen, some to keep watch on the enemy, the rest to survey the land. If we march now, we can choose our battlefield, but we must approach unseen." He started to rein away.

"What about me?" asked Jo. Since they had left the City of the Firebird, Mother Mahaliel had kept him by her, but he was not part of her bodyguard and he chafed at being held back with the women when a real battle was on the way. He had not wanted to fight the king of Aztlan, but Elaya was an old enemy.

"Does the fighting cock want to use his spurs?" Marsh's teeth showed white in a brief smile. "Very well. If Her Holiness permits, Red, you may come with me."

For a long moment Mother Mahaliel held Jo's gaze. Even in the darkness her face shone. Then at last she smiled. "Take him. He will bring you victory."

<hr />

Hail thou resplendent and sovereign sun,
Adore we thy glory, oh thou holy one,
So help us and heal us until as above,
Below, all is beauty, and all know thy love. . . .

At noon, the sky above the Father of Mountains was a great bowl filled with light. Those students who had remained at the College of the Wise through the August holiday stood with eyes closed and faces uplifted as the last notes of the chant resonated into silence. They hailed the sun as a healer, but what Luz saw through her closed eyelids was a victorious and destructive power that made her want to shrink whimpering into the nearest dark hole.

Or perhaps that was only last night's dream come back to haunt her. She shuddered and opened her eyes as the gong signaled the end of the noon meditation. For three nights the same nightmare had wakened her, soaked in sweat and afraid to close her eyes lest it return.

I should have gone home, she thought grimly. *Perhaps if I was with my family the dreams would not come.* And it would be cooler in Seagate, where the mist-cloaked coastal hills could protect her from the tyranny of the sun.

Here on the slopes of the mountain, she felt naked before that glory. That was the point, she supposed—to let the light search out and purify all shadow from the soul—but it made her afraid.

She started back toward the kitchen, stumbled over her own feet from exhaustion, and stopped again with a sigh. She would have to seek help from someone; she could not go on this way. As if her thought had called him, a figure in a gray robe moved from the shadow of the porch into her path.

"Come," said Master Granite, and she had no choice but to follow him.

The walls of the College of the Wise were thick stone, and the master's chamber was blessedly cool. He poured water from an earthenware pitcher and offered it to her.

"The sun has great power. Here on the mountain we are very close to his light, but you must not allow yourself to become dry."

Luz nodded and drank, feeling her tissues revive and her head clear. This year she would begin her studies of the element of Water. That seemed a great blessing just now. She set down the cup, eyeing the master uncertainly. Since their first unfortunate encounter she had tried to avoid the Master of the College, but it was difficult when there were so few in residence here.

"The light is hard to bear, but it is not the sun out there that I fear, it's the one I see in my dream," she said finally. "The same one has come for three nights now, and yes— I've tried the chants and the meditations. They give me some ease, but I can't go forever without sleep. . . ."

His gaze sharpened; she felt a pressure against her awareness and instinctively armored herself against it.

"So you have learned something, Frederic's daughter." His eyes slitted in a smile. "Now show me if you know how to let those shields down."

For a moment she faced him with defiance—she had thought of him as an enemy for too long. But the master waited, patient as the stone from which he took his name. She frowned at a sudden recognition, remembering a time when Julian had visited Seagate during the annual ritual to the spirits of the land and she had seen just that rooted stillness in the king. Was she surprised, she wondered, to realize that Julian was like a master of the College, or that Master Granite might in some way be like the king?

She took a deep breath and then another, determined to show him how well she had learned. Awareness slipped and shifted, and suddenly she was no longer alone. With an effort, she kept herself from thrusting him away again. His touch was curiously impersonal, cool, steady. Luz stilled, wondering what would happen now.

"Show me. . . ."

She heard the command, and in response, the images came—

Two armies face each other across a plain of golden grass. On one side, the banners are blue and silver; on the other, white and gold. Above, the noon sun blazes, striking sparks of flame from spearpoints and armor. They begin to move, and from the white banner a red dragon rises, roaring. A tide of blood floods across the land; a tide of grief rises in her soul.

Here was where the dream had always ended, but now the heat faded even as the light became more pure. Within that radiance she glimpsed the rounded limbs of a child that even as she perceived them lengthened, becoming the anguished body of the god self-sacrificed upon the Tree, who in the next moment robed himself in the golden splendor of the sovereign. For a moment then, her awareness of the master was thrust aside by something Other. She viewed unguessed vistas beyond the sky, and perceived a greater Presence that regarded her with laughter and with love. Then, gently, it withdrew, and she was alone within herself once more.

Luz felt her own tears cool upon her cheeks, looked up and glimpsed astonishment in Master Granite's eyes. Then his barriers went up as well.

He cleared his throat. "The message has been delivered. I do not think the dream will come to you again."

"Who was that—?" She faltered as he turned his back to her.

"The higher spheres have also their Guardians." He spoke so softly she could hardly hear his words. "In times of great danger, they may appear to reassure us that there is a reality beyond our own. But I know of nothing—" He stopped. "Perhaps your dream was a warning of something that is yet to come. . . ."

<hr />

The remnants of the army of Elaya stood in a dispirited huddle, surrounded by Sun guards. With the approach of dusk, a fog bank was rolling in from the sea, as in the Cataclysm the great wave had swept away the works of the Ancients that had once filled this plain. It rose like a gray wall, cutting off the sky, and Jo shivered at the touch of damp wind. In that pallid light, the prisoners looked corpse-pale. But the dead were whiter still.

The bodies of the slain lay sprawled on the plain of the Tambara. Jo supposed that he ought to be accustomed to the sight of slain men by now. It had been easier when he was the Dragon, whose kills were always tidied away before Jo came to himself again. But a man should take responsibility for his deeds, and some of those who lay so still on the field had fallen to his spear. He had expected to feel triumph at this victory over Westria's old enemy, as heroes always did when the bards told their tales, but no decent man could rejoice at such carnage. And when his guts churned sickly at the sight of a battlefield, at least Jo knew that he was still in control.

He wondered if the lions that were said to lurk in the hills beyond would come down to feast on the carrion when night fell. Decency required the victors to bury their enemies, but that would take time, and meanwhile, the scavengers would eat well. The crows were already busy, and from time to time he glimpsed the gray shape of a coyote skulking through the high grass. The lion was the totem of Elaya's princes. Was it an honor to be eaten by your totem, he wondered, or the final loss?

Garr would know. Jo had been grateful to have the older man beside him in the fighting that had won them Elaya, a steadying presence in battle, who always seemed to be ready with another lance when Jo's was lost, so that he did not have to draw his sword. Jo wore the red armor and rode the red stallion, but the Dragon slept.

Commander Anaya came trotting up, and General Marsh moved his mount forward to meet him.

"Of the prisoners, two hundred and seventy-seven have made full submission and will swear allegiance to the Sun. Another four hundred have sworn not to take up arms against us. Almost that many more lie dead on the field."

Once more, thought Jo, Sun discipline—and desperation—had brought them victory against a greater number. Since Mother Mahaliel had adopted him, Jo had sat in on more strategy sessions than he liked to remember. General Marsh knew his business—and to him, it *was* a business, based on careful planning, supported by drill. Jo wondered if his father and Lord Robert could have done as well. He had heard plenty of bards' tales, but the men and women who had fought in it rarely talked about Caolin's War.

"And how many escaped?" the general asked.

"One of the *impis*—that's their crack infantry, the ones who fight with *assegai* and cowhide shields. Some cavalry—" Anaya shrugged dismissively. "Enough to skulk in the hills, but I do not see how they can do us much harm."

They all looked toward the mountains, which were covered by a dark tangle of live oak and ceanothis, chamisa and sage. It would be easy for men who knew the country to lose pursuers there.

"Is Prince Harun among the dead?"

The commander looked uncomfortable. "We have not found him, sir."

General Marsh sighed, his dark face setting into even sterner lines. "Then they can still hurt us."

A coyote howled from the hillside, and from the field, more answered. The bard Piper used to sing an Elayan song about how the coyotes chose their king. Perhaps it was neither the serpent nor the lion, but the coyotes, who were the victors here.

It was growing dark, and the wind from the west was cold. *Fall is coming, even to this southern land,* Jo thought with a sigh. *Los Leones is ours now. We'll lie snug through the winter there.* And after that? His mind shied away from wondering. They had reached the golden west. Surely the Suns would be content to rule the lands they had won.

"In the names of Earth, Air, Fire, and Water and the Maker of All Things, let the Autumn Sessions of the Estates of Westria begin!" The herald brought down his staff with a jangle of sweet bells. Cloth rustled as the men and women who sat on the benches of the Council Hall settled themselves more comfortably.

Twenty years and more had mellowed the new timbers with which the hall had been repaired after Caolin's destruction. It looked now, thought Rana, as she remembered it on the day when Julian had been acclaimed as Westria's king. The benches on each of the hall's eight sides narrowed into a wedge whose point was the seat of one of the counselors. But now she sat enthroned beside Julian before the section reserved for the Royal Domain, and a new generation observed their elders from the upper benches, a generation that had never known war.

But the bench reserved for the royal heirs was empty. It was hard to believe that almost a year had gone by since Johan . . . disappeared. She had waited throughout the winter, but there had been no sign of the storm that Coyote, or Someone, had promised her. Her son was gone.

Frederic, his robes glowing richly crimson in the light shafting through the high windows, rose from his seat before the royal officers on the southeastern side. He paced to the stone hearth in the center of the hall, bending to kindle the cedarwood laid ready there. In another moment a fragrant curl of smoke twined upward toward the opening and they saw the bright leap of the flame.

"The elements are in balance; in the sacred center the hearthfire burns." His low voice carried throughout the chamber. "The Council is met. Let the business of the day begin. . . ."

Reports were always first on the agenda, the bi-annual accounting of trade and transitions, triumph and trouble from every part of the land. There was little here to surprise her. Rana had not realized that the fires in the coastal mountains had been so extensive, but she was glad to learn that the storehouses in Sanjos had sufficient supplies to support those whose holdings had been burned until their gardens were producing again.

She allowed her eyes to wander around the Council chamber as Master Kieran the goldsmith gave the report for the Free Cities. In the north, Julian's cousin Elinor sat beneath the black and white banner of the Corona. Her mother had been sister to Julian's mother, but she had the fair hair her grandfather had bequeathed to Lady Rosemary as well.

Rana transferred her gaze to the bench where the Master

of the College of the Wise sat, as still in his gray robe as if he had been carved from stone. Frederic said that the letters he got from Luz these days sounded cheerful, and the girl had not wanted to come home for vacation, so she must have worked out whatever problems she was having with the master before. Would it have been a comfort to see her, wondered Rana, or would watching Frederic with his daughter have renewed awareness of her own loss?

In the east, William and Jeanne sat with their father at the desk reserved for the lords of the Ramparts. Rana grimaced, knowing that more than regional solidarity had brought them here. Would one of them be sitting in the empty seat behind her when the Council met next spring?

To Frederic's right, Alexander of Las Costas, having spoken already, was talking to his own heir. Today, Carola's ginger hair lay loose on her shoulders, but she gazed at the rest of them with the same supercilious expression Rana remembered from the archery competition the year before. Alexander had been loyal enough in recent years, but Rana had never been able to warm to him after his early opposition to Julian's bid for the throne.

Master Kieran was finally concluding his report. Rosemary straightened and poked her husband in the ribs. Only then did Rana realize that behind the papers in his hands Eric had been dozing. She hid her own smile, wondering if Julian had seen. But he was watching Frederic and scowling. She tried a mental touch, but his mind was armored, even against hers. Well, that should be no surprise to her, these days.

And now the seneschal was rising once more, the agenda in his hand. Rana closed her eyes, but she could not close her ears to his words.

"My lords and my ladies—the next question before us is the designation of a new heir for Westria. Since the disappearance of Prince Johan, nearly a year has passed. Our gracious king is in the prime of his strength, and will, with the blessing of the Guardians, reign for many years, but in his father's time we learned the importance of providing for all eventualities."

Frederic stopped and sipped from the cup of water on his desk, and Rana saw that his hand was trembling. It eased her a little to know that it was as hard for him to say these words as it was for her to hear them.

"My lord king, your next heirs by blood are your cousins Philip and Robert of the Ramparts, and Philip's children, William and Jeanne. They are all descended from House Starbairn. Are they willing to serve Westria, and is it your will to choose from among them now?"

Faintly from outside came the sound of some commotion, but now everyone's attention was fixed on Julian.

"For the good of Westria, which we all serve," he said harshly at last, "I will not take Lord Philip from his province, and Lord Robert—"

"—wouldn't take the crown if you handed it to me on a plate!" muttered Robert from behind his brother, sending a ripple of shocked laughter around the room.

"It is best, in any case, that heirs should be chosen from among the young, so that they may be both well trained and still vigorous in that—as you have so tactfully assured us—far distant future when their service shall be required," added the king. This time the laughter was louder, and some of the tension eased. "For that reason—" he began, but the shouting outside could no longer be ignored. The doors to the Council chamber slammed open and a rather disheveled young woman in a seneschal's red tabard hurried in.

"Cordelia!" exclaimed Frederic. "What's wrong?"

Her harried gaze passed him to fix on the king. "My lord, there's an envoy. I think you should—"

The rest of her words were lost as three men pushed past her. Two of them fell to their knees before Julian; the third, whose skin beneath the dust was the color of polished wood, swayed where he stood. The king was on his feet as well, the shepherd's staff gripped tightly in his hand.

"What do you mean by intruding here?"

"Prince Harun," the man croaked, "calls to his brother of Westria. Men came from the east, a migration, an army! We could not stop them. Prince Harun fights on, but Al-

Kaid has fallen. Help us, we beg you, or Elaya will be no more!"

Frederic steadied the envoy and offered the cup of water. "Who has attacked you? Was it men of Aztlan?"

The man gulped thirstily, then shook his head. "The high prince of Aztlan is dead. They killed him. They are a new folk who have no king, only a priestess and a general, but they fight like demons from the pit. They call themselves the Children of the Sun."

Piper was right. Julian took a step back, hand going out for support, and Rana grasped it. In that moment of un-shielded contact she felt his fury and his fear, set her feet, and willed strength into him.

"Your Majesty," the envoy's cry rose above the tumult that had erupted around them, "will you help us?"

"Silence!" Julian's command cracked through the hall. He looked from one sector to another, catching and hold-ing their eyes until all were still. "Yes—I will come."

He waited for the new babble of query and protest to die down. "I believe these men because I have had reports of the Sun people already, though I never thought they could come so far. Elaya has been our ancient foe, but I tell you that if we do not fight these new enemies there, we will have to face them in Westria."

"My King," objected Alexander, "war cannot be de-clared without a vote of this Council." The hall had erupted into a babble of debate, but Rana was not sur-prised. After Piper's return Julian and Robert had started planning.

"Then vote," said the king. "But I am going with who-ever is willing to follow me, whatever you decide." He looked around the circle and sighed. "Given that my life is about to become rather more uncertain, I choose both Jeanne and William as heirs presumptive. Lady Jeanne, if she wishes, shall come with me, and in my absence I would leave William to assist the queen."

Now, at last, he turned to Rana, and in the stress of the moment the barriers between them were gone. *"My heart . . . I know that you would follow me, but only you can watch over Westria."*

She reached up and smoothed back his dark hair where it lay crushed beneath the weight of the crown. *"Take care, love. . . ."* And then, *"It was easier when all you sought was the Jewels."* At the thought of them, she felt a reflexive tingle at brow and throat and waist and groin, connecting her to the physical expressions of the elements they ruled.

"Rana, the Jewels are yours as much as mine." He kissed her hand.

She should be glad of that, she thought, as a word from Robert drew the king's attention away from her. She suspected that this was going to be a war not only of men, but of powers.

☞ 10 ☜

CONDOR'S VICTORY

The palace of Al-Kaid rested like a crown on the golden bluff above the plain of the Tambara. From its highest tower, you could glimpse the misty glitter of the sea. At the foot of the bluff, a broad avenue cut through the tangled streets of Los Leones to cross the highway that ran toward the blue mountains. Once, the princes of Elaya had stood here to survey their domain. Now the banner that flared from the tower was the white and gold of the Children of the Sun.

In the weeks since the city fell, Jo had come here often. Those mountains stretched to Westria's border, and her coasts were washed by that same sea. After the great battle by the river when they had broken Prince Harun's army, he had expected to enjoy seeing Elaya humbled, but his de-

tachment was beginning to fray. Westria and Elaya might
be old enemies, but over the years they had traded goods
and songs as well as blows. His grandfather's memories
were of a worthy enemy. Jo found it unsettling to see its
people ground beneath the invader's heel.

Of course, some of them were not ground down but
groveling. When Jo descended from the tower, he found
that another delegation had come in, this one from the Nippani farmers of the coastal plain. Their daimyo was still
skulking in the hills somewhere with Prince Harun, but one
of his cousins was only too eager to serve the invaders. Jo
had wondered how the Children of the Sun would hold this
land, but Elaya had always been a gaggle of competing
chiefdoms; perhaps they did not care who ruled in Al-Kaid
so long as they were protected from their neighbors.

As Jo entered the audience hall, Mother Mahaliel beckoned him to her side. The markets of Los Leones were
rich, and she sat now in new garments of spotless white on
a dais beneath a canopy of white and gold. Tadeo Marsh
was seated before her, with the senior clan-fathers and division commanders as a council.

The doorkeeper had drawn breath to announce another
delegation when a courier pushed past him, one of the many
whom the general had sent out as soon as they had taken the
capital. Good intelligence was a weapon, Marsh was fond
of saying, perhaps the most important weapon in war.

"Live in the Light!" The man saluted the general.

"Destroy the Darkness!" the others in the room replied.

"You are Nathaniel Akenson, are you not? What is the
news?"

"Ye sent me t' the coast," the courier nodded to the council, "t' talk with traders. When I got there, a ship come
from the north, from the land o' Westria. They say Prince
Harun sent envoys, asked for aid an' alliance."

Jo's breath caught, but all eyes were on Tadeo Marsh.

"And will they grant it?" the general asked softly.

"Their king swore he would, soon as he c'n gather
forces. That'll take time, but they're arming. Word is

they'll march down the Great Valley, attack through the Dragon's Tail pass."

Westria was coming. . . . Jo shuddered at the onslaught of memories he had thought locked away. His father was coming. He felt Mother Mahaliel's gaze upon him and tried to hide his fear.

"I thank you for the warning," the general said softly. "We shall have to prepare a delegation to welcome him. . . ."

In springtime, the Great Valley would have been jeweled with flowers, the pools and channels of the marshes overflowing with snowmelt, and the whole land clamorous with migrating birds. But at the end of the dry season, the Darkwater was a trickle. High tule reeds rustled in the wind. When Julian patted Shadow's black hide, dust puffed up from his hand. Spearfoot, the big brown charger he would ride in battle, was with the remounts somewhere in the rear. Even the grass had faded, and a dun cloud marked the road that led toward the Elayan border. The birds were back, though, heading south for the winter. They rose from the muddy pools in shrieking flocks as the army passed.

Actually, thought Julian, as he looked back, it was stretching a point to call this an army. The thousand fighters that marched behind him would have made up no more than one wing of the force Robert's father had once led this way.

As he watched, Robert himself came cantering back up the line. He reined in beside the king, untied the scarf that had protected his nose and mouth, and used it to wipe his brow. Dust grayed his hair and filled lines in his face that Julian had never noticed before. It looked odd—the king had accepted that the rest of them might be middle-aged, but it had seemed impossible that Robert should ever grow old.

"How are they doing?" asked Julian.

"Well enough. One of the mules has gone lame, but they've redistributed its load. So far, it is managing to keep up. If it can't—" He shrugged. "Fresh mule meat is none so bad, and if we don't eat the beast, the coyotes will."

Now, at the beginning of the campaign, they were still well supplied, and the farmers whose holdings they passed had come out to offer more. They had better enjoy the fresh food while they had it. The dried and salted rations the pack train was carrying would be needed once they reached Elaya. It would not do for the Westrians to seize whatever food the invaders had left from people who were supposed to be their allies.

"Water?" Julian unhooked his skin and offered it. Robert took a long gulp, held it in his mouth for a moment, then swallowed with a sigh.

"Why couldn't we have waited until spring?" he said crossly. "I've been reading the accounts of my father's campaign against Prince Palomon. Plenty of water, plenty of forage—half the sheep in Westria are pastured down here once the rains have brought up the grass."

"And when the rains do come, you'll wish for dry weather." Julian grinned. "We're a week from the end of October now, so they should hit right after we reach Elaya."

Despite his proud words in the Council Hall, even a small force could not be raised overnight, not in a land that had gone for more than two decades without war. If not for the yearly martial games that each province was required to hold, it would have been impossible. But Seagate had sent heavy cavalry under Frederic's brother Orm, which made some two hundred knights, combined with his own. From Las Costas came a hundred archers mounted on sturdy ponies. The Ramparts had sent lighter riders and a contingent of axe-men from the mountains, with Lady Jeanne to lead them. In the van rode Julian's own household troop from the Royal Domain.

"Anyway, it's time you earned that commander's baton!"

Robert groaned. "Sleeping in a bedroll on the ground was a lot easier when we were twenty. But at least we are making good time."

Julian nodded. "Two weeks from Laurelynn, and another day should bring us to the site of the Battle of the Dragon Waste. I've always wanted to see it—you know the battle was fought on the day I was born."

His gaze moved from the plain to the mountains that marched to the east, where lay another path he had never taken, that led to the sacred valley of Awahna that was not entirely in this world. That road was for adepts, not for kings.

"Look at it then, and make an offering at the cairn where Brian of Las Costas died. But we won't camp there." The laughter left Robert's eyes. "That army was betrayed, and some say the place is haunted still."

"Surely their spirits have gone back to the land. That's what I would do—"

"You," Robert said shortly, "are the Master of the Jewels; and Guardians, how I wish you had stayed home!" Julian raised one eyebrow as his cousin went on. "I understood when you had to lead the army against Caolin while I stayed to guard Laurelynn, but this is only a war against men! You could have simply sent *me*."

"If I had not committed myself, who else would have come? They haven't heard Piper's reports; they don't really believe in the danger," Julian said softly. "Robert, don't torment yourself over what happened more than twenty years ago. I thought I might have to give my life to stop Caolin; and if I had failed, you would have avenged me." He reached out to grasp the other man's arm and gave the hard muscle an encouraging squeeze. "But we are going to war together this time."

"Yes." Robert's blue eyes held his with an intensity that Julian remembered from long ago. "And that's better than watching you ride off without me. But I warn you, if anyone dies on this campaign, it is not going to be you!"

The road that Westrians called the Dragon's Tail rose steeply from the plain into the great mountains that were the beast's body. To Julian's right, the foothills of the coastal mountains lay brown and bare and the higher ranges behind them marched away to the west in lines of hazy blue. Beyond the marshes of the valley, only clumps of sagebrush grew. A horse shied as a tumbleweed bounced across the road, driven by the ever-present wind. The mountains curved northward to either side, but the valley faded away into brown haze, as if Westria itself were disappearing even as he left it behind.

Before them, the blue bulk of the Dragon Range loomed. The mountains rose abruptly from the end of the valley, first a long slope, then the gold velvet-covered knees of the hills, and then the sheer slopes behind. Were they a wall to keep enemies out, as he had always believed, or to keep Westrians in? The entrance to the pass was guarded by a long, dun-colored ridge. As the road curved around it, he saw the pale line of the Dragon's Tail snaking up through the pass.

As they started up, Julian pulled up his scarf to shield nose and mouth from the gusting wind. He had come this way once in the first years of his reign to inspect the fort at its foot, but he had never taken the ancient road. He was glad they had brought pack horses. The garrison at the fort earned a little income by renting extra teams of mules to help traders hoist their wagons up the slope or keep them from running away on the way down, but it was a slow and dangerous process. There were no wagons on the road now, only the long line of men and beasts toiling up the hill.

Slowly they climbed the road that clung to the hillside above the ravine. Live oak and bay laurel clung to the walls of the canyon that rose so steeply to either side. On the slopes above, he could see the darker feathering of pines. It would be a bad place for an ambush, but the scouts he had sent out that morning had seen no enemies. Before the Cataclysm, men had carved earth like cheese, shaping a natural fold in the mountains into this smooth gash that climbed for five miles to the tree-clad ridges above. For a moment the view wavered dizzily.

"The altitude bothering you?" Robert, who was riding beside him, reached out to touch his arm.

"I grew up in mountains higher than these," snapped Julian, extending inner senses to anchor himself to the earth once more. He must have made some sound then, because Robert's grip tightened.

"What is it?"

For a moment Julian was silent, trying to understand. The energies of the earth were balanced in an uneasy tension, but he had ridden over such places in Seagate and the Royal Domain without being disturbed. There was something different here—

"Now I understand," he said suddenly. "The earth spirits here do not know my name. . . ." He tried to laugh. "If we ever post a sign to mark our border, it should go there— just where the road curves. I should have expected to sense the change in energies, but since I mastered the Jewels I have never been out of Westria."

"Now that you mention it, I do feel something strange." Robert frowned. "I'd best send word down the line. Some of the men will be noticing it too."

He stiffened, and Julian followed his gaze. Perhaps they had been too quick to assume safety, he thought then. Lucas Buzzardmoon, who had turned his talent for investigation to scouting, was urging his pony down the hill. Behind him came a dark-skinned man in blue and white livery.

Closer, the king could see that the livery was worn and faded, the high-bred horse gaunt as if it had been ridden for too long. But the courier's face brightened as he recognized the circled cross of gold on the green banner and the circlet on Julian's helm.

"I found him coming down a back trail," said Lucas, taking off his hat and pushing his sandy hair back from his brow. "He feels all right to me—" He drew his pony aside so that the other man could move forward.

"My lord of Westria." The Elayan bowed in the saddle. "Prince Harun welcomes you to his land—"

"Is it still his?" asked Robert.

The courier's face stiffened. "The land is always ours, though the invader sits in our cities. But I bring warning— they got word of your coming, lord, and they've sent an army to stop you."

"Where?"

"Two miles from here the road gets level, goes through a valley with a little stream. It would be a good place to make camp. There used to be an old fort there. The road narrows again, then opens out into a flat about a mile across with a lake on the eastern side. Like this—" He pulled out a piece of paper on which a rough map had been drawn. "They call the place Condor's Rest. That's where they wait, lord, with their demon-priestess. They left some men to garrison Los Leones, but the best of their troops are here. By our count, General Marsh has some fifteen hundred foot soldiers who fight with sword and spear."

"And where is Prince Harun?" Julian asked then.

"The Nippani archers harry the enemy. The prince is taking the last Tambaran *impi* and a few dozen Drylands crossbows and three troops of light cavalry from Las Palisadas over the mountain." He pointed to the east. "There's a road that comes in beside the lake, but he can't get there 'til evening, and he'll need to rest men and horses."

"So will we," answered Robert grimly.

Julian had hoped to get through the mountains to the lowlands where he would have room to maneuver before making contact, but his foe had chosen the field, and neither side could avoid battle now.

"We'll continue on to the fort, slowly, so there's no chance of meeting until tomorrow morning, and make camp there. Go back to your prince and ask him to post signalers. He should keep his forces out of sight of the enemy and be ready to hit their flank once battle is joined."

The king looked up as a shadow flickered across the road. Against the pale blue of the sky a black shape circled, only its height above the mountains giving a clue to its real size. The messenger followed his gaze and made a sign of protection on his brow.

"A condor—," said Julian with interest. "I have not seen one since I was in Awhai."

"He knows what's coming . . . ," muttered the Elayan. "He's the spirit of these mountains. Tomorrow his kin will feed well."

The condors had been wheeling overhead all afternoon, swinging over pine-clad heights folded one upon another till they were blue with distance and then back again. From his vantage point on the hillside, Jo had a good view of their maneuvers. It was better than watching the warriors of the Sun prepare to fight the men of Westria. The sound of steel on whetstones and the tink-chink of the armorer's hammer drifted upward, an overture to battle that had become all too familiar. Other men were moving across the hillside with bags and forked sticks, seeking snakes for tonight's ceremony.

A muscle cramped in his back and he stretched to ease it. As he shifted position, the man who had been set to watch him tensed, then relaxed as Jo sat back again. He ought to be grateful that Mother Mahaliel had ordered so courteous a bondage; he did not think he could have endured being chained. But his own thoughts were a greater torment—he had been a fool to believe he could simply ride out of Los Leones. He should have hidden his feelings, waited until the confusion of departure offered him a chance to get away.

But the Mother had new servants now who had identified his accent as that of Westria, although, thank the Guardians, she did not know his real name. They still called him Red as they had in the circus. Had she dragged him along on this campaign to torment him? He should have slain himself before they could bring him here, but now they had taken his weapons, and his guard had been instructed to keep him from harm.

Dusk fell, and campfires blossomed among the neat rows of canvas tents set around a central square as the spear-wives cooked corn and beans for their men. Tonight they had been issued beef as well; the rich scent of roast meat hung in the air. The Children of the Sun had camped on a flat where two narrow canyons joined the road. Beyond the notch where it passed through the trees lay the broader field where they would fight in the morning. An advance guard had been left to hold the field, but no general wished to fight in darkness. Tonight, the Children of the Sun danced for their god.

With full dark, a new fire was kindled in the center of the campground. The leaders of files and companies formed a circle around it, with their followers ranked behind them. A chair had been set for Mother Mahaliel near the bonfire, with her general beside her, and it was here, as the drums began their muted thunder, that they made Jo sit as well.

He could not meet her eyes; she had loved him and he had tried to leave her. But he was still unbound, and the men came unarmed to the ceremony. Perhaps, when the dancing turned to frenzy, he might be able to get away.

The drumming crescendoed and then ceased as Mother Mahaliel rose, lifting her hands.

"My beloved children, my radiant warriors, five great battles you have fought since we left the Sea of Grass, and soon you will win once more! And this sixth battle shall be your greatest triumph, for six is the number of the Sun!" She smiled at the ullulation that shook the air in reply.

"To the pure in heart comes victory," she went on. "When you face your foe, that knowledge will kindle fire in your hearts and lend strength to your arms. But how shall you know if you are worthy of the favor of the Sun?"

A ripple of anticipation ran around the circle. The rough fiber bags set beside the bonfire were beginning to quiver as the snakes inside them were roused by the warmth of the fire.

"The Sun has blessed us, bringing us into a land where His messengers abound. So dance, my children! Those who lead shall take up the serpents and not be harmed, and those who follow will see the sign of victory!"

She turned to the drummers, and hands slapped the taut skins in a steady rhythm that vibrated through the ground. This was something more primal than the Sunday services. The men in the circle were beginning to sway, and Jo felt his own pulse beat faster in reply. The sudden shrill of a flute lifted the hair along his arms. A guard brought one of the bags to Mother Mahaliel. For a moment she lifted her arms in prayer, and it was not the firelight that set her face aglow. Then she opened the mouth of the bag and reached in.

There was a collective gasp as she brought out a writhing serpent in each hand. For a moment the wicked triangular heads darted frantically. But as she paced around the circle, the snakes seemed to relax, coiling gracefully along her arms.

"The tooth of the serpent shall not wound you, the edge of the sword shall not gash you, the point of the spear shall not pierce you!" she cried. "For you are the Children of the Sun!"

Two captains strode forward and received the rattlesnakes from Mother Mahaliel's hands. She took two more, passed them to the warriors who were crowding around her, and reached into the bag again. Presently she offered one to Tadeo Marsh, who gripped it firmly behind the neck as he marched around the fire, then passed it to one of the men. Jo blinked, dizzied by the energy of the dancers who spiraled around the fire.

Someone screamed—a man had been bitten. In the next moment the soldiers of his own file were striking him down. Presently, one of them came forward, blood-spattered, to receive a serpent from Mother Mahaliel. Jo watched in appalled understanding as the man staggered off, eyes white-rimmed in ecstasy as the rattlesnake twisted in his hands.

The circle had become a surging mass. Jo had no need of a guard now—only a madman would try to push through. Most of the dancers had stripped off their tunics; firelight gleamed from smooth scales and sweat-sheened skin. Red gleams swirled through Jo's vision—someone had told him that they called this mountain range the Dragon. . . . He groaned and shut his eyes against the image of a red dragon coiling around the fire, then jumped as something cool and smooth moved across his thighs.

"Be still, and he will not hurt you—you are his brother, after all," said a soft voice at his ear.

Jo opened his eyes and saw the rattler coiling in his lap; but before he could move, Mother Mahaliel seized his arms.

"Look at me. . . ."

His gaze flicked upward and was held. Terrified, he could feel the snake twining up across his chest and around his shoulders. *Move!* The spirit gibbered within him. *The snake will bite you and you will be free!* But he was the bird and she was the serpent, and he could not look away.

"The dragon is coiling around you," she hissed. "Do you feel its power?"

His answer was a wordless moan. His muscles locked as he felt on his neck the soft tickle of the rattlesnake's tongue. Was it the fire or some inner light that pulsed in her eyes, dark and bright, until that was all he could see?

"The dragon belongs to me . . . *you* belong to me. . . . You hear only my voice . . . respond only to my words. . . . Do you understand?"

"I understand," he heard himself answering. A vein in his temple throbbed as the blood pounded in his brain. She released his arms. Was it the snake that caressed his cheek or her hand?

"Stand up." Jo's body obeyed her command. "You will dance, you will fight, you will think as I tell you until I restore you to yourself again. . . . Red Dragon, I call you! Bring us victory!"

Mother Mahaliel gripped his shoulder and spun him hard, thrusting him into the dance, and the Red Dragon spread his wings.

———

The condors returned with the dawning, gliding above the battlefield on wide black wings. Julian shivered and turned his gaze back toward the foe who waited on the other side of the killing ground. Condor's Rest, they called this place. . . . He would be happy to leave it to the birds. The valley formed a rough oval about three miles by one, sloping slightly toward the east where a triangular lake gleamed in the sun. The marshy ground in that direction might be a problem for the Westrian cavalry. The peaks to the east still cast their shadow across the valley, and the morning air was chill even through the blue surcoat with the starburst of his house that he wore over his mail. Spearfoot stamped impatiently, and Julian patted the stallion's brown neck. He had always hated these last moments before battle, when you wondered if you had disposed your men to best advantage, and whether your enemy had any surprises in store.

This time, that was almost a certainty. Prince Harun's messengers had babbled of the enemy's ferocity but could tell him little about their training. They looked disciplined, standing in four neat double squares, sixty men on each outside face and forty on each side within, armed with spear and shield, white surcoats covering hardened leather or mail. He could see something white on the hill behind them. Was that where the priestess the Elayans feared so greatly sat with her general? Julian's commanders had argued that he ought to be directing from the rear as well, but his forces had too little training. His presence was needed to hold them together here.

As the wind shifted toward the Westrian lines, the stallion's ears twitched uneasily. "What am I hearing?" muttered the king. "Sounds like a hill full of rattlesnakes over there."

"Just about," replied Osleif, his page and trumpeter, the silver threads that formed a winged unicorn glinting against the red of his surcoat as the light grew. "The Elayan said they take the snakes' rattles after they dance with them, and tie them to their ankles."

Julian nodded. "The snake may buzz—" He pitched his voice to carry down the line. "But we will tread him down! We stand upon Elayan soil, but we are fighting for Westria. May the Guardians ride with us and guide our swords!" He made the sign of the circled cross upon his breast and caught a flicker of motion as others did the same.

The rattling grew louder as the Suns' squares began to move. Julian tightened his rein, glancing to the left where Robert and Jeanne commanded the two divisions of infantry. A purple banner with a golden bear fluttered above the men from the Ramparts; the Las Costas contingent was marked by a golden sun on azure blue. A company of spearmen from the Royal Domain marched beneath the blue banner with House Starbairn's silver star.

The Westrian light horse would be able to do little against the enemy spears, so Julian had ordered them to fight on foot and leave their mounts in the rear. His heavy cavalry were massed on the right, leaving room for Prince Harun's riders to attack from around the lake on the left. Behind him, his house guard followed the banner of Westria while the riders from Seagate rode under a forest green flag with the white horse rising from a white wave. The Westrians were outnumbered, but if his knights could break the enemy center, that might not—*would not*—matter, he told himself as he swung his spear high. As the sun lifted over the eastern ridges, the point flashed silver. The clear blare of Osleif's trumpet split the air, and the Westrian infantry began their quickmarch forward.

For agonizing minutes Julian waited, giving his spearmen the head start they would need. Arrows hummed toward them; he saw men fall. Then he dug his heels into Spearfoot's sides and the hiss of rattles was swallowed up in the thunder of hooves. Peripheral vision caught the green and gold flicker of the Westrian banner as its bearer moved up beside him. Scarcely a half-mile separated the two forces, the gap narrowing rapidly as they hurtled forward. A deeper-toned horn blatted from behind the enemy. The center squares halted; the two on either side marched a spear's-cast farther and stopped, overlapping their shields, the soldiers on the outside kneeling and digging the butts of their spears into the ground while those behind them braced their own shafts so that their squares bristled like giant porcupines.

Arrows with wicked obsidian heads hissed overhead, the volley from the archers he had placed on the western hillside crossing those of the enemy like two swarms of hostile bees. A horse screamed behind him; his helmet pinged as an arrow glanced off it. For a moment longer, Julian could see the geometry of the battle plan unfolding, his own forces extending into a wedge as they wheeled left toward the center of the crescent his enemy was forming to receive them.

If we can break those squares, our spears can take them. . . . Then the time for thought was over. Spearfoot faltered as the horse sighted the enemy spearpoints, but momentum carried them forward. He braced his own spear against his stirrup, dropping the knotted reins on the stallion's neck and covering his body with his shield.

Julian rocked in the saddle as his spear struck, stuck, and was ripped from his hand. He wrenched sword from sheath, swung at the snarling face before him, gripping hard with his knees as the stallion came to a plunging halt surrounded by screaming white-clad warriors. Reflexes honed by years of training took over, shield shifting to guard as he stabbed into the mob around him again and again.

⟶⟶⟶

Horn calls shrilled discordantly from across the field. Julian looked up, finding himself for the moment at the edge of the action. He reined in, willing his pounding pulse to slow. The cavalry that had survived that first charge had struck again from behind and found the enemy squares as strongly defended in the rear. Cutting back and forth, they had been pushed aside so that his back was now to the lake. The sun stood almost overhead, glaring down from a cloudless sky; in the timeless urgency of battle, the hours had flown.

The green banner of Westria tossed among the struggling figures, then its bearer broke free. Osleif followed, with several of the other riders behind him.

"Sound the rally," said Julian. An occasional arrow still thrummed downward from the enemy side, but the king had told his own archers to stop shooting once battle was well joined. Three enemy squares remained. Each had become the focus of its own battle, against which the attackers flung themselves in vain. Among the white-clad Sun soldiers in the nearest square, he could see one warrior in red whose sword flickered in and out like a flame. Crimson plumes danced on his helm. If the Suns had more like him, thought the king, the battle would already be won.

"Where's Prince Harun?" He shaded his eyes with his hand.

Shortly after the battle began, the Elayan charge had completed the Westrians' disorganization of the fourth square. The survivors of the *impi* were doing their best to repeat the feat against the third, plumes thrashing, assegais flashing past their cowhide shields. Now the Elayan riders, men in desert robes on high-bred horses, were following the Westrian knights who had turned toward Julian.

"My lord of Westria—" A man on a white horse trotted toward him. The robes that covered the warrior's mail had once been richly embroidered in blue and silver, though they were blood-spattered now, and a silver coronet banded his helm. White teeth flashed in a dark face as he bowed. "I give you my thanks for coming to our aid—"

"Thank me again when this is over," Julian said grimly. His mail had kept his skin whole, but bruises and stressed muscles were waiting to complain. His shield dangled in two pieces from his arm. He shook it loose and let it fall, and one of the other men passed him his own.

"Our horses are heavier, so I invite you and your men to fall in behind us. Let's see if we can put a dent in that middle square with another charge."

He nodded to Osleif, who blew the notes that would signal his own men to get out of the way, then picked up the reins. Spearfoot's response was slower now, but the brown ears pricked, and after a few moments of bone-jarring trot the stallion jerked into an uneven canter. Hooves thundered behind him.

As they neared the foe, a new call blared out from the hill. A ripple of movement ran through the Sun square; all the squares were moving—the men on the edges spreading out as those behind stepped inward, extending toward each other until suddenly they had formed a line that continued to shift, its center thickening to receive the Westrian charge as the sides began to curve around.

Julian glimpsed a blur of blue and silver—the Elayan

prince was moving up beside him. Robert, his blue eyes blazing, swung up his sword in salute as they passed, and Marcos, guarding his back as always, grinned. Then they struck the mass of white-clad bodies. Spearfoot plunged, clearing a path with his hooves, and as his head came down again, a flung spear crossed it and smashed into Harun's side. Julian saw the prince fall, his foes' roar of triumph followed in the next moment by a cry of dismay from the Elayans. The warriors of his guard closed around his body, but the other Elayans were turning to flee.

As the Sun line continued to close, the king found himself forced back as well. The dismounted Westrian warriors might manage to form a shield-wall, but it was no place for horses. As he wrenched Spearfoot's head around, spears flashed in the sunlight and enemy fighters surged around him. The stallion screamed as the wicked points struck home. Someone grabbed Julian's leg; he kicked the man in the head, slashed at the arm of another, used his shield to batter a third away.

Spearfoot lurched, but there was open space before him; knees buckling, the stallion lunged forward. Julian kicked his feet from the stirrups and threw himself free as they hit the ground, sword trapped under his body, trying to cover himself with his shield. He felt a sharp pain along his outer thigh as a blade stabbed up under his mail. His head rang from a blow that was stopped by his helm.

Then someone in a purple surcoat stepped between him and the sun. Steel sang as rescuer and assailants traded blows, and he heard Robert's battlecry. The king rolled into a crouch, then managed to get upright. Guarding each other's backs, he and Robert cleared the space around them. The Westrian banner was down, its young bearer crumpled beside it. Julian shifted his sword to his other hand for a moment and grabbed it.

As Julian bent, he heard a grunt from Robert. He looked up, saw a spear spinning away; blood spouted where Robert had severed its wielder's hand.

"Are you hurt?" he asked as Robert staggered.

"He didn't get you. . . ." Robert managed a smile, but the shield was sliding from his arm.

"Westria! Westria! To me!" cried the king. The attack faltered as more of his own warriors saw the green flag and fought their way to his side. "Blow the retreat," he snapped as Osleif pushed through.

Now his own men were all around him, urging him away from the enemy. The warrior in red whom he had seen before shouted incoherently, struggling to reach him, but there were too many Westrians between them now.

"You'll be all right now, Julian," Robert said hoarsely. Julian saw blood on his cousin's side, but everyone was bloody; Marcos was hauling him along. Julian pressed forward, leading them toward the valley from which they had come. The enemy's horns blared furiously, but though the Westrians had not been able to break the Suns' line, they made them pay for every foot of ground.

Once more Osleif sounded his horn. Julian heard the clatter of hooves as the horses they had left in the rear were brought forward. He had not expected defeat, but he had planned for the possibility, and as the animals came into view, his archers released their remaining arrows. Taken by surprise, the enemy faltered long enough for the retreating Westrians to clamber into the saddles. Those first mounted took others up behind them, and the archers loosed their last bolts and scrambled down the hill. The cries of their foes grew fainter as they galloped down the road.

"My lord, you must come—"

Had the rear guard been attacked? Julian looked at Lady Jeanne in alarm, but it was sorrow, not urgency that he read in her eyes. After the first frantic dash, their pace had slowed. Now the road was growing steeper and they had to go carefully, but so far there was no sign that the enemy was following. The sun was sinking, and ahead, the Great Valley lay veiled in golden haze.

"Marcos said to bring you," she added. Julian felt his gut

twist with apprehension as he reined his horse around to follow her back along the line.

Marcos was kneeling by one of the litters they had made from cloaks and spearshafts to carry those worst wounded. On his brown cheeks, silent tears cut through the battle grime. Julian dismounted, staggering as his weight came down on his wounded thigh, and limped forward to kneel at his side.

Robert lay with eyes closed, but he roused as Julian breathed his name.

"Did we escape?" A little blood bubbled at the corner of his mouth. "Are we in Westria?"

The king reached out to the earth and felt the familiar energy answering him.

"Yes," he whispered. "Can't you feel it?" He reached deeper, drawing up the power, seizing Robert's hands and trying to will it into the wounded man. A shadow flickered across his face; Julian glanced up and saw the spread wings of a condor dark against the glowing sky.

Robert shook his head a little and smiled. "No use . . . I told you once . . . sometimes another . . . must die for the king." The setting sun flared through the clouds in a last burst of splendor, lending an illusory color to his skin.

"You are not going to die!" Julian exclaimed. Long ago he had feared this and been reprieved. But now the payment was falling due.

"I failed you before . . . not this time. . . ."

"You never failed me, Robert! Your love—" Julian's throat closed. Even as the words left his lips, the life was fading from Robert's eyes, fading from the world. The men of the retreating column seemed no more than ghosts as they filed past.

The king struggled to his feet, fist clenching as the condor circled once more. "Go back to your eyrie, ill-omened bird! This is no meat for you." He turned to the waiting men. "Take him up. We will bury him in Westria."

Julian gazed northward, but the sun had gone down, and the shadows were lengthening across the land.

Jo stood on a darkening field, aching in every muscle, eyes dimmed by the lassitude that told him the Dragon had been fighting. He could hear the moans of the wounded and the calling of spear-wives searching for their dead. But still louder were the cheers of the survivors. The Suns had won again.

He wondered which battle this had been. He did not recognize the shape of the hills. Blood dyed the rest of him as red as his armor, but he seemed unwounded. He flinched as a darker shadow passed above him and a condor glided down to settle on one of the bodies, the bald head dipping to tear at the outstretched hand of a warrior who lay beneath a crumpled flag.

The banner was green; from its bloody folds the circled cross of Westria gleamed. Jo stared, and recognition stabbed like a sword from ambush. He sank to his knees, understanding in a single convulsion of despair where he was and what he had done.

Behind him, someone was boasting they had seen the Westrian king's war-leader carried from the field. Jo's chest hurt as if a blade had found his heart. And so it should, he thought numbly. *Was it my sword that brought Robert down?* It was the work of a moment to set the hilt against the ground and slide the point under the front plate of his brigandine. He leaned forward, forcing the sharp blade to pierce his skin. . . .

Someone shouted, hard hands seized his shoulder and flung him backward. Screaming, he tried to fight, but his weapon had been ripped away. A weight pinned his legs; they grabbed his wrists and he felt the cold clasp of steel. His heart pounded as if it would burst his breast, his anguish turning inward as a trapped beast gnaws its own flesh. But even the Dragon could not save him now.

"Come," King Jehan's voice called from within. *"I will keep you safe, my child. Let go your memories and come with me. . . ."*

11

TWO OF SWORDS

The patter of rain on the roof slates of the College of the Wise merged with the flutter of the cards as Mistress Iris shuffled them. To Luz, the sorrow of the skies seemed a fitting reflection of her mood. In their second year, the students studied the element of Water and were nicknamed "weepers," but since the battle at Condor's Rest, all Westria had been weeping.

The images of the Seeker and the Adept, Guardians and Staves and Blades, Cups and Platters and the Four Jewels of Westria, flickered past the adept's graceful fingers. Then Mistress Iris tapped the cards into a neat stack and set them down on the table beside the green velvet cloth on which an outline of the circled Cross of the Elements had been stitched in gold. The deck was a variant version in which many of the traditional figures of the tarot had been replaced by images from Westrian lore. It was said to have been commissioned by the Master of the Junipers when he was Master of the College. One of this year's tasks for the weepers was to create their own decks of cards.

"There is always more power in an answer when need impels the question," said the priestess. "What shall we ask?"

"What will happen because we lost the battle?" offered Kamil.

Luz was not sure whether her shiver came from the question or because even with a fire going in the small classroom she could feel a draft. She had been looking forward to learning divination, but there were some questions whose answers it might be better not to know.

"Very well—that's a good question to put to this deck. Cut the cards now—once or twice will do—and then lay the one that lies on top in the center of the cross. That will signify the questioner."

Kamil bit his lip in concentration and took the first card, turning it over as he laid it down. The figure on its face wore the blue robe of a Westrian justiciar. On one side, the background showed a landscape of tilled fields; on the other, the view was of mountains wild and bare.

"What card has he drawn?" Their teacher's dark eyes moved around the circle.

"It's one of the trumps. He has picked Justice . . . ," answered Radha.

"And what does it mean?"

"Integration and balance, decision and integrity," the girl replied.

Well enough, thought Luz. Certainly the country could use the focus it implied.

In their first year, the lessons had been all aimed at grounding and control, but now they were being told to open up, and divination was one of the tools they used. It had proved harder than she expected, even after so many months of discipline, to release only those powers that were wanted, and only on demand.

"Very well. Now, Joffrey. Set the next card at the northern point of the cross, the place of earth and stability."

The card he picked was the Wheel, in this deck represented by a wreath whose flowers were in all stages from bud to blasted bloom. In good times, it meant that things were about to change; to see it here seemed to confirm the end of the stability that Westria had known.

Possible meanings for *that* were only too clear. The Elayans had always been a potential enemy, but they had been equally matched with Westria. The enemy that waited beyond the southern border now was of another order entirely. Having repelled Julian's army, would the Suns be content with the conquest of Elaya, or would they consider the land to the north easy game?

The southern point of the cross signified fire and passion. Mistress Iris handed the deck to Luz. The image she turned up was the Hanged Man. For a long moment she simply stared at it. The picture showed a naked man hanging head-down from a great tree. The picture seemed to imply that he was supported as well as suspended there. Vefara had told her about a god who gained wisdom by hanging himself from the tree. What wisdom could she find in this sacrifice?

"Luz," Mistress Iris said softly, "what do you see?"

"He suffers . . . but in his torment there is ecstasy." She looked up unhappily. "What does this mean for Westria? Lord Robert is dead already! Will we all have to be sacrificed?"

"Turn up the next card," begged Radha. "The west is where the tides roll in. Maybe we'll find more hope there."

"It is so," said the mistress. "The repeated cycles of the sea bring renewal. Vefara—choose again."

The image on the card was of a woman bound in chains and surrounded by flames. Eight daggers flew toward her. Her situation seemed desperate, but her expression was hopeful.

"My people have a story about a goddess who was stabbed by swords and burned by fire and yet lived—" Vefara's voice wavered. "But what does the card mean here?"

"It is not a single trial that awaits us, but many. . . ." Still staring at the layout, Luz spoke without intending it, and heard in her own voice the certainty of prophecy. "But we will survive them."

Mistress Iris frowned thoughtfully, but without commenting, directed Joffrey to draw another card and set it at the eastern point of the cross. From this direction blew the winds of change. They seemed to have overturned the three cups that lay at the feet of the young man on the card, although two more still stood upright behind him. Much had been lost, but something remained, if they could only turn and see.

"The spread is complete, but another card may point to a conclusion. Luz, draw the card and tell us what you see. . . ."

Obedient, Luz turned up the next image and put it down on the corner of the cloth. Here, another female figure was portrayed, her arms crossed, each hand grasping a sword whose edges were wreathed in flame.

"It is the Two of Swords. Her decision hangs in the balance. A crowd swirls around her, yammering counsel, but she is blindfolded and cannot see her way."

"And what will happen?" Was it Mistress Iris who asked that question, or Westria?

"There are too many swords in this reading, but she cannot stay where she is. She will have to do something soon."

The sword struck the leather-padded post with a satisfying *thunk*. Tadeo Marsh felt the vibration all the way up his arm and shifted his weight, letting the momentum draw the blade out and up in a smooth swing that brought it slashing across the second post and around as he settled to guard once more. Men who had paused in their own exercise to watch him began to move again. They should not have stopped, but he supposed it did no harm for them to see their commander sweating like any other soldier. Actually, he was sweating more than he should have after such a simple combination of moves. Too much desk work was stealing his wind. He drew breath, widened his stance, and blurred into motion once more.

When Tadeo broke off at last, the sun was high in a pale sky washed clean by last night's storm, though burgeoning clouds to the west promised more rain to come. This morning the mountains showed clearly. The top of one peak glinted white—the only snow, the natives had assured him, that they would see. It was a far cry, he thought with satisfaction, from winter on the Sea of Grass. January on the delta of the great middle river where he was born had been this mild, but wetter. The climate of Elaya was altogether splendid, he told himself, stretching in satisfaction.

But the time he had allowed himself for exercise was over. The general sheathed his sword and turned back toward the fortress. All around him, men continued to work in files or squares, practicing the maneuvers that would become instinctive in battle. The Children of the Sun had claimed the central plaza of Los Leones as a practice field, exiling the markets to lesser squares around the town. They needed the space, and controlling the number of people who could gather at any point discouraged any thoughts of rebellion, not that they had had much trouble with the natives thus far.

The Children of the Sun had begun to send priestesses out to the nations of Elaya along with their warriors, preaching the doctrine of their all-powerful deity, and new recruits were responding. Tadeo's veterans had their work cut out to integrate these newcomers into their army. But it was needful. The Westrians had been defeated, but the Suns had burned the bodies of a third of their own men on the field.

A gruff voice shouted, and two files that had been thrusting at each other with padded pole-arms came to a confused halt. The air sizzled as the man called Garr, who had once been armsmaster to Master Marvel's circus, explained just what species of idiots they were. A strange man, thought Tadeo, but useful. After all, the fellow had trained the Dragon, who was one of the best swordsmen he had ever seen. The boy was there now, watching—no, serving as a model—he noticed, as Garr had him demonstrate a move with a wooden stave.

But thinking about the Dragon made Tadeo frown once more. He would never have criticized Mother Mahaliel aloud, but he could damn her silently. The tricks she had played with the boy's mind at the snake dance had well nigh ruined him. Red could still fight—he had proved that at the battle—but he had become . . . unpredictable. Tadeo hoped that Garr could handle him if he started to confuse the drill ground with the battlefield.

Yet in the larger scheme of things, the Westrian boy had no importance. Tadeo shrugged on the coat his aide held out for him, his mind turning to the agenda for this afternoon's meeting with Mother Mahaliel and her advisors.

"What do you see when you look into the fire?" asked Mother Mahaliel.

"Scarlet the wings of the dragon who slays . . . red for the trickster whom nobody blames . . . blue for the ruler who secretly stays . . . gold for the phoenix who soars from the flames," Red chanted, and she smiled at his foolery.

There was one who was not listed in the rhyme, the one who had just begun to learn who he was when the slavers captured him, but the scar on his breast was still healing from the last time Jo had wakened. Better to leave him safely sleeping, guarded by King Jehan.

Cedar and juniper glowed in the belly of the clay stove, lines of flame interweaving in sigils of shifting complexity. It was raining again, and Elayan houses, even the chambers that had once housed the princesses of Al-Kaid, seemed to have been built for a perpetual summertime. On a winter evening everyone was glad of a fire.

Red picked up the poker and stirred the burning brands. "What do *you* see?"

"A burning city . . . ," said Mother Mahaliel. "Last night I saw it once more."

"The City of the Firebird burned beautifully." One of the logs broke in a shower of sparks and he laughed.

She gave him an odd look. "It is no mortal land I visit in my visions. The city of my god burns with Light and is not consumed, and then I wake, and I am . . . here."

Red nodded. In *his* dreams, Jo lived in a golden land.

"It is so beautiful there, my child," Mahaliel murmured. "Everything is clean, pure. . . ." She glanced around the room with its tile floor and smoke-stained walls and sighed. Bett looked up from the game of chess she was playing with one of the virgin guards, and seeing that their mistress did not call, returned her attention to the board.

"*That chess set was Prince Palomon's,*" commented King Jehan from within. "*I saw it at the peace talks after we took Santibar.*" Red ignored him. In Caolin's War the Elayans had taken Santibar back again. He supposed that now it belonged to the Children of the Sun.

"Does your god speak to you?" Red asked. These days his own head held a chorus. It was ever so much better than being alone.

"He sings, my child. He sings. . . ."

"How did He come to you?"

She looked at him in surprise. It was not, he reflected, a question that many would dare to ask her. But he could dare anything now.

"I had a husband and family once, long ago. A son like you. . . ." Her face sagged, suddenly remembering its years. "Their love was enough for me. But we were driven from our home, and outlaws caught us as we fled out onto the Sea of Grass. They killed—" She stopped. "They left me for dead. My soul *was* dead. I walked away empty, under the empty sky. For many days I was alone.

"And the Sun rose. . . ." Suddenly her face was radiant once more. "He filled me. He burned away the pain. He told me to bring all the world to His light. Men make so many complexities of their religions, but the truth is simple. We have only to submit to His will. He has led me here. He has promised me a home where the hills rise golden beside the sea."

"Westward lies the ocean. Shall we build you a temple there?"

"Not yet. . . ." Gently, she stroked his shoulder. "This land has beauty, but in my dreams I see a place where the fields are rich with crops and the mountains with game. There was a bard who traveled with us for a time. He used to sing about the western land." She hummed softly, and Jehan's memories, awakening, provided the words.

> The hawk soars high o'er yonder hill,
> The stag bells in the glen,
> The whale chants wild in waters chill,
> The bear dreams in her den.
> They call me to return again,
> They set me on my way,
> Where the twilight seals the day.
> To the West, to the West,
> I am summoned,
>   As the Dreamers come before,
> With my wounds all healed away,

Like the sun I will rest
Where my vision leads,
  Along the Western shore.

Mahaliel's fingers tightened. "Westrian boy, do you know where that land lies?"

As she spoke, he could feel her god awakening within her like a great glaring light, its power spearing into his soul. Jehan drew his blue cloak between them, cool as twilight.

"This country is too well populated already. There is no room in here for gods."

"My lady—" He offered Jehan's charming smile. "The Land of Dreams can only be found within. . . ."

"Watch out—the sword! So much blood . . . Robert, no!"

Startled from her own dreams by Julian's cry, Rana jerked upright. He shuddered, flailing, and she caught his hands in her own.

"It's all right, I'm here. . . . It's all right, Julian."

Like an echo, Rana remembered another man shouting such words, tormented by memories of a battle where he had failed to save someone he loved. Then, it had been Robert whom she had nursed through his delirium. But Julian had only been lost, and he had come back to them. Robert's ashes mingled now with the earth of the Sacred Wood, for he had died in the place of a king. He would never ride up the road to Misthall again.

Julian's grip tightened painfully; then he came to himself with a gasp and let her go. "Sorry . . . I'm sorry. . . . I should sleep in a separate chamber. I'm afraid I'm a poor bedfellow."

"No," she answered. "I would still hear you, and to comfort you I would have to get up in the cold." She pulled the covers over both of them once more. By the silence, she guessed the hour to be close to dawn. Most of the bedrooms in the old house had small fireplaces, but the fire in this one had burned out long ago.

"He took the blow that was meant for me," muttered Julian. "And all those others—they died because of me, because I led them there. . . ."

This, too, she had been hearing since the November day when the king returned from his ill-fated expedition to Elaya with what remained of his army. Rana had hoped that moving the royal household from the palace in Laurelynn to Misthall, the old royal dwelling in the hills that overlooked the Great Bay, might make it easier for Julian to deal with his sorrow.

But now it was January, and though heavy exercise or alcohol could send him into a sleep too deep for dreaming, they did not help for long. She had learned to rest lightly, anticipating the nightmares, as she had learned to waken long ago, after she returned from a journey to the north to find Phoenix a prey to night terrors he could never name. The reasons for Julian's agonies were only too clear.

"Some of them died on our retreat," he went on. "We burned the bodies outside of Risslynn. The smoke went up in a black column so high they must have been able to see it from Elaya. The great condors fly above those mountains—did I tell you? I hope the bastards buried the men we left on the field. I hope they didn't let the birds scatter their bones. . . ."

"Yes, Julian, you told me." She took his hand. A little light was growing beyond the curtained windows. She could make out the bedposts, and her husband's dark shape against the gloom. "But even the condors serve the Guardians, and the spirits of our dead know the way home."

Julian shuddered. "Oh yes. They followed me . . . they follow me. Will I ever be free?"

"I don't know," she answered a little more tartly than she had intended. "But you are not the only one who is grieving."

"I am the one responsible. I led them there," he said softly, turning away. "And I didn't lead well enough to bring them back again."

"Then learn!" The accumulated pain of these past weeks overwhelmed her. Rana bit her lip, shocked at her own words, but her pity had not helped him. "You were outgeneraled and outnumbered. Perhaps, having repelled you, these Sun people will be content to stay in Elaya. But what if they don't?" she said briskly. "You had better prepare to fight more effectively next time, and justify the sacrifice Robert made to save you!"

He jerked as if she had struck him. But whether her words would prick him into some more useful response than brooding or simply make him bleed, she did not know.

The prisoner staggered forward, leaving smears of blood behind him on the sand. As the man passed, Red caught the stink of urine. Had the guards given the fellow no opportunity to relieve himself, or had he pissed himself in fear? Red breathed shallowly, wishing himself elsewhere. Mother Mahaliel liked to keep him by her for entertainment, but he did not see any way to make a joke out of what was going to happen here.

He glanced at the grim profile of the woman who sat in her chair of state above him. Perhaps the Mother would not wish to be amused just now. In the wan winter sunlight they could see that the prisoner was a small man, sallow-skinned, with lank black hair, clad in the filthy remnants of what had once been a convert's white robe. An ordinary criminal would have been flogged or exiled, but this was a recusant, one who had accepted the religion of the Sun and then gone back to the worship of his old gods.

Red's smile twisted as he glanced down at his crimson vest and breeches, startling as a splash of blood against all these white robes. No one seemed to have noticed that *he* had never vowed himself to Mother Mahaliel's god. But then, formal commitment was not required of children or of the mad, and he surely included both among his several selves.

The guards shoved their captive up the mound that had been raised opposite the platform on which Mother Mahaliel was enthroned. Swiftly they locked the chain from his manacled hands to a ring bolted into one of the stones, then scrambled back down to join the circle of men who kept the crowd away. Thus elevated, he was clearly visible to those who had been called to watch his trial. For a trial was what Mother Mahaliel persisted in calling it, though everyone was anticipating an execution. They would have a good view. A brisk wind had driven away the mists that so often veiled Los Leones, and the blue mountains that surrounded the basin were revealed in unusual clarity.

When all were in place, the priestess rose to her feet. Reason told Red that it was her aura, not her body, that had expanded until he felt like a child beside her. Slowly she surveyed those who waited below, her white veils fluttering in the wind.

"Chien-Lu Lin, listen to me—" Her voice rang out like a golden bell. "You came to the Children of the Sun, and like a brother they welcomed you. With my own embrace I brought you into the Light, but now you have turned from us and returned to your darkness. How could you do it, my child? What deception could have seduced you from the Truth we bring?"

The man on the mound trembled, but he raised his head at last, gazing around him at the waiting crowd. "I thought she is Lady of Compassion, walking among us as old tales say. But it's a lie—all this you do, only a lie to trap us in a world of illusion once more."

"It is your apostasy that is the lie, my child," said Mother Mahaliel, a boundless sorrow throbbing in her words, and Red, crouching at her feet, could feel her sincerity. "I beg you to turn again. Give up your superstition. Even now, will you not recant your error and be saved?"

The man turned to face her, his dark eyes wild in his bruised face. "My Lady of Compassion gave up her arms and eyes to save father who persecuted her. She stop on brink of Nirvana to hear cries of those who suffer in this world, turned back to pray for them. Till all are saved, she stays. *Your* light is delusion; you say you want to help, but you kill—"

"You speak blasphemy!" Mother Mahaliel lifted her arms. "If your demon has power, let her save you! By the fire we are purified! By fire you shall be tested, *now*!"

Red pulled back as the air around the priestess shimmered suddenly with the heat of a desert noon. Through his fingers he stared, expecting to see her draperies aflame. But it was the man on the mound who cried out as the first spark kindled in the rags that covered him.

"Namu Kuan Shih Yin Pu Sa'a!" His words became a rapid mumble as the fire took hold. The Children of the Sun said that the soul who was innocent and pure could walk through fire unharmed, but Chien-Lu Lin was *becoming* fire, his body beginning to combust from within. And still, impossibly, his chant went on.

Red recoiled, seeking some other self to face the pain. From amidst the crowd Garr watched with bent brows, as if he could sense that the Red Dragon was about to break free. But the dragon was already in the smoke that swirled around the burning man, a white dragon, on whose back Red glimpsed a slender female form wreathed in floating draperies. Did no one else see her? Here and there among the crowd someone cried out and sank to his knees, and Garr lifted his hand in what looked like a greeting, but Mother Mahaliel's expression was unchanged.

The spirit woman reached out to the dying man, and when she straightened, her arms cradled a spark of light. Her radiant gaze swept the crowd, slowed, fixed on Red as he cowered beside Mother Mahaliel's throne.

"I am the Iron Goddess of Mercy, and in my heart there is compassion for all beings—even for you." As She lifted Her hand in blessing, the monster within him sank back into the depths and Red followed him. *"Be at peace, my child. I promise you this—when the Red Dragon meets the White, he will find peace."*

As the clamor quieted, it was Fix who sat up, gazing around him with grave curiosity. Mother Mahaliel sat slumped on her chair, her eyes wet with tears. In the ashes on the mound, all that remained was a pile of blackened chains, and a wisp of white smoke that whirled away toward the west and disappeared.

"My king, your summons came, and I'm here." Marcos straightened from his bow and stood waiting.

Julian gestured to the younger man to take a seat by the hearth. Rain dripped from the eaves of the palace and the river was high; he fancied he could hear its roaring even above the crackle of the fire. Ruddy light gleamed on the tile of the arms of Westria set into the bricks of the mantelpiece and the pile of military texts the king had gleaned from the palace library.

"Not a summons, Marcos, a request. When we returned from the south, there was so much—" Julian searched for words. He would not admit it to Rana, but her words had stung him into coming back to Laurelynn, and in the midst of the many other affairs that awaited him he had found time to write to Rivered, asking Philip if he would send Marcos here.

"I wanted to be sure that you were taken care of," said the king. Marcos had always been the lovely young man who was Robert's consolation. When had the silver begun to thread his hair? "Will you have some wine?" Julian rang the bell on his desk without waiting for the answer.

"There's no need for concern." Marcos warmed his hands at the flames with a hint of his old smile. "A long time since, my lord Roberto gave me a holding. My sister an' her man keep it for me now."

"Do you wish to return there?" The man's face was worn by sorrow, but his eyes held none of the anguish Julian knew must live in his own.

One of Prince William's sons appeared in the doorway, carefully balancing a tray that bore two clay cups and a bottle of robust red wine from one of the king's own vineyards in the Royal Domain. Julian thanked him and poured.

"Does my lord need me?" Marcos asked.

"By the Guardians!" Julian exclaimed, offering him the cup of wine, "I think I do, though whether for my torment or my comfort I do not know. Do you not hate me, Marcos? Robert died in my stead!"

Marcos turned the cup between his fingers, then looked up at him.

"My king—you spoke clear to me, an' I think I must do the same. Roberto, he was my heart, but always a part of his soul belonged to you. He wasn't sorry to die, if it were to save you. Also," Marcos sighed, "for him, this was th' easy way. Roberto never wanted to grow old. . . ."

For a moment Julian found it hard to breathe. Death had looked like an escape to him often enough these past two months so that he understood Marcos's meaning. He cleared his throat.

"The man who took care of my gear was killed in Elaya. The traders tell me that the Sun army is preparing to move north. To take the job now I need someone who can fight." In one swallow he emptied his own cup. "Marcos, will you stay with me? To see you will remind me that my life is Robert's gift, and I dare not waste it. . . ."

"The king of Westria fought brave enough, but he be no general." Vincent Chiel led the line of clan-fathers toward the dais that had been set up in the square.

"Not a good enough general," Tadeo Marsh corrected, keeping pace at the head of the commanders who marched onto the parade ground. "He did not know what he was facing. Against an Elayan army his battle plan might have worked well. We have not come so far by underestimating our enemies."

Earlier that day it had rained, but now the clouds were parting. Yellow light angled through the clouds, lending the faces of the soldiers who stood in their ranks to either side a sickly glow. Tadeo had hoped that the discussion would come to an end when they left the Council meeting for the ceremony, but Chiel was a man of fixed ideas, and this review of the Suns' military might had inspired him.

"But is Westria an enemy?" wondered Commander Anaya, whose square had sustained the fewest losses in the battle in the mountains. "After such a defeat as we handed them, surely they'll be happy to let us alone. . . ."

"Ah, but do we mean t' let *them* alone?" Loris Stef, the oldest of the clan-fathers, asked then. "I've been talking with the traders. The rest of the country's not like what we saw from the mountains. Along the coast and farther north is rich land. Maybe that's where the god means t' lead us."

The god, or good sense? wondered Tadeo. Either way, he admitted it had delivered them from a part of the world where they would have been constantly threatened by populous nations who already had reason to be suspicious of any religion that came out of the Sea of Grass. Ever since the battle, they had been debating whether they should be content with their conquest of Elaya or move on.

"Then I trust He'll give us time to train replacements for those we lost in our *first* encounter with the Westrians before sending us off to fight them again," the general commented dryly.

"Reckon He will," observed Stef. "Here they come now. . . ."

Tadeo realized that the steady drumbeat had been amplified by the slap of sandals on the muddy ground, not so precise as might have been wished for, but an improvement over the confusion that had marked their first attempts at drill.

As they shuffled into the open space before the dais, Mother Mahaliel rose from among her attendants—ten maidens and one red-headed young man, a reverse of the structure of the army's files. But unlike the spear-wives, Red did not sleep with Mahaliel's guards. Perhaps he could not. The last time the general had visited Mahaliel's quarters, the boy had been playing at jackstones, laughing like a little child.

"My beloved children—" Her golden voice rang out across the square, "Live in the Light!"

"Destroy the Darkness!" From three thousand throats came the reply.

"You who have been faithful through many battles are like a field of golden wheat, heavy with grain. You who are newly come among us are like the first green shoots, striving toward the sun."

The simile, thought Tadeo, was not entirely happy. The fate of grain, after all, was to be cut down. But perhaps the priestess did not see it that way.

One by one, the files who had lost men in the battle were called forward, and their spear-wives moved along the line of recruits, choosing men to fill the empty places.

Mother Mahaliel stood once more.

"Now we are whole again. Now we are one, an Army of Light before which no foe can stand. To you who still mourn for fallen brothers I offer vengeance, and to you who are unblooded I promise victory."

Tadeo frowned. What was she on about now?

"The light that has purified your hearts will blaze across this land, purging it of all that is unclean! Our god has spoken—our way lies northward. He has shown me our banner floating above the city of Laurelynn."

The general caught for a moment an expression of anguish on the face of the Westrian boy. Then it was gone, and a different man seemed to look out of his eyes. *Something strange there,* Tadeo thought. *If the woman thinks she can keep the Dragon chained, she is welcome to him; but I think we will not allow that one onto the battlefield again.*

But Tadeo had more critical concerns than the mental state of one Westrian captive. The men were cheering; the ground trembled with the intensity of their response to the priestess's words. They had become a single being, animated by a single soul whose voice was Mother Mahaliel.

I am sorry for you, Westrian king, thought Tadeo Marsh. *I would have spared your land, but I can only direct this beast, not stop it.*

"To glory I summon you! We march on the Golden Land!"

12

THE WAY TO WESTRIA

The road wound north between the mountains and the sea. Looking back, Red could see the long line of men and beasts, like some impossible, many-legged creature whose steel scales gleamed dully in the fading light. The white and gold banners of the Children of the Sun fluttered in a wind that was carrying more rain clouds in from the ocean. General Marsh had delayed their advance until March, waiting for the grass to grow higher and hoping for the weather to improve. The clouds were not cooperating, but the army that took the ancient road was better trained and far better supplied than any force the Children of the Sun had fielded before.

Habañero danced as the banners snapped beneath a stronger gust of wind. Red reined him back with unconscious skill and bent to give the red neck a soothing pat. "At least I've kept you safe, Baby," he told the horse, then wondered where the thought had come from. He recalled a promise, but could not remember to whom it had been made, or where.

"Storm's coming," said Loris Stef, coughing. He had been complaining about the damp almost since the rains set in, which was pretty much as soon as they left Los Leones. Bett, who had an acid tongue for everyone except her mistress, called him an old auntie and said he ought to have been counted among Mother Mahaliel's women instead of the fathers of the clans.

"Do you wish you'd stayed in Santibar, old man?" she asked now. "*She* would give you leave, and I daresay the Iron General would be glad to see you go!"

Santibar by the Sea, with its broad avenues and graceful palm trees, had been a welcome refuge after the trek through the valley beyond Los Leones. The town had surrendered to the general's advance guard without resistance. After so many years as a bone of contention in the endless rivalry between Elaya and her northern neighbor, they were not minded to play the same role in a conflict with this new and more formidable enemy.

"So he can give the spoils of Westria to his own men?" said Loris. "I'll stay, if only to keep an eye on him."

Cho-cho, the dark-eyed girl who had joined the household in Elaya, looked scandalized and hid nervous laughter behind her hand.

It was true that one way or another, very few of the throng that had set out from the Sea of Grass marched now in Mother Mahaliel's train. Some, the most hardened and fanatical, remained as the backbone of the army, but most of the survivors who had brought their families or earned the right to marry had been left to garrison the conquered lands. Some of them had won brides from Mother Mahaliel's household, leaving Bett senior among those who served her now. Red had sometimes wondered if Bett stayed because she loved her mistress or because no man would have her.

But he was not sorry to leave Santibar, stripped now of supplies, behind him. At the sight of the blue sea backed by those gracious hills, King Jehan had wakened, keening for the city now doubly lost to Westria. Only by getting drunk and staying that way until it was time to march had Red been able to get them safely away. Now Jehan lay almost as deeply buried as the Dragon. Red could allow Fix time out to enjoy the ride, but the child was likely to do something foolish if left too long alone.

Red was the only one who could be trusted to keep them all safe, and he was feeling more unsettled the farther north they came. When wind ruffled the surface of the water he blinked, sure for a moment he had seen a face forming there. He turned toward the hills where the ceanothis was in blue bloom, and clapped his hands to his ears as the wind whispered a welcome through the pleated leaves.

I don't know you! He tried to imagine himself behind a barrier of stone. *I have never been here before. . . .* But recognition was stirring. *Go to sleep,* he told it sternly. *For you, this place can only bring pain!* Habañero began to sidle nervously, picking up his anxiety. Grateful for the distraction, Red applied himself to getting the stallion back under control.

By the time the second day's march from Santibar ended, the voices had become a chorus. Red's head throbbed with the effort to keep the self who knew them asleep within. The Suns made camp on a sheltered sandy space between the hills and the sea. Beyond it, the road turned sharply into a rock-warded pass that wound inland through the hills, where a rampart of golden sandstone seemed to bar the way. When darkness fell, the earth offered back the warmth of the day on a soft wind. Scents of damp earth and new grass wafted gently among the tents that were being set up on the sandy ground, and brush and small trees grew along a shallow watercourse that led to a beach where the waves sighed softly as they rolled up across the sand.

He was leading Habañero down to the horse-lines when Cho-cho called to him.

"Oh, Red, this land is lovely!" she exclaimed. "Just stand still for a moment and breathe the air!"

Unthinking, he obeyed her, and in that moment, all his defenses went down. Suddenly it was Jo who was drawing in that sweet air with a delight so piercing it was almost pain, Jo who for that moment knew only that he had come home.

From time to time he had sensed the spirits of other lands, but not since he had been carried off by the raiders had he felt this sense of connection with all that lived. Astonished, he gazed around him. The sights and sounds of a Sun encampment were familiar enough, but what were they doing here by the sea? Habañero butted him and he clung to the stallion's neck, trying to understand. They had been in the mountains above the Dragon's Tail pass. . . . He stretched out his hand—the last time he had seen it, he had been covered with blood that was not his own.

Around him he heard only the murmur of conversation as men pounded in tent stakes and laid out gear. But he remembered bonfires and the excitement of an army drunk on victory, shouting that the Westrian king's war-leader had gone down.

Jo ground his face against the stallion's coarse mane, remembering the many times the man who had been like a favorite uncle had been kind to him. More memories were returning. He felt at his side and realized that he carried neither knife nor dagger, and a twinge in his solar plexus brought back the reason why. He rubbed the ridge of scar tissue across the muscle, remembering the inner agony that was so much worse than the body's pain. *Why did they stop me?* he thought despairingly.

Habañero tensed, gathering himself to lash out as someone passed too close behind them. Automatically, Jo took his rein and began to lead him forward once more. Time must have passed, for that battle had been fought at midwinter. The smell of the air here told him that it was spring. He could remember nothing of what had passed in the months between.

But it must be close to the Equinox, and they were at the borders of Westria. Memory of a long-ago trip with his parents identified the road from Santibar. The Children of the Sun were about to invade his homeland—it was too late to warn anyone now. The camp was full of armed men, all of whom had been told to stop him if he tried to run away.

They didn't understand. The last thing in the world he wanted now was to go home. But home was where the Children of the Sun seemed determined to carry him. Westria called with a sweetness Mother Mahaliel could never match, but he dared not return to her. He was doubly damned. Whether or not he had killed Robert, Jo had certainly killed Westrians.

The wind dropped and he smelled the sea. A line of white lace lapped the shore. The general had already placed sentries up and down the road, but there was no need to guard the beach. Some of Jo's anguish began to ease as he realized that there might be an escape for him after all.

He settled Habañero for the night with special care. The horse was the envy of half the army. They would take good care of him. After supper, he sought his tent, to lie in a kind of waking dream that was sweeter than sleep, reaching out in love to the land that had borne him, and the sea that would receive his bones. And in the dark hour after midnight, when even his watchers might be expected to drowse, Jo slipped out of his tent and made his way down to the shore.

Water hissed across the sand, whispering his name. The waves gleamed faintly in the light of a young moon, sinking already toward the sea. *Like me . . .* , he thought, saluting her, and moved on until the little waves snatched at his ankles. For a moment the water seemed shockingly cold. Then it became merely bracing. In a moment, he thought, it would seem warm. . . . He began to wade forward.

A faint shout echoed behind him, but by then, the water was breast-high. Laughing, he dove through the breakers and began to stroke forward with all the strength he had.

Sea Mother, to you I offer my body; let your creatures feed well, and give my regrets to the Lady of Westria. . . .

It was harder than he had expected. The tide was coming in, and each surge seemed determined to bear him back to shore. But soon it would not matter. He was too far out to touch bottom already; cold weighted his limbs and he was growing tired.

Now, Mother, he thought as a billow burst over his head and pushed him down. *Receive me into your blessed darkness, and take away my pain.* For a moment it seemed to him that he was a child once more, lying in his own mother's arms. The queen had always loved the sea. But she had not been there when he needed protection. He reached out again to that Mother who was both greater and older than his own. The water bore him up; instinctively he sucked in air, but he refused to struggle. When the next wave thrust him under, he abandoned volition, consciousness, and identity, and allowed himself to sink into the embrace of the sea.

But instead of those endless deeps, he found himself borne up by the smooth lithe flex of dolphin bodies that carried him shoreward, slipping away as men splashed into the water to drag him back to captivity.

Rana dreamed that she was floating on a dark and gently heaving sea. Cold numbed her limbs, and she knew it was time to surrender. She released her hold on the piece of wood that had sustained her and began the long slow slide into the depths. With the logic of dream she found herself accepting the fact that she did not need to breathe, as she recognized the dark and sparkling swirl of octopoid tentacles that resolved themselves into Sea Mother's cloak.

She curved in homage to the Guardian of the creatures of the sea, a little surprised to realize she had her own, middle-aged body here—she usually returned to her adolescent slenderness when she dreamed of the sea.

"Queen of Westria, what has come to your son?"

Shock threatened to dispel the dream, but Rana clung to the image of Sea Mother's wise eyes.

"Mother, I have lost him," she wailed.

"I found him, but I sent him back again."

"What do you mean? Where—when?" Anguish broke the dream, and this time she could not capture it again. As she sped toward consciousness, Sea Mother's final words drifted up to her—

"He must find his healing on the land, not in the sea. . . ."

Luz fought for breath, struggling against the arms that held her. Water splashed her face; she choked, gulped cold night air, and opened her eyes.

"Luz—" Radha's frantic face showed pale in the light of the setting moon. "Are you all right?"

"I'm all wet!" She plucked the cold fabric of her gown away from her skin.

They had come out to practice moon-seeing on the eastern terrace below the great hall. Radha pointed at the up-ended silver scrying bowl. The rest of the water that had filled it glistened on the stones.

"Holy Guardians, what did you *see*?"

"I saw a great army camped beside the ocean, and then I thought I was drowning. . . ."

"How terrible," said Radha, setting the basin back on its stand.

"You don't understand," said Luz as more memories returned. "I didn't want to come back. I was—it was Johan. He wanted to die. . . ."

"You must tell Master Granite!"

Luz shook her head. "He would think me hysterical,"—or worse still, he might believe her. Ever since she had told him about her dream the previous summer, the Master of the College had been watching her with an interest she found more disturbing than his previous hostility. "Everyone believes that the prince is dead."

"But you don't think so?" It was not, quite, a question.

"He's not dead yet," she corrected, "though if he keeps trying. . . . Anyway, I think I would feel it if he died. But that's all I am sure of. I thought I was seeing those Sun people—our enemies—but how could Jo be among them?" Her heart still ached with an echo of his pain.

"If they are coming, King Julian will stop them," Radha said stoutly. "And if Johan is with them, the king will find him."

"Yes . . . ," Luz agreed. But her tone lacked conviction. The enemy had looked very strong.

———※———

"There seem to be rather more of them than we saw in Elaya. . . ." Lady Jeanne brought her horse up alongside that of the king. The winter's hard training had built even more muscle onto her sturdy bones. She stood in her stirrups, shading her eyes with her hand. Their position just below the crest of the hill gave them an excellent view of the line of men and wagons winding along the road through the Gaviota Pass.

"Yes. General Marsh took a selected force to the mountains, picked for the job. This . . . is an invasion."

"Well, *we* spent the winter building up our forces," Osleif observed brightly. "I suppose we shouldn't be surprised that the enemy did too."

"There's another difference," said Jeanne. "Last time, *they* chose the battlefield." Her tone was dry but her curling brown hair was beginning to escape its severe braids, always a sign of excitement.

"We're still outnumbered," warned Julian. "We are not going to be able to stop them here. But we can hurt them."

A damp wind stirred the brindled mane of Shadow, the roan stallion who was his warhorse now. The king looked up and saw clouds rolling in from the sea. It would rain before nightfall—that would make his enemy's progress no easier. He was painfully aware that he lacked the enemy general's experience, but he had spent the past month working his way through every volume on military history the palace library could provide. Now his observation of the pass through which the enemy was approaching focused on cover and gradients. Julian had fought in his youth, but for more than half his life what he had needed to know when he visited a place was whether the beings that lived there were in balance and its spirits were happy. Now when he looked at a hilltop he wondered whether it would be defensible.

"Get back to the troops. I want the Ramparts axe-men stationed among the rocks where the enemy has to pass single-file. Put archers on those ridges—" he pointed— "and send the Las Costas and Seagate cavalry in from the side canyons where the pass broadens. Mass the spearmen just beyond the exit to the valley to tempt them forward. The Danehold scouts will show you the way."

"And you will be where?" Jeanne frowned.

"He will be on that hilltop," Marcos assured her, bringing his horse up beside the king, "screened by the live-oak trees."

Julian nodded. "I'll take Osleif to blow the signals."

"And he will take *us*," added Edwin of Registhorpe, Rana's younger brother, who now commanded the king's personal guard.

Julian looked around at his keepers and sighed. Another thing he had learned from his books was that a general could not afford to get embroiled in the fighting, but even if military doctrine had allowed it, his own forces were determined to keep him out of danger. With Robert's death to avenge, they did not need Julian to motivate them. Only if things became desperate would the king lead his fighters into battle again.

"I wish you had ordered the jarl to evacuate the Danehold," said Jeanne. He had meant to train her as an heir, but instead she had inherited Robert's role as field commander.

"They've always been our first line of defense against Elaya. I couldn't persuade Anders that this is not just another raid. But the village has walls and ditches, and the hold is ringed by stout walls. If the Suns turn aside to attack them, we can hit them in the rear."

Edwin nodded. "Their young folk have certainly been useful. They know every foot of this land."

As he spoke, a slim blond boy in a green tunic slithered back through the brush and popped up at Julian's side.

"Hurry, m'lord—the big wagon with the sunburst painted on its canopy is coming through now."

The demon-priestess would be in it, thought Julian. If Tadeo Marsh was the enemy's brains, she was its heart.

"Get up the hill, Thorolf, and tell the archers to start shooting when they hear my horn." Julian set heels to Shadow's sides and urged the horse down the winding path.

* * *

Tadeo Marsh heard the horn-call with grim recognition. This was the Westrian border. His troops already had their orders, for he would have been more surprised if they had *not* been waiting for him here. The Suns were more vulnerable than they had been when they faced Westria in the mountains, but they were not without defenses. They had survived attacks while on the march many times before.

He ducked and grabbed for the helmet that hung from his saddlehorn as the arrows began to fly, and grinned again as he saw that they were targeting the wagon with the sunburst. The bales of supplies packed inside would be no worse for a few punctures. Mother Mahaliel and her household were safe in an old wagon with a weatherstained cover, farther down the line.

At the thought of her household, his expression soured. Some of his troops had asked her to send the Dragon to fight with them again. But the general would not have permitted it even if the boy had not lain half-drowned and raving in her wagon. Disciplined, battle-hardened troops were what won victories. Heroes and madmen could be equal liabilities on a battlefield.

Ahead the land opened out into a rolling valley, its pastures vividly green with spring grass. Before the palisaded settlement at its far end, a glitter of spearpoints showed the position of the Westrian infantry. They were welcome to wait, the general thought wryly. Another commander might have been tempted to attack them, but he would make his stand here.

More arrows snicked past, but by now shields were up and those without them had taken cover beneath the wagons. Even the mules and oxen that pulled them were protected by coverings of thick rawhide. The files detailed to guard them had spread out in a long line, kneeling behind their shields. The others had dismounted and were pressing forward, forming rectangular blocks a hundred men long and two wide, the inner rows standing with spears braced against their insteps, while the outer lines knelt, their own weapons angled toward the bellies of the horses who were now charging from the ravines that sloped toward the road.

"Steady—steady, boys. Let them come."

The general trotted down the lane between the lines with his aides behind him, smiling as he saw his strategy begin to unfold. He had one of the fine red horses they had inherited from the circus, but he was riding the rawboned brown gelding that had carried him for so many miles, and his helmet bore no plumes. His soldiers knew him well enough, and there was no need to make himself a target for the enemy. The men nodded and grinned as he went by, though their eyes stayed on the foe. They had defeated these people once already, after all.

The Westrian riders were pounding toward them in all the splendor of their chivalry. Marsh scanned them through the eye-slits in his helm, but he could not make out the blue shield and white starburst of the king. He grinned once more. Apparently their first encounter had taught the man caution—or it had taught his army to fear for him. The Westrian king had fought bravely. It remained to be seen whether he could command.

The general lifted his gaze to the hilltops, wondering where Julian was hidden, but he was no mystic to speak soul to soul. It hardly mattered—he could see the shape of his foe's mind in the attack that was almost upon them. Then they hit in a tangle of men and horses, some beasts refusing when they saw what awaited them as others were impaled upon the spears.

A few horsemen broke through the line, swords scything the unprotected backs of the spearmen. A horseman— no, a young woman—charged through the gap, her face set in battle-rage. Tadeo drew his own blade, but before he could strike, she was past him, trampling through the line and back again to rally her men.

"Form your line!" he bellowed. "Form the lines again!"

Spears rattled as they got back into position, pulling the wounded behind them. Men from the wagons came running down the passage to drag them to safety.

"Now forward!" General Marsh signaled to his trumpeter to sound the advance. The ground ahead looked level enough for them to form their squares. Against those formations, these gnats could buzz all day without doing them much harm. And when the Westrians had exhausted their horses and their arrows, the Children of the Sun would march on.

"To take the path to the Otherworld is not like going for a walk on a fine spring day." Master Granite's deep voice echoed from the stone walls of the underground room. Black cloth hangings covered the walls. Beside the well in the center stood a tall, three-legged chair.

Luz huddled into her woolen cloak, uncertain whether she was shivering from anticipation or because of the chill. She had heard stories about the Chamber of Visions, but this was the first time the second-year students had been inside. Snow still covered the slopes above them, and the well was fed by an icy spring.

"Answers come most clearly when the question is impelled by need. Given the message the last courier brought, I doubt that there will be much difficulty finding a question. . . . ," he added, and someone laughed nervously.

"You are all now familiar with the lesser levels of divination. You will encounter the art of the seer at a deeper level when you sit in the Seat of Seeing by the sacred well." He laid his hand upon the stool.

Luz had reason to know that one could receive visions anywhere, but it was also true that some locations had a power of their own. Surely this spot, where several ley lines crossed just below the peak of the Father of Mountains, was one of them. And it was not only the flow of energy along the leys that would help them. The great mountain had once been a volcano, and power still welled upward from its core.

"So, who shall see for us first?" He looked from one to another of the students gathered there. "Vefara, will you try?"

The brown-haired girl was usually the first to volunteer, but this time she shook her head. "Master, you have told us the Suns were heading toward the Danehold. Last night I couldn't sleep for wondering what might be happening to my home. I tried . . . to far-speak them, but what I heard was all jumble. I wouldn't know if I were seeing truth or my own fears."

"So—" His gaze swept the others. "Are there some who would think less of Vefara for refusing? She has obeyed the first rule for seeing for others, and that is to be sure you are mentally, spiritually, and physically fit for the task."

"But we've learned how to focus and empty our minds," objected Kamil.

"Yes, you have. And that is why I believe Vefara. Even those skills are not enough when the emotions are deeply engaged."

Luz bowed her head as if the hood of her cloak could hide her from the master's view.

"Come then, Luz," he said softly. "You shall sit in the seer's seat today. . . ."

She had no valid reason to refuse him, only the suspicion that it might be wiser not to succeed. But she could already feel the power in this place pulsing against her barriers, and countering her reluctance was the longing to fly free.

This fear is foolishness, she told herself as she stepped up onto the stool and settled herself in the chair. *What can he do to you? He is the Master of the College of the Wise, bound by oaths that would constrain a Guardian.*

"Are you willing to go out on the spirit road?" he said softly. "Will you see for the people?"

"I will," she answered steadily, pulling her hood farther down to hide her eyes. The chair had a low back that curved around to support the arms. Even as she relaxed against it, she felt her consciousness lifting. She could hear the others settling themselves on the floor, but all that mattered now were the master's instructions, familiar phrases she had practiced with Radha until her response was nearly instinctive.

Her breathing deepened; her limbs loosened. She sat in balance, present at the same time in the depths of the earth and on the pinnacle of the world. And now her spirit was following his direction to the inner reality where the Tree of Life stood in splendor. He called her by her name and she answered, her voice hushed as she tried to describe how its mighty branches upheld the worlds.

"That is well." The master's voice grew stern. "Now

look until you see a gateway. When you go through it, you will fare out where you may tell us how goes the war."

Even as he spoke, she could see the black pillar and the white like a frame with the Tree between them, its image wavering as if seen through water.

With increasing intensity, the others began to sing—

> *Behind the Veil you go,*
> *Wisdom's way to show,*
> *Speed onward, seer,*
> *Fare without fear,*
> *Till all we need we know. . . .*

With a rush, the song lifted her, as if sound had become energy. She felt herself propelled through the Gate, and the lurch and shift of consciousness as she moved pushed her ever deeper into trance.

"I'm being drawn to the Tree," Luz whispered when he called to her again, "up through the spheres. The sphere of the Foundation is a sea of pearl and purple, and that of Glory is a wind of poetry. Victory burns me with emerald fire and still I am rising, born and sacrificed and healed by Beauty, blazing with all the power of the Sun. But I cannot stop—it is red, all red here. . . . The sphere of Strength . . . ," she groaned. "I am in the realm of war and war is what I see. Blood is on the ground, blood everywhere. . . ."

"It is not yours, it is not you," he said firmly. "A cool light surrounds you, separating you from the pain. Let it protect you. Draw back a little and tell us what you see."

Luz drew a shuddering sigh, clinging to his certainty. His voice was her lifeline. She understood now why this was not a practice to be pursued alone.

"I see the Danehold. I think the battle is over. Smoke rises from the village, but it is beginning to rain. The ground all around is trampled to mire. The great gate of the stronghold is in splinters. . . ." She heard Vefara weeping, but even her friend's pain seemed distant now. "They are not all dead. People are standing around a new grave-mound. There are a dozen spears stuck in it, and one pole with the banner of a silver hammer on a green field. This is what I see."

"Lord Anders has fallen," came Vefara's voice. "It must be."

"You have answered well," said the master. "Now follow the road north. Follow the track of the army. Find them."

She felt herself soaring like a bird above the green hills, and though she knew that she was talking, sight became speech without her awareness. Her consciousness had moved onward, perceiving a shining being half angel and half serpent that fought against a radiant figure she recognized as the Lady of Westria. Above them both sat another being, cloaked in red and armed in shining mail. His face was stern as he watched the battle, waiting, *judging*. . . .

And then the vision began to fray. She was being pulled back like a fish on the end of a line, only this line ended beneath her breastbone. Now she saw the two pillars before her, and with a jerk she was through. The master was speaking, his voice a little rough with tension, leading her back to the world of humankind.

They were outside on the mountain before Luz could get anyone to talk to her. The air felt blessedly warm after the chill of the Chamber of Vision, even though they were above the tree line and patches of snow lay among the tumbled stones.

"What did I say?" Her stomach growled as if she had gone all day without food, though it was only noon. "I remember a question about the army, but I was somewhere else, and—"

"You said the Suns are marching north in the rain," Radha interrupted. "Our men are shooting arrows from ambush, worrying at their flanks, then ducking away."

"But that's not what I was seeing," Luz began, then fell silent as Master Granite motioned the others away.

"I know what you saw," he said in a low voice, "or rather, Who. I shared some of your vision, as the Guide must do, but only got glimpses—echoes—while you—"

His gaze bored into hers. "You saw the Guardians as They are in the Otherworld." She tried to look away, but his will overbore her own. "You have great gifts, Luz, but such abilities require special training. From now on you will take your lessons with me. . . ."

<hr>

"We have taught them a lesson, my lord." Young Thorolf's flaxen hair lay in ashy strands against his skull. His pale face was wet with rain and tears. "Those Snakes will remember the Danehold when they lick their wounds."

And they will laugh, remembering that we could not stop them, thought the king, but he did not say so. The reek of smoke caught in his chest and he suppressed a cough. Moisture was working down beneath his collar; he tugged at his wool scarf to cover it. Rana had made it for him the year before in one of her periodic attempts at knitting. Lumpy though it was, he was glad of it now.

The skies were weeping with the folk of the Danehold, gathered around the new mound to mourn their fallen jarl. Even the hills that surrounded the long valley seemed sodden now. The Suns had broken through the palisade and tried to burn both it and the jarl's half-timbered hall, but the rain had defeated them. Though the thatch smouldered and the whitewashed walls were stained with smoke, the great beams were still strong. *May it be an omen,* thought the king.

Thorolf was the oldest of the fallen jarl's sons. The others clung to the skirts of his widow, standing straight as if she had been carved from one of the pillars of the hall.

"Lord Anders fought well," Julian answered. "Surely this night he will feast with his fathers in the High One's hall." In the more remote districts of Westria, people mixed a variety of local beliefs with the official religion. So long as they honored the Covenant, no one objected, and as king he had learned enough to say the right words on occasions like these.

"Not he—his folk have held this valley since before the Cataclysm, and it is their way to die into the land!" said

Lady Ragnhild with bitter pride. She was a tall woman with a blond braid fading now to silver. A smear of blood darkened her gray gown. "From the mound he will watch over us, but it will be hard. We got our cattle to safety, but those trolls trampled down the grain."

"If it is any comfort," said Julian, "I do not think that the invaders will trouble you again. If they do show up, you must promise to take to the hills. I will send supplies to tide you over until you can get another crop in."

"Nay, my lord, you will need all you have to feed the people north of here. This"—she gestured toward the ruined fields—"is only a foretaste. But the stream still flows. We can plant more peas and beans and corn. There is game enough for our needs."

Including ostriches, remembered Julian, survivors of some odd experiment in farming from before the Cataclysm, whose offspring now ran wild in the hills. They were good eating, but uncatchable. Only a very patient stalker could succeed in bringing one down.

He nodded to the lady. "When your sons are grown you may pass lordship to one of them, but for now I would set you as jarl over the people here. Lead them well."

For a moment Ragnhild held his gaze, then she slid the silver armring down over her wrist and held it high. Julian remembered having seen her husband wearing it at feasts when he was here before. Overhead, the clouds were hurrying northward. Behind them, a band of brightness showed beneath their gray pall. The last of the daylight woke the dark hills to rich color and touched the ring with gold.

"Hear me, Thunderer, and all you holy gods." Her voice rang out with sudden strength. "On this ring I swear to keep faith with you and with my people and with the wights of field and hill who are the soul of this land, so long as my life shall last!" She offered the oath-ring to the king.

"And so swear I in return," he answered. Was the silver warm from her body, or had her oath wakened it to power? "And this I pledge as well. I will pursue those who slew your lord to their destruction or my own!"

From the blue clouds to the north came a long rumble. Thorolf looked up with a sudden fierce smile.

"The Thunderer hears us, Lord King. Surely His Hammer will strike our foes!"

┅ 13 ┅

THE FALLING TOWER

"Westrian infidels, keep silence! You are most blessed, for the Mother herself has deigned to teach you. . . ."

Tadeo Marsh heard the guard's barked orders with a grim smile. It was a scene that had become familiar on their march north. Most of the natives fled before them, but some had stayed to defend their homes. For different reasons, he and the priestess were agreed on the desirability of taking captives. The general needed information to defeat the Westrians. To rule their country once he had conquered it, Mother Mahaliel needed souls.

They should be camped here long enough for her to win some. The Children of the Sun lay now in Sanjos, the first city of any size they had encountered here. The Danehold had put up a good fight, but despite the rain that bogged down the Suns' wagons and constant harassment by the Westrians, their northward march had continued. Madona and Montera and Salt River were only hamlets, taken with ease, and the army of Westria seemed to be on the run. Tadeo grimaced at the mud stains on his tunic. At least April seemed to be taking the clouds with it as it ended. On the hills the grass was richly green, and the sky a pale, rain-washed blue.

The provincial lord commander could not stop the Children of the Sun from overrunning his city, but the fortress was another matter. Its walls had been rebuilt after an attack by an Elayan army over twenty years before, and they were tall, strong, and stoutly defended. Still, the weather was fine, and the city's storehouses well supplied with food. General Marsh had brought down stronger citadels. All he needed was a little time.

Two of Mother Mahaliel's virgin guards laid down a piece of carpet, then unloaded and pegged into place the pieces of her great chair. The prisoners, an odd lot of farmfolk and captured soldiers, were seated in a semi-circle on the damp ground. Well, that would do them no harm—his own men fared the same. But there was one who caught his eye, a dark-skinned girl who reminded him of his sisters. Tadeo had seen many folk of his own race in Elaya, but in Westria the peoples seemed to have mixed more thoroughly, and those whose looks identified them with one ethnic group or another were rare.

He motioned to his aides to continue on without him and headed toward the live-oak tree that shaded the wagon. Perhaps he should listen for a time. He had never needed to worry about governing when he served the Empire, where an overdeveloped bureaucracy stood ready to move in behind the soldiers. He had fought over borderlands, accustomed to being ruled alternately by the Empire of the Sun and the Iron Kingdom. But even so, without the support of natives who saw the advantage of cooperation, no invader could hold a land.

A ripple of interest ran through the crowd as more guards escorted Mother Mahaliel to her chair. These Westrians differed from their conquerors in history, manners, and above all in religion, Tadeo thought with a grim smile. She was going to have her work cut out for her. But if she failed to win these people, he was the one who would have to deal with their rebellion.

"My children, I want you to listen." Mother Mahaliel's voice was so soft they had to still their own mutterings to hear. "You are shocked and afraid because you are prisoners, but to me you are children who have been brought up in error, constrained for your own good until we can set you free."

"We *were* free—" The whispers died under the glare of the guards.

"Bonds are most effective when the prisoner does not know he bears them. Because you serve the false gods you call the Guardians, you are like blind men who do not know there is anything to see," Mahaliel replied with the same golden patience. "You walk in shadow, but the light of my god will open your eyes to the true way."

"Your way, maybe, but we already follow the way that's right for Westria," said one of the men. He was young, like all of those Mother Mahaliel had chosen for this meeting. The young were adaptable, and more likely to be frustrated with the status quo.

"There is only one truth, as there is only one sun in the sky, and it is the same for everyone," said Mother Mahaliel. "But I wish to understand what you believe, and what use it has been to you."

"Didn't no one tell you of the Covenant that saved us after the Cataclysm? You know, in the times when all the old ways was destroyed?" asked the dark girl.

For a moment the general was distracted as a wagon laden with lumber rumbled by. The sound of hammering echoed across the camp. The outskirts of Sanjos had been easily overrun, but the lord commander still defied them from behind the walls of his hold. It would take siege engines to knock them down.

"What is your name, my daughter?" Mother Mahaliel was asking now.

"I'm Sarina of Oakhill. Our farm is"—she faltered—"was just north o' Madona."

In a way, Tadeo found the difficulties comforting. The towns from which these prisoners came had submitted with suspicious alacrity. Though he had left small garrisons to ensure their loyalty, he did not trust them.

"I've got no learning, lady," Sarina added as Mahaliel gestured to her to go on, "but 'tis only a few years since I swore the Covenant an' took my name, an' I remember the teaching there."

"You choose your own names? How charming—and the one you have taken is beautiful, my child."

That was true, thought Tadeo. Even in her anxiety, the girl who bore it had a serenity that went with the name. Now he was listening because he wanted to hear her reply.

"We was taught the Ancients tore up the earth so bad that everything broke down. There was earthquakes, wildfires, tidal waves—most o' the people died. The Guardians had t' take back their old powers, an' our people swore they would never do those things anymore." Sarina spoke swiftly, as if repeating something memorized.

"And who are these Guardians?" Mahaliel's gaze swept the circle.

"They're the Powers," an older man spoke up. "Earth an' Water, Air an' Fire."

"And the spirits of every kind of beast and plant and tree," added another young woman.

"Bear Mother who guards the north and Coyote in the south, the Eagle eastward in the Snowy Mountains an' Grandmother Salmon in the sea," the older man went on. "There's others, they say, that the adepts know. But the Lady of Westria rules 'em all. She came to our king an' lay with him, I've heard. An' then he found the lost Jewels of Power that the kings use to keep the balance in Westria."

"Or say they do . . . ," Mother Mahaliel said softly. "Can you really believe that any truly spiritual power would grapple in the sweaty embrace of a mortal man? In the name of these 'Guardians,' your priests impose rules upon you, is it not so? They hedge you about with prohibitions, saying when and where you may graze your beasts and build your homes."

"That's so," muttered one of the men. "My cousin staked out a holding in the High Cross Mountains, an' they drove him from it. The beasts killed all his stock and his fields were taken by the trees. The priestess at Sanjos said she couldn't do nothing, cause the Covenant don't give us that ground."

"Those are false rules," replied Mother Mahaliel, "made by false gods."

"How can they be?" objected Sarina. "They have th' power!"

"Only if you give it to them. . . . You call yourselves children of this earth, children of Westria. But you are bound by superstition. *We* are the children of the Sun, who shines on all the lands. Your gods are false because they pretend to rule, whereas we know that it is the Sun on whose light all life depends. He is the only Power worthy of worship."

That was not entirely true, thought Tadeo. His parents had set out offerings in the fields to the spirits of growth and harvest, as all men must who till the soil, and in the Empire's armies there were always altars to the Lady of Victory and the gallant soldiers' god. The emperor called himself a son of the Sun, and at his coronation was ritually married to the Lady of the Land. But his gods had not helped him against the battalions of the Iron Kingdom. In those lands the war god had the head of a wolf and loved all things made of metal. But it was true there had been plagues—it was one reason the Iron men had needed to annex some of the Empire's rich farmlands, so perhaps those gods were flawed as well. The one thing he knew for certain was that Mahaliel's Sun god had given him an army of disciplined, dedicated soldiers with whom he could win victories.

"We know our god is greater because He has given us the victory."

Tadeo's thought was echoed by Mother Mahaliel's words.

"You worship Him only 'cause He's powerful?" Sarina's soft voice brought his attention back to the prisoners.

"No, my daughter," Mahaliel's voice throbbed like a viol. "I worship Him because He is Love. . . . He loves *you,* my child. . . . Rest in Him, and His radiance will banish all your fears away. Deny your false gods. Give up your struggle with all these superstitious obligations. Your only rule shall be His will, and that is Love!"

She reached forward to seize the girl's hands, and Tadeo

saw the glow that surrounded her at such moments flow out to encompass Sarina as well. The dark girl was weeping; some of the others were tearful as well. But Mother Mahaliel's gaze was fixed inward, her features made beautiful by joy.

"She's done it again," murmured the guard. "At least for some of 'em. 'Tis always amazing to see 'em come in fighting an' go out her slaves."

"What will happen to them—to the dark girl?" Tadeo asked.

"I suppose she'll make a spear-wife. We'll want more for the new men."

"No—" Tadeo grasped his arm. "I need a cook for my staff. When the Mother is finished with them, send the girl to me."

The guard lifted one eyebrow, but Tadeo had no time to correct his misapprehensions. A man in the gold baldric of a division leader was striding toward them; as he drew closer, the general recognized Commander Anaya, who had been supervising the men who were building the siege engines.

"Sir, the third catapult has been completed, and the last of the ladders. The big trebuchet is almost ready, but we've been able to find only one stone of suitable size. However, we have a captive who worked on repairs to those walls whom we've—persuaded—to discuss their weaknesses."

"Excellent. Call all officers to meet for the evening meal at the house I've taken in town, and ready the men for an assault at dawn."

The thought of dinner reminded Tadeo of the girl—he really did need another cook—and he looked over his shoulder. The other prisoners had gone, but the guard had Sarina by the arm. Her eyes met his, and he was the first to look away.

———

You cannot see us, you cannot hear us—Julian mouthed silently. *Look away . . . you see only the fog. . . .*

He stilled, scarcely daring to breathe, as the sentry

turned and began his regular march back along the road, his torch a bobbing sphere of brightness in the misty air. The man was a fool, thought the king, to blind his night vision thus, but these people said the hours of darkness were haunted by demons. *Demons like me. . . .* Julian touched the mud that masked his face and grinned. For this mission he carried a shield of plain wood, and a dark tunic covered his mail. He had prayed for such a night as this, when the sea wind that began to blow at dawn would carry in a fog to hide him from his foe.

As the torch dimmed, he turned back toward the bay and closed his eyes, drawing on the power of the Wind Crystal that he bore within. It was legitimate, he thought, to use the power of the Jewels to encourage the elements to act in a way that would be useful. He would not have tried to summon a storm in summer just to serve his need, but he had certainly urged the rain clouds to flood the Suns' advance this spring, even though it meant that his own army was as wet and cold and muddy as the enemy.

"Come wind—" he whispered, "draw a veil of mist between us now. . . ." He waited until a breath of damp air kissed his cheek and he could scarcely see the reeds, and then, with a burst of wordless thanks to the sprites who had sent it, he whistled softly to the men behind him.

Three more such groups were already infiltrating the town. This was the last of them, two dozen men including the king and his guard. Swiftly they crossed the road, silent as shadows in the fog, and made their way through the back streets of the town. Badly as Sanjos had been damaged when it fell, the streets were yet recognizable to those men of Las Costas who had managed to join them. Julian did not have the forces to recapture the city, but if they could retain surprise, the troops converging on the tower should be able to overcome the circle of sentries that ringed it now.

They halted to regroup in the courtyard of a ruined mansion near the citadel's shattered outer wall. Alexander had been in a hurry to rebuild after Caolin's War, and his walls, for all their splendor, had been of adobe brick faced with granite instead of solid stone.

The men detailed for the diversion slipped away, and they settled down to wait once more.

"Will you not at least stay here, my lord, with a guard?" whispered Edwin, continuing the argument that had raged since the king proposed his plan. The rest of the guard murmured agreement.

"Unless I order him out of there in person, Alexander may not be willing to come."

"Then let him pay the price for it!" muttered Edwin. "And leave the province to his heir."

"M'lord, ye must not risk yourself," Marcos added his plea.

Julian sighed, aware that he was being as stubborn as Alexander. Six weeks of skulking at the Iron General's heels and being beaten off like a pack of mangy curs whenever they did attack had galled him past enduring. But that was not the only reason he was here.

"Alexander lost this city to Caolin thirty years ago," he said finally, "because I did not come to his aid. He ran then—he will not want to do so again. And I do not wish to fail him a second time!"

From the other side of the keep, they heard a sudden clamor of arms and the shout of "Fire!" As the nearest sentries started toward the commotion, Julian leaped to his feet and led his men to the wall. Fog still swathed the city, but it was growing lighter. There wasn't much time. As figures appeared out of the mist, whistles identified the first and second troops he had sent in.

Then he heard a cry and the sudden clash of steel. He cursed, but they had come farther than he had expected before being opposed. One of the Sanjos men came pelting toward them.

"The Snakes are coming—half the army—get back! Get out while you can!"

The tramp of booted feet echoed from the walls of deserted shops and houses as Tadeo Marsh led his troops toward the citadel. This had once been a beautiful town of white-washed adobe and warm red tiles, built on the ruins of a city that died during the Cataclysm. The rich coastlands of Las Costas had raised it to glory, and now the Children of the Sun had killed it again. Most of the former inhabitants had fled during the fighting, and the wind sighed now through empty byways, tearing the fog into ghostly streamers.

Or almost empty, he realized, ducking as he heard the familiar snick of an arrow and something dark flicked past. A man cried out behind him and fell. From somewhere ahead he could hear the clangor of swordplay. He shouted to his men to close ranks and broke into a swift jog.

They came out into the plaza. The general's back still twitched beneath his armor, but no more arrows came. The walls that had once fronted the far side were rubble now. And between him and those walls he saw a tangle of struggling men. He cursed the sentries who had not seen them and the guards who had not stopped them. He had grown accustomed to choosing his battlefields. But Tadeo had been a soldier before he was a general; and even though he had not expected to fight, he had put on a gambeson of riveted leather scales as well as his helm.

Beneath his anger he was surprised to find himself eager to come to grips with his elusive foe. Grinning fiercely, he reached over his shoulder to the sheath strapped across his back and drew his sword.

Julian felt the shock along his arms as his sword struck the rawhide hauberk of the soldier before him. Then the leather yielded; as the blade crushed the man's shoulder, he screamed and dropped his spear. The king jerked his blade free, wheeling to face the next man, the next blow. For the first few moments, he had hoped his force would be strong enough to complete his mission despite the enemy. But there were too many of them. He cursed the chance that had brought him here on a day when the Snakes were mounting an attack. The Westrians would be lucky to get out alive.

He twisted his shield to deflect a spearpoint, ramming forward to thrust beneath an unprotected arm. If they could prevent the Snakes from getting into formation, they might have a chance; but he had learned not to pit swords against infantry squares.

But not all of the Snakes had spears. Ahead of him, three Westrians had engaged a single enemy swordsman, a big man who swung his long blade two-handed with blazing speed. His gear bore no decoration, but what Julian could see of his skin was black as new-turned earth. Guardians! It was the general! The king felt his lips curling back in a feral grin as he ran forward. As he reached them, one of his own men went down.

"Leave this one to me!" he cried.

Julian had never been a fancy swordsman, but he had learned his fighting in a hard school, chasing reivers on the borders of Westria when he was Lord Philip's squire. Caolin's War had polished his technique only a little, and any airs and graces he might have picked up since then had been knocked out of him in the last six weeks of war.

He caught a flash of white teeth in a curling black beard as the general wheeled to face him, sword coming up in mocking salute before it whipped around. Taken by surprise, Julian managed an awkward leap backward as he got his shield up. The enemy blade crashed down, bending the metal rim and biting a great chunk from the leather-covered wood. Julian blinked. If he took many more such hits, the shield would not last long.

He got his feet under him and met the next blow with his sword, blade scraping along blade with a screech of steel, arm straining against arm. For a moment that seemed endless, they swayed, matched in strength and will. Then one of the Snakes fell and rolled into his commander's path, and the general leaped away. Julian followed, settling into a crouch with shield up and sword angled back. His opponent turned back to face him, feet apart and knees slightly bent, with the sword upright before him.

Both fighters stilled, drawing breath in deep gasps. Julian felt his awareness rising to a pitch of intensity he had rarely known. He knew, before the movement was visible, the moment when his enemy decided to attack once more. As the general blurred forward, Julian moved to meet him, ducking as the great blade swept across and up, so that the slice came out of the shield instead of his thigh. In the same instant, his own sword flashed out, and only a swift twist brought the general's blade down in time to deflect it from his side. Not quite far enough—the blades scraped; then Julian's weapon twisted free and slashed through the boot across his opponent's left calf.

"My lord! My lord! Fall back—we're outnumbered here!"

As the king straightened, he sensed a shadow at his elbow. Edwin was bellowing in his ear. The general had staggered backward, and for a moment Julian was safe. But more and more white-clad Sun soldiers were pouring into the square. His gaze went back to the general and he raised his sword in salute. His opponent was using his own blade to keep himself upright, but he lifted the other hand in reply.

Julian's smile faded as he reached the entry to the first street and looked back at the men who were fighting to cover his retreat before the yet unconquered tower.

"Alexander!" He cupped his hands around his mouth, putting all his anguished spirit into the call, and even in the midst of the conflict, men stilled to hear. "Alexander, forgive me! I tried!"

"Alexander of Las Costas!" cried the general. "I offer you one last chance to surrender before we batter down your door!"

"Never while I live, outland dogs!" came the answer from above.

"Then die! Destroy the Darkness! The infidel must die!" From hundreds of throats came the cry.

Every fortress must have an entrance, and they had finally found the man who knew the location of this one, shrouded in vines on the south side of the tower. With the trebuchet, the Suns might have knocked it down, as they had done with the wall, but if they meant to settle as well as conquer, they would need strongholds of their own, and to capture was easier than to rebuild. Now that the Westrian attack had been beaten off, it was time to finish the conquest of Alexander's city. Tadeo limped to one side, and the men who carried the ram trotted forward. Behind them, more men were spreading out to surround the site. He savored the moment of silence before the storm.

The ram plunged forward, a many-legged wooden beast with a head of steel. It struck, crushing the vines that had hidden the door. Dust rose to mingle with the last of the fog as a hollow boom resounded through the morning air. Again and again it swung, and its booming became the scream of rending wood and stone. The door fell—they were in! Tadeo started after them and nearly fell as his leg betrayed him. Swearing, he backed up until he found a piece of wall to lean on. He could hear yells and the clangor of steel from within.

"Remember!" he cried. "I want their lord!"

He could track the attackers' progress through the keep by the muffled clamor as they fought their way from one level to the next. The top was a flat platform guarded by a parapet, where the banner of Las Costas still flew: a golden sun on a blue field—*almost the same,* he thought wryly, *as that of his conquerors.* Now the general glimpsed a commotion up there—the banner was coming down. His smile died as he caught a flash of blue and gold on the parapet, where a man maintained a precarious foothold as he wrapped the banner around his body.

"You Snakes will get neither my banner nor me!" he cried. For a moment no one dared to move. "But I leave you this legacy—" Alexander's words were carried by the breeze that tugged at the flag's silken folds. "The earth of Las Costas shall not nourish nor the waters quench the thirst, the winds shall not cool nor the fire give warmth to those who seize it by the sword! As I am Lord of Las Costas, with my blood I bind this curse to the land!"

White-clad warriors rushed toward him as he bowed—
no, he was plummeting—toward the stones of the square.
In another second he hit with a sound Tadeo never wanted
to hear again. Blood spread beneath the broken body and
soaked into the earth of the land Alexander had so proudly
ruled.

Exulting soldiers ran to maul the body, ripping away the
bloody banner, finding a rope to tie to Alexander's ankles.
If Tadeo had captured the Lord of Las Costas, he would
have treated him with honor, but there was no point in
fighting over a corpse. Let the men celebrate their
victory—they had earned it. And no doubt Alexander's
soul was already winging its way to whatever paradise
Westrians believed in.

"Sir, you're bleeding!" Commander Hallam pulled off
his scarf and knelt to bind it around the ruined boot, its
leather dyed crimson now.

Tadeo looked down at the pool of red. Like Alexander's
blood, it was sinking into the ground. *And so we all feed
the earth in the end.* . . . He felt dizzy, and wondered just
how much blood he had lost.

"We'll get a wagon to take you back to your quarters."
Hallam hurried off, and Tadeo leaned back against the wall
and closed his eyes until he heard the creak and groan of
wooden wheels on the stones.

One of the Westrian converts ran forward to help him
into the wagon. "Great Guard—I mean, Holy Light, sir!
Did you know that man you were fighting—that was *him*,
the king himself! I saw him when he came visitin' here
some years ago."

"Was it indeed?" Tadeo tightened the scarf around his
calf. The wound was beginning to ache. He would have to
get it seen to soon. He saw that strong-featured, mud-
streaked face once more in memory and smiled. It had
been a good fight. He was not entirely sorry his foe had
gotten away. For the first time in many years he had met his
match, and he realized how much he had missed having an
equal.

This country breeds brave men, he thought as a horseman dragged the body of the lord commander down the road, followed by a cheering throng. *If I take you, king of Westria, I won't let them treat you so.* He himself had been captured at the end of the war with the Iron Kingdom, and he still felt a sick fury at the memory. Remembering the resolve in the face of the man who had faced him so fiercely, he thought that both he and Julian would choose Alexander's way out rather than be paraded as a prisoner.

———⟫•≼⟪———

Julian staggered as the grass, the live-oak trees, the very earth of Las Costas convulsed in a silent scream. He fell to his hands and knees, fingers digging into the soil. For a moment he could hardly breathe. Through blurred vision he glimpsed astral figures limned in lines of light overlaying each bush and tree.

"My lord, my lord, are you injured? Is it your heart?" Marcos was at his side, his voice tight with concern.

My heart, yes—but not the heart in my body. . . . He let his breath out slowly, feeling the first shock subside. "Alexander is dead," he said aloud as his own tears began to fall.

"And you can feel it?" Edwin asked in wonder.

"Didn't you know when your father died?" Julian eased back, grateful for Marcos's strong arm.

Edwin nodded with dawning comprehension. "It was like a fist squeezing my heart, and every tree and rock in the holding seemed to be crying out his name, and then all his awareness of the land came to me."

"Just so. Eric of Seagate felt your father's loss too, just as I know it when death comes to those who hold their lordship from my hands."

He had felt an echo of this grief when Sandremun died in the Corona, but that passing had been a distant pain. And the mourning of a land whose lord passed in the course of nature was a gentle thing compared to the anguish of the province to which Alexander had been bound. Its rage resonated around him.

Julian shivered. The willing sacrifice of blood could preserve a land—surely Robert's death must have left some blessing for Westria—but the converse was also true.

"Lord Alexander has left his death-curse in his province. We must find Lady Carola. He could not have warned his heir of this, if he told her what to expect at all. He was only a child when his own father died."

Eric had once told him that Seagate had grieved when his son Ulric, who had been sworn as heir when Frederic renounced his title, died in a rockfall. Julian was aware of a momentary surprise as he realized that he had felt nothing when his own son was lost. Had some defect in himself created the barrier, or had Phoenix never truly belonged to Westria?

Now other men were weeping, tears streaking pale runnels across cheeks still smeared with mud. The king gazed back across the marshes toward Sanjos. He could still see the blur of red tile roofs and the shape of the tower where the blue and gold banner no longer flew.

He heaved himself to his feet, refusing the aid of Marcos's arm. "Come—Alexander has bought us a little time, but the general is too good a commander not to send a force after us. By nightfall we must be in the hills."

As he started to turn, a flicker of white on the tower caught his attention—white, with a hint of scarlet banding a sphere of gold. The banner of the Children of the Sun flew now above Sanjos. But it seemed to him that the shadow of Alexander's curse already dimmed the air around it. The Suns had captured Sanjos, but it would give them little joy. Swallowing bile, he started up the trail to the hidden refuge where the new Lady of Las Costas would be waiting for news.

"Yes, yes, the keep has fallen," Tadeo snapped as the folk of his household thronged around the wagon. Carefully he swung his legs over the side and slid down, putting all his weight on the unwounded limb. He should have reported to Mother Mahaliel, but his wound made a good excuse to avoid joining in what he would consider an indecent exultation over a fallen enemy.

"Here now," exclaimed Commander Hallam. "The man's been hurt—give him some room!"

"I can walk!" protested the general, but he was glad of the support of Hallam's shoulder as they climbed the steps to the broad veranda that ran across the front of the dwelling.

"I'll bring you a healer," said Hallam as Tadeo sank into a chair.

"There are many worse hurt than I. Have them care for the others first and come here when they are done."

"Perhaps one of your household—" Hallam began, and paused as Sarina pushed through the crowd.

"I will tend him," she said briskly. "This be only a slash, yes? I treated worse on the farm—both beasts and men! You, boil up some water"—she turned on the head cook—"and I will need clean cloths! This boot is ruined, lord," she said as she knelt before him. "It will hurt some, but best we get it off now. . . ."

There were several moments that made Tadeo's senses swim before he was free of the boot and the cloth of his breeches, and the wounded limb had been propped on a bench. He lay back, breathing carefully as Sarina worked over him, aware of the cool competence in those long fingers even through his pain, and blessing the day he had taken her into his household.

"Tell me 'bout the battle, lord. 'Twill take your mind off the hurting."

The general had not thought he could speak of it, yet to this Westrian girl it seemed right to admit his admiration for a fallen enemy. But when he came to Alexander's last defiance, he felt her grow still.

"He cursed you?" she repeated. "Lord, that is very bad! That must be what I felt—all of us who are from here felt something, like a shadow over the sun."

"It will pass," he said briskly. "When the tower is cleaned up, I mean to make my headquarters there."

"No!" She looked up at him. "You must not do it! That will be a bad-luck place now." The steward handed her a bottle of whiskey and she poured the spirits over the wound. He swore at the sting, but the pressure of her hands was a blessing.

"Best if I sew the edges together now, lord, so it heals tight."

He nodded. "Give me some of that whiskey to drink and I won't feel the pain."

"No spirits," she replied, her dark face growing stern. "I'll make some tea of chamomile an' white willow with honey to sweeten it. You must lie still, give it time to heal. Don' go back t' the keep, lord. You run your army from here!"

He felt the first prick as her needle drew the strand of sinew through his skin and wished she would make that tea soon.

"It won't be a problem," he said breathlessly. "Mother Mahaliel will exorcise the evil and all will be well."

"Oh yes!" The air seemed to brighten as Sarina smiled. "The Lady is so wonderful! She's like a bright light coming into a dark room! She will drive the curse away. You ask her to come an' lay hands on your wound."

Tadeo nodded. No doubt the tales of Mother Mahaliel's miracles had lost nothing in the telling, but he had seen people who had been carried in on litters walk rejoicing from her rituals. When, he wondered, had he become so reluctant to be one of them?

"The Lady has many more important demands on her energy," he said carefully. "I would rather trust to your wise heart and clever hands."

Mahaliel's miracles seemed rather selective. Certainly she had not done much for her pet Westrian boy. Red had recovered from his wetting; but whether he had been trying to drown himself or had simply chosen the wrong time to go swimming, no one seemed to know. Anyone with half an eye could see the boy was loonier than ever—a sardonic shadow who had lost his soul. Didn't the priestess see it, or didn't she care?

Would I do that to you, Sarina? Tadeo wondered as he

gazed down at the soft waves of the girl's dark hair. Was she tending him so attentively because she liked him, or because she was his servant and in his power? *I would have you forever happy, my dear,* he thought then, *and always free. . . .*

✦ 14 ✦

THE DEFENDER

Rana looked up from the papers scattered across the table as William came into the tower room.

"What a wonderful view." Sunlight glinted on his curling hair, fairer than his sister Jeanne's, as he leaned out the southern window. "The Red Mountain looks huge from here, and you can see the river road all the way to where it joins the one from Walnut Valley."

"Laurelynn is a lovely place in May," she answered, "most years. . . ." Her smile faded.

The papers before her bore tallies of apples and arrows, bricks and salt beef, halbards and healing herbs, all that a careful mind could imagine might be needed to supply a beleaguered city. She worked until she was exhausted, and at night fought nightmares in which they were besieged by Caolin's army and she listened to Julian's delirious mutterings as he relived his torture in the dungeons of Blood Gard. The days were not much better. The king's last message had said he was about to mount an attack on Sanjos, and it had been three days since the courier had arrived.

Rana rubbed tired eyes. "How are they coming with the western wall?"

"Well enough," William replied. "They've repaired the foundations and laid three new courses above. But it's still only brick, you know. Even catapults will do some damage, and if they bring a trebuchet that can fling really large stones—" He did not need to add that on the Red Mountain there were boulders of any size an attacker might ask for, needing only to be set rolling down the slope to the shore.

"Yes, I know," said the queen. "But we are fortifying the hearts of the people at the same time, and really, they are our best defense. . . ." She stopped. William was leaning out the window. "William—what do you see?"

"Riders. . . . Their banners are green. Coming at a fast walk, so pursuit is not too near. Oh, here's someone in a hurry—a messenger," he added, but Rana was already on her way down the stairs.

It took until nightfall for the whole army to arrive, though their numbers were halved from the three thousand that had marched away the February before. By that time Julian had already ordered the first contingents to continue on to Rivered, William, still hotly protesting, with them. "It's just because you and Jeanne *are* my heirs that I want you away from here," he had told them, and Jeanne, her face gaunt and a bloodstained rag tied round her arm, had taken her older brother by the shoulder and hauled him away. Osleif had been left at his home near Misthall. Those who came after were sent northward to join Eric at Bongarde, where Frederic, who had also protested, had been staying since March. Only Julian's house guard and those who were too badly hurt to travel farther were brought into the town.

"With the city guard and the training William has been giving the citizens, we've enough folk to man the walls," Julian said between bites of the stew Rana set before him. "And we have the supplies you've gathered." He gnawed at the piece of bread in his other hand.

"Julian," Rana laid a hand on his arm—"you are babbling. If you don't want indigestion tonight, stop talking and pay attention to your food." She feared he would have nightmares anyway, new ones, but she had to try.

"I'm sorry . . . ," he sighed. It really had not been a trick of the light—most of his beard had gone gray. "It's been . . . three . . . days since I've had a hot meal." When he pushed the dish away at last, Marcos appeared at his elbow with the wine pitcher and refilled his cup.

"Have *you* eaten?" Rana asked the younger man. "Go get something now. That's an order. We have plenty of food."

When Marcos had gone, she poured wine for herself and sat down.

"Now tell me. . . ."

Julian looked up, and Rana winced at what she saw in his eyes.

"I couldn't save Alexander. We did not have the men to stop the Snakes from taking the town. Well—I had expected to lose it. I assumed they would continue right on to reduce the citadel, but once they had knocked down the outer walls they left the tower standing. Alexander was still holding it with his guard; they were besieged, but I thought that if I hit hard and without warning, I might at least break through and get him out of there. But that was the moment they chose for their final attack. We were outnumbered. There were Westrians among them, Rana—men I knew— fighting under the banner of the sun! That was two weeks ago. . . ."

"And Alexander?" she asked then.

Julian shuddered. "Dead. I knew when it happened— Guardians, the whole province felt it! The landspirits nearly went mad! And poor Carola—she didn't know what was going on. I stayed an extra day with her, told her to come here if she needed to, but she's determined to continue the fight from the hills. She'll be all right—she's got all her father's stubbornness." He gave a short laugh. "And the land itself will help her. It makes the spirits very angry when the blood of the one who has served them is spilled on their ground. A man who made it out of the city told us Alexander laid a death-curse on the invaders. People were putting flowers on the spot where he fell. The Suns forbade it, but the flowers keep appearing there." The king sighed. "I hope he knew I didn't betray him. I hope he knew I tried. . . ."

Rana nodded. "He was their lord." *And you are the lord*

of Laurelynn, she added silently. *Will you have to die if this city falls?* But as she tried to think how to ask him, the door banged open and Marcos burst in.

"My lord, my lord—" He paused to draw breath. "There's torches, lots of them, on the river road!"

"Ah . . . they must be finding Las Costas even more unfriendly than I expected. Well, at least they let me finish my meal." Julian stood up, his worn features hardening once more into the mask of the warrior king. "Go down and tell the wardens to close the city gates and set fire to the bridge. The Snakes are here. . . ."

———≫◦≪———

Tossed by the wind, the serpent on the white banner seemed to writhe in and out of the rays of the sun. Crouched in his usual place at Mother Mahaliel's feet, Red tipped his head to watch it, letting Fix look out of his eyes. Fix enjoyed things that moved—the flutter of flags, sun on water, the flicker of flames—and in an armed camp there were few places where the child could safely come out to play. But at least they were out of Sanjos. He had just begun to get his several selves under control when that idiot Alexander had killed himself, and the resulting psychic blast had sent them all cowering. It was easier here in the Royal Domain, where the landspirits did not cry out for vengeance from the very ground.

He had found that it was possible for them to live in Westria—so long as he kept an eye on Jehan, and all of them kept Jo buried very deeply indeed. At the moment, Red needed to retain only enough awareness to track the discussion. Since the Suns had settled down outside Laurelynn, he had become the safe sounding board for the tirades that often followed the Lady's weekly meetings with General Marsh and the clan-fathers, and she would expect him to be ready with sardonic commentary afterward.

"Yes, the trebuchet has broken down part of the southern wall," said the general, "but the breach is already partly filled in. They were well prepared for the siege, and they work hard and fast."

"But if we throw *enough* stones," said Loris Stef enthusiastically, "they'll have piles of rubble instead o' walls!"

Red rubbed his palm over the smooth skin of his head and moved back out of the sun. It was almost time to shave it again. He had cut his hair soon after they entered Westria. He told Mother Mahaliel it would be cooler under a helmet or the hooded mask he liked to wear when he went out, but he had another reason for wanting to hide his hair. *If I cut away enough,* a thought surfaced, *there will be nothing left of Jo at all. . . .*

He opened the door to let Fix shift his gaze to the play of sunlight on the waters of the Dorada. The command post had been set up on a hillock just out of range of the catapults that returned fire from the city's walls. It offered a good view of the surrounding hills whose grassy slopes, at the beginning of June, were entirely golden, and the orderly rows of tents along the shore. He avoided looking at the rose-red city where the green banner flew.

The general shrugged. "It does no harm to keep them busy. Constant attack wears down their will and encourages our men, but until we have built enough boats to make an assault, it does little good."

"How long 'til the boats are ready, then?" asked Vincent Chiel.

"Not until Midsummer," came the reply. "It is not the building that is holding us up—the craft need be little more than rafts if we attack where the channel is only an arrow-shot wide—but we need timber. We are tearing down every farmer's barn we can find and sending woodcutting parties to the hills, but that takes time."

Between woodcutters and foragers, a good part of the army was away from camp, and often, Red recalled with a secret smile, not all of those who went out returned.

"You know my opinion—we should not be here at all," the general went on. "While we sit still, the main part of the Westrian army has escaped to the other provinces, where they are regrouping and building new strength. To hold down a conquered people we need to make their strong points our own. It is those fortresses we should be attacking, not Laurelynn."

"And raise the siege?" asked the head of one of the smaller families.

"Laurelynn is no real use to us," repeated Tadeo Marsh. "Not now. When we begin to rebuild the country we will need it, but for now we need places to garrison our soldiers, and there's not room enough there."

"They have food," said Chiel.

"So do the provincial towns," observed one of the others. "As we found at Sanjos."

"But the city is richer!"

The general shrugged. "When we have reduced the rest of the country, its capital will fall like a plum into our waiting hands. Better by far to take the population without too much bloodshed. We will need those people after the war."

"Laurelynn holds their king," Mother Mahaliel spoke at last. "You despise him because you have defeated him at every encounter—"

"No—," General Marsh began, but she was continuing.

"I have talked to his people. You yourself, my general, have counseled me regarding the need to understand an enemy's soul. Laurelynn's value is symbolic, not strategic, but that makes it all the more valuable. And they will never stop fighting us so long as their king is alive."

A shiver went through the one who was listening, and when he looked up again it was Jehan who gazed out of his eyes.

"Well, that may be so," the general agreed. "Most of the men we have captured have shown a commendable loyalty."

"The lord of Las Costas fell to our hand, and the king of Westria will do likewise," Mother Mahaliel said with absolute certainty. "The god has told me that at Midsummer we will enter the city. Send heralds and offer terms—say that they will be treated gently if they open their gates to us. But I think they will refuse, and we will treat them as we did Sanjos, and the river will run red with the blood of the slain. Either way, the king and all his household must die."

"It shall be as you command," said Tadeo Marsh evenly. Vincent Chiel began to laugh.

———⟫•⟪———

The archers stationed near the catapults were laughing, too, as they aimed across the channel at the men who were repairing the broken wall. Target practice, they called it. The range was extreme, but occasionally one of the workers would fall. The sun was sinking toward the western hills, and the shafts flared golden as they soared through the air.

Jehan, walking along the shore with one of the guards who had watched Jo since they crossed into Westria pacing behind him, saw one shaft fall short and bob away downstream.

"I could do better," he said to the archer, a blunt-featured fellow from Aztlan.

"Could ye, now?" An uneasy note crept into the laughter. Did the man think he was talking to the berserker or to the fool?

But there was nothing to disturb him in Jehan's smile, and presently he had the longbow in his hands, and was slinging on the quiver of arrows. As he reached the shadow of the fencing that had been raised to shelter the men from the Westrians' return fire, he tripped, and suddenly arrows were clattering everywhere across the grass.

"No, no—I was clumsy—I'll gather them!" Before the archer could move, Jehan was on his knees, grabbing at arrows; and as the man turned scornfully away, he slipped the piece of sticky paper, the same pale brown as an arrow, from his sleeve. Swiftly he wrapped it around one of the shafts, binding it with a few horsehairs that were also tacky with boatbuilders' glue.

"You cannot even hit one of those men," he boasted as he got to his feet, the arrow in his hand. "I'll wager you I can pierce the banner that waves from the top of that tower!"

"And what will ye bet, boy?"

"How about a flask of wine?" It was well known that

Mother Mahaliel got first pick of the casks looted from the vineyards of the Royal Domain. They would assume her household shared the bounty.

The archer's eyes brightened. "Well enough, an' I'll put up this bracelet I found—"

Jehan's eyes narrowed, recognizing the lovely red and white of polished manzanita and wondering if the Westrian woman who had owned it was still alive. But he could not afford to care about that now. He drew on Jo's memories as he considered the tower, for it had been built after his day. He would soon need Jo's skill with a bow as well. But it was Jehan who had borne the Jewels, though he had rarely used them, and he extended the awareness the Wind Crystal had taught him to test the air.

The wind on the river would hamper the first part of the arrow's flight, but not once it reached the lee of the tower. *"Windlord,"* Jehan sent out a silent prayer, *"let this bolt speed true!"*

Then, as the creak and thrum of the catapult for a moment distracted the archer's attention, he nocked the arrow, braced himself, and began to draw. And as the pull stretched the muscles of his chest and arms, he released them to Jo; and it was Jo who took aim at the tower where he had said goodbye to his father a year and a half before, who heard the wood of the bow creak as it bent, knew the moment of balance, sighted and let the arrow fly.

He was still Jo as he watched the perfect golden flight of the arrow arc high over the water, and descending, bear its message through the tower window where he had always intended it to go.

"Ah, well, t'was a good try," the archer said cheerfully. "I'll be along when I get off-duty to see about that wine."

"Yes . . . ," Jo said distantly. "It will be waiting for you." Even with the sad, charred remnants of the bridge before it, Laurelynn had never seemed so beautiful, its walls glowing every shade of carnelian and rose in the light of the dying sun. *If I threw myself into the river, I might be able to reach the island's shore. . . .*

"And you'd serve as a target for both sides," Red replied.

Ruthlessly he thrust Jo's consciousness back down and turned toward the path. The catapult men were winding the arm back for another try. His eye followed the flight of the missile and he winced as it bashed a new pink gouge in the brick walls. As he made his way back to his tent, he could hear the irregular clatter of stone on brick as they continued to hammer at the walls of Laurelynn.

———◦————

The long summer day was giving way at last to a purple evening. The general heard the battering of the catapults cease as the dimming light made it impossible to aim. In the sudden quiet he could hear the ordinary noises of the encampment— oaths and laughter, the sound of a hammer as someone reset a tent peg, a spear-wife's song. It was something to be proud of, he thought as he surveyed the orderly rows, to have transformed the rabble who had followed Mother Mahaliel when he first met her into an army that could overcome whole nations.

Before him, the pale canvas of the awning they had stretched next to the command tent glowed in the light of the lanterns, and beneath it he could see Sarina's white gown. Tadeo quickened his pace, trying to suppress the limp King Julian's sword-slash had left him. The girl had been waiting for him. As he approached, she came forward with a mug of something cool and minty in her hand.

"You been walking on that leg too long?" Sarina asked as she handed him the drink. "Sit down," she added. "Let me see."

The hide that covered the folding stool creaked as he sat down and extended his leg for her examination. The sultry June weather had encouraged Tadeo to revert to the kilt and sandals of his childhood. And bare legs did make it easier to deal with his wound.

"It's all right," he told her, though the healing muscles were aching as they usually did at the end of the day. But it *was* healing, as well as such things usually did, the scar a livid pink against the dark brown of his skin. And the healing had progressed more quickly since they left Sanjos. By

the time they had dealt with the ruined supplies and lame
mules and a host of other unexpected disasters and got
moving, even he had begun to believe in Alexander's curse.

The last of the light picked out the angular shapes of the
rows of tents, set a sheen on the moving surface of the river,
and turned the brick walls of the city to an even garnet, with
all the scars his catapults had given it smoothed away. A
beautiful place, Laurelynn—the general hoped he would
not have to damage it too greatly to make it his own. The
pennon above his tent stirred in the strengthening wind off
the river. There was beauty in this land of Westria. He wondered what it would be like simply to live here, without
having to constantly think of war.

As always, the touch of Sarina's hands was a blessing.
How did she stay so cool in this heat? She had dressed for
the weather in a shift of undyed cotton held in by a woven
sash. As she bent to examine him, the neckline bloused
open. He felt abruptly thankful for the loose drape of the
kilt as his body responded to the sight of the pointed
breasts thus displayed. He had begun to realize how much
she attracted him when they were in Sanjos, as soon as the
worst of the pain of his wound began to fade. But by then
he had become too accustomed to her sweet ministrations
to consider letting her go.

Had he been wrong to take her into his household? In
any other army, Tadeo thought wryly, he would simply
have ordered the girl into his bed. But among the Children
of the Sun a man could be flogged or worse for taking a
woman outside of the rules set by Mother Mahaliel. And
Sarina was one of the most enthusiastic of the Westrian
converts, in the forefront of the congregation whenever the
priestess preached to her people, one of the sweetest
singers in her choir. If Sarina had cause to complain of
him, she would find it easy to get Mahaliel's ear. But that
consideration was secondary to the need for discipline. An
army whose leader disregarded his own orders rotted from
within. Tadeo told himself that it was a poor general who
could not command his own desires. But his palms tingled
with longing to cup those sweet breasts in his hands.

He could not take Sarina as a mistress, but he had begun to think seriously about marrying her. Most of the clan-wives had been left in one or another conquered town, but a few still traveled with the army. Would Sarina consent if he asked her, scarred and grim as he was, and twice her age?

She got to her feet and stood looking down at him. "I'll put on more ointment of aloe before you sleep, lord. Maybe we can make it heal without even a scar!"

"Sarina"—Tadeo spoke before he could lose his nerve—"I've been thinking. You have done so much for me. I wondered—"

"But you don' need to, lord!" she replied as she arranged cold meats and greens and slices of tomato on a wooden platter. "I asked the Mother can I serve in her household, but she says that I serve the Light best where I be, takin' care of the one who leads His armies to victory!"

"Yes," he began, "but I am a man as well as a general, and—"

"We are all the children of the Light . . . ," she said serenely. "It's been such a joy to me, knowin' we're all safe in His care. I always feared I might do somethin' wrong, get the Guardians angry. My dad, he used to tell stories 'bout the Cataclysm, an' how if we don' do right it will come again. But I'm safe now!"

Damn the Light! thought Tadeo, seeing her face grow radiant with enthusiasm. *I want the darkness of my bed with you in it, your dark skin against mine. . . .*

But he could see he would get nowhere talking of love to her now. There was none so devoted as a new convert. He had seen it many times before. And perhaps it was just as well. Absently he reached down to rub his scar. To break this city and the king who had given him that wound would take all his concentration. He had no doubt that he would succeed. Brick and stone could only take so much battering, and what other defenses did Laurelynn have now?

<hr />

The steady beat of the drums reverberated from the walls of the palace and the other buildings that surrounded the square. As Julian followed the high priest of Laurelynn through the crowd, it buzzed in his bones. The red cloak they had found for the king to wear dragged at his shoulders. Rana paced by his side, similarly clad. For most Westrians, religion focused on family rites at hearth and field. The clergy had needed to search their records to find out how the Guardian who ruled war should be honored—even when Caolin was besieging the city, they had not felt the need for a public ritual of this kind. But on the night when Julian kept vigil before his knighting, the Defender had come to him. He could only hope that the Guardian would bless them now.

In the center of the square, a platform supported a black pillar and an altar covered with crimson cloth. As Julian handed Rana up the steps the drums fell silent, and like an echo, he heard a wild throbbing from across the river. It was the sun's day, and the enemy had suspended their attack in order to perform their own strange rituals. Even now, the masons were working to repair the breaches their trebuchets had made in the walls, but the king had judged it safe to allow the rest of the population to gather for this ceremony.

The banner of the Defender dipped and bobbed as it was set in place against the pillar. On the stone altar, coals were already smouldering. Between the fire and the midsummer sun, the king felt himself beginning to sweat beneath the red wool. The high priest, a rather quiet little man named Martin, who had risen to his present eminence mainly because he had a gift for settling quarrels, handed the smouldering bundles of sage to his priests and priestesses to pass among the people in the crowd.

Julian moved to face Rana across the altar and lifted his hands for silence, but the people were already still. A month of siege had left its mark. Food was not yet scarce, but it was being rationed. The day of fasting for which he had called had practical as well as religious advantages.

"People of Laurelynn—" He pitched his voice to carry across the square. "We come to the altar of the Defender as suppliants, purifying ourselves as He is pure. Breathe in the smoke of the sage and let it carry away all fears and frustrations that would impede us." He spread his arms wide as Rana fanned the smudge smoke toward him, then did the same for her. Master Martin was already purifying the other dignitaries who stood on the platform.

"We ask for the courage we will need to fight and to endure. We ask for wisdom to understand what the best course may be. I know how swiftly rumor can fly in this city"—he paused for the ripple of amusement to pass— "and so our decision will be made before you all. Thus far you have resisted the enemy with great courage—but is that the best, or the only, choice we have? Master Kieran Druson is representative for the Free Cities to the Estates of Westria, and Mistress Pateri Fall your lady mayor. Jorge of Linhold captains the City Guard. I ask their counsel now."

As the goldsmith came forward, the king fingered the pommel of his sword, remembering a day long ago when this man had pulled the bellows in Master Johannes's shop to forge the blade. There had been no silver in Kieran's brown curls then, but the steady gaze in those gray eyes was the same.

Kieran cleared his throat. "My friends, this is our situation. Our storehouses are full—we can hold out for nigh on a year if need be, but not forever. While the enemy spend their strength on us, they're not out destroying other cities. We are not warriors, but by resisting, we serve Westria."

Captain Jorge nodded. "That's so, and those who are not bred as warriors can still learn. There are weapons in the armory, and we can teach you to use them, but the river, not our walls, has always been our real protection. If the Snakes break down our walls faster than we can repair them, and if they can build enough boats to cross the water, even the bravest defense won't stop them for long."

A ripple of unease passed through the crowd. They had been aware of this, but no one had set it out so starkly before. And they knew the threat was real. The fortress at Sanjos had resisted, and the Suns had burned it to the ground.

Mistress Pateri took her place beside them. She was a

vigorous woman in middle age who had once clerked in the Office of the Seneschals, then married a river trader whose business she administered with equal efficiency. She surveyed the crowd before her and sighed.

"It falls to me to make the case for surrender," she said boldly, and waited for the murmur of shock to cease. "The Suns have treated those towns that gave in to them gently. If we cooperate, there's no reason to believe they would not deal with us the same way—"

"Yes, and kill our priests and make us worship their god!" came a shout from the crowd.

"That's so; and before we let them in, we must get all those who would be in danger away," said the mayor. "And that includes our king and queen," she added, lifting a hand to still the crowd once more. "What King Julian hasn't told you is that we've had a message from someone in the enemy camp. Despite their promises, the Suns will kill any of the royal kin who falls into their hands. Laurelynn may be the heart of Westria"—she smiled—"but the king belongs to *all* of Westria. Whether we resist or surrender, my counsel is that he must go!"

"Can we believe the message?" someone cried. The king and his advisors had spent some time debating that question. The slip of paper had been signed with a starburst and wrapped around the shaft of an arrow shot with great accuracy or considerable luck through the window of Julian's tower.

"We have reason to believe the informant is a Westrian who knows the city well," Mistress Pateri said calmly. "So you see, the king has more to lose than we."

"Then why doesn't Master of the Jewels use 'em to blast his enemies?" an old woman shrilled.

Julian felt Rana's shock and lifted a hand to still Master Martin's instinctive protest. From the crowd came a conflicting buzz of horror and speculation.

"Because I am not the *master* of the Four Jewels," Julian's voice rang out across the square, "but their keeper, as I am the protector of Westria. And more important than my survival—or the survival of any one of us here—is the future of this land. So long as this is only a conflict between men, I must not invoke the primal powers or I risk breaking the Covenant that has preserved us since the Cataclysm."

"Then you get your kingly arse out o' here, lad, and you be sure they don't get the Jewels!" the same voice called again.

As the laughter spread, Julian tried to see who had spoken, and fixed on a browned and grimy face beneath gray hair. A tattered shawl that might have been any color or all covered a blouse of muddy blue and a skirt of dull green. As she turned, he glimpsed in the borders of her garments a glint of gold, and stiffened, teased by a fragment of memory.

After a moment he found his voice. "The Jewels themselves are far from here, mother, but I would have all of you know that my queen and I carry their energies within, so have no fear."

"Do not forget that, when this becomes a war of Powers. . . ."

The answer was in the same voice, but his eyes widened as he realized that it had not been spoken aloud. Rana's glance met his in shocked surmise, and together they turned to search the crowd, but the old woman had disappeared.

So, one Guardian has answered, he thought, remembering now how the Lady of Westria had looked to him the first time they met. *But there is another whose favor we need.*

The pounding of his heart began to slow and he looked up at the red banner with its bound wolf and the circle and arrow sigil of the planet of war. All these crimson draperies and wolves had given him a turn when he first saw them, as if he had gone back twenty-five years and Caolin had won their war. But in his tortured way, Caolin had loved Westria. The enemy that threatened now was alien to this land.

"You have heard the arguments," he said when the murmurs stilled. "As I would not insult you by deciding the fate of this city without consulting your leaders, I will not act without seeking help from the Guardians of this land. Or rather, it is *we* who must seek that help—all of us. Let us call upon the Defender."

He stepped back, and flames flared up suddenly as Master Martin poured pure alcohol on the coals.

"As we sing the invocation," said the priest, "open your hearts to the god."

> *Bright the light that blazes scarlet,*
> *Striking, searing, quick to cleanse*
> *Evil from the flesh or spirit,*
> *Cauterizing all offense.*
> *Passion that empowers perfection,*
> *Strength that serves the cause of Right,*
> *Sword of Justice, stern protection,*
> *Warrior, ward us with thy might!*

The square grew quiet as the last notes died away. The fluttering banners snapped overhead. Someone coughed, a baby whimpered and was stilled, the incessant whisper of the river that was the constant backdrop to life in Laurelynn was suddenly as loud as the rush of blood in his veins.

The light that blazed red through Julian's closed eyelids intensified; his heart drummed in his breast. In the next moment his skin prickled, and he recognized the Presence that had guarded his knighthood vigil long ago. His eyes flicked open and he blinked, for suddenly little Master Martin seemed much taller, and his crimson cope had become a mantle that fell to his feet in sculptured folds. Around his head light glanced as if from a helm of steel.

One of the priests folded in a faint as the figure moved forward. Julian would have knelt, but he could not move.

"I am courage that does not count the cost. I am the slayer and the slain." The deep voice resonated through blood and bone. "I am the wolf and the power that binds him. I am the impeccable warrior, strength restricting its own severity. I am the eternal Champion, the Defender, fire in the blood and fire in heaven, consuming all that attacks integrity. In your hour of need have I come to you. What would you have of Me?"

"Lord"—the king found his voice—"what must we do?"

"Bleed . . . sacrifice . . . endure. . . ."

"The best among us has been sacrificed already," Julian said grimly. "How shall I save my city and my land?"

"If you fight for your city you will lose your land, but if you leave them, the people of your city may save Westria. If you have the courage to yield yourselves"—the Defender took another step forward, his steely gaze transfixing the silent crowd—"you may become a snare and a distraction for your foe."

"Will You protect them?" Rana moved to Julian's side.

"I will armor their spirits. . . . They have more strength than they know. Believe in your people, sovereigns of Westria, as they believe in you. . . ."

───────•═▶◀═•───────

Faith was all they had left, thought Rana as the last rope was loosed and the boats slid away from the island. It was the gray hour before dawn, when vision blurs and they might hope that the enemy would be sleeping off their celebration. But they huddled low, making no sound as the current sped them downstream. Even from a few lengths away, the other boats were no more than darker blurs on the water's gray surface; but though she could not see Julian, Rana could feel him, almost as strongly as she had felt the presence of the Guardian that afternoon.

Beside her, one of the priestesses sobbed and was hushed by her companions. They had brought with them most of the clergy, both the city guards and Julian's warband, and any others who might be in especial danger or too useful as sources of information to the foe. But Master Kieran had stayed, and Mistress Pateri, and Master Martin, though they had begged him to go. Had the little priest always been so courageous, or had the Defender, in leaving his body, left with him some of his steel? The Suns killed Westrian clergy when they found them, but if even Rana had not suspected Master Martin's strength, perhaps they would not suspect such a mouse of a man, once he was out of his priestly robes.

By the time the sun rose, they were past Spear Island and grounding the boats in the brush of the marshes on the northern shore.

"Look—," said someone, pointing. The rose-brick walls of Laurelynn were still in shadow, but the morning light caught the speck of green that fluttered from the tower. Even as they watched, the banner began to descend. They ought to get on, but no one could move. Then came another flicker, and suddenly a new banner flared in the wind. It was white.

One of my bedsheets, thought Rana, but her heart was weeping. Laurelynn had opened its gates to the Children of the Sun.

⚯ 15 ⚯

RESISTANCE

After Midsummer, Westria became in truth a golden land, when the hillsides ripened and the last green grass clung only to the dwindling streams. While Tadeo Marsh sent out troops to search the countryside for an enemy who seemed increasingly elusive, Mother Mahaliel tightened her hold on Laurelynn.

In the middle of the day, it had become her custom to climb into a palanquin and progress through the town. Fix remembered finding it in a storeroom and pretending it was a fort when he played with Sombra and her sister. Her brother, even then, had felt it beneath his dignity. But Mother Mahaliel had refurbished it with cloth of gold.

Red wished that Master Marvel had still been with them to see. But the circus-master had died of a fever in Elaya. Manofuerte had been killed at the Danehold. Of the circus-folk who had joined the Children in Aztlan, only Ezequial the juggler remained to dance ahead of the gaudy palanquin as it paraded through the streets, keeping a flickering

array of gilded balls—and whatever else people flung at
him—aloft.

Only Ezequial remained, and of course the Dragon, clad
in tight red breeches, a gladiator's harness of red leather
crossing his bare chest, his face hidden behind a snouted
mask. Mahaliel thought the mask was to impress the people, and laughed. Red had meant it as a disguise. But even
the palace servants who knew Jo's face had noted only the
shaved skull and lumpy nose, and these days, another man
looked out of his eyes. The sword he brandished was of
gilded wood, and if he had tried to run, a spear from one of
the Mother's virgin guards would have brought him down.
This would not have mattered if he had truly been the
Dragon, but the berserker did not surface until his hand
held steel. It was Red who mocked a gladiator's feints and
passes, moving with a sinister, sinuous grace he had
learned from Ezequial, and Jo had no desire to escape from
anyone except himself.

Each day they would take a different route through the
city, often stopping while the men-at-arms the general had
left with Mother Mahaliel burst into some house where in-
formants had told them of a shrine. Soon smashed remnants of altar and images and offerings would be burning
merrily in the street while their owners screamed beneath
the lash. The building belonging to Laurelynn's community of clergy had been the first to go. The whole house
burned; however, there had been surprisingly little of value
left inside. Rumor had it that the high priest was still in the
city, but if so, he had not been found. Of the priesthood,
only three were captured, too stubborn to escape with the
others or to hide afterward. Mother Mahaliel's faith, or
perhaps her obsession, was proof against whatever magic
they tried against her, and the three had burned as well,
their martyrdom witnesssed by a silent crowd. "By fire we
are purified," said Mother Mahaliel.

Jo's internal community had served him well, each personality emerging to play its appointed role. But the only
one of them who had felt obligated to watch the priest-

burning had been Jehan, and for a long time afterward he had been silent and refused to come out at all.

The procession always ended at noon in the city square. Each time they came there, Red halted at the edge, nerves quivering as he sensed the impress of an implacable and incorruptible power. Mother Mahaliel was a priestess—could not she feel it? But she ascended the platform without hesitation, filled by her god.

"Children of Westria—" she cried, "you are here because my warriors have made you come, and you gaze at me with frowns. But consider—does not my very presence in your city prove the truth of my faith? Your gods change with the seasons, but mine is eternal. Your gods hedge you about with rules, but mine sets you free. Your gods cannot understand human frailty, much less forgive your sins, but mine burns them away. And when you die, you fall as the leaf falls, with no more meaning. Those who have embraced the Sun's glory will live in His light eternally!"

Her face shone with enthusiasm as she preached to the crowds who had been herded to hear her, but the familiar golden glow did not extend beyond the platform where she stood.

The color that filled Red's vision was crimson; the voice he heard was stern, with a depth that made Mother Mahaliel sound shrill.

My son, take refuge in the fortress of your spirit. Wait and be still. . . .

———————

The hillside's quiet was shattered as a boulder bounced past and crashed through the manzanita toward the horsemen below. Julian ducked, swearing. Screams told him where it fell. Bending his bow, he rose to his knees, glimpsed a target, and in a single smooth motion released the arrow.

"Sacred Sun, Captain's hit!" came a yell from below.

Julian grinned. Combat archery was another skill he'd relearned this past month. From all around him came an eerie shrilling of willow whistles.

"Retreat, retreat!" came another voice. "These hills be devils' country! Throw him cross saddle an' let's be off home!"

A slingstone whirred overhead and the king ducked again, then piped a sharp trill. When his own men ceased firing he could hear the disorganized clatter as the survivors of the Sun raiding party took off down the trail. He got to his feet, but all he could see of them was dust, trailing down the narrowing valley where vineyards basked in the sun. Around them the mountains rose sharply, clad in fir and pine. High to his left a mighty palisade of brown stone frowned above the valley. Before and below, steam from the geyser floated toward the blue summer sky.

Devils' hills indeed! This part of Seagate was rich in natural springs, some of them sweet and pure, while others had the throat-catching sulfur stink he remembered from the pools of Awhai. There were no devils here, but spirits in plenty, for even before the Cataclysm, this had been a volcanically active land.

Brush crackled, and a wiry young man with a mop of black hair slid down to join him, a sturdy tow-headed boy at his heels. Others, both from the king's warband and local people who had joined them, began to emerge from the undergrowth. Most of these mountains belonged to the elder kindreds, but a scattering of human families had won permission from the Guardians to gain a modest living from the forest, and they were quick to resent any who might threaten their tenancy there.

"Good work, Khelys, though that last boulder nearly flattened *me*! Was the slingstone yours as well?"

"Nay—'twas Turtle." He grinned at his son. "He's a good aim, aye? He slings little stones to frighten the deer from our fields."

"Well, you've scared the Snakes from your forest, at least for a while. I think we'll let them be off to spread the story without further interference. Is there a path we can take westward? It's time I was paying another visit to Bongarde."

"Aye, lord, I know all the trails. Ye may lie the night with my folk at Midvale, and come morning I'll lead ye over the hills."

Rana let out her breath in a long sigh of relief as the king's warband came trotting through the orchards below Bongarde. The watchers who were posted on all paths these days had sent word that he was approaching from the north, though only the Guardians knew what route he had followed to be coming that way. As the news spread, shouts rang through the fortress. Frederic came to a halt beside her, breathing as if he had just run down from the tower, with Lenart a half-step behind him.

"Look at Julian!" said Frederic, between exasperation and laughter. "He might be coming in from a day's hunting!"

"He is," murmured Lenart, "only now he hunts men."

Whatever he'd been doing hadn't hurt him, Rana thought as the horsemen drew closer. Julian's leather vest was scarred and stained, but he was brown as a nut, and nearly as fit as the young man she had first seen fighting for his life in a wood near her home. Marcos, on the other hand, seemed to have aged, no doubt from his efforts to keep his lord alive.

The king reined in as they neared the gate, evaluating the new logs that reinforced the defenses above the ancient stone foundations with a warrior's calculation. Then his gaze moved down to those who awaited him, and he was only a tired warrior coming home.

"Lady of Earth!" Julian exclaimed when they were all gathered in the great hall. "Sitting here, even I can hardly believe in the war!"

The table was laden with the remains of a noble supper, which they were finishing off with tankards of a dark and robust beer. Following his gaze along paneled walls hung with faded banners and embroidery samplers, cast antlers and trophies of old weapons, Rana understood his reaction. After their escape from Laurelynn she had felt the same.

Even Eric and Rosemary, sitting at the head and foot of the table, seemed unchanged, and for the first time since Luz had left for the College of the Wise, all three of Frederic's children were home, his youngest daughter having arrived unexpectedly a few days before the king. They sat together now, fair, red, and dark of hair, but all with their mother's golden skin and something of their father's sweetness of expression in their eyes.

"Some scouts came," grunted Eric. "My own warband gave them six feet apiece of Westrian soil. Bera tracked down the last one—" He nodded toward his middle grandchild, a sturdy young woman in the black robe of a priestess.

"Did you indeed?" Julian gave her an approving smile.

Bera shrugged. "The bears found him for me. They don't like these invaders either—they cut down trees where they should not, and kill too much game. The word has gone out among the elder kindreds, and they will help us where they can."

"You can speak with them so clearly?" asked the king.

Frederic laughed. "The problem is getting her to communicate with humankind."

"The Snakes are not men," muttered Lenart, and Bera turned on him.

"Brother, don't you dare use that name! The Sun warriors kill the rattlesnakes they dance with, and wear their rattles when they go to war. It is an insult to the serpent-folk to call them so. The Guardian is not pleased with them, not at all!"

Julian looked thoughtful. "Mistress, do your duties hold you here? I dare not wield the Jewels against a merely human enemy, but if these—foes—are breaking the Covenant, I think we are justified in asking the elder kindred to be our allies. If you rode with my warband, we might offer the Guardian a chance to avenge his kin. . . ."

"And what opportunities will you offer Lenart and me?" asked Frederic with an uncharacteristic bitterness. It occurred to Rana that he, who had given his birthright as Eric's heir to his brother in order to become an adept and put that calling aside to serve as Julian's seneschal, had suffered most in their exile from Laurelynn.

Julian must have heard it too. "It is true, you have probably done all that you can from here. . . . Where is Ardra now?"

Frederic blinked at the non sequitur. "Somewhere along the coast, carrying information and supplies to Carola of Las Costas." Though Sanjos had fallen, Alexander's daughter was rallying the countryside.

"When she gets back, I'd like her to take you to Queen Alyce in Normontaine. No, I'm not making up a job to get you out of danger!" Julian exclaimed. "I need an ambassador. Alyce is a fighter herself—she'll like Ardra, and she'll listen to you. I can't imagine she wants Mother Mahaliel and the Iron General as southern neighbors. Persuade her to send whatever force she can raise to the Corona, and wait for word. . . ."

By the time the king had finished, Frederic was looking considerably more cheerful. Lenart, on the other hand, still frowned. Julian sighed.

"Do you want to come with me?" he asked Frederic's son. "There's no glamour in it. I'll use you as a courier, envoy, supply clerk, whatever the need."

Lenart turned, a new light in his eyes. "My lord, to serve you is all I have ever asked."

The king blinked as if he had not expected quite so much enthusiasm. Rana wondered why, considering how often Julian's friends had followed him into danger over the years.

Luz, who had been remarkably silent throughout the meal, looked up as well, and Rana wondered if she were about to volunteer too. The queen had always had a kindness for Frederic's youngest daughter. The childish roundness that had blurred the lines of the girl's face had gone. Aside from that, Luz had at first seemed unchanged. But Rana realized now that one of the things the child had learned was how to hide herself behind a mental shield.

She turned back as the king laughed.

"Well, Eric, now that I have disposed of the rest of your family, I hope that Orm and your own fighters will be enough support for you here. You've done a fine job on your fortifications, but I want you to promise me that if the

Suns send an overwhelming force, you'll get yourself and your folk out and take to the hills. Our strength is not in our cities, but in our land and people!"

Lord Eric snorted, but Rana thought that Rosemary seemed relieved. "I was fighting battles before you were born, Julian. Never fear for me!"

"No, of course not," responded the king, holding out his tankard. "My real worry was that we might run out of beer!"

⋙━◆━⋘

The beer held out, but Julian wondered if he would. Eric and Rosemary had gone up to their chamber long ago. Even Rana had given up at last. But Julian had stayed to talk with Frederic by the fire, though the fatigue of the day's ride weighed on his bones. He surveyed his old friend with weary affection, recognizing that to wait in safety while others were risking their lives might be easier on the body, but it could be harder on the spirit than the ceaseless warfare he had been engaged in since they lost Laurelynn. He had not allowed Frederic to share his dangers. The least he could do was to give him his attention.

"Should I have sent you to the College of the Wise?" Julian said at last.

"It's too late for that. It has been a long time since I chose to wear the Red Robe instead of the Gray." There was a painful sweetness in Frederic's smile.

"Or I chose it for you," Julian said harshly. "I needed you to be my seneschal, and I laid that burden upon you, never considering what *you* might need. I thought you could be both seneschal and mage—" He looked at Frederic in appeal.

"So did I . . ." the other man said softly. "But I doubt that the College would welcome me now. Luz got into trouble for defending me when Master Granite questioned whether I should be called a master at all. And yet I did go to Awahna, Julian! The Guardians know the truth, and that is all that matters in the end."

The king nodded. Those who made that journey did not

speak of what they had seen. But it was said that the mark of Awahna was apparent to those who had been there.

"You were not the only one who hoped I would forget the idea once Caolin's War was won. Ardra nearly left me when I wouldn't promise not to go—" Frederic shook his head ruefully. "Once you have heard that call, it does not leave you alone. But there was so much to be done. I delayed, and delayed, until the master's message came. . . ."

Julian sat up, all desire to sleep leaving him. There were many masters at the College of the Wise, but for him and Frederic, *the* master would always be the Master of the Junipers, the adept who had watched over him through his childhood and been his wisest councilor during his quest for the Jewels. Julian had made him Master of the College of the Wise.

"I hurried north as fast as I could. He was nearly eighty, after all—in those days that seemed old to me. He wasn't ill, as I had feared, but the stress of the war was catching up with him. He looked desperately fragile, as if the sunlight shone through him."

Julian bent forward. "He wrote to tell me he was resigning as Head of the College and sent me his love and his blessing. It sounded like a farewell. By the next morning I had a courier pounding north to ask if I should come, but by the time she got there you were gone."

Frederic's lips twitched. "I am sorry, but you know you would have tried to stop us. The master wanted to return to Awahna, and he said he was not strong enough to travel alone. I've always wondered if he asked me to go with him because he feared that otherwise I would never do it, and be haunted by my failure forever."

"Maybe not," observed Julian. "I know he was heading for Awahna when he turned aside to try to save my mother. He may have had it in mind for many years. But I thought that the journey could only be made once."

Frederic nodded. "In general that's true. Those who survive the quest come back, whether they succeed or fail. In any generation there are only a few who even try. Besides Master Granite, Master Badger, and Mistress Iris at the

College, there is only the Mistress of the Waterfall, who withdrew into the mountains above Mist Harbor to meditate years ago and may no longer even be in the body; and if I still deserve to be counted, there's me." He held up a calming hand as Julian started to protest, and went on. "It is said that some masters have attempted the journey a second time. No one knows if they got there, because none of them ever returned."

"I have to admit, I did try to stop you," Julian said then. "I sent men to search the roads, but you and the master had disappeared."

"That is probably why he insisted that we cut across country." Frederic grinned. "We skirted the foothills and followed the Eagle River into the mountains all the way to the divide. Then we turned south to pick up the Peak Road at Lake Tao. After that, we were on the same road you took to find the Wind Crystal, only going the other way. The weather was good, and we had a steady mule for the master to ride. The journey seemed to make him stronger. I learned a lot from his talk, and even more from his silences. But it was nearing the end of summer before we reached the Pilgrim's Road." He fell silent, staring into the fire.

"That trail can be uncanny sometimes—," Julian prompted at last. "What happened when you got there?"

"We stopped for the night beside a lake," Frederic said softly. "The master was in good spirits. He said we were getting close, and I knew it was true. I could feel the power of the Valley the way you feel where the sun is even when your eyes are closed. It was a beautiful night—very calm and still. The master said he was going to sit for a while, to meditate. I meant to join him, but I fell asleep instead. When I woke in the morning, he was gone. The mule was still hobbled—" Frederic looked up. "The master could not have walked far. I searched, but I never found him. In the end, I set the mule free and went on alone. . . ."

Frederic looked back at the fire, but Julian sensed he was seeing something more than those dancing flames. He sighed, for he too had camped at Lake Tenaia and seen the reflection of the mountains glimmering in the light of the moon. And when he had climbed farther, hoping to glimpse the Sacred Valley, for a moment he had seen . . . something . . . through the mists that hid the vales. The memory haunted him still.

"They say we are not allowed to talk about Awahna, but in truth there is no way to speak of it in human words," Frederic said at last. "They say that to reach Awahna is to become enlightened, and it is true—while you are there. The difficulty is to bring that knowledge back to the world. I learned many things, and met those who dwell there, but if the master ever came there, it was not revealed to me."

"He was old." Julian sighed. "I knew I must lose him soon. But he might have lasted longer if I had not sent him to rule the College. Who gave me the right to use up the lives of those I love?"

"The Lady of Westria gave you the right to ask. And we answer because we love you!" Frederic's laugh was that of the boy Julian had known long ago. "Surely you have used yourself harder than anyone else. We have to beg you to let us share your dangers!"

Julian felt his face grow warm, and knew it was not from the heat of the fire.

"Listen, my dear." Frederic's tone sobered once more. "The Master of the Junipers is gone, but I was trained as a priest too. This vacation you have enforced upon me has given me the leisure to remember that. Let me counsel you now. You bear the weight of Westria, but you must not try to bear it all alone." He lifted a hand to still Julian's protest.

"I am not even telling you to let your friends share your burdens. At the College we were taught that the Sun is a great power. The sphere it rules is a central axis on the Tree of Life, where the energy swings around to descend into the physical world. But it is not the only power. Call on the Guardians!"

"Are you telling me to use the Jewels? This is a war of men—"

Frederic shook his head. "It is also a war of Powers. If you will not command, then *ask* them to help you defeat the Suns. Surely the Guardians have an interest in maintaining the balance in Westria!"

Was it the fire that filled Frederic's eyes with light, or did the glow come from within? Frederic and Robert had been closer to Julian than brothers. Now Robert was gone. At least Julian could protect the friend who was left to him.

"You are right, of course," he said finally, remembering how the Lady of Westria had challenged him in Laurelynn. "When I am fighting, all I care about is the next threat, the next need. I have been thinking like a warchief. I will try to remember that I am also a king. I only hope I don't have to go all the way to Awahna to get the Guardians to listen to me."

Frederic laughed. "Indeed—but it grows late. Rana will not thank me for keeping you from her bed 'til dawn."

Julian felt another pulse of heat at the thought. At dinner, his awareness of her, awakening after so many weeks of warfare, had been a pleasant torment. "Lady of Fire, it will serve me right if she makes me sleep on the floor! But I don't regret this conversation, Frederic. . . . Thank you."

———※———

"Julian," Rana murmured when they lay together in the big bed at last, "you offered that girl a place in your warband—why won't you take me? I can shoot, and you said yourself that this kind of hit-and-run fighting is mostly work for the bow. Or if I cannot go with you, let me lead my own company."

"Guardians, no!" He raised himself on one arm to peer down at her, a dark shape against the light of the waning moon. The warmth of the day still lingered in the valley, and the windows had been left open to the night air. "Rana, don't even think about risking yourself in this war!"

"Why not?" she snapped. "You've given everyone else their orders. I am the queen."

"Yes!" Julian exclaimed. "And that is why I cannot risk you! At least Frederic will be safe in Normontaine . . . ," Julian settled beside her again. "Do you know, at this moment I can almost be grateful that Johan is lost, or my heart would be breaking with fear for him, too. I'm taking two of Frederic's children into danger, but Luz will be safe at the College. If the worst happens and the rest of us fall, the masters will know how to get their students away. But you . . . if you want to leave Bongarde, perhaps you should go there. I thought you would be happier here because it's nearer to the sea."

He does care what I feel, she thought in some surprise. She rested her head on his shoulder, welcoming the rasp of his beard against her skin. She found herself acutely aware, after so long apart, of his scent and the feel of his flesh against hers.

"You do understand why one of us must survive?" he said presently.

"Yes," she sighed. It wasn't a masculine instinct to protect his property that was driving him, but a king's need to protect his land. "William or Jeanne could sit on the throne," she said aloud, "but someone would have to teach them how to bear the Jewels. . . . I understand."

"With all this fighting, I had almost forgotten the other duties of Westria's king. It took Frederic to remind me— that's what we were talking about for so long."

For a few moments they lay in silence, but she could feel the tension in the body beside her.

"Sleep now, my love. You are strung as tightly as your own bow. For this night at least, you are safe with me." She reached up to stroke the thick hair back from his brow.

"Rana. . . ." He turned suddenly and gripped her hand, bearing it back down as he kissed her. For a moment, surprise held her still, then she reached out with her other arm to bring him closer still. As Julian's hard strength pressed her into the pillows, her own need answered his. The movement of his flesh within hers became her only sensation, the rasp of their twinned breathing the only sound.

A light wind from the west whispered around the top of the tower. From that vantage point Luz gazed northward, where morning light blessed the meadows of the long valley in

whose center Bongarde lay. To the south, a blur of mist
marked the Great Bay. The Master of the Junipers had lived
here when he stayed in Seagate long ago, and it was still
called the Master's Tower. When she was a child, this place
had been the solid center of her world. Now, it seemed to
sway in the September wind whose warmth, even at this
hour, promised a hot day. If she extended her awareness she
could still feel the power in the land that was her heritage,
but it no longer anchored her here. She gripped the rough
stone of the parapet with the sudden fancy that if she once
let go, that wind would whirl her away.

She had come home from the College of the Wise for a
short holiday, hoping that the familiar suroundings would
settle the doubts that more and more often assailed her. But
although the golden meadows and the dark green of the firs
and redwoods that clothed the hills looked no different,
everything was changing here as well. And now her father,
whom she had thought rooted safely for the duration of the
war, was going away.

As if her thought had summoned him, she heard Frederic's voice from below.

"It is all very well to counsel *me* to caution, Julian, but
you are sending me away from danger while you intend to
ride right back into its jaws."

She heard the king murmur some reply, and then the two
heads, one dark, one silver-fair, appeared in the stairwell.
If the powers they taught at the College were as great as rumor reported them, Luz would have made herself invisible,
but instead she straightened. After all, she had as much
right to be here as they.

"Good morning!" she said brightly as they emerged,
blinking, into the sunlight. "It is going to be a beautiful
day." She sketched a curtsey in the direction of the king
and started to move past them.

"My dear, there's no need to go—" Her father gave her a
hug and smiled. "Julian and I have been arguing this point
since before you were born."

Luz glanced at the king, and thought he reddened beneath his tan.

"I have lost two of those I loved. My son is gone, and Robert died in my arms," Julian said in a low voice. "Do you wonder that I am somewhat anxious about those who remain? But I am trying to put my own fears aside, and choose for the good of Westria."

Luz nerved herself to speak. "Isn't that what we all must do? I didn't come home before because I thought I should stay at the College to learn as much as I can. But I'm no longer sure where my duty lies."

"It lies at the College!" exclaimed the king, as if appalled to find he might have to start worrying about her, too.

"Why do you say so?" Her father's question crossed the king's reply.

"Many of the students have left already. My friend Vefara went back to the Danehold, even though she knows that if the Suns catch her she could be burned alive. I feel like a coward sitting on that mountaintop and studying the lore, as if what happens below has nothing to do with me."

"You have been fighting in your own way," said Frederic. "Master Granite may have his failings, but has he not led you in the rituals that bring power into the world?"

"Master Granite!" She could not deny that he was a master of magic, but how much of what he did had any relevance to what was happening to Westria? She managed a wry grin. "Did I tell you he has taken me as his special student? Though I am not sure that's such an honor. With so few of us remaining, everyone is getting extra attention. I finished the work for my Water year by Beltane and now I'm halfway through the training for Air. But why should I memorize all the rituals if Westria is overrun by this new religion and no one is left to celebrate them?"

"The land will remain," King Julian said with sudden authority. "The Guardians will still watch over each beast and tree. If the Estates of Westria had not chosen me to be their king, I would still have been bound to the land and served it from the wilderness. It will be your duty as a priestess to do the same."

"Go back to the College, Luz." Her father held out his hand. "Your sister has finished her training and I cannot deny her this chance to use it, and your brother has already chosen his path. But you still have a chance to be something more—"

An adept? she wondered, thinking of the gray robe her father so rarely wore. *Was Master Granite right? Do you want me to fulfill your failed destiny?* But she loved him too well to ask aloud, and by now she could shield her thoughts well enough to prevent him from hearing what she would not say.

"I have had to tell Rana to stay in safety for the same reason I ask it of you." In his voice Luz could hear the king's pain. "Our enemies are strong, but they cannot triumph forever. The land itself will reject them, and when that happens, someone must survive who understands how to make peace between men and the other powers."

Luz bowed her head as if she agreed, and certainly there was no point in arguing further. What the king said made sense, but she had heard Lord Eric discuss his battles often enough to know that a general who refused to commit his reserves could forfeit his chance at victory.

I am a woman grown, though they think me a child, she thought proudly. *And I have my own power. When the time comes, I will decide where it should be used!*

———◆———

A hot wind from the northeast was snapping the banners as Tadeo Marsh rode across the new bridge and entered Laurelynn, two troops of soldiers trotting at his heels. At summer's end, the Great Valley baked beneath a tyrannous sun. At least on the river the fiery wind was countered by a cool breeze. He suspected that the Westrian capital might be dismal in winter, but just now it was a welcome change from the army camps where he had spent the two months since they captured Laurelynn.

Less welcome was the message that had brought him here. One did not expect enthusiasm from a conquered city, but Mother Mahaliel's reports had assured him that the conversion of the populace was progressing. To hear that someone had managed to poison the wine meant for the priestess had been an unpleasant surprise. Mother Mahaliel was unharmed, but three women in her guard had died.

With distaste he realized that the dark lumps set above the gate were human heads, black with flies. No doubt their presence assured the people, and more to the point, the garrison, that Steps Had Been Taken, whether or not justice had been done. As he rode up the main avenue toward the square, Tadeo realized that he was scanning the area around him as if he were on patrol in hostile territory. And of course it was true. He had too much hard-won experience to confuse acquiescence with agreement. This city had submitted entirely too meekly.

White-robed devotees flocked to take their horses as they pulled up in the courtyard. The carvings of the Guardians of the Directions embracing the arms of Westria that had graced the arch above the big double doors had been smashed, to be replaced by a crude banner of the serpent and sun. A good wind, he thought, would blow it away.

And what if some accident blows away Mother Mahaliel? he dared to wonder as he started up the stairs. His soldiers would fight when and where he asked. But it was Mother Mahaliel who gave them the reason *why*. He had rather enjoyed being able to conduct his campaign without the priestess looking over his shoulder; but without her, the Children of the Sun would be like one of their own serpents once its head was off. And he would dwindle to a warlord, raiding settlements from some fastness in the hills. It was time he gave thought to the future. The next attempt on the woman's life might succeed.

He found Mother Mahaliel in the chamber at the top of the tower where the light came in through windows on every side. It had been the king's workroom. When they took the city, they had found it littered with the detritus of a hasty departure, the hearth full of ashes and papers scattered across the floor—remarkably few papers of any value, however. He would have appreciated some maps.

Westria was a large land. Now the table was covered with a white cloth and a lamp burned before the beaten gold sundisc on its stand.

"Hard campaigning suits you," said Mother Mahaliel, smiling as he bent to kiss her hand. She had put on weight, but her eyes still glowed. He had forgotten how it felt to be in her presence, like coming into the warmth of a firelit room out of a storm. Her women had set out cakes and wine.

"Drink. In this weather you must have a thirst."

"Nay, lord, it is safe," said one of the women, seeing Tadeo's hesitation. "I have drunk from the bottle myself with no harm. I and my sisters will be the first to taste what is offered to the Lady from now on."

The general nodded and accepted the glass. His men would die for him in battle, but at a word, *her* followers would leap from the top of this tower. Yet that would not save her from an arrow. Her guards might have destroyed all the shrines in this city, but he doubted they had found all the swords.

"Holiness, I would feel better if you were surrounded by our army."

Mother Mahaliel shook her head. "Have I taught you so little? I am the vessel of Light. While my god is with me, the darkness *cannot* prevail."

Was this a divine serenity or only a serene complacency? Best to change tactics.

"Of course. But this city, as you have assured me, is pacified. We have extinguished all resistance in the towns and villages along the river, but that is only a military victory."

"You have not found the Westrian king?"

"No, Holy One. But if he still lives, he is reduced to skulking in the hills. His cousin's family in Rivered are the only leaders left to them. That is our next objective. We can conquer them for you, but you must win their souls. . . ."

16

POINT OF BALANCE

Luz took a deep breath and released it as a tone, feeling the vibration through her throat and chest, hearing it reflected by the perfect acoustics of the oak-paneled room. Master Granite's voice joined hers an octave lower, as if they had become one spirit in two bodies, his breathing matching hers.

"Very good," he said softly when the note had diminished to silence, "but this is no more than any priest can do. Try again, and this time begin by focusing the vibration at the base of the spine."

Luz nodded. When she returned to the College, her training had resumed with even greater intensity, as if Master Granite were trying to cram everything he knew into her head before the enemy arrived at their doors.

She tried for a deeper sound, but it was hard to say where it was coming from. As she paused to draw breath once more, the master cut in with his own note, and this time she felt the vibration in her own body. At first it was only her spine that buzzed in sympathy, but as he increased the volume, she felt the pulse expanding, throbbing in the sacred place between her thighs.

She looked up quickly, and his gaze caught hers. She felt her cheeks heating, but she could not look away. His gray eyes were at once intent and dispassionate, but Luz was certain that he knew precisely what he was doing and what she was feeling now.

Anger intensified the sensation to a flame; then she opened her lips and matched the note, an octave higher. Slowly she sang it up the scale— and with it, the vibration in her flesh—until she could channel the energy through the top of her head and dissipate it into the air.

When the sound faded, Luz felt her heart pounding as if she had climbed to the top of the tower and back again, though neither of them had moved. Without waiting for permission, she sat down beside the table. The music room's insulation was as good as its acoustics. They might have been alone in the world.

"Now do you understand?" he said softly.

"I *feel*, as you know very well," she answered furiously, "but I do *not* understand!"

"You may move the energy in your own body or in that of another by directing sound, to harm or to heal, to elevate consciousness or return it to the body once more."

"And what," she asked tartly, "is the purpose of directing it *there*?"

"Sexual energy has great power," he replied in the same dry tone. "In your Fire year, you will learn how it may be raised in the Great Rite and used to increase the fertility of the fields. But I think that such sweaty grapplings do not attract you, is it not so?"

Luz felt herself flushing again, but she did not reply. Master Granite began to pace slowly around the room.

"For those who would follow the Way of Renunciation, there is another path to power, that belongs to the Mysteries of Sound. When a priest and priestess, properly trained and purified, use the power of tone to drive that energy all the way up the spine, they may meet in a congress of the spirit whose power can move the world." He stood still at last, watching her.

"That is what you mean to teach me?" Luz said steadily. She had the odd feeling that the wooden walls were drawing in.

"You have the potential to be such a priestess as Westria has not seen in centuries. I have said it, and you are proving it."

And you will be my priest? Is it for this you've been preparing me? Even from him, she had the skill now to keep that question hid.

"The Guardians give such gifts only when they are needed," Master Granite added, frowning, "as Westria needs them now. Our land is being overrun by a deadly enemy, and the king will not, or cannot, use his powers. His son was flawed, and in any case he is lost, and William and Jeanne together have about as much talent as my mule!"

"What do you mean?" she asked aloud, a little stung by the reference to Jo. The Master of the College had scarcely met the prince. What could he know?

"Only the College of the Wise can save Westria." He set his palms on the table and leaned forward. "With your power directed by my skill. But true power requires more than learning. On the heights we find clarity and perspective, but there is a danger in too much detachment. To complete your training, you must learn to apply your skills in the world. And indeed, it has come to me that in such a time of emergency, none of us has the right to cling to this safety. Everyone else in the kingdom is fighting the invader. The College of the Wise should offer more than prayers!"

He did not touch her—he never touched her. When Master Granite first began to teach her, Luz had wondered about his motives—liaisons between master and student were forbidden at the College, but in these troubled times, who knew what traditions might fall? Now that she knew what he wanted of her, it seemed to her that honest lust would have been a simple and wholesome thing.

"What do you mean to do?"

"I think the time has come to close the College. Masters and students alike should be using their skills to support the bands who are fighting. We will go together to Rivered, to offer our services to the king. This is a holy war."

"That . . . is a rather overwhelming proposition," she said softly. *If only,* she thought with hidden hysteria, *my grandfather Caolin could see me now!* But the decision she had made at Bongarde must now be made again. King Julian would not be able to forbid her to fight if she came as acolyte to the Master of the College of the Wise. "You will understand that I must meditate—" She rose, bowing her

head in the obeisance due a master. The most delicate of
mental touches encouraged him to let her go.

"Of course, but you will continue to develop your skills,"
he answered her.

"Oh yes . . . ," she breathed as he opened the door.

When Luz left the building, she took one of the wooden
walkways that crossed the fragile soil of the meadow and
continued up the mountain, not stopping until she could
look down and see the great hall of the College and the
dormitories, the temple and teaching halls and green-
houses, laid out like children's toys below. The wind that
blew her fine hair about her face carried the chill of the gla-
cier on the peak above her. The lower slopes of the Father
of Mountains fell away in swathes of evergreen whose far-
thest vistas were dimmed by the Great Valley's haze.

Somewhere out there, men were fighting and dying.
What had they to do with Master Granite's grand plans? Or
with her own fears? Luz stood on the mountain for a long
time, breathing deeply of the clean wind.

⸻

In the windy dawning of the day of the Autumn Balancing,
the king of Westria came to the Red Mountain. He had led
his band south from Bongarde to the Great Bay, crossing
the main road by night when the Children of the Sun stayed
safe by their fires and passing through the hills into the
Royal Domain. Now they followed a path that dipped in
and out of the folded valleys until it began the last winding
push to the peak.

"We're almost to the top now," said the Lady of Heronhall. The summit of the Red Mountain was a dark mass
against the paling sky. They had rested at her holding during
the day, and when she learned that Julian had never approached the peak from this direction, she had volunteered
to be his guide. Even at this hour, when the rest of them
would so much rather have been in bed, she radiated energy.

"And not a whisper of an enemy!" observed Lenart
with satisfaction.

"No," murmured the king, his gaze on the sky. "The Children of the Sun come from the plains. They don't understand the power of high places, and they fear the darkness."

The sky was gray now; he could see Bera's sturdy shape on the pony ahead of him, and in the lead the slight, fairhaired figure of his guide.

"Take the path to the saddle between the peaks and wait for me there. The rocks will shelter you. I will go up to the summit alone."

Julian had not been to the Red Mountain since the Autumn Sessions the previous fall, the last moment of peace the land had known. In the spring, Rana had performed the rites alone. In this place the king was, at every level, at the center of his world, for this was also a nexus for the invisible currents of power that flowed through the land. For that reason, Caolin had chosen the peak for the site of the fortress whose ruins had provided the stones for his tomb.

It was the grave mound to which Julian's steps led him now, covered, at this season, by a few wisps of grass as golden as the sorcerer's hair. The king sank down upon one of the larger stones with a sigh.

"Hello, old enemy—," he said softly. "I could use your counsel now. You once tried to draw me into your darkness. The foe we fight now would destroy us with too much light. Their god blinds them with brilliance; they cannot see what it is they are trying to win. . . ." Awareness overwhelmed him suddenly and he groaned. "They will shatter the Covenant without ever having understood it, and if I use the Jewels to fight them, *I* will be breaking it! Either way, everything I have loved and fought for will be lost!"

He rested his head in his hands. Before his men he had to show confidence. Even for Rana he had to pretend certainty, though she must suspect his fear. But in Caolin's dungeons he had been pushed to the edge of despair and beyond. Here, he dared to weep, and when he came to the end of tears, to be still.

And in that place beyond sorrow, it seemed to him that

he was not alone. In a place of shadow a fair light was shining. *Luz* . . . , a child's voice chanted. *Luz.*

Was Caolin's spirit telling him to return to the simplicity of the child he had been when he himself bore that name? Julian did not know, but he felt obscurely comforted.

Presently he sat up and wiped his eyes. In a few moments the sun would be lifting above the Snowy Mountains. The base of Caolin's grave mound was edged with identical flat stones. Out of habit, Julian began to count them, but he could have identified the one he wanted by its aura of power.

He gripped the rough edges and gently set the slab aside. Dry roots webbed the redwood box beneath it, attesting that it had not been disturbed. This close, the Jewels resonated in his flesh as if he already bore them. Unexpectedly he laughed as he felt the heady rush of power.

He picked up the box and climbed to the top of the mound. Carefully he drew the Jewels from their wrappings. As he set the Earthstone in the north, he felt his feet rooting in soil, was abruptly aware of every blade of grass, every bush and tree on the mountainside. Placing the Jewel of Fire in the south brought him a link with all the beasts that roamed these hills. He cropped grass with a deer and stalked it with the mountain lion, smiled as he sensed Bera charming a rabbit from its burrow nearby. He laid the Sea Star in the west and touched the deep thoughts of a whale, set the Wind Crystal in the east and breathed in the ecstasy of the eagle as it mounted the skies to greet the day.

The Red Mountain was the highest peak in central Westria, the point from which even the Ancients had measured their land. The curve of the earth hid the Father of Mountains, but from here he could see the white tip of the Mother of Fire to the northeast, and in the south, the tangle of hills that hid the Danehold. In the east, the highest peaks of the Snowy Mountains blazed silver as they caught the first rays of sun. Westward, the view extended to the Far Alone Islands.

By now Frederic and Ardra were out there, sailing northward. Would his friend recognize the moment when the ship passed out of Westria? During the journey south from Bongarde, Julian had meditated on Frederic's words. Surely it was more than time to invoke the land to her own defense.

"Westria, can you hear me? Will you help us to defend you?" The intensity of his need made him blink away tears.

When he opened his eyes, a woman stood before him, formed from all the colors of the day. He tried to speak, but his heart was pounding too furiously and he could only bow. He heard her laugh.

"With your human eyes you see so little. . . . I am not always peaceful and smiling. Fire and flood are also part of my nature, but they pass, and the flowers bloom again. It is the same for the Guardian of Men. He is the child of hope and the ruler and the sacrifice who is always hanging on the Tree. His blood heals the land."

Julian found his voice. "Robert died for me, and the child of my hope is lost."

"There is always hope," she replied.

The warmth in the Lady's voice eased him, and he was able to look at her fully at last. But even in the moment of vision, her form was becoming transparent, a window through which he saw the land laid out below. Then there was only Westria, but her voice spoke in his heart.

"Your tears are my tears. But from the blood that has been shed will spring new flowers. Do not be afraid of change—it is needful if you are to grow."

Julian reached out to her, arms flung wide. And for a moment, despite the enemy who had made him a fugitive in his own land, the Master of the Jewels held all Westria in harmony.

"King Julian gained mastery of the Jewels through a series of initiations such as no king of Westria since the first Julian has undergone, but what has he done with it?" Master Granite sounded almost excited. His mule twitched its ears and moved a little faster along the causeway that parallelled the Dorada River, and the beast Luz was riding followed. "Surely he was not given such gifts to do no more than maintain the status quo in Westria!"

Face shaded by her broad straw hat, Luz ventured to raise one eyebrow. It seemed to her that leading the fight against the Children of the Sun ought to count as a sufficient challenge for any king. When she was growing up, she had been the one to wonder why the king didn't revel in the Jewels' magic, while her father explained the hazards of using Power. It seemed strange to hear the Master of the College ask such questions now.

"But how should he use them?" she asked. "They were never intended as weapons of war."

The mules jerked as a flock of ducks took flight from the rich feeding at the edge of the slough, wings churning the water in a series of bright splashes. To either side, the land rose and fell in a patchwork of marsh where blue water gleamed from among the reeds. Beyond lay golden grassland, broken now and again by a brighter patch of green where some farmer had dug ditches to irrigate an orchard. The fields were stubble now, gleaned by the hordes of waterfowl who fared south at this season. Each day the clamorous flocks darkened the sky—geese and swans, teal and wigeon, and ducks of every kind, and at night every patch of open water became a mass of chattering feathered bodies.

Luz wished she could fly with them. They had left the College just after the Autumn Equinox, and three weeks of plodding travel had brought them far down the valley. Behind them, the Dorada Buttes rose in contorted splendor from golden slopes whose only crops were cattle and stones, a landmark visible for miles up and down the northern half of the Great Valley. Their rust and ochre spires of stone rose stark against a brilliant autumn sky.

"It is true that the king never had formal training. One would have expected the Master of the Junipers to have taught him more, but Junipers was, perhaps, too—spiritual—to be truly effective in this world."

"Did you know the Master of the Junipers?" Luz asked

tightly. He had disappeared long before she was born, but her father had spoken of him so often and with such love that he had always been one of her heroes.

"Ah—I forgot—your father was rather a protegé of his," the master remarked with uncomfortable acuity. "Well, I will speak no ill of the man. And no matter how much he taught the king, it is the journey to Awahna that opens the gateway to real power. King Julian had Junipers's counsel in his youth. It is only fitting that the College come to his aid once more."

You are not the Master of the Junipers, thought Luz, her old dislike of Master Granite momentarily returning. *Don't you understand that what the king learned from him was not power, but love?*

At first they had journeyed in company with the other teachers and students who were leaving in obedience to Master Granite's command. But since the parting of the ways at the Hold they had traveled alone.

Was it lack of initiative that kept her following the master, or had he gotten more of a hold on her than she knew? It felt right to be here, despite the fact that Luz distrusted his intentions more strongly the farther they rode. Her anxieties were for a moment forgotten as a heron lifted suddenly from among the reeds, the blue feathers that edged his gray wings bearing the shimmer of the water into the sky. Then she sighed and turned to her companion.

"When we reach Rivered, what do you mean to do?"

"It depends on what we find—that is why I insisted that we change our robes for ordinary garb. These Sun worshipers kill Westrian clergy. Regular priests and priestesses, that is. I do not believe they have come up against an adept before." His assurance verged on complacence, but he might well be justified. "Nonetheless, there is no reason to make ourselves a gift to them. I have better uses for my energy."

Master Granite had donned a patched tunic and breeches with an old felt hat that any farmer might wear. Luz wore an innkeeper's daughter's old gown. She found it hard to believe, though, that even foreign barbarians would mistake Master Granite for a peasant. His back was too straight; his gaze was not that of a man who works with the powers of the earth, but one who commands them.

And would she fare any better? If she had learned anything these past three years, it was how to veil her power, even—or perhaps especially—from Master Granite. She might be able to pass as an ordinary farm girl.

"If the city is still free, I will seek out Lord Philip at Hightower. He must be in communication with the king."

"And if it is not?"

"Julian was on the Red Mountain on the Equinox—you will remember that we felt the shift in energies when he completed the balancing. If necessary, I will go out on the spirit road to find him."

Luz glanced back at the Dorada Buttes. The stories about Caolin's War had become legend; they seemed much more relevant now. It was said that the wolfriders had pursued the young king south from the Mother of Fire and brought him to bay somewhere among those weathered upthrusts of stone. But before Julian could be captured, he had hidden the Jewel. It was Rana who had found it again. Luz wondered if the impress of its power could be felt there still?

In theory, both king and queen were masters of the Jewels, but Rana was the first queen in many years to exercise that power. Had she realized, even then, what her destiny would be?

Dust was rising from the road ahead. Luz stiffened, pointing.

"They're in a hurry, whoever they may be," Master Granite observed.

The land here was open, fallow fields sloping downward toward the meandering line of the upper Dorada. The cottonwoods that lined the shore stood too far away to reach in time. Luz edged her mount up beside the master's and reined in, waiting.

The dust cloud grew, resolving into a troop of white-clad riders with brigandines of riveted leather. Children of the Sun. With frightening speed they surrounded the travelers, lance points swinging forward.

"Oh, sirs, I'm naught but a farmer from near the Hold, an' this is my daughter—no danger to you!"

One of the men laughed. The troop leader directed a quelling glance his way.

"But you might be some use to us," the commander replied. "Where are you bound?"

"We were going to Rivered to visit my sister." The master slumped in the saddle, his figure blurring.

"Rivered be in our hands now," said the captain. "An' the stronghold's under siege. . . ." He looked at the adept doubtfully.

"This 'un's no use fer digging trenches," said one of the men.

Luz blinked, realizing that the image of an old man veiled the massive figure of the man she knew.

"You do not want me. I am too old. You want to rein aside and let me pass. You want to let me go. . . ."

Luz suppressed a grin as the troop leader turned his pony's head away.

"True—he'd just eat up supplies. Let him be."

The master nudged his mule forward and Luz lifted her rein to follow.

"What about t' girl?" said one of the other men. "She looks healthy—an' easy on th' eyes. Our wife died o' flux two weeks past. *She'd* do—"

Luz flinched as the other men of his file surrounded her, eyeing her with an uncomfortable combination of resentment and need.

"That's not for you to decide!" the captain said sharply. "We will take her to Mother Mahaliel!"

From the corner of her eye, Luz saw the master turning his mule. She felt the pressure of his fury like an oncoming thunderstorm. He might be able to slay one of the soldiers with that force, but could he overwhelm them all?

"No!" She projected her mind-voice with all her will. *"You cannot take them all! Escape! I can protect myself until you rescue me!"*

"They cannot escape from the fortress," said the general patiently. "But it will take time to break in." The chair creaked beneath him as he leaned back. It was made of woven willow, one of the furnishings of a house that had belonged to the richest merchant in Rivered before it became headquarters for the Army of the Sun.

"Why not take it by storm like we did with Sanjos?" asked Loris Chiel.

"Their walls were adobe, faced with stone, pretty to look at but not really that strong. We have solid granite to deal with here," observed Commander Hallam. "There's timber enough for ladders and the like, but a direct assault needs a lot of men. With one division left to hold down Las Costas, and another to garrison Laurelynn, we don't have the numbers."

Nor do we want another suicide to raise the land against us, thought Tadeo with an inner shudder, remembering how the lord commander of Sanjos had died.

"So we will do it in a way that is slower, but just as sure," he said aloud. "This Lord Philip who commands there is a stubborn man, but that's no match for starvation. I want his surrender. Of course, if we can knock down their walls, we can just walk in, but this is the kind of stronghold we ourselves will need. I would rather not have to rebuild it. And we are not in a hurry. I am told that the valley will be too marshy to move troops through once the winter rains begin. We might as well make ourselves comfortable here. Either way, by spring the fortress will be in our hands."

The house was a rambling frame building on the edge of the bluff above the Silvershine River, on whose southern side the town of Rivered lay. Even in October it was still warm enough to make the broad shaded porch more comfortable for councils than any room inside. The porch had been intended as a place from which to watch the sunset, but from here he could look down on the barracks they had built for the troops on the level ground beside the river, or turn and survey the houses that clung to the tumbled hillside below the fortress.

"Come spring, maybe we'll have an army of Westrians,"

said Commander Hallam. "That last patrol got bloodied up some, but they took prisoners. They were half convinced t' join up by the time they got here. And now the Mother's doing her magic on 'em."

"They pissed on a tree yet?" asked Stef, laughing as Commander Hallam looked confused. "That's what those Westrians do t' prove they's converted. They go out in th' woods, hack down a tree, an' piss on it. Then they jus' leave it lie. Insults the spirits, I heard."

"How can ye insult a *tree*?" someone muttered, but in a moment all grew silent. Up the street a white sunshade was approaching, borne by four woman warriors. Its golden fringes shimmered to each step, veiling and revealing the woman beneath. Mother Mahaliel had decided to attend the staff meeting after all.

"Holy One—" Tadeo rose with the others, and offered his hand to lead her to the most imposing chair, its arched headboard carved with a frieze of poppies and lupines.

"Tell me, what progress have you made with the fortress?" she asked, looking up at the gray stone walls set on the rise above the town. Hightower had a fine view over the plain.

"The trebuchet is doing its work, but those walls are made of granite. They will not crumble like brick at the first blow." Tadeo sighed. The Suns were plainsfolk who understood neither sieges nor cities. "And though at this season the streams that feed into the river are dry, I am told there's a good well within the walls."

"But we took the town easily—" Mahaliel frowned.

"Rivered has no defenses. By the time we arrived in force, most of its folk were inside the castle or dispersed into the hills. They abandoned the town, just as they gave us their capital, knowing we would have to leave a force to guard and feed it. This siege ties down more of our men. But with winter coming on, the time for swift victories is past."

"At least there's food enough," said Loris Stef. Like Sanjos, Rivered had storehouses to get the people through bad times.

"For us!" The other clan-fathers laughed.

"Trust me, Holiness—the fortress *will* fall," said Tadeo Marsh. "Once we hold it, the Ramparts will be the base from which we will advance on the north as soon as the ground is dry enough for marching. We will take the Corona, and then move down into Seagate."

His commanders nodded and the clan-fathers smiled in satisfaction. Despite an occasional reverse, the Iron General's hold on Westria was tightening steadily. Some of them, thought Tadeo, might even understand his strategy.

"Will their king not try to stop us?" asked Vincent Chiel.

"I wish he would try," answered the general. "He will not escape me so easily a second time!"

"Where *is* he? asked Commander Hallam. "Do our scouts bring no word?"

"Plenty of word—about where he *has* been. . . . The man does move around."

That morning a rather battered troop had ridden in from the south, where they had been attacked by Julian's warband. They were still trying to understand how the king, who had last been seen in Seagate, could have gotten there without having been sighted by any other patrols.

"The Ancients taught that to defeat an enemy, one must know him," Tadeo said firmly. "I do not yet know this king, but when I do, I will be able to predict his movements, and then he will be mine. Every move he makes now is a message to me. In the meantime, we are laying the groundwork for our permanent possession of this land."

"After midwinter the tide will turn," said Mother Mahaliel with disturbing certainty. "As the sun strengthens, our enemies will fail. I want that fortress, General. You must make it so. . . ."

She gazed up at the castle, above which the gold bear on the fluttering purple banner of the Ramparts seemed to be enjoying a breeze that only occasionally reached them below. But once winter came, they might find themselves more snug in the town. Tadeo repressed a sigh of regret for

the sunny quarters they had left behind in Elaya. But even
the fortress was bound to be more pleasant than winter on
the high plains.

Mother Mahaliel was holding forth on the glory of the
rites with which she would celebrate their victory. He wondered if she had understood a word he said.

"Even the gods must be patient sometimes," Commander Hallam muttered, too softly for the clan-fathers to hear.

In the days when the Children of the Sun were a ragtag
collection of wanderers at the edge of the Sea of Grass,
Mother Mahaliel had understood that; and Tadeo recalled
that in those days she had shown flashes of humor as well.
When had that changed? He listened to her impassioned
description with a flicker of unease. So long as they had
been marching toward the same goal, there had been no
cause for conflict; but in the days when the Empire of the
Sun had been stronger, he had served with an army of occupation, and he knew the difference between conquest
and rule.

So long as the clan-fathers supported her and the army
worshiped her, he was bound to Mother Mahaliel as well;
but once the Children of the Sun spread out to take possession of the land, they would become more concerned with
their own interests. Who would rule Westria then?

A clatter of hooves in the street below roused him from
such speculations. A patrol was coming in, leading a string
of laden ponies and one captive, a slight young woman in
nondescript clothing who rode a brown mule. As they
paused below the porch, she looked up. For a moment
Tadeo met the acute glance of a pair of huge dark eyes, set
in a pointed face with creamy skin ripened to gold by the
sun. Then the brim of the straw hat hid her face as she lowered her gaze to her bound hands once more.

That one's not nearly so cowed as she pretends, he
thought with an inner smile. She was the kind of girl he
liked, but to him Sarina was more lovely still.

"So what have you brought me, my fine lads?" Mother
Mahaliel bent over the railing, smiling brilliantly.

"Fine white rice for your dinner, an' dried apples, an' other things—" The commander gestured toward the mules.

"And a girl," observed one of the clan-fathers.

"That's so," answered the commander. "But my second file has lost their spear-wife an' wished to claim her, if it's your will."

Mother Mahaliel's gaze shifted to the captive. "You, girl—look at me." The note in her voice compelled them all. "What is your name?" Oddly, it was the prisoner who took longest to respond, and when she did look up, all the fire had faded from her gaze.

"My parents called me Sombra, m' lady . . . ," she said softly.

Mother Mahaliel's gaze had narrowed. What was she seeing there? "Are you a virgin?" she asked suddenly. "Have you lain with a man?"

The girl's eyes widened. "Nay, m' lady," she answered, as if surprised that anyone should care.

Mahaliel smiled. "I'm sorry, lads, but I've needed another maiden for my household since I left Laurelynn, and virgins are hard to find in this land. We'll get a good wife for you, never fear, but this one belongs to me!"

This is no hound bitch to fawn before you, Mahaliel, thought Tadeo, his amusement deepening, and then wondered why this girl should make him think of some creature both shy and dangerous. But advising the priestess on her household was neither his right nor his duty. He was still smiling as he watched them depart, Sombra following obediently at her new lady's heels.

———❖———

Luz kept her eyes on the road as they made their way through the town, less for concealment than because her vision still swam with blurs of light from the moment when she had met Mother Mahaliel's eyes. When she realized that this was the enemy's sorceress, she had expected a monster, but the woman's aura blazed like a fire. She could only bless Master Granite's schooling, and trust that the shielding that had held against *him* would keep her from being consumed.

Time for me to be a shadow, she thought, understanding now the instinct that had moved her to give her childhood name. *There is only room for one "light" among the Children of the Sun.*

When she could focus again, she found that Rivered looked heartrendingly the same. She could almost imagine that in another moment she would see her father riding with Lord Philip through the square. But if she had understood his mental call aright, he was now on his way to Normontaine, and Philip and Elen were safe, if one could call it that, in the castle above the town. But one thing had changed—the priest's house and the garden shrine that had stood beside it were in ashes. Luz tightened her shielding, reminded of what would happen to her if Mother Mahaliel learned she had come from the College of the Wise.

The Sun priestess had taken over the house that had once belonged to Rivered's mayor. Clerks were busy in the front room, but once they reached the living quarters on the second floor, the place seemed oddly quiet after the constant bustle that Luz remembered from before. The guards who had carried the sunshade dispersed to join their companions as Luz followed the priestess into the long dining hall, empty except for three women, and a man who sat with his back to them at the other end of the room, gazing into the coals of a small fire.

"Live in the Light, my children," Mother Mahaliel said briskly. "I have brought you another helper. Her name is Sombra." She turned to Luz. "These are Bett and Irina and Cho-cho, who serve me. They will show you what you are to do."

Luz nodded in response to their greetings. Cho-cho had the straight black hair and almond eyes of the Elayan Nippani. She guessed by their accent that Bett and Rina, both of whom looked to be in their thirties, were from the Sea of Grass. They were big women, growing plump from lack of exercise, Bett with brown hair and Rina with fair. But when they looked at Mother Mahaliel, all three pairs of eyes held an identical reflected glow.

"Is she of the Faith?" asked the one called Bett, eyeing Luz like a tabby who sees a strange cat come into the room.

"She will be," answered Mother Mahaliel.

Don't put up your back at me, Mistress Bett, thought Luz. *The last thing I want is to steal your place by this fire.* She bent her head humbly, visualizing her spirit swathed in a smoke-colored veil.

The priestess moved closer. "Look at me. . . ."

Unwilled, her gaze lifted, but her spirit stayed hidden. Just in time, for the light she had faced when Mother Mahaliel chose her blazed forth with redoubled power.

"Oh, mistress, oh mistress, you are too bright!" Luz cried. "I'll be burned to ash by that fire!" Behind those words came a mental whisper—*"Let me be. You don't want another slave."* All she could sense in the woman's mind was light. It was like trying to talk to a forest fire. *"Use reason to convert me and you will prove your faith is true!"* Luz focused her will and pushed again with a force that would have been a shout addressed to Master Granite, but among the Suns the Mother was the only one who used mind-power, so when would she ever have learned to hear?

Mother Mahaliel blinked, and that dreadful radiance eased. For a moment she looked confused; then she set her hand on Luz's head in blessing and turned to leave the hall.

"It's all right, dear," said Cho-cho, when Luz had stopped shaking. "It is natural to be overwhelmed when you first feel our Mother's love."

I have convinced the handmaidens, thought Luz, *but did I deceive Mother Mahaliel?*

"Have you served a lady before?" asked Bett.

"I have worked in noble households," Luz answered truthfully, grateful that she would not have to maintain a country accent, and blessing her grandmother's insistence that she and her sister should learn to perform, as well as to direct, *all* the work of a great lord's hall.

"Sun be thanked for that," muttered Irina. "The last Westrian slut we tried seemed to have been brought up in a cow shed. And she *sniveled. . . .* Are you a sniveler, girl?"

"No, lady," answered Luz. *Not after two years at the College of the Wise.*

"Very well," said Bett. "I'll show you where you'll sleep, and I suppose"—she eyed the faded blue tunic with disfavor—"we'll have to find you some clothes."

Mother Mahaliel had paused to speak to the young man who sat by the hearth. As Bett led Luz toward the other door, something in the way he stood set her heart to pounding. He was a tall lad with a shaved head, in a splendid sleeveless tunic of crimson embroidered at neck and hem with gold.

Luz stopped, staring. "Who's that?"

"The Mother's pet gladiator." Bett sighed with something between annoyance and resignation. "Red's a bit simple, but harmless, so long as you don't let him have steel. We picked him up from a circus in Aztlan."

He's from Aztlan. Luz told her heart to slow. *It was just a chance similarity.*

"But they say he came from Westria," the woman went on. "Do you recognize him?"

Luz dared to lower her shields enough to reach out, and felt her mental touch not so much repelled as deflected by a mind that flickered in as many directions as the fire.

"No. He just looks like . . . someone I used to know."

"He can be amusing when he's in the mood." Bett started off again.

The man turned, and once more the movement stopped her breath. Luz knew that lean height and breadth of shoulder and the red glint of the brows, but the nose was wrong, and his bare muscular arms bore far too many scars. She willed him to lift his eyes. Blue as House Starbairn's shield, they met hers with bitter laughter and a sardonic twitch of the brow.

"Jo!" her spirit called. No one else in Westria had such eyes. But the man who looked out from behind them was no one she knew.

17

SHADOW PLAY

"Oh yes, mistress, I do indeed believe I have been brought to you by a Higher Power . . . ," said Luz.

Mother Mahaliel nodded thoughtfully. As the winter drew in, she spent more of her time by the hearth in the long hall with her women around her. While they kept busy embroidering vestments for the clergy who were being sent out to preach the Mother's teachings, Mahaliel herself addressed the training of her newest acolyte. So far, she did not seem to realize that her initial attempt at conversion had been deflected—and why should she, when everyone around her treated her as the Voice of God? When you had no equals against whom to measure yourself, self-evaluation must be difficult.

Strictly speaking, Master Granite was responsible for getting Luz here, but as that had not been his intention, she had to suppose that some other power had moved him. In any case, it was clear that she had arrived exactly where she was most needed, if she could stay hidden in plain sight long enough to win back Jo's soul without losing her own.

"So, your people believe in the High God, but they do not worship Him—how can that be so?" the priestess asked.

"How can *worship* be needed by the source of all? The Maker of All Things just *is*. All I know how to do is to . . . open my heart . . . and . . . be there . . . ," Luz whispered, remembering how Master Granite had punished her for doing just that. And now Mother Mahaliel was *encouraging* her to seek that ecstasy. She might despise the Mother's theology, but the power that the woman served was real.

The cheerful pop and hiss of burning logs punctuated the intermittent rattle of rain against the slubbed glass in the high windows. Yet it was not the warm red glow that she saw with her eyes that Luz both desired and feared, but the radiance she sensed with her soul, a locus of power that was both within Mother Mahaliel and beyond her.

"Once more you have answered well. You have a simple wisdom, my daughter, that I wish my clan-fathers could grasp," said Mahaliel a little tartly.

There was nothing simple, thought Luz, about presenting the theology she had learned at the College of the Wise in terms suitable to a simple country girl. She was still trying to decide whether she was more frightened by Master Granite's vision of her potential, or Mother Mahaliel's.

"We worship the Divine Being as the Sun because He is Light," the Mother went on. "It is an image that all men can understand, and men do need images, *personalities,* through whom they can communicate with that which is beyond all individuality. Even to me, He comes not as the One, but as the Beloved. I do not speak of this to everyone," she added, and Luz averted her gaze from what she glimpsed in the older woman's eyes, "but I think that you might one day be able to understand. . . ."

Mahaliel leaned forward and Luz felt the warmth of that golden aura surrounding her. She had seen the Mother heal a woman who was hemorrhaging in childbirth, and restore the mind of a man willing himself to death because he had lost his swordarm. If the Mother could not raise the dead, the whisper ran, it was because she had not yet tried. And now, Luz felt behind the aura the radiance from which it came: pure, uncompromising, so completely *itself* there was no room for any other awareness. And it was awakening, beginning to look at *her.*

Nodding, she drew shadow around herself once more. Oh yes, she could understand! She was certainly beginning to understand the power that had brought the Children of the Sun all the way to Westria, and why the Mother's women had accepted her. No one, once brought into the circle of Mother Mahaliel's love, had ever resisted her. No one, except, in his own strange way, Jo.

That it *was* Jo, she now had no doubt, though she understood how he could pass unrecognized by those who did not know him well. Whether he knew *her*, she could not yet tell. When she first joined the household, he had ignored her. Then it seemed that he was avoiding her, spending all his free hours in the practice ring. But a series of storms had made that impractical, and now he sat with the rest of them by the fire.

The Mother patted her shoulder and rose to get ready for one of her interminable meetings, leaving Luz with a bowl of walnuts to shell. Hightower still defied the army that lay before it. Even the trebuchet seemed unable to make much of a dent on its stone walls. But eventually its storerooms would give out. No doubt Mother Mahaliel and the general were discussing some new way to hasten the day when the fortress would fall.

She gripped the nutcracker carefully, but despite her care, from time to time some of the meats would go flying along with the shell. Luz swore and snatched as one chunk arched toward the fire, and jumped as a strong hand gripped hers and pulled it away.

"No, Sombra, you know you mustn't touch the fire!"

She stared, recognizing the high, childish voice and the spirit that looked out of Jo's blue eyes.

"Fix?" She cleared her throat.

"Of course. I'm glad to see you. There was no one to play with here. . . ."

"I'm glad to be here too," she answered carefully. "You always help me. I bet you can't shell these walnuts as fast as I can, though."

"Can too." He grinned back at her with the same smile that had won her heart when she was three years old.

Luz swallowed hard and handed him the bowl.

Fix cracked a walnut with an expert flex of his strong hands and took up the pick to extract the nutmeat. His bowl was filling fast, though there were still unshelled nuts in the basket. When Sombra came back she would be pleased.

He flinched as the general reached down and snagged a piece of walnut. Fix was not exactly afraid of the general, but the big man reminded him of someone else who—he tensed as the memory began to surface, felt the Dragon sense his fear and stir, and relaxed as Jehan intervened to thrust it away.

"An odd thing happened to Division Four's sixth file when they were on patrol," the general was saying to Mother Mahaliel. "They were camped on the open prairie, and one night something gnawed through every bit of rope or leather they had. Bowstrings, saddle girths, and of course the hobbles. By morning their horses were all over the plain. They were half the day catching them, and some still had to ride double on the way home."

"The guards were alert?" asked Mother.

"Most of the file were old-timers," said the general. "One of them said he saw a shadow flowing over the ground. In the morning they found tracks, some kind of gophers—but what would make animals act that way?"

Fix giggled, and flinched again as their attention shifted his way.

"What do you know? You are a Westrian. Could their king command the beasts to attack us?" Mother asked.

"He summoned sea otters to fight pirates once."

That had always been one of his favorite stories about Caolin's War, though neither his father nor his mother would ever talk about it. A memory surfaced of how Sombra's sister had once persuaded a whole family of mice to take up residence in the bed of a prune-faced woman Rosemary had hired to teach the girls embroidery. *I bet Bera is up to her old tricks again!* He suppressed a snort of laughter and looked up again.

"But he wouldn't do it—" Frightened by the general's gaze, Fix fled. "Not as Master of the Jewels," Jehan, who had been observing from within, picked up the thread. "Their power is meant to maintain the Covenant between men and the elder powers, not to set them at odds."

"Ah, yes, this Covenant about which we hear so much," said Mother Mahaliel. "The witch we executed last week was chanting it as she died, but no help came. No wonder we are conquering these people, when they fear to use even what power they have!"

No help that you could see, thought Jehan, but in truth, the prayer he had made to the wind to quickly overwhelm the woman with smoke could do no more than shorten her suffering. Happily, by this time, most of the Westrian clergy had melted into the general population or sought refuge in the hills. Only when one was betrayed by a new convert did a priest or priestess fall into enemy hands.

It was said that Julian could wield the Jewels as Jehan had never dared to do when he was king. *I could not, even if I would,* he thought. *He will not, even though he can. . . .*

"But there are others in the priesthood who would not scruple to make alliance with the lesser powers," he said aloud. He might as well do what he could to increase the Suns' fear.

"An' then Mistress Bera told one o' th' gophers t' tunnel right underneath where their leader was lying!" Marcos exclaimed. "You should of seen him! He sat bolt upright, started banging on th' ground, then moved his blankets. An' damn, if a few minutes later the same gopher wasn't working away right under him again!"

Lenart led the others in a gust of appreciative laughter. The king's warband had taken refuge from the rain at Loren Farwalker's holding, tucked behind a ridge in the foothills a long day's ride east of the Dorada Buttes. Julian was glad to see them under shelter. Winter weather was not kind to men who lived in the wild.

"Kept 'em all busy while the others was gnawin' through the horses' hobbles," put in another of Julian's riders. "An' when they was all chasin' th' ponies, the beasts come into the camp an' trashed whatever they could find."

"Nice to have them on our side for once," said Loren,

who had carried on his family's tradition of creative gardening on a succession of plots carved into the side of the hill.

"You could ask my sister to have a word with your land-spirits before we leave," said Lenart. "She'll tell you what the Gopher Guardian would like in the way of offerings." He leaned forward to pass Marcos the mulled wine.

Frederic's son looked fit and more relaxed than Julian had ever seen him. They were all tired, but the men seemed to be in good heart. And he was relieved to see a measure of peace in Marcos's eyes.

"Blessings on Mistress Bera!" Lucas Buzzardmoon lifted his mug in salute, and the others drank in enthusiastic accord. The girl herself had gone out walking, as impervious to weather as any of the beasts she loved so well.

"You will have to make a song about it, Piper," said the king to the bard, who had recently joined them.

The younger man nodded. "I will—we all need to smile!"

"I'll smile more easily when I understand my enemy," said Julian. "You must have seen a great deal of the general when you were their captive. What can you tell me?"

He understood that to hit the foe and then flee might not be glorious, but it preserved his forces. The military historians were unanimous on the need to put results above reputation. When Julian was still in Laurelynn he had used his enforced leisure to continue exploring the volumes on warfare in the palace library. Defeating Caolin had required a shaman-king. Now what was needed was a general.

"General Marsh made quite a reputation for himself in the war with the Iron Kingdom," Piper said after a moment's thought. "He's a careful leader, they said, strong on discipline, more interested in success than glory. So long as the Empire kept him supplied he won more consistently than most of their other leaders, which probably saved him from being strung up by the crowd when things went sour, though it didn't save him from being run out of town by the families whose scions actually lost the war. They were cav-

alrymen, as I recall, whereas the general handles infantry
particularly well."

"Oh yes . . . ," murmured Julian. "He does indeed. . . ."

"One thing, though—he's no fanatic," Piper said then.
"Whatever keeps him with Mother Mahaliel, it's not devotion to her god."

"Then maybe we can reason with him," said the king.
"Guardians save us from mystics with a direct line to
heaven!"

"Isn't that what everyone is supposed to be looking
for?" observed the bard.

"Yes, and each of us has to find his own path. What I fear
is the man, or woman, who thinks there is only one way to
get to the truth and he's the one with the map in his hand.
Even Master Granite—" Julian stopped. It would do them
no good for men to see the king and the Master of the College at odds.

The master had turned up in October, gibbering about
having lost Luz on the road. He also was outside, meditat-
ing, and the king had to admit that the gathering was more
convivial without him. They had mounted a raid on
Rivered in an attempt to rescue the girl, but Mother Mahaliel's quarters were too well guarded. Spies told them
that Luz was using her childhood name of Sombra, and
warned against revealing her identity while she was still in
the Mother's hands. Another of those strange star-signed
messages had ridden an arrow into their camp, saying that
Luz was safe and well. There seemed little they could do to
free her, for now.

Julian rubbed his temples and took another swallow of
wine. The thought of Luz was one more sorrow to haunt his
nights. When he saw her at Bongarde he should have tried
harder to convince her that she must stay in safety. But who
would have expected the Master of the College of the Wise
to run off this way? Fortunately Marcos seemed to have
persuaded Lenart not to try infiltrating Rivered all by himself. He would never be able to face Frederic if *two* of his
children were lost in this war. Master Granite was a differ-

ent kind of problem. The Master of the Junipers had taught his king to fear the consequences of misusing his power. Now it seemed to be the king's turn to keep the Master of the College from misusing *his*.

It was easier, if no more rewarding, to go back to wondering just who their secret informant in the enemy camp might be. The messages had come at irregular intervals, reporting troop strengths and patrol patterns. The only signature was the same eight-pointed star Julian bore on his own shield. Could it be some old retainer of House Starbairn who had been swept up by the enemy? At times, Julian almost thought he recognized the man's scrawl. Whoever he might be, he clearly was, or had been, a fighter, and he was certainly a fine hand with a bow. Perhaps Philip would have some clue to his identity.

"You mean to get Lord Philip out of Rivered, do you not?" said Master Granite as Julian passed the campfire where he was sitting, a little apart from the other men. "I want to go with you."

The king surveyed the Master of the College with a sigh, then beckoned him to follow. He could evade this discussion no longer, but it was not something the men needed to hear.

That afternoon they had fought a brief action with a company of Suns who were checking on the condition of the northern roads. So, of course, was Julian. Both sides understood that the conclusive encounter would take place somewhere in the northern part of the Great Valley once the land dried out sufficiently to support the passage of an army. The marshlands they had seen today were still half-drowned, and snowmelt would keep them that way even after the skies cleared. But everyone would be on the move once summer arrived.

The outcome of this skirmish had been inconclusive—the enemy had learned to seek safety in numbers—but enough of them were returning home slung over their saddles instead of sitting upon them for the king to feel reasonably pleased. Now it was time to move south once more. The lord commander of the Ramparts had held his fortress bravely through the winter, but even the strongest castle must eventually fall when assailed by determined men.

Julian could hear the master squelching after him as he led the way through the cottonwoods to the banks of the stream, which rushed noisily over rocks and driftwood brought down by the recent rains.

"It will be little more than a raid—secret and swift," said the king. "You would be very much in the way." He sat down on one of the larger logs.

"I think I proved my worth when I rode out with the patrols," Master Granite said stiffly. I can work the weather, create distractions—"

"So can I," the king said gently, "when it is the right thing to do."

The adept swallowed whatever he had been about to say. *Good*, thought Julian. *He has remembered who I am.* But it was true that on patrol the man had sometimes been useful.

From the camp, they could hear Piper's fluting, soft with distance as if the night had begun to sing.

"But I *must* do something," Granite said finally. "That girl—"

"The only thing you *must* do, sir, is obey!" Julian said sharply. "You have been giving orders at the College for too long with no one to question you, and you have forgotten how to follow them." The king tried to inject a little humor into his tone. "It is quite understandable. If I had to serve another commander, the same would be true of me. But I *am* the general here."

"You are more than that—my lord." The honorific seemed forced between rigid lips. But Julian could not see—Granite was no more than a darker shadow in the darkness beneath the trees. "You are the Master of the Jewels," the adept went on. "You tell us that you cannot use them in a war between men, but this is also a war of Powers. The Suns' single god denies all others. If his followers defeat us they will break the Covenant. Why will you not call on the Guardians for aid?"

Because when I asked them to find my son they failed me! before Julian could command his thoughts, his deeper self replied. Was that the reason, or was it simply because, as he had told Frederic last summer, the demands of leading his soldiers distracted him from spiritual things?

"Bera calls the other kindreds to aid us when it will do them no harm. To nudge wind and cloud in a useful direction makes little difference when they are already moving," the king said aloud. "But a time will come when we face their priestess. If she calls down the power of her god, as I have heard she summons fire to burn our priests and priestesses, I will use the Jewels against her then."

"That's so . . . ," the other man said thoughtfully. "These folk she leads are no more than sheep, deserving our pity, not our hatred. The woman is the priestess of evil. You say I am unaccustomed to a master, but so is she. Mother Mahaliel will not have encountered anyone trained as I—as we—have been trained. You must bring the war to her, my lord, to a place where she cannot escape our power."

"The time will come," repeated Julian. He could not be sure he had convinced Master Granite of the need for restraint, but at least the man had ceased to badger him. "But for now," he added, "we must be content to fight with weapons of wood and steel."

———————

Red ran his hand along the leather straps that crossed over his torso, feeling the Dragon twitch beneath his bare skin. Bronze rivets glinted in the pale light of the winter sun, and bronze plates glinted from his vambraces and greaves and ornamented his helm. But he had no blade. They let him have a bow to shoot at waterfowl, but the sword belonged to the Dragon. Garr held it now, his other hand a steadying pressure against Red's shoulder. The armsmaster would not give him the sword until he entered the ring.

He stood in the passage that led to the arena. Above its

timbers he saw banners rippling in a chill wind from the
Snowy Mountains. It tugged at the crimson feathers on his
helm, lifted the cloaks of the people who were filling the
benches above the ring—an uneasy, hungry sort of wind,
like the people whose murmurs, compounded equally of
apprehension and excitement, filled the air.

*Despite their pious protestations, they want to see blood
spray through the air, a body opened by the blade, lopped
limbs hitting the ground.* Images of carnage, ordinarily
locked in the depths with the Dragon, crowded his vision,
driving Red under. A ripple ran through his body and his
head jerked to release the tension. In that moment of transition he was Jo once more.

Garr's grip tightened. He was the only one who was not
afraid to handle the Dragon, and the Suns had been only too
happy to give him the job. It was fitting, thought Jo. The old
swordmaster had been the first to suspect the presence of
the beast within.

"It's all right, lad. Be easy. It will be over soon."

"It is not all right." Jo's voice cracked. "It will never be
all right until one of them kills *me*. Why do the Guardians
allow me to live?"

"Because they still have work for you. . . ." The man's
voice deepened.

Jo turned, saw the old man's familiar features becoming
a mask for something Other. It was a transformation he had
observed many times before. Was this spirit just another
personality sharing the old man's body, as Red and Fix and
Jehan and the Dragon shared his own, or at such moments
did the armsmaster play host to something more? Into the
shadowed socket of Garr's damaged eye he could sink forever. The stern compassion he saw there brought tears to
his own eyes.

"Go forth and do what you must. Even here we are with
you. Trust me."

Unwilled, Jo's lips drew back in a snarl. The Dragon was
ready. His brain pulsed with pain and pleasure, revulsion
and ecstasy. At such moments, he wondered if the Dragon

was the real one, and the rest of them servants whom the beast had created to make sure he got fed. But for a few moments longer, Jo was still master.

Among Mother Mahaliel's people, holidays were times of purification, during which no criminal might remain within the community. In their early days, the Children of the Sun had dealt with the problem by exiling the offenders. But now they had a more efficient solution. To combine execution, entertainment, and exercise for her pet demon, Mother Mahaliel had hit upon the idea of having the Dragon destroy malefactors in the ring.

From the other side of the wall came a rattle of drums. The criminals were being brought in. Garr moved Jo forward. Today's victims were three men who had gotten drunk and raped a spear-wife belonging to another file. They had narrowly escaped being torn apart by the woman's husbands. But to allow that to happen would have hurt the morale of the army. Better by far to let everyone see them chopped to bits by the Dragon. If by some chance the men were unjustly accused, the god would give them the victory. If even the god could not defend them from the Dragon, their blood would be on *his* hands, not on those of the Children of the Sun.

And there is already so much blood there . . . what matter a little more?

The gate at the end of the passage swung open. Jo looked up from his clenched fists to the stands where the people had once gathered to watch the warriors of the Ramparts compete in martial games. Now they were filled by the Children of the Sun. His gaze moved along to the shaded box where Mother Mahaliel sat with her white-clad maidens around her, fixed on one of them—

"Luz! What are you doing here?"

And then Garr set the cold hilt of the sword into his hand, and Jo fled gibbering into the dark.

———

Luz jerked upright, staring. She had put up all her barriers to shut out the avid anticipation in the minds around her, but that mental call had pierced them like the blade of the sword in Jo's hand.

No, not Jo, she realized as her response to his cry rebounded. For a moment he had been there, but the energy that surged through that lithe figure was not even human now. There was a deadly beauty in the way he paced forward, head a little bent, body moving in a perfect balance that extended to the gleaming sword.

The three rapists moved into a triangular formation to meet him. When the guards had first shoved them into the ring they had shuffled miserably, but now they were straightening, resolving to meet their fate like men. And their situation must not seem so hopeless—they were three trained and experienced soldiers against one foe, and they too had swords in their hands.

But though their opponent walked in human flesh, he was not a man. Luz blinked, seeing with doubled vision a gladiator in a bronze helmet and a sinuous, scaled serpent with one shining claw.

The drums rattled again. The soldiers settled into position, swords ready. The Dragon had come to a halt, knees flexed, his sword gripped two-handed, tip angled back over his left shoulder. It was the most active stillness Luz had ever seen, like a crouching cat or a hawk at hover, myriad tiny flexions holding him in the balanced stillness that watched for the first movement of the prey.

She glanced at Mother Mahaliel, who had leaned forward, a little flushed with excitement and eyes bright. *Does she know what kind of elemental she has summoned here?*

Then one of the soldiers, emboldened by that stillness, charged in, a companion guarding each shoulder a half-step behind. Steel clanged and hissed as the Dragon's sword met his foe's and slid along it. A quick twist released it, and as the soldier's blade fell out of line, the Dragon's continued onward into the man's gut.

Luz recoiled, then forced her eyes open once more. *He must be it. . . . The least I can do is to see it. . . .*

The other two leaped around him, swords swinging. The Dragon ducked beneath the blows, ripping upward. The first man's ribcage opened as the blade jerked out; he collapsed and threw the soldier on his left off-stride as the Dragon leaped back, crimson drops spraying in an arc from his sword.

Now the other man was moving in, face contorted in a rictus of rage. A sudden clangor of metal rang across the ring as blades clashed again and again. Luz glimpsed a flash of white teeth below the bronze helmet. Why didn't the Dragon finish off this opponent as he had the first? In the next moment he danced back, waiting for the other unwounded man to join his companion. In a different combat, one might have suspected a gallant gesture from a superior foe, but here the similarity to a cat came once more to mind. The Dragon was not minded to grant too swift a release to his toys.

The two soldiers now stood back to back, white-rimmed eyes following the Dragon's easy pace as he circled them. From time to time the long blade darted in with no change in stance to signal whether it was going to come in high or low. Now the men were bleeding from a dozen pricks. Only a few splatters marred the Dragon's pale hide. Those who watched from the stands scarcely dared to breathe.

It was neither the Dragon nor his foe who finally broke that tension, but Mother Mahaliel. Striking the gong, she released a single pulsing note into the air.

"Finish them—"

Before the reverberations had died away, the Dragon moved. One man's sword went flying, a blur of brightness in the sun. Then the Dragon's blade whirled around and back again, striking off the rapist's head and slicing through the spine of the man behind him.

For a moment the two bodies still supported each other, though the one spouted a red fountain and the head of the other flopped upon his breast. Then they collapsed. As the last untidy twitchings ended, the Dragon stared coldly around the ring. The tension had grown greater, and in front of the other gates now stood archers with drawn bows.

And no wonder, thought Luz. *How do you get the Dragon caged again?* But her heart cried, *Jo . . . Jo. . . .*

An old man with a scarred face was coming out of the gate from which the Dragon had entered. Behind him shambled several scared-looking fellows holding a net. The Dragon turned to face them, fine tremors running through the long limbs. The old man spoke, his single gaze fixing the eyes beneath the helm. The gladiator swayed, and the armsmaster snatched the blade as it slid from his hand. Then he was falling in a boneless crumple, more swiftly than any of his foes. As the men lifted him, the helm slipped off his hanging head and Luz glimpsed his pale face, emptied of any personality at all.

It was more than a week before she saw Jo, in any of his personas, again. Bett told her in one of their rare conversations that it was always like this after an execution. Of late, the older woman seemed increasingly hostile, whether because she was less convinced than her mistress of Sombra's faith, or out of jealousy. And Bett didn't like the girl's friendship with Red. Certainly she had taken a sadistic pleasure in telling her how hard it was to drive out the Dragon. After a fight, Red was kept in the old armsmaster's cabin, and sometimes when he returned he would bear contusions that had not come from the fight. No one dared to ask what old Garr had to do to banish the beast, but when the boy came back he was always very gentle for a while.

Luz had gone into the garden to pick thyme and savory for the evening's stew and found him walking there. She stopped short, wondering if she would meet Fix again. Bett had said that often when Red returned from his convalescence he seemed like a little child. But the body language was different, more contained than the child's abandon, and more balanced than Red's casual slouch. But neither, she realized with a release of nerves, was it the sinuous strength of the Dragon. She cleared her throat, and he turned with an unexpected smile.

"My lady—I will go—"

"No! I didn't mean to disturb you. I only came for herbs," she faltered, indicating her basket. The mind she touched was no one she knew, but he seemed friendly. "May I talk to you?"

For a moment he considered her, his frown that of a much older man.

"Yes . . . perhaps it is time." He swept the sodden leaves from a bench with a courtly grace that made her blink, and laid his cloak across the bench so that she could sit down. Beyond the garden walls bare branches netted a cold gray sky, but on the peach tree beside the bench, buds were swelling with the first hint of green.

"Sir, I have met Fix and Red, but who are *you*?" she ventured at last.

"Ah, now that is a very . . . theological . . . question," he observed ruefully. "Would you believe that even I am not entirely sure?"

"Well, who do you *think* you are?" she said tartly. He turned, and she understood where Jo had gotten his smile, and with that, began to guess the answer. "You're King Jehan. Jo's grandfather. That's why he took the name." She stared at him, overcome once more by the strangeness of all these courtly graces expressed through the body of the boy she knew so well.

"That is, indeed, who I feel myself to be, or at least, a part of him. The Master of the Junipers used to say that the *person* we think we are is only a constellation of thoughts and habits, along with the memories that provide continuity as we go through life. So everyone is really several people—most of the time sequentially, it is true, rather than all at once like Jo. But there is another part that goes on from life to life, deeper and more enduring, of whom we live mostly unaware."

"As Fix and Red and the Dragon are unaware of Jo—"

"Red knows, and tries to protect him, though to some extent that is because he needs him to stay alive. My own role is somewhat different."

"Are you King Jehan reborn?"

He shook his head. "If so, I should not have my old memories. I remember being in the Sacred Wood. I failed as king, or at least I thought so," he added as she shook her head. "Perhaps in my grief I left an echo, a ghost, as it were, unable to rest until I expiate my sins."

"And you are doing so by watching over your grandson?" Luz asked gently.

Jehan shrugged. "It is *his* sins that should worry you. You came here hoping to save him, did you not? Can you absolve him from the knowledge of what he himself has done?"

"What do you mean?"

"He has tried to kill himself twice. Can you stop him if he comes to himself a third time?"

Luz swallowed, remembering her vision of Jo drowning in the sea.

"My lord," she whispered, "what did he *do*?"

"You saw the Red Dragon in the ring—" He rounded on her suddenly.

"Yes . . . but that was not Jo!"

"The Red Dragon is the incarnation of Jo's rage, and at Condor's Rest, the sorceress unleashed it on the field. He fears he killed Robert. He knows he killed Westrians."

Luz sat back, wide-eyed. She had been afraid of her own potential for power. She could only dimly imagine how much worse it must be for Jo.

"Do you imagine that your love will save him?" Jehan asked bitterly. "Faris could not save me! If you do succeed in escaping with him, where will you go? Is there anyone at the College of the Wise with the wisdom to heal such a wound?"

Luz shuddered. Not Master Granite, surely. And though her father was a good man, he had spent his life dealing with the welfare of men's bodies, not their souls.

"I don't know," she said softly. "But I will find a way. . . ."

18

THE FORTRESS FALLS

"General, you promised that Hightower would be ours by the turning of spring!"

Tadeo Marsh suppressed a wince as Mother Mahaliel's voice shrilled. Angrily she gestured to her tame gladiator to shove another log onto the fire. The general had never seen her so agitated, but as the winter wore on he had heard that note more often. The greatest hardships of their migration had not caused her to quail, but many warriors who never failed in battle found it hard to endure a siege. He hoped that this outburst was only a response to the frustrations of a long winter, and not a symptom of the deterioration he had suspected the summer before.

"It will be, Holiness." He forced his tone to calm. "You must come and see how well the trebuchet we mounted on the hilltop to the east of the fortress is working. The crack in the wall has nearly reached the foundations, and the rock above is beginning to fall. By tomorrow we'll have a breach the army can pass through."

"If there's anyone left for them to fight. The defense is failing," Commander Anaya put in. "Starvation has sapped their will, and every day fewer faces appear on the walls."

"I'm hungry too," said Red brightly, rising from his place by the fire. "Mother, may I take my bow down to the river and shoot a fat duck from the southlands for you?"

"If any will come to this benighted land!" the priestess grumbled as the boy slipped away. "I will be glad to move to better quarters." Her tone now was merely petulant, and the general began to relax. "Rats can't eat through walls of stone."

Spring might be a season of new life, but it was also a time of emptying storerooms, and mice had nibbled much of what was left in Rivered. Vermin, too, were a hazard of warfare, but it would do no good to say so to Mother Mahaliel. The woman had grown too dependent on miracles.

"Tomorrow, you say, we will be in the fortress?" asked Bett, laying a soothing hand on her mistress's shoulder. Behind her, the Westrian girl opened the door and started to come in, and the older handmaiden waved her back with a glare.

The Mother's household was as troubled as the rest of the city, thought the general. If this siege went on much longer, they would all be as hysterical as Mother Mahaliel.

"I swear to you, my lady, by evening it will fall." Tadeo shivered despite the fire. Outside, it was beginning to rain.

Luz held out her hand, wondering if that spot of chill she had felt was a drop of water. It was supposed to be spring. The hills around Rivered were green, but in the city garden no blossoms had appeared for the Feast of the First Flowers, even if that feast had been celebrated by the Children of the Sun. Somehow she had assumed Lord Philip would be able to hold out forever. But the winter had been wet and cold, with snow all the way down to the city, and thick fogs that lay like a clammy blanket across the sodden land. When they lifted, one could see the gleam of water dappling the valley. Even if help had been forthcoming, it could not reach Rivered until the floodplains dried.

The massive outer wall of the fortress looked as if it had been attacked by a regiment of monstrous rats, yet still it stood. But now, in the seventh month of the siege, the situation was becoming desperate for the Children of the Sun as well. As mice plagued the city, rumors of Westrian witchcraft were everywhere, the most lurid from the converts, for whom guilt added its load to their fear. When she could, Luz offered her own wide-eyed embellishments—in the case of rodents, she found it only too easy to convey disgust and fear.

Beyond the clouds the sun was getting higher. Luz had told Cho-cho she would go see what food could be found in the market. As she hurried down the street, she passed Jo, or rather Jehan, heading toward the riverside, bow and quiver in hand. He nodded, but she pretended not to have seen him. Bett had already threatened to tell Mother Mahaliel about their conversations. She would have to take care.

When she came back from the market, Mother Mahaliel was waiting by the door.

"Where have you been?"

Luz stopped short, awareness twitching at the suspicion in the woman's tone. "To the market to buy eggs, mistress. I told Cho-cho I would be gone." She held out her basket to display the eight brown eggs inside.

"And is that all you were doing? Did you, perhaps, *meet* someone there?"

"I met all sorts of people," retorted Luz. "What do you mean?"

"Red went just before you," said the Mother in a low voice. "Did you see him there?"

"Oh, *him.*" Luz kept her tone deliberately light. "I saw him across the street—but not to speak to."

"But you have spoken to him before. Did you think you could keep it secret from me? Long talks in the garden, whisperings by the fire. . . . His mind is not that of a whole man. Why do you spend time with him?"

No, he has the minds of several men, thought Luz as she searched for an answer. "Why shouldn't I? He seemed lonely. He reminds me of a boy I used to play with when I was a little girl."

"But you are a child no longer," said the Mother, "and he has the body of a young male. I will not have his innocence corrupted. You will avoid him."

What had Bett been telling her? As the winter wore on, Mother Mahaliel had begun to snap at everyone, but she had been kind to Luz, until now.

"How can I, when we all live—" Luz began, but the

older woman's face darkened, and she felt the first tremor of fear.

"If you do not have enough tasks to keep you busy, I must give you more." She frowned. "Bett tells me that the mice have been into our storeroom. Clean up the mess and sort out the different grains. By tomorrow morning I want it cleared."

A branch cracked as some small creature scuttled through the underbrush before him, and the king shifted nervously. Like an echo, from across the river came a *thunk* of stone hitting stone. This was the first evening the Suns had continued the attack after sundown. The message he had received must be genuine. Julian unfolded the scrap of paper and strove to re-read it. *"East wall ready to come down. Final assault tomorrow eve."* For a moment, his gaze lingered on the eight-pointed star scrawled at the end. The light was going, but it hardly mattered. The king had memorized the note's contents by now.

"I am sure Lord Philip got your message," Lenart murmured.

The king nodded, peering through the willows that screened their hiding place, and shivered as a cold wind rustled the new leaves. Sun patrols were sporadic on the northern bank of the Silvershine, especially now, when the general had pulled in all his forces for the final assault.

"I admire your calm," he whispered back. "Unusual in a man your age. Or perhaps I am thinking of Phoenix. That boy never could sit still." He stopped, wondering where that had come from. Anxiety must be distracting him more than he realized if he was talking about his son.

"My lord, may I speak freely?" Lenart broke the silence.

"So long as you do it quietly." Julian kept his tone intentionally casual, remembering that this young man had been his son's friend. Most of the time, Lenart kept his feelings hidden behind a formality that bordered on pomposity. Perhaps the tension was weighing on him, too.

"Johan . . . was not always at his best in your presence.

But no man who does not know how to find his inner stillness can be as good as he was with the bow."

Julian realized that he was crushing the message that had arrived wrapped around an arrow shaft and carefully let it go.

"You may not quite realize how overwhelming your achievements can be," Lenart added.

"The tales have grown in the telling," muttered the king.

"Johan wanted very much to be worthy of you, my lord."

I was not worthy to have a son. But it will not matter whether or not I have an heir if we lose this war.

Dusk was veiling the land, but fires glowed on the lower hill to the east of the fortress where the enemy had positioned the great trebuchet. They would give light enough to aim—the fortress was not going to dodge or run away.

Fortunately the same was not true of its defenders. The king's gaze fixed on a tangle of trees on the far bank of the river, well beyond the line of enemies who kept watch on Hightower's walls.

"Did something move, there among the trees? No," he corrected himself, "they will wait. If we can see, so can the Suns."

"I'll just slip down a little farther and look," said Lenart. Moving with surprising grace for so large a man, he disappeared into the undergrowth.

Hidden by those trees was the worn stone slab covering the entrance to the tunnel that Robert had shown him so long ago. For several months Philip had been using it to smuggle out his wounded and bring in supplies. It had been built originally as a channel to lead water from the river to a cistern deep beneath the fortress, but someone had had the happy idea of carving a ledge above it, just wide enough for an active person to move along. Robert had rediscovered its other end in the fortress when he was a boy, exploring where his brother, the lord commander, had forbidden him to go.

And even as Julian smiled at the memory, he heard Philip's voice, and allowed himself a relieved sigh. He had failed to rescue Alexander, but the lord commander of the

Ramparts would be saved! The branches shivered, he saw
Lenart's bulk against the dimming sky, followed by that of
another man, and then his cousin was beside him. He
glimpsed other shapes emerging from the tunnel and scuttling forward to fade into the willows. For a moment, he
and Philip clasped arms.

"Is Jeanne with you?" After the fall of Sanjos she had
gone to help defend Rivered while her brother tried to or-
ganize some defense for the rest of the province. He was
somewhere in the mountains now.

"She'll come with the last group. Only a hundred are left
up there now. They're keeping the torches lit and moving
the dummies on the walls."

"She knows she must be out before nightfall?"

"If she doesn't, it is not for lack of telling," Philip said
with a father's bitter pride. "Jeanne has borne half the load
of defending Hightower. I could not deny her the right to
cover our retreat at the last."

"Both of your children have earned our gratitude," said
Julian. *And either would be worthy of Westria. Would I
have the same pride in Johan and the same fear for his fate
if he had lived to see this day?*

"Yes . . . ," said Philip, "and if you wish to earn mine,
you will take me somewhere out of this cold!"

The air in the storeroom was chill, with a distinct, musty
smell that would have told Luz mice had been at work here
even without the spilled seeds and the droppings everywhere. As she set the lantern down, shadows skittered
about the room. Luz suppressed an involuntary shudder.
She had put on breeches and tucked them firmly into her
boots, but she fancied she could already feel tiny clawed
feet dancing across her skin.

Ordinarily a broom and a waste-bin would have solved
the problem, but with food growing scarce they could not
afford to throw anything salvageable away. If she could
separate the grains, they could be sifted and washed and
earmarked for uses that required boiling. She pushed her

fears back into the shadows, considering how to address the task.

It took until evening to transfer the beans, wheat, barley, oats, and peas remaining in the bags the rodents had chewed open into new, whole containers and set them in the kitchen. The mouse kindred had been busy indeed, and beyond the paths she had cleared to walk on, dunes and drifts of mixed grains covered the floor. Damn the creatures! They should be made to clean up the mess they had made! She reached for the hammer and a piece of board to block the hole where they had come in, then stopped, considering.

In her Earth year at the College they had learned to talk to the Guardians of the plants in the garden and the animals in the pens. And there had been that time when Mistress Melissa called on all of them to send out a request to the Rat Guardian to leave the chicken coops alone. Luz had conquered her fear well enough to help with that—could she do something similar now? She listened carefully. The house was quiet. No one would know. And after five months of pretending submission, she *needed* to prove she could still master her fears.

Luz rewrapped her shawl against the mice as well as the chill. When they talked to the Rat King, they had asked him to take his people *away*. Would she be able to maintain her focus when she heard the whisper of tiny feet on the floor?

I have the skill if I have the will! she told herself with a resurgence of her old pride.

She closed her eyes, forcing her breathing to deepen and slow as inner senses unfolded. The energies of the humans in the house fluctuated in the regular rhythms of sleep, but beneath the foundations she sensed the movement of other minds. She conquered a twitch, knowing they would never come if they sensed her revulsion, then built up in her mind the image of a fine, sleek gray mouse. Very softly, she sang—

> *Listen, listen, Mousie Man—*
> *I will help you if I can!*
> *Good companions we shall be,*
> *If you do this thing for me.*

For a moment then, she found her balance in a place beyond fear, and sensed, with a dawning of wonder, the focused, fearful, busy construct of the mouse-kin. She opened the eyes of spirit and body together. Before her, a mouse-shaped swirl of light elongated until it took the form of a little round man with gray whiskers, wrapped in a garment of velvety gray fur.

"You are not much like your sister." His voice was high and whispery.

"No, sir." She cleared her throat. "But if your people will help me sort this grain, they may have a portion to carry away."

He wrinkled his nose. "Whatever for? Have we not been doing what Mistress Bera asked, spoiling the food of your enemy?"

Luz nodded. "And you've done well. But I have to protect the heir to the Jewels, and if I don't please his captor, she will send me away." Luz tried not to think about what else Mother Mahaliel might do.

"Hmm." Master Mouse looked around him. "The tradition is for you humans to help one of us first, but you have feared us, not so?" His whiskers twitched in a smile at her wary agreement. "Well then, you must promise, wherever you dwell, to make the offerings. I don't know why you fear," he added, eyeing her with amusement. "You are a mouse yourself, is it not so? Your spirit is great and bright, but you always hide."

Luz stared at him, realizing that it was true. Even at the College, she had played the part of Master Granite's meek apprentice. When would she dare to claim her own power? Perhaps tonight was a beginning.

"Hold out your hand . . . ," the Mouse King said then.

As Luz complied, she realized that mice, hordes of them, were swarming into the storeroom. She braced against panic, but what she felt was an expansion of consciousness—not Master Mouse, but all mice, alert and eager and half-drunk on the scent of all this food. One of them scurried up the side of the bin and jumped into her open hand. She felt the essence of life, soft and warm and surveying her with very bright eyes. When she looked up again, the Guardian was gone, but the floor was a seething mass of mice, sifting through the grain.

By dawn, the different seeds had been sorted and the mice were gone with the tithe she had offered them. Only the little female who had been her companion remained, perching on her shoulder as she shoveled the piles of sorted grain into bags and then swept and scrubbed the floor. She leaned the board across the hole but did not nail it closed, and set the little mouse down.

"Go now to your people with my gratitude," she whispered. "And take care."

She was stacking the last bags, appropriately labeled, onto the shelves when the door opened and Bett looked in.

"Well, and how have you—" Her voice faltered. "You're done already?" Wonder changed to suspicion in her voice.

"I work hard," Luz said brightly, trying to make out the woman's expression.

"My lady, my lady," called Bett. "You must come and see!"

With awareness sensitized by her communication with the Mouse King, Luz felt Mother Mahaliel's approach as heat. She heard voices at the door; instinctively her eyes squeezed shut as a pillar of fire in the shape of a woman came into the room. But to close her eyes only allowed her to perceive the priestess more clearly, and by that she understood that she was seeing with the eyes of the spirit. In sudden panic she tried to ground her own aura, wondering if the Lady could see her in turn.

I've grown careless, serving her day by day, she thought bitterly. *"And proud,"* came Master Granite's voice in her memory. *I was deceived by all the small indignities that living in a body entails, and forgot the strength of the soul within.* Or some souls—Bett still seemed little more than a shadow to the inner eye.

Luz knelt to set down the last bag, body and spirit huddling earthward. *"I am no threat to you,"* she shaped thought into spell. *"I am only a little brown mouse hiding here. . . ."*

"My lady—" She stayed on her knees with bent head. "I have completed the task you set me."

"I see that you have." In that warm voice, approval warred with something else. Surprise, or suspicion? "A . . . remarkable . . . achievement, to be sure."

"Run," said the Mouse King in her mind. *"She is a cat, and she will spring!"* Luz felt her heart sink. She had been so determined to please Mother Mahaliel by succeeding in this impossible task. Clearly, it would have been safer for her to fail. . . .

———

"Sombra is a witch, mistress. You must see that now!" Bett's voice carried clearly from Mother Mahaliel's chamber.

Red, who had just come in from the stables, lifted one eyebrow. The old girl was on a tear this morning, for sure. He held cold hands to the hearthfire, then sorted through the heap of odds and ends of wood piled beside it and added a few more logs. As he did so, a chunk of manzanita rolled across the floor. He picked it up, seeing its possibilities, and pulled out his belt-knife, still listening to the voices from the other room.

"She has been trading on your good nature, your kindness. But she still holds to the native superstitions. She has invoked those evil powers here in our very household. How else could she have accomplished that task?"

Ah, he thought then, they must be talking about what Sombra had done in the storeroom. He pared a chunk of wood away, perceiving in the red and white grain the shape of a crouching animal whose nature careful carving might reveal.

"Yes, I do see that. . . . ," Mother Mahaliel said slowly. "She seemed so bright, so insightful—I had great hopes of her. But the Dark One is never more dangerous than when he comes in a fair disguise."

"She is in the herb garden now. When she comes in, we will hold her. She must be *tested*. . . ."

The undertone of malice in Bett's voice sent a chill up

Red's spine. He stilled, staring down at the piece of wood in his hands. The Suns released the spirits of their dead by fire. It was a punishment and a disgrace to rot in the earth, a fate feared more than death by those ordinary criminals killed by the Dragon in the ring. But those whose sins were spiritual—witches and heretics—must go living to the pyre.

"The fire is holy. It will suffer no evil," Bett said softly. "If Sombra is innocent, she will pass unhurt through the flames."

Do you believe what you are saying? he wondered. *Have you ever seen one of your heretics come living from the fire?*

"It cannot harm the pure of heart," Mother Mahaliel repeated. "But she is so young. . . ."

Red had seen three trials for witchcraft during his time with the Suns. The memory of the victims' screams sent him scuttling back to the protection of his other selves. He jerked to his feet, and the carving dropped into the fire. Before he could rescue it, the wood blazed up in a spurt of flame.

My father passed alive through the fires of Blood Gard, came a thought from the place where Jo waited, deep within. *But he was Master of the Jewels, and Luz is only a half-trained girl.* Now it was Luz he saw burning amid the dancing flames. . . .

"Mistress, why do you waver? It must be done," Bett said then. "I think this will be a test not only of Sombra's faith, but of yours."

"Do you dare to question me?" Mother Mahaliel spoke sharply, and for a moment he hoped her wrath would fall on Bett instead. There was a tense silence; then the priestess sighed. "No, it is I who should question myself. The Sun has told me that the fire is the way to His Light. Let the girl find it, if she can. . . ."

Jo's head swung back and forth in anguish as he felt the Dragon waking. *"Be still!"* he begged. *"Your rage will only get both of us killed!"* The Dragon must not be freed, but Red was afraid of the burning, and Fix was simply afraid. Jehan waited in the shadows of his mind.

"We take from you the burdens you cannot bear . . . ," he heard his grandfather speaking within. *"I can advise, but what's needed now is a thing that only you can do. Get out swiftly, before Mother Mahaliel sees you here—"*

Have to find Luz and hide her—but where? Jo's thought began as he slipped out the door, but already memory was showing him the shack near the barracks where the old armsmaster lived. *She will be safe with Garr. . . .*

"Yes, I understand that Garr cannot hide me here for long," exclaimed Luz. "But I want *you* to understand that I won't go anywhere unless you come too!"

The old man's cabin was set by itself between the arena and the barracks the Suns had built on the level ground by the river. The local people said that long ago there had been a great prison there, that the ghosts of inmates haunted it still. But Garr did not look like a man who would be disturbed by spirits of any kind.

With the door shut and barred behind them, the only light in the room came from the fire. Jo's face was a pale blur. But she could see him well enough to know that at least it *was* Jo, and not one of his alter egos. That was a wonder to balance the fear that had struck her to the heart when he gave his warning. It would seem that her danger had summoned his true self from the depths in which he had been hiding. If she left him now, Jo might never surface again.

"Do you really think we managed to get away without being seen? When Mother Mahaliel finds out you helped me, what do you think she will do?"

"I am her pet," he answered bitterly. "She will not harm me."

"Maybe not, but when a pet goes unpredictable, it's caged," Garr observed, gesturing toward the shackles hanging on the wall. Luz suppressed a shudder, wondering just what means the armsmaster had used to control his charge, and whether the manacles were intended to keep Jo from harming others, or himself.

Jo followed her glance with a mirthless laugh. "Oh, yes, Garr knows how to chain the Dragon." He turned back to her. "Do you think I have stayed here for love of Mother Mahaliel? If the beast breaks loose, I would rather it savaged the Suns than Westria." He leaned toward her, and she saw a red light dancing in his eyes. "Do you truly wish to find yourself alone in the wilderness with me?"

Luz stared at him. She had known she would have to wrestle Red and Fix and Jehan for his soul, but she had thought the Dragon a creature of the arena. What if they had to fight on their journey? Who, or what, would she have to deal with then? By the time she found her voice, Jo had already started to turn away.

She cleared her throat. "At the College of the Wise they teach that we have an immortal spirit that exists before our bodies take shape and that survives their destruction. I believe that. I'm not trusting myself to Jo, or the Dragon, or whoever else is in charge on any given day, but to that spirit in *you*."

"Then you're as crazy as I am," he began, but she went on.

"Mother Mahaliel is right—fire purifies. You are in the flames right now, but the Phoenix will rise from the ashes. I'm willing to risk my life to prove that. Are you?"

Garr gave a short laugh. "Well, lad, there's a challenge for you!"

Jo turned on him. "You *agree* with her?"

"Oh, I would never counsel you to refuse a challenge."

His laugh this time was different, and Luz felt the hairs rise along her arms. In the firelight, his missing eye was a well of shadow. Who was he? Could she be sure who anyone was anymore?

"Besides, the girl should not go into the wilderness alone, and only in the wild lands can you hope to avoid the general's patrols."

Luz lifted one eyebrow. She would have been expected to make the journey to Awahna alone. However, the hazards on the Pilgrim's Road did not ordinarily include being pursued by enemies.

"The fortress will be taken by nightfall. There is nothing we can do to alter that outcome," Garr went on. "General Marsh will need all his men for the final assault. You must leave in the confusion after Hightower falls. You will need horses, supplies—best that I be the one to get them."

"Won't that be dangerous for you?" said Jo.

"Nay, lad—there are some who owe me favors and will keep silent for their own sakes. And once *you* are gone, I can disappear."

"Then why not come with us!" Jo exclaimed.

"I must stay to cover your trail," Garr said patiently. "And your time under my care is ending. You will have to watch out for each other now."

"Commander, I'm going back to the town to report to Mother Mahaliel. I'll leave you to keep an eye on things here." Tadeo Marsh glanced back at the fortress and sighed.

Beyond the broken wall, the courtyard of Hightower was illuminated by several fires. Dark figures darted back and forth before them, looting, not fighting. When the Suns had finally burst through, the only defenders they found were stuffed dummies propped atop the walls. The rain was beginning to fall in earnest now, and Tadeo pulled up the hood of the thick cloak he wore.

"Watching is about all I can do," answered Hallam. "The men have waited for this for a long time, and there will be no controlling them until they've stripped the place bare."

The general nodded. Even the disciplined troops he had commanded in the Empire of the Sun turned into demons once a city fell.

"If anything worth having survives the fires," he replied. Before escaping, the Westrians themselves had set the fortress ablaze. That they *had* escaped, he was certain, and once he had a chance to examine the fortress by daylight, no doubt he would discover just how. He suspected a tunnel whose exit the patrols had missed, although the men were already muttering about witchcraft.

"Well, they will recover all the sooner if they don't find any wine. Perhaps the Mother will be able to persuade them that our foes didn't vanish into thin air," said Hallam.

Mother Mahaliel was more likely to agree with them, thought the general as he started down the road with his aides behind him. But at least she should be pleased that Hightower was taken at last. With the fortress in their hands, they could begin to prepare for the summer campaign.

Word of the victory had reached the town before him. Despite the weather, the spear-wives had built a bonfire of their own in the square, and were serving out food and drink. When the soldiers did come back to the town, they would find a warm welcome here.

He was a little surprised not to see Mother Mahaliel holding court among them, but there was light in her windows. As he approached, someone called out, and a pale figure hurried down the steps.

"Sir, thank Father Sun you're here!"

"Cho-cho, what's wrong? Is your lady ill?" Tadeo took her arm, his mind already calculating what he might say to the troops if it were so. He had thought about what he would do if Mother Mahaliel died, but he was not yet ready to rule in his own name.

"Ill with grief, with rage," the girl babbled. "Come to her, sir. Maybe you can make her calm."

"Stay here. I may need you soon," he murmured to his aides.

A blast of heat met him as he followed Cho-cho inside. A roaring blaze filled the fireplace, and Mother Mahaliel crouched beside it, throwing more logs into the flames.

"Mahaliel, what are you doing? Come out to your people and bless our victory!"

She tipped her head to gaze up at him with a crafty smile. "I must build up the fire. . . . I must build up the fire to burn the witch who has stolen him away. . . ."

He took an involuntary step backward. It was she who looked like a sorceress, with her hair unbound and the firelight glittering in her eyes, a sight more shocking than the destruction of the fortress.

"Hightower is ours, Mahaliel," he tried again, standing his ground with an effort as she reared up, the lighted brand she held scattering sparks across the floor.

"Our luck is gone! She has taken my Dragon. What is a fortress to me?"

"That Westrian bitch has seduced the boy to run off with her!" hissed Bett. "I told her how it would be! We searched the town. They're not here. You must send out trackers."

"Not until morning," he answered, and likely not for some hours afterward. The general could not deny the men their celebration even if he wished to.

In his opinion they were better off without the Dragon, but the boy had been Mahaliel's pet, and he needed her sane. As soon as he had men fit to ride, he would send squads out along the roads. He turned to tell her so, but Mother Mahaliel was back on her knees, feeding more wood to the hungry flames.

Hightower was burning, casting a lurid light on the clouds and turning the raindrops to a shower of fire. The reek caught at Luz's throat as she and Jo followed Garr through the town. Despite their danger, she was profoundly grateful to be out and moving at last. Cooped up in the cabin with an increasingly silent Jo, Luz had found the afternoon very long indeed.

Except for a few other hurrying figures wrapped up against the rain, the streets were empty. The soldiers were sacking the citadel, and everyone else was celebrating in the square. Nonetheless, they held to the back alleys until they reached the thickets on the south side of the town. Among the trees, Luz could make out the shapes of two horses and a laden mule.

"There's a road just over that rise that leads up into the hills." Garr tossed the reins of the red stallion to Jo and gave Luz a leg up onto the dun gelding. "If you take my advice, you'll go east. The Suns will be expecting you to head up the valley to lands the Westrians still hold. They're plains people at heart, and they won't like following you into the mountains. Don't stop 'til you've put some miles between yourselves and this town. The rain will cover your trail."

Indeed, the rain was falling heavily now. Luz pulled her hood forward, shivering despite the heavy woolen tunic she wore over her linen gown. But the wet was surely preferable to the fire that awaited her if she stayed here. Jo was still standing by his horse, trembling with something more than cold.

"You heard what he said, Jo—get mounted! We've a long way to go!"

"I can't. . . ."

Luz stared at him. Suddenly the patter of rain on the leaves seemed very loud. Above it she could hear shouting, closer now, as if some of the soldiers were returning to the town. She glanced at Garr, and saw that the old man was watching her. *He wants to see if I can handle this,* she thought grimly. She turned back to Jo, pitching her voice very low and clear.

"Then in the name of the Guardians, give way to someone who can!"

⇜ 19 ⇝

SPRING STORMS

On the second evening after the capture of Hightower, Tadeo Marsh set off for his daily visit to Mother Mahaliel. Soldiers brought fist to breast in salute and whispered as he passed. Rule of the Suns was his—if he could hold on to it. Men had admired old Garr's ability to control the Dragon, but an army could turn into a monster that was more fearsome still.

Since the fall of the fortress, town and camp had been full of rumors. Mother Mahaliel was dead, said some, or she had gone into seclusion to bring them a new revelation. But the most persistent stories were of witchcraft. Some whispered that the Mother had withdrawn to fight the powers of darkness who had spirited the Westrians out of their fortress and stolen the Red Dragon away. Others believed it was the Dragon, empowered by her magic, who had carried off the soldiers who had been defending Hightower. The general rather liked that one, but he did not much care which story gained credence, so long as the Suns accepted his right to speak in their prophet's name.

But that depended on what happened to Mother Mahaliel. As Tadeo mounted the steps to her house, he wondered what he would find.

"How is the Lady?"

"She is resting well." Bett spoke loudly enough for the general's aides to hear her, though Tadeo saw no hope in her eyes. "A few more days, and perhaps she will be restored to health."

"The men will rejoice to hear it," said Commander Hallam. After the Mother's servants had finally gotten her to rest, the army had been told that she had a fever, which was one way of describing her madness. "Go in to her, sir. We will wait for you here."

The bedroom smelled of sickness. As Tadeo's eyes adjusted to the dim light, he realized that the silent shape tucked so neatly into the white bed was Mother Mahaliel.

"Mahaliel, how are you—," he began, but as he moved closer, he realized that he was unlikely to get a reply. Lamplight lent an illusory color to skin like dough, the slack flesh sagging on her bones. Her eyes were open, but she did not appear to be seeing anything in the room. He turned to Bett, who stood with arms crossed defensively.

"How long has she been this way?"

"Last night she finally stopped raving. We were relieved,

but—" She shook her head helplessly. "It is all the fault of that Westrian witch. You must catch her, General, and make her lift her curse!"

"I have sent trackers along the main roads—," he began, his eyes still on Mother Mahaliel. She looked sick and old, but that was not what he found disturbing. The golden aura that had been so powerful an aspect of her presence was gone.

"The girl is no fool, General," Bett was saying, "she'll know better than to go where we're likely to follow. It's the back roads you must search. Send men into the hills."

"You may be right . . . ," he answered, thinking hard.

He would have been just as happy to let the fugitives go, but if Mother Mahaliel died, the Suns would need a scapegoat for their rage. When he caught Sombra, he would burn her himself, and the gladiator with her. The people would follow Mother Mahaliel's avenger, and by the time the Suns realized that they had traded a mistress for a master, it would be his own fault if they did not also recognize that they had gained by the exchange.

A wet camp in the wilderness is a poor trade for my snug bed at Bongarde, thought Rana, waking as she felt the first spatters of rain. But then there was little sense of any kind in the course she had chosen, only compulsion.

Five days ago she had awakened with the conviction that it was time to leave the sanctuary in which the king had left her. If she had told anyone she was going, they would have found some way, queen though she might be, to stop her. But because she was queen, she could persuade the spirits of the land to cover her tracks. When Eric and Rosemary calmed down, they would realize that they should have expected this. Once more, she had run off to follow Julian.

It was the beginning of April, late for a winter storm to lash the land, but under cover of darkness the clouds had blown in from the sea. If Rana had seen them coming, she would have sought shelter at one of the holdings she had passed this afternoon instead of seeking to avoid pursuit a little longer by camping on Healer's Hill. She shoved her gear closer to the trunk of the live oak underneath which she had been sleeping, rolled up her bedding, and crammed it into the oiled-cloth bag. She had gathered plenty of wood before she slept, and she would stay dry enough wrapped in her cloak beside the fire.

She shoved several pieces into the fading flames. Raindrops hissed as they hit, but a big enough blaze would defy the rain. Anyone who saw the light would think the ghosts had been awakened by the storm. And in a way that was true—trapped in this middle-aged body was the ghost of the girl who had watched Julian do battle with Caolin from this hill almost thirty years before.

Lightning blinked; the flames flared wildly and sank as a more powerful gust shook the trees, carrying with it a sustained rumble as if those long-ago armies were charging once more across the plain. Light flashed again; overhead she glimpsed the horsemen themselves, plunging through a roil of clouds.

She laughed through the crash of thunder that followed. "Ride on! I don't fear you! I have a ghost or two of my own to call if you trouble me!"

Silverhair had died in her arms not so very far from here. If the harper's spirit lingered, she might summon him to sing the ghosts to sleep. But first she had better put some more fuel on the flames.

When she turned back with the wood in her arms, a man whose sodden hair and beard glinted silver was sitting on the other side of the fire.

"Silverhair . . . ," she breathed. But this man was too solidly built. His shoulders were broad, and muscle corded the arms he held out to the fire. Yet there was something very familiar about that battered old hat and the threadbare gray cloak he wore. Her eyes narrowed. "Coyote Old Man? Is it you?"

His answer was a dry chuckle that set the skin prickling along Rana's forearms. "Don't you know me? Through many lands I have wandered, but I come, as I promised, on the wings of the storm. . . ."

And now she was afraid, recognizing the Power into whom Coyote had transformed on the Red Mountain two and a half years before.

"I remember, *Wanderer* . . . ," she said slowly. "And indeed the world has changed. Will you restore my son to me?"

"I restore nothing." He laughed once more. "I guide, and sometimes I guard."

"Are you the Guardian of Men?" she asked then, searching through her memory for bits of old lore.

"Ah, now that's a title that has been attached to many names. . . . It's true that I was hanged on the Tree, but not to save *you*. You must save yourselves. What I offer is the wisdom to choose. . . ."

Rana sat back with a sigh of recognition. The Guardians always insisted that humans must be responsible for their own deeds. It was one reason so many Westrians had been seduced by the simpler theology of the Children of the Sun.

"I have been guarding your child," the Wanderer said then. "But he must make his own choices now." The single eye that she could see bored into her own.

For a moment she stilled in shock, understanding that until this moment she had not truly dared to believe Johan lived.

"Where is he? How can I help him?" she asked when her voice would obey her again.

"He is where he needs to be. If he has the strength I believe is in him, you will see him again. You will want to choose for him, but you must not do so. All you can offer him is your love."

With an effort, Rana pulled herself together, seeking some action to release the surging confusion of joy and fear within. "And what can I offer *you*? I have no whiskey with me, Wanderer, but I can make tea." She filled the pan with water and threw in some mint leaves.

"A gift deserves a gift again. But give the drink to the man whose body I'm wearing. You should not make this journey alone. He'll serve you as escort on the road."

"*He,* not you?"

"Oh, no—this body is flesh and blood." He stretched out

his hand to the fire and jerked it back as if surprised when it burned. "It has served me well, but he has not the strength to bear me all the way to Elder."

"Is that where I will find Johan?"

"It's where you will find your husband—and the choices that are waiting for you." For a moment longer he met her gaze, and she felt herself being drawn into the galaxies that swirled in that single eye. Then it closed, and as the energy that had upheld him was withdrawn, the body of the old man slumped to the ground.

Rana leaned over, made sure that he was still breathing, and turned back to stir the pot, which was now beginning to boil. When she looked at her companion again he was sitting up, rubbing his forehead.

Rana poured the hot liquid into a cup. "The rain is passing. Have some of this tea. It will warm your insides, and your cloak will dry if you spread it before the fire."

The act of swallowing seemed to steady him. "A blessing on you, good lady. I must have been more tuckered than I thought, to fall down in a faint like that before your fire. . . ." He blinked, as if he were trying to understand how he had gotten there.

As well he might, thought Rana, thinking over the conversation that had just ended. She could see now that his left eye was not missing, only half hidden by an old scar.

"What shall I call you, now that you've accepted my hospitality?" she asked.

"My name is Garr, and until a few days past, I was an armsmaster with the Children of the Sun."

———————

Luz woke with a sob, grasping at fragments of dream. She had stood in the heart of Light, as if she had walked into one of Mother Mahaliel's sermons, encompassed by the tyrannous radiance of the sun. For a moment only the hard point of the rock that dug into her back through the blankets reassured her that she was not still a prisoner.

"Sombra, what is it?" asked Fix as she sat up, heart pounding.

At the end of their fifth day of travel they had camped just off the road in an oak wood above a rushing stream. Through the trees she could see the long blue ridges that guarded the Snowy Mountains. As the sun lifted above them, the dew that clung to the thick grass in the meadow gave back its light in a million points of flashing gold.

"A dream," she answered him. "Just—a dream." And indeed she could not quite class it as a nightmare, even though she had been with Mother Mahaliel.

"Come into the Light, my Daughter, and forget all your fears. . . ." The Mother's words reverberated in her awareness. The effort to wrench herself free had whirled her back toward consciousness, but Luz could still see the woman's triumphant smile.

Is she dying, or only lost in vision? she wondered. Either way, the Mother had been trying to drag Luz along. *I will have to ward our campsites,* she thought grimly. *She pursues me, even in my dreams!*

Fix, the only one of Jo's inner family who liked to get up in the morning, was already unhobbling the horses and leading them down to the stream. Yawning, Luz poked at the campfire, blowing the banked coals into new flame. At least traveling with Jo was not boring. He traded personalities as a vain woman might change her clothes to suit her mood. Jehan knew the country best, while Red had the most experience camping. Fix viewed each new turn in the road with a child's wonder. Only Jo himself had not reappeared.

Responding, Luz found herself courtier, sparring partner, and big sister in turn. She wondered if Jo's collection of selves was simply a more evolved example of the constellation of responses everyone contained. The thought helped her to keep at bay her fears that she had only managed to free Jo's body, while leaving his soul enslaved by Mother Mahaliel.

After that first, frantic night of travel, another day had brought them to the road that wound the length of the foothills. None of Jo's personalities questioned her decision to turn south. Luz told herself it was the last direction pursuers would expect her to go, but now, remembering her dream, she realized that she had another reason. Nowhere in Westria could they be assured of safety, and she dared not take Jo across the border. There was only one way to find certain sanctuary not only for the body, but for the soul, and that was to go out of the world of men entirely and seek Awahna. And Master Granite had been right in one thing, she thought grimly; if the Master of the Jewels dared not call on the Guardians to aid in this war, then someone else would have to do it for him.

And she would find them, she thought with a flash of her old pride. She had listened carefully to her father's stories and studied the maps at the College of the Wise. Why should she have been given the knowledge, if not to undertake this task? Master Granite would not boast so loudly of his plans for her when she returned with the heir of Westria!

She glimpsed the prince now, the fuzz of red-gold where his hair was growing back glinting in the sun. But when he came into the clearing he was still Fix, laughing as he offered her an armful of nodding golden flowers.

"Daffodils!" she exclaimed, admiring the precise curves. "Wherever did you find them?"

"Over there—across the stream." He grinned. "There's a whole field of 'em, just opening to the sun."

The morning was indeed beautiful, but when they got out from under the trees, all the Great Valley was obscured by banks of gray cloud, and the wind from the west blew damp and cold. Down there, it must be raining already. But even though she could no longer see the valley, Luz could feel something from that direction—an avid, inimical energy that she felt certain was looking for *her*.

Had Mother Mahaliel sent one of her priests with a search party? That searchers would be ordered after them, Luz had been sure; but she had not sensed their presence until now. As they rode southward, she continued to hope her unease was no more than a carryover from her dream, but when they passed the turnoff for the old road that led back to the valley, her sense of danger grew acute.

"Will you look at that, now—" The voice was Red's.

Luz turned from her fruitless scanning of the road behind them to see him waving toward a pointed peak that rose from a tumble of hillock and meadow between the hill along whose side they were passing and the blue ridges beyond. It looked as if it ought to have a castle on top of it, but though black cattle grazed on the meadows below, no human habitation could be seen.

"From the top of that butte we could get quite a view," she said carefully. *And see if anyone is following,* she added silently. She was never quite sure whose side Red was on. "That trail seems to lead in the right direction. Let's climb it and see."

It took them nearly two hours to find a path through the tangle of trees that covered the slopes, but the view from the top was all that Luz had hoped for. The remains of a stone tower on the summit bore witness that this place had once been used as a watch hill. From here she could see past the bend where they had left the road all the way back to the turnoff to the valley. And as she gazed, the approaching clouds parted and sunlight sparked from something moving there. She stared and saw that wink of light again. Her instinct had been right—there were horsemen on that road.

"They're following us, aren't they?" Her companion's voice had changed again. "And we'll have left a pretty clear trail."

Luz turned and her eyes widened as she realized it was Jo. It was interesting that danger should have summoned him. "Yes . . . I'm going to try to do something about that."

"You'll have to do it fast," he said in a level tone. He went to the red stallion and untied his bowcase from behind the saddle. Garr had given him plenty of arrows, but he had neither armor nor sword.

If he has to fight, will the Dragon appear? Luz wondered. *And will I be glad or sorry if it does?*

But that was a fear for the future. She had work to do. Luz set her feet firmly, extending awareness to anchor herself to the hill's ancient volcanic core. Then she took a deep breath and reached out to the approaching clouds. As they neared the mountains they were billowing upward already, dark with pent rain. For a moment there was nothing, then came a sudden twitch, as if she had got a fish on the line.

It was time to see if she had mastered the spell-work she had learned at the College of the Wise. Putting all her will into strengthening that contact, she began to sing.

> *West-wind driving, ever striving!*
> *Bring the waters, wet and wild,*
> *Swirling, whirling, clouds unfurling,*
> *Widdershins, the storm's sweet child!*

Luz laughed as a damp gust of wind lifted her hair. The clouds had heard her! They were close now, a purple-gray wave sweeping over the hills. No fisherman had ever hooked such a catch! Her outstretched arms shook with strain.

> *Rain comes sweeping, skies are weeping,*
> *Raindrops in a silver veil!*
> *Clashing clouds, release your floods—*
> *Waters, wash away our trail!*

And roaring, the clouds answered her. Luz brought down her arms to break the connection just as the full force of the wind hit the hill. In the next moment it sent her sprawling, fighting for breath as water sheeted down. She heard a horse squeal. Then she felt Jo's hands hard on her arms.

She managed to crawl after him, dropped with a little shriek over an edge she had not seen, and slid down to fetch up against the gnarled trunk of an oak tree. She glimpsed the horses below her, heads down and rumps turned to the blast.

"Guardians, Luz!" gasped Jo when the first fury had passed. "Did you have to call them so *loud*?" He was soaked to the skin.

She brushed ineffectually at the mud plastered down the front of her gown and shook her head. "Didn't know . . . it would work so well!" Suddenly this struck her as hilarious, and the look of exasperation on his face was funnier still. Jo grabbed her as she tried to stand and slipped again. She clung to him until she felt his shoulders begin to shake and knew he was laughing too.

The general's mood was as grim as the rain. Since Mother Mahaliel had fallen ill, he had visited her when he finished the work of the day. When he returned to his own quarters Sarina would be waiting, always with the same question in her dark eyes.

"The Mother is no worse," he said gently, sitting down to the meal the girl had prepared for him. "She sleeps." A few days of sunshine had given them all hope, but overnight the clouds had rolled in again and the land cowered beneath the storm.

"Will she get well?" the girl asked softly, her eyes bright with tears.

"My dear, I do not know," he answered truthfully, although recovery seemed less likely with each day that passed. "Perhaps the Sun will take her to Himself."

Sarina was not the only one who was grieving. The men he had sent out to seek Sombra and Red along the valley roads had come back empty-handed, though a second group was out somewhere in the mountains still. Town and camp seethed with anger and anxiety. He almost hoped the Westrians would attack and take the Suns' minds off their fears.

Rain drummed on the roof. He saw that the girl was shivering, got up and draped her shawl around her shoulders. "Are you cold? Shall I put more wood on the fire?"

Sarina shook her head, turning to him with a sudden sob. "Not cold, sir—I'm afraid!"

"You have no need to be." He put an arm around her shoulders. "I will take care of you."

"It's like the sun's gone out and everything's dark," she murmured. "The Mother made—makes—everything so clear. Without her . . . what if she was wrong? I've broken the Covenant, cut myself off from th' land."

"Does the Westrian religion damn you to torment for apostasy?" he asked curiously.

She shook her head. "I'd still be myself in Hell. Our priests say that souls uprooted be like tumbleweeds blowin' in th' wind, never resting, 'til they fall to nothin' at all. Good people go to a place like Westria, only more so— the 'world within the world' they called it, an' after awhile they might get born again. But t' do everything right so you can get there is hard. Mother Mahaliel, she said all we need do is love th' Light. But it's all shadows 'round me now."

"Sarina—" He cradled her slim body, acutely aware of the softness of her breast, and the longing he had suppressed for so long burst free. "I won't argue theology. But you can believe that I love you, girl, and nothing's going to hurt you while I'm here!" He waited, heart pounding, feeling her grow still within the circle of his arms.

"Love?" she said finally. "All I wanted was the Sun, but I can't hear Him now."

"What you've got is me—not so bright, maybe—but I'm listening. I would have you be my woman, Sarina, if you think you could love me, but I'll take care of you, either way. If you believe in nothing else," he added grimly, "believe in the strength of my right arm." That arm was trembling now, holding her as if he held some wild bird in his hand.

"You're a good man. . . . I feel safe when you're holdin' me." She touched the taut muscle of his bicep, then reached to his face. "I loved you 'cause you served the Sun."

"Would it be so different to love me for my own sake, girl?" Tadeo said hoarsely.

Her answer was a shy kiss. Despite his resolution, Tadeo's grip tightened, and he kissed her back. His own heart pounded as loudly as the falling rain, but the storm outside was cold, whereas he glowed with a heat far older and more fundamental than the passionless radiance of Mother Mahaliel's Sun as he felt Sarina grow warm and willing in his arms.

"I tell you true, woman—" Red turned in his saddle to glare as Luz sneezed again. "You fall off that horse and I'm not going to carry you!" Her misery served her right, he thought as a touch sent the red stallion jogging down the road. Ever since that rainstorm she had been as smug as a hen with one egg, and cackling just as loud.

Likely as not the storm would have come anyway, at this season in these hills. From the looks of it, this one had been a real gully-washer. He was just as glad to have missed it. They had stayed on the Watch Hill until the rain stopped, and taken another path back to the road. By the time Red took over again, Jo's clothes were nearly dry.

Luz said their pursuers had given up, and he supposed she would know. He was not sure he cared. When they passed a small holding, she had even been confident enough to send him to trade some of the silver pieces Garr had given them for a bag of dried meat and pine nuts to eke out their supplies. The girl swore she was all right, though she shivered every time the wind blew. He had guessed even then how it would be, and now, four days later, when she wasn't shaking with fever she was coughing or blowing her nose. Since the road turned east the day before, they had been climbing steadily. They were in the wilderness now, where the elder kindreds ruled. The Big Oak Inn lay somewhere ahead, but it would not be safe to show themselves there.

What if Luz died out here? Even the thought was enough to shake Red's control. He recognized now the deficiency in his inner arrangements. Protecting Jo had been their only purpose. Until now, first Mother Mahaliel and then Luz had provided direction. Without Luz, Jo would have to emerge and make the decisions, and Red did not think it was safe yet to let Jo out alone.

All right, then, he thought, scanning the tree-clad slopes ahead, they would have to find shelter, and soon. The road was descending alongside a rushing stream. Ahead, it opened into a grassy flat, where some homesteader had tried to scratch out a living from the forest. Apparently the Guardians had not blessed his efforts, for the roof of the log house was missing shingles, and in the corrals the grass grew high. But it offered shelter, and from the look of the sky, they had reached it just in time. This high in the mountains, even in April such clouds could bring snow. He wondered if the storm spirits, attracted by Luz's summoning, were now tagging after her like stray cats who had unwisely been fed.

Red repaired one of the corrals well enough to hold the horses and cut fir branches to replace the decaying mattress of straw inside. There was still wood in the shed. As he brought the last armload inside, the first flakes of snow began to fall. Luz had thrown off the blanket and was tossing restlessly. When he touched her forehead, it burned.

He had not expected to need an alter ego who understood nursing. Once he had set water heating to make broth from the dried meat, Red could think of little else to do. It was time to let someone else take a shift, anyway. He sat down with a sigh and opened the doors of his spirit to Jehan.

Luz opened her eyes and saw a man's face, familiar blue eyes framed by dark hair and short-clipped beard. She blinked again and the hair was a brush of red, but the face was still Jehan's. She realized then that she had been seeing with the eyes of the spirit. *At least,* she thought muzzily, *I can tell who I'm talking to.* It was a relief to realize that the changing faces were not an artifact of her delirium. If only *she* had another self to escape into. Her rest had been haunted by nightmares, and she ached in every bone. She swallowed, struggling to form words.

"How long . . . have I been ill?"

Jehan smiled. "It has been two days since we got here. Drink this—" With one arm he raised her head and shoulders as the other held a wooden cup to her lips. She swallowed, coughed, and tried again. The broth tasted familiar, though she could not remember having drunk before.

"This is the last of the dried meat, but we shot a deer this morning, and there will be more. I know little of healing. Is there anything else I can do for you?"

"In my saddlebag there's some horehound and a little

white willow bark," she whispered when he had laid her down again. "In the yellow leather bag. You can find birch leaves outside, and dandelion. If there was a garden, you might look for feverfew."

To speak even so much made her head swim. She closed her eyes, hearing the liquid rattle in her chest. *Stupid girl,* she thought, and felt the easy tears sting her eyes, *so proud of your skill! You're just as vulnerable as any farmer's child.* She felt a breath of colder air as the door opened and shut again, but already she was sinking back into her tormented dreams.

She wanders in darkness, fighting her way through a tangle of writhing trees. She is wearing the familiar coarse cotton robe of a student at the College of the Wise, but she realizes without surprise that her body is tall and thin . . . and male. Is this how Jo feels when one of his other selves comes in? But it is only the body that is different—she recognizes her powers, and her pride. . . .

She has lost her cloak and she is shaking with cold, but surely the gateway to Awahna must be near. Soon she'll see it! The Gate will swing open, and her flight will be justified. Master Granite will admit that she's no toy to serve his ambition then! But when she thinks of the head of the College, the image that forms is that of a woman, small but unyielding, with skin the color of earth and a fuzz of silver hair. The Mistress of the Madrones . . . memory supplies the name.

She plunges forward, but mist swirls, obliterating the path. She forces her way through the tangling branches and teeters on the edge of emptiness. She has escaped the tyranny of Mother Mahaliel's Sun, but the dark gulf that yawns before her now will consume her soul!

"Child of Light, go back! You cannot pass!" a great voice cries, and in that moment she knows that she and Caolin are one.

Sobbing denial, she clings to the hard hand that has seized her own.

"Luz, Luz, come back!" That is a boy's voice, harsh with strain. With a knowledge beyond reason she recognizes it, and hears, and turns to him.

Coughing, Luz opened her eyes and saw the desperation in Jo's blue gaze give way to an astonished joy.

There's hope for both of them, thought Jehan, waiting for the pot of birch-leaf tea to boil. Jo had retreated again once the girl's crisis was past, but so long as her need could call him forth, he was not lost. And Luz herself was sleeping peacefully, her fever broken at last.

The congestion in her lungs was breaking up as well. He heard her stir and helped her to sit up, then held her as she coughed. When she was finished, she remained sitting, the first time she had been able to do so in days.

"You should sleep again," he said as he brought her the tea.

"I know, but I'm recovered enough now to fear it. I've had nightmares enough to last a lifetime!" Luz shuddered, sipped at the tea, then looked at him once more. Her voice cracked. "Jo is more fortunate in his grandfather than I. In my dream, I was Caolin. . . ."

Jehan blinked, all his own old guilts swirling up in memory. "I suppose it makes sense. He told me once that 'Luz' was his milk-name. Did you know?"

She shook her head, her face contorting in revulsion. Then she sighed. "Tell me about him, my lord. I think you are the only one who can."

"I know what Caolin *was.* Of those who are now living, only Julian really knows what he became." Jehan stopped, but she was still waiting, her eyes huge in a face whose roundness had been fined down by illness until the lovely contours of her bones showed clear.

"I met him first when I was taking my year at the College of the Wise, and again when he turned up after he tried to reach Awahna, and failed," Jehan said then. "Caolin was brilliant, full of energy, always there to help me—just the man to support a youngster who was not ready to be a king. We got lost once when we were out hunting and took refuge in an abandoned cabin—" He looked around him, frowning. "It could even have been this one. That might explain why you picked up the contact here."

Luz shuddered and drank more tea, waiting as he nerved himself to go on.

"I made him my lover," Jehan said at last. "For me, it was a simple, friendly thing. Caolin was only one of many. I'm afraid that the reputation I got in those days was deserved. I never understood until it was too late how singular and complete was his love for me. If I had known how to love him—if I had not laid the burden of Westria on his shoulders while I played at being king—we might all have been saved. But I was too blind, and he was too proud to show me his need."

"*Pride!*" The girl's bitterness echoed his own. "That's surely one thing I've inherited from him. Master Granite warned me, and I learned to hide it, but then he took me as his personal student and I decided that I must be something special after all. I was going to storm the gates of Awahna and force the Guardians to make Jo well." She shook her head in disgust. "At least Jo knows that he is broken. That's the first step in healing. Let this be a beginning for me."

"May it be so—" Jehan turned back to the fire. Just now she looked too much like Faris for his comfort. Faris and Caolin . . . the two people he had loved the best wrapped up in one package! Perhaps he had begun to make amends for failing them, but from now on it might be wiser to let Red take care of her.

And in any case, the closer they came to Awahna the more uneasy he became. If the essence of the man he had been had gone on to the world beyond, then he himself was only an echo. There would be no place for him in that land where only our true selves can go.

———

Luz huddled into her cloak as Red moved carefully down the path. Drifting veils of icy mist blurred both shape and voice, as if he were already fading into the Otherworld.

"It's hopeless. We can't go on if we can't see." Shaking his head, he scrambled back toward her. The stallion, hearing his master, pulled at the lead-rope she held, while the dun stamped nervously.

"No," Luz objected as he took back the reins. "We've come too far." Wind gusted suddenly and she clutched at her hood.

"Woman, you're crazy! Don't expect me to nurse you if you take the fever again!"

Foolish she might be, but when they left the cabin, the weather had been fair. They had set out in the afternoon three days before, ascending to a realm where silver firs two hundred feet tall reached out to a brilliant sky. Ahead, the high peaks shone in snow-clad splendor above lofty ramparts of bare gray stone. It reminded her of the austere splendor of the Father of Mountains. With each exhalation, Luz seemed to leave more of her mortality behind. When Red grew surly and silent she scarcely noticed, so exhilarated was she by the vistas revealed by each turn in the road.

But clouds had gathered overnight, and the view that had been so fair the day before now seemed cheerless and grim. That was when Red began to argue in favor of turning back, but Luz refused to listen. Soon they must leave the caravan trail. She did not know if it were a vain hope or Awahna itself that summoned her; but even if it cost her life, she had to heed that call.

They had gone scarcely a mile when Luz glimpsed a path leading off to the right. But mile by mile the air had dimmed and thickened, until they had to dismount and lead the horses, feeling their way along a path they could no longer see. She did not think the mist that surrounded them was any weather of the world. The illumination shifted with each change in the wind. She glimpsed mountaintops streaming snowy banners; then the wind whirled whiteness around them once more.

"We don't have a choice," she cried. "Surely it will be more sheltered farther down!"

"At the bottom of some cliff!" he exclaimed.

That was quite likely, Luz thought grimly. The last hour had gone far to destroy whatever pride her illness had left to her, she told herself as another shift in the wind showed sheer wall above and a drop below.

"I'm going back. This wind will strip me to the soul!"

"Maybe that's what is supposed to happen on this road," she replied.

"You're crazy. Can't you hear the wind demons calling you?"

Luz *did* hear them. But she had already faced those accusations in her dreams.

"Fix wouldn't let me go on alone," she replied, and recoiled at his laugh. She pulled on the reins and led the dun horse a few steps forward, slipping on slick stone.

"This place is too scary for him—and Jehan has already deserted you."

It was true that Luz hadn't seen the king since he had told her about Caolin. She had tried not to feel hurt by his defection.

"You're the one who has been abandoned," she snapped back at him. "You're the only one left, except for Jo!"

"If only that were so!" The edge of hysteria in his laughter was more chilling than the blast.

Luz turned, a new fear displacing the old. The red stallion whinnied in panic and plunged back up the trail. Through wind-blurred eyes she glimpsed Jo's white face, and now, at last, she dropped the dun's lead-rope and reached out to him.

"I'll die if I go farther," he said hoarsely. "And the Dragon will try to protect me! Run, Luz!" He tried to push her away. "He's coming! He'll kill you—he—"

The mist began to glow red around them as tremors ran through the whipcord muscles of his wiry frame. The precipice of her delirium yawned before them. He roared, the firm flesh writhing beneath her hands. Still Luz hung on, reaching for the courage to open her own soul to the terrible powers that ravaged his. The will and pride that had upheld her through so many dangers flung up one wall after another, but need wrenched them aside. And from somewhere deep within, power uncoiled in a sinuous swirl of white radiance, meeting his red rage and matching it in a supple interlace of energies. With delight, she recognized the power she had met in vision, and knew that she needed neither to control him nor to surrender, for they were one.

"Release me! I am the Serpent of the Sun!" The demand beat against her awareness.

"I am the Child of Light, and I will never abandon you!" her spirit replied. *"White Dragon meets Red, and the Phoenix rises!"* Consciousness exploded upward in a coruscation of rainbow light.

➻ 20 ➻

VEILS OF LIGHT

Luz opened her eyes on a whirl of rainbow veils spun from the spray of a waterfall. Its singing thunder throbbed in the air. Jo lay beside her, his breathing steady and profound, all the pain that had marred his features wiped away. She sat up, a little surprised to find she had neither wing nor claw, and flexed her fingers.

Before her, a swift stream flowed through green meadows; from the heights leaped a second waterfall. Then a new shift in the wind brought her the resinous scent of burning pine and a hint of garlic, and she realized that the drift of white she had taken for more mist was woodsmoke.

"Jo—" She shook his shoulder. "Jo, wake up. I think we're in Awahna."

His eyelids fluttered, and he raised himself on one elbow. "Oh, Guardians," he whispered. "Are we dead, Luz? We must be—I don't hurt anymore!"

"I don't know, but I feel quite substantial, and more *myself* somehow. And I am hungry." How odd that her body should seem so solid when, like Jo, she had expected to be a spirit by now.

"Look, there's a fire."

The wind changed as they approached it, and they saw a small man in an adept's gray robe stirring the pot that hung over the flames. Luz blinked. At first she had thought him bent and old, but as he smiled she saw that he was slightly built but vigorous. Beneath bushy brows, his brown eyes were as clear as the waters of the stream.

She paused, not quite certain who, or what, she was dealing with, and offered him the salutation of a student to a master of the College of the Wise. Jo's own training surfaced in his most courtly bow, and Luz felt his movements as she felt her own.

"Welcome to Awahna—" The master motioned them to sit on a log on the other side of the fire. "I always used to offer my visitors tea, but I suspect you could do with something more substantial." His voice was like coarse brown bread with honey. She tried to remember why that simile seemed familiar.

"Would you like some soup?" he continued. "You have traveled far."

That's true in more ways than one, thought Luz as she took the bowl. It was solid enough, carved from a redwood burl whose smooth whorled grain was a delight to the hand, and the soup he ladled into it was thick with barley and vegetables, seasoned with garlic and bay.

"I never heard that spirits ate garlic," whispered Jo. "We *are* alive!"

"Oh, yes," said the master. "You are still wearing your bodies. You will need them when you go back again."

Is that a promise or a warning? wondered Luz as the stew spread a warm glow through her limbs.

Jo nodded in thanks as the master handed him a bowl. "Are you the gatekeeper here?"

"'Gatekeeper'—that was well said, my prince, for my task has always been to open the door to the Mysteries. . . ."

"You know who I am?" Jo asked.

"Oh, yes. Do you?" In the master's brown eyes, light shifted as it did in the river's depths, yet he, like the river, remained the same.

Jo sat very still. "No. . . . All my life I have worn masks, until finally the masks wore me."

But I know, thought Luz, seeing in his blue gaze the fracturing of personality that had been his torment transformed to the faceting that reveals a jewel's essential fire.

The master nodded. "That is the question you must answer here. . . . To reach Awahna, you had to face the truth of who you have been. Some die of that testing. The great task of each life is to learn who you really are. In Awahna, your true self is the only person you *can* be. . . ."

"Is that why those who make this journey take new names when they return to the lands of men?" asked Jo.

"I think I know the last name that belonged to *you,*" Luz said suddenly. "You are the Master of the Junipers. My father loved you."

The master nodded. "You must tell Frederic that I got to Awahna safely. I know he grieved, but it would not have aided his progress for me to be with him. Nor, for that matter, would it have helped my own." He turned back to Jo. "I loved your father too. As I loved Jehan and Caolin," he added then. "Caolin survived his journey, but the wound of his failure to complete it never healed. Perhaps now both he and Jehan will be able to rest. But this time is for you." He rose to his feet.

"Come with me—"

"But what in the name of the Guardians possessed you to come here?" Julian swung his staff angrily, realized at the last moment that he was about to decapitate a bunch of poppies, and deflected it, wincing, against his leg.

"The Guardians themselves, or one of them, let me know it was time to leave Bongarde," said Rana calmly. "Put that thing down, Julian, before you hurt something. Foolish man—the reason I came *here* was because of you."

The stone houses of Elder clustered on rising ground where the Gold River joined the Eagle, between the Dorada Buttes and the foothills of the Snowy Mountains. When Julian had drawn his wife into the garden behind the headman's house so that they could quarrel in private, he had forgotten to lower his voice. They could probably hear him in Rivered.

"At least you had the sense not to come alone!" the king added a little more calmly.

"Garr's a good man. I'm hoping he will stay and ride with you," said Rana. This did not seem quite the moment to explain just how the old armsmaster had come into her service. But he had indeed proved useful, scouting out alternate routes and finding them places to hide when they sighted Sun patrols.

In the week and a half it had taken them to catch up with the king, there had been plenty of time to mull over what the Wanderer had said to her. He had known where she would find her husband. She clung to the hope that he would prove to be right about her son as well. Should she tell Julian what Garr had said about the Westrian boy who had been his pupil and his prisoner, or would that hope be too great a burden to add to those he already bore?

"So tell me what you have been doing here," she said instead.

The king, having relieved himself of an ill temper which she knew owed much more to anxiety than to anger, seemed relieved to shift the conversation to his army.

"I've spent the winter showing men the basic drill and then sending them home to teach their neighbors. They may not match the Suns' infantry in precision, but they can hold a shield wall and maneuver in close order now. And I told them to make arrows. They have been ordered to muster as soon as the spring planting is done, and may the Guardians get them here before the Suns arrive."

"And when is that likely to be?"

Frowning, the king gazed toward the valley. "As soon as the ground begins to dry, the enemy will head northward. But General Marsh can't afford to leave me undefeated at his rear. When the men of the Corona and Normontaine arrive, we'll have the numbers to match the Suns. Until then, our job will be to buy time." He broke off as Rana steered him to a bench beneath a willow tree whose masses of yellow catkins glowed gold in the light of the sinking sun.

"Sit, Julian. You'll do your army no good by fretting yourself to flinders before you've even sighted the enemy. Breathe. Listen to the birds. Remember what you're fighting for."

"You're right, of course." He took her hand. "This land is so fair it breaks my heart sometimes."

No, she thought, *it is not the beauty of the earth that breaks the heart but the deeds of the men who walk upon it.*

April was nearing its end. Birdsong rang from every tree and fencepost. Even here in the town, lark and mockingbird and robin poured forth a hopeful song. They were building their nests in the conviction that life would continue; could the rulers of Westria do less than they?

"The headman tells me I have arrived just in time for the festival," Rana said aloud.

"I tried to dissuade him," muttered Julian. "I'm more concerned with battlefields than barleyfields just now."

Rana slid an arm around his waist and he laid his own across her shoulders with a sigh. Her heartbeat speeded a little at the familiar weight and scent of him. He was all sinew and hard muscle now. Last summer he had come to her bed like a conqueror, but then he had been fresh from a victory. Now, despite his strength, he was worn with worrying. Could she awaken him, and with him, the land?

Above the new green that hazed the trees, the sculpted peaks of the Buttes were outlined in flame by the setting sun. Once Julian had nearly died there, but Rana had found the Jewel of Fire where he had hidden it, and awakened to love. Perhaps its power could work for them again.

She cleared her throat. "Yet the fields must be ploughed, and you are not only the leader of Westria's armies, but Master of the Jewels. I did the rites on the Red Mountain at the Spring Turning, but this festival needs both of us. Will you dance with me on Beltane Eve?"

———◆◆◆———

It must be almost Beltane, thought Jo. His heart lifted as he watched the play of light across the great split dome that dominated the valley.

"We've seen several sunsets," Luz replied. "But it *is* hard to keep track of the passage of time here."

Jo nodded. He was becoming accustomed to hearing his own thoughts on her lips, or finding that his sentence finished hers, when they even bothered to use words.

It was hard to say at what time of day Awahna was most beautiful. The log shelter in which they slept was only an antechamber to a hall whose grandeur outstripped any edifice of ancient times, walled in gray granite, curtained in waterfalls. In the early morning, when the sculptured face of the dome hung mirrored in the lake, its stillness brought healing to the soul. But as the day wore on, the sun woke the falls to noisy life. Sunset turned them to a torrent of jewels, but they seemed most exquisite shimmering in the light of the full moon. To pass from the contemplation of such beauty to dream was so gentle a transition that he wondered if he slept, and yet he was filled with energy each time he woke to a new day.

"Do you suppose we died on the journey without noticing?"

"We still eat and drink—spirits would have no need of such things."

Jo nodded, remembering the bowls of acorn mush sweetened with honey that had been waiting for them that morning. Here, eating was an experience that fed the spirit as well as the body, flavors and textures sending messages so vivid that he could *feel* their essence becoming part of his own. Luz was filling out again, her hair a dark cloud which no braiding could entirely tame. Her skin, normally a color somewhere between brown and cream, had a golden glow, and her eyes, as deep as the lake's dark waters, drew him inward until he touched her soul.

"I expected this place to be unearthly."

"But it is as real as our own flesh," her thought replied.

"And as close. I wanted to die when the Suns brought me back to Westria because suddenly I could feel my bond to

everything that I thought I had betrayed. But I don't feel that way here, even though the connection is a hundred times more profound."

He looked up as the bird that balanced on the pine branch above him sang out his name. Here, each drop of water and blade of grass hailed him, not as prince or master, but as one part of a body might recognize another, all of them together making up the entity he called Westria.

Luz belonged to it as well. He knew her now in a way quite different from their childhood friendship or the abrasive intimacy of their journey through the mountains. He was aware of her location even when they were apart, yet they were more than ever distinctly themselves. It was not the same way that his several selves had interacted; her essence complemented his own.

They sensed the Master of the Junipers's approach and turned to greet him.

"In the sunlight he looks solid," came a thought from Luz as the master moved through the shafts of light between the pines, *"but his shape shimmers when he passes through the shadow of the trees."*

"I see it too," Jo said aloud. "I thought that living in Awahna had preserved his life, but maybe he's a spirit after all. Not that it seems to matter here. . . ."

"It never occurred to me before," Luz said then, "but without darkness you can't see the light."

Jo laughed. "Someone should tell Mother Mahaliel."

Then the master was before them, eyeing them as if to gauge the progress of their internal transformations. "The air of Awahna agrees with you, my children. I think you are ready for another meeting now."

He led them toward a glade at the foot of an outthrust of granite that soared like a bastion into the sky.

"Are you taking us to the Guardians?" Jo asked.

"Does that surprise you? If they can be said to have a home that touches the physical world, it is here."

"It is your home, too," said Luz. "Are you one of the Guardians now?"

The master's stillness overflowed into laughter as the

snow-fed river overflowed its banks, a mirth so compelling that in a moment both Jo and Luz were laughing too.

"Not yet, not yet, though if you children from the College of the Wise continue to call on me, that is what I may become! It is a mistake, you know, to assume that once you have done with the body you have finished with choices. There are always more—to continue learning in this realm or to seek the lessons of another lifetime, or else to dwell on the threshold between." He looked back at Jo and Luz with a smile. "When I came here I wanted only rest from the labor of leading the College, but it seems I am so made that I cannot refuse those who ask my aid."

"Thank you," Luz said simply. "There is no one I would rather have had as our guide!"

As they crossed the meadow, a group of black-tailed deer looked up from their grazing, like all the animals here, quite unafraid. If deer was what they were. When Jo looked back, instead of the great stag who had guarded them, he glimpsed a tall figure crowned with horns of light.

"What are the Guardians?" he asked.

The master cocked his head at Luz.

"At the College they taught us that they are of more than one kind," she answered obediently. "Some arise from the energies of those plants or animals that they guard, while others express forces or elements. But some are born from the need of humankind."

"Not quite," the master replied. "The Powers have their own reality—it is the faces they wear that come from the minds of men."

"Like the Defender," Luz said then. "And the beings we call gods."

"And of which kind is the Lady of Westria?" asked Jo.

"Look, and see . . . ," the master said with a smile, gesturing toward a glade surrounded by tall fir trees.

From the outside, the place had seemed no different than any one of a dozen other spots whose beauty he and Luz had admired; but the moment Jo set foot within, he felt the difference, in the same way that he had known when he passed over the border of Westria. This was holy ground. Yet what he saw were the common things of earth—trees and grass, stone and sunlight—although he viewed them with a more reverent attention than ever before. Then, of a sudden, all the beauty of the glade coalesced into the shape of a woman with hair like sunshine and flower-decked robes that shimmered with every green the springtide could show.

"*Welcome, my prince.*" The words came from both within and without, and he remembered that thoughts need not be spoken here. "*You two have been brought to us so that we may all take counsel. What we have learned from your minds we add to our own knowledge. It is time to do something about the Children of the Sun. . . .*"

Beyond the Lady waited a tall, reddish-skinned figure with a green cloak, whom Jo recognized as the Lord of the Trees. Jo bowed as the air glowed crimson and the tall figure of the Defender strode up to join them, recognizing the Power he had sensed in Laurelynn. There was another close behind him, who for a moment reminded him disturbingly of Garr. Jo peered more closely at the single blazing eye beneath the Guardian's broad-brimmed hat, and realized that he had it backwards. The old armsmaster had sometimes looked like *him*.

"You know all of those here except, perhaps, the Wanderer," the master said then.

"Oh, he has met me, though he did not know my name. . . ." The gray-cloaked Guardian laughed as Jo stared open-mouthed. His tunic was the deep blue of the evening sky. "I gave you what help I could, lad," he said more gently. "I could not take the pain for you, but I did not leave you to bear it alone."

Luz took Jo's arm, gazing at the Wanderer suspiciously. "What are you doing here? You are no Guardian of Westria!"

"Am I not?" He cocked his head to gaze at her. "Your friend Vefara would recognize the shape I wear. Wherever men think and create and strive to know, I wander. This is a war of ideas as well as men. That makes it my business too."

"So what have you all decided?" Jo found his voice at last.

The air seemed to brighten as the Lady laughed. "Why so suspicious, my champion? We can only work through those who are able to hear us, after all," she answered his astonished stare. "It is not the way of the Guardians to interfere in human quarrels; but if the Suns prevail, the Covenant will indeed be broken. We may not bring down a second Cataclysm to defend you, but we would not send you to war unarmed."

She looked around her. "There is one more who should be with us—ah, there you are—" As she turned, a shadow uncoiled from the ground, upper body becoming that of a man with slitted yellow eyes and scaly patterned brown skin while the lower part retained the form of the snakes whose Guardian he was.

"It's the Rattlesnake!" Jo winced as Luz dug her fingers into his arm.

"Señor Serpent, be welcome," said the Lady of Westria.

"Thiss iss the prinsse?"

Jo made a wary bow.

"Sscared? But you are sserpents—both of you. Dragon iss sserpent too!" A rattle of laughter set the guard hairs prickling up and down Jo's arms. "Your foess make you fight, but they kill my sonss and ssteal my name! Will you take vengeansse for me?"

"The Red Dragon is a monster," Jo said in a shaking voice. "He kills friend as well as foe. I would rather die than allow him to devour my mind again."

"It is true," the Wanderer said then, "that it would be unwise to send the boy into battle with a sword in his hand. He has been trained too well. . . ."

Rattlesnake hissed thoughtfully. "But when White Dragon and Red fly together?"

We were one, and we were free. . . . Once more Jo and Luz were united, as they had been in that moment when they confronted the abyss and won entrance to Awahna.

"It might be possible," said the Defender. "One to be the weapon and one to wield it, as I am the Wolf's nurseling and the Wolf's binder—force by force still balanced and controlled. . . ."

Rage controlled by Love.

"Let him bear the power of Awahna," said the Lady of Westria. "Let us give him a Spear!" She turned to the Lord of the Trees. "Old One, your children feed on his fathers' bones. Will you give him a spearshaft to channel the power that is in the earth of Westria?"

The sound of the Guardian's laughter was the whisper of wind in the trees of the Sacred Wood. "That I will, and gladly—"

Even as he spoke, his form was stretching upward in a column of ruddy bark. Tiny needles showered down as his cloak extended into a green canopy. But the great Redwood was still shaking. Skeins of golden light ran sparkling up the trunk and out the branches, intensified, and suddenly an eight-foot branch came rattling down from above.

"Is redwood strong enough?" asked the Defender.

The Wanderer picked it up and laughed. "This branch will be—this piece might have come from the Worldtree itself."

"But a shaft without a point is only a staff, however strong," the Defender replied.

"The Dragon needs a fang," said the Lady. "Brother, I believe it is time for you to make your contribution."

"Lay down the sstaff," Rattlesnake replied.

As the Wanderer set it down, the Guardian seemed to sink in upon himself. Limbs became loops that uncoiled as he stretched along the branch until the wicked triangular head projected above its end like the point of a spear. A scintilla of light ran through wood and serpent alike. When it faded, the wood of the shaft shimmered with a faint pattern of scales, and from its end had grown a sharpened point that gleamed like hammered bronze.

For a moment they all stood looking down at it. Then a glitter in the air shaped Rattlesnake's outlines, as if he could not be bothered to manifest fully a second time.

The Lady of Westria laughed softly, then bent to take up

the spear. "Behold, my prince, the weapon of the Champion. You shall wear the red cloak of the Defender into battle, and wield the spear with the skill of the Wanderer. When you strike, the earth of Westria will strengthen your arm, and those who have stolen the name of Snake will flee or fall."

"And the White Dragon will be with you," thought Luz.

The Lady set the spear into Jo's hands. *"But for tonight, at least, you may forget your fears. This eve is the feast your folk call Beltane. Come, and join the dance!"*

The green of her robes swirled outward to become one with grass and tree, but her body grew brighter, shaped from a host of moving points of light. *That is her true form,* thought Luz. But even as Jo agreed, it too began to shift, interpenetrating a patterning of other lights that revealed the inner shapes of rocks and trees. The Awahna in which he and Luz had wandered was as tangible as any other place in Westria, but its apparent solidity was no more than a surface, behind which other modes of being might stretch to infinity.

Jo understood now why he and Luz had not met the Guardians until now. First, Awahna had to transmute their spirits and refine their senses until they could see with the inner eye.

———⊷◆⊷———

Luz was viewing everything in multiple levels now. Above the valley, a million points of light pulsed in time with the bright shapes that circled below. She blinked as a whirl of sparks coalesced into a canine shape with knowing eyes and a brush of tail, and from there became a wiry man with a mocking grin who still moved in a fiery glow. Coyote was here. Was that massive woman whose dark fur cloak glistened with silver Bear Mother? The green shimmer of a tree shrank suddenly to man-high, still clad in bristling dark green, dancing with a woman made of flowers. It was said that at Beltane those priests who served in the Sacred Wood joined the spirits of the trees in the dance, but every Guardian she had ever heard of seemed to be here.

From time to time one of them would approach her, and Luz would grow still beneath the measuring weight of that regard, only to be caught up again by the music of wind and water, birdsong and the percussion of galloping hooves. She had not been willing to dance at the College of the Wise, but here, to dance was as natural as breathing. She and Jo met and parted only to meet again, and she saw his spirit flowing through his long limbs like a trail of sparks kindled by his fiery hair.

The dance grew wilder, spiraling to a climax in whose center pulsed four vortices of light like living jewels. But even as Luz focused on those shimmering forms, they were changing. Now she saw a dark-skinned woman robed in leaf green. A slim, pale man in robes that flowed with all the colors of water appeared beside her, and another whose garment seemed spun of cloud. Last, light blazed up in the form of a woman whose draperies flashed with crimson and emerald fires.

"*Earth and water, air and fire, on these four all life depends. . . .*" The words of the initiation hymn echoed in memory.

The Guardians of bird and beast and plant surged around them, sweeping Jo and Luz forward. The Lady of Earth held out her hand.

"One day you will bear the Jewels, but for now, let our blessing armor you against your foe."

Linked in mind to Jo, Luz could not be sure to which of them the Lady was speaking. Perhaps it did not matter here. Now all the Guardians were gathering around them. Jo, already more open than she was, staggered, and she extended her own shields around them both to temper the intensity.

The enduring strength of Earth rose up to hold them as they received the fluid power of the Lord of the Waters. Inspiration set every particle to singing as Windlord fanned them with his wings. All these were powers to which Luz had been introduced at the College, but now the knowledge resonated within. Then heat seared her soul as she faced the fourth element, the one for whom no training had prepared her, and met the knowing smile of the Lady of Fire.

"Blessings you have had," she said softly, "but none has asked what you desire. . . ." She took Jo's hand. "Do you love this girl who stands by your side?"

Luz knew she ought to be indignant, but only truth was possible here. She had known that she loved *him,* and hidden it through all that time when he had not even known himself, much less her. But now the truth was as obvious as the light in the Lady's eyes.

"I love you. . . ." Were those words his or hers?

"For some, the fire of love does no more than warm the hearth and bake the bread," said the Lady, "and those are no small things. For some the fire kindles lust in the loins, or rage in the head." Her green eyes rested for a moment on Jo. "But for some it burns in the heart, and the world is blessed by its light. When the time is right for passion, I will surely bless your bed. But when you leave Awahna, much of what you understand now will fade. So tonight, let the heartfire burn!"

She set one hand on Jo's chest, with the other touched Luz. Radiance arced between them as two auras became one, and that, a part of the larger pattern as they were swept into the dance.

As the world turned toward midnight, the light of Awahna intensified and began to swirl outward, following the channels where energy radiated through the land. And where the people of Westria had gathered to bring in the May, that power flowed out to touch them, and they too became part of the dance.

"Rana, you know I was never much of a dancer," Julian complained as his wife drew him toward the bonfire. "At least let me finish this beer!" He hung back long enough to drain the earthenware cup and hand it to one of the brightly clad youngsters who was circulating with a pitcher of the same yeasty brew that he had earlier poured out as an offering.

"That's all right." Rana grinned at him. "If you are out of practice, the Guardians will appreciate the effort all the more!"

The musicians, seeing the king and queen approaching, began to play with renewed vigor, fiddles and woodwinds tossing the sprightly tune back and forth while the drumbeat galloped on. It was a simple round-dance of the sort country people enjoyed. A few wrong steps here and there made little difference so long as you kept moving.

Most of the townsfolk had gathered on the broad field that Julian had been using for a drill ground to drink and dance and welcome in the May. All over Westria, household and hamlet would be doing the same—except in those places that were held by the Children of the Sun. The invaders spent this night in prayer and fasting, warding themselves against the wild powers of the land.

It was not only Rana's arguments that had persuaded the king to bless the festival with his presence. Beltane was one of the great holidays of the year, and what good would it do to defeat their enemies if they forgot what they were fighting for? Whether or not the Guardians liked his dancing he could not say, though surely they must appreciate this celebration of the old ways now, when those ways were threatened by their enemy.

And whether it was the beer, which was quite good, or the music, the king was finding it easier to dance than he had expected. For one thing, he was in better training than he had been for years. As one dance followed another, he began to find release in stamping out the beat. And he could take pleasure in Rana's enjoyment. The exercise had brought color to her cheeks and a sheen of moisture to her skin. She had always been graceful, and with the firelight coppering the silver strands in her red hair, she could have been twenty years old once more. He would have to tell her so—he turned, but the musicians were bringing the piece to a close.

Murmuring, the people faced westward, where the jagged silhouette of the Buttes rose against the night sky. On the nearest peak, flame sparked as if a star had descended to signal hope to Westria and defiance to her enemies.

"The Beltane fire!" The cry went up around him. "Bring in the May!" Everywhere people were streaming toward the fields to find the branch of greenery that would bring the power of springtime into their homes.

Julian looked for Rana and saw her already mounted on the sorrel mare she had ridden from Bongarde.

"Where are you going?" he cried.

"To bring in the May—catch me if you can!"

As the queen reined the horse away, he saw a groom bringing up Shadow. She had planned this, damn her! Bemused, he noted the cloak tied behind his saddle and the green and yellow ribbons braided into the black mane. All around him people were smiling at the byplay between their king and queen. He would never hear the end of it if he refused her challenge now.

He swung into the saddle. Rana was already a flicker of red at the edge of the field, but Shadow was dancing with impatience to be after her. Julian could only trust that Rana knew where she was going, and that the night vision of the horse would be good enough for him to follow.

The queen had taken the road that led toward the Buttes. As Julian rode after her, he passed groups of laughing young people off to collect more substantial armloads for garlands. Soon most of them would separate into couples to encourage the fertility of the earth through the oldest of rituals. In this, as in so many other things, it was the duty of the king and queen to lead, and this year Rana had made sure they would do so.

Or at least he hoped so. For so long his mind had been bent wholly on fighting. It seemed months since he had looked at a woman with desire. Rather than fail on this of all nights, it would be better not to try; but Rana had enchanted him to a bed in the wilderness once long ago. He could only hope that she would find the power to awaken him again. She had been—strange—since her unexpected arrival, her manner an unsettling mix of anxiety, suppressed excitement, and joy.

As the town fell away behind him, the night seemed full

of whispers. The flicker of Shadow's ears told the king that the horse heard them too, but did not fear, though he plunged in surprise as a stag leaped across the path. They went on more slowly, winding up the oak-studded slopes at the base of the Buttes. *Histum Yani,* the people of this place had called it long ago, the "mountains in the middle" that linked this world with the one beyond. Julian was beginning to wonder if his wife meant to lead him all the way to the Otherworld, when Shadow lifted his head and whinnied and he heard the mare reply.

Rana was waiting for him in a circle of oak trees, her body a white blur against the dim grass. Julian tethered Shadow beside the sorrel mare and began to remove his own garments. Sparkles of light swam across his vision as he strained to see through the darkness. It took him a moment to realize they were not random. The spirits were wakening. He was seeing the life force in the trees and grass as he had learned to do when he first mastered the Earthstone. And now he realized that he could see Rana quite clearly as well.

He had forgotten that she could be so beautiful.

"Once you hid the Jewel of Fire in this mountain. I found it," the queen said softly. "Come to me, and I will give it back to you. . . ."

The king laughed, but his heart was pounding as his body responded to her call. "Lady, I am here to serve you."

He came to her, and she drew him down beside her on the grass. Now he could feel the magic in the night. It was Beltane, and the Guardians of Westria were putting forth their power.

As her kiss laced sweet fire across his skin, he realized that he did not need the power to take, only the willingness to give. *I am the one who offers, and I, the offering,* he thought as he moved upon her. *As I would give my blood for Westria, I pour out my life for you now.* And as he did so, he became a conduit for the magic, and it passed from king to queen, and thence to the land.

21

NIGHT BATTLES

"The Ancients had a story about a man and a woman who were expelled from Paradise," said Luz as she guided the dun gelding along the trail. "There was even a snake. I know just how they must have felt when the gates swung closed."

"At least the Guardians did not send us out empty-handed," Jo replied, fingering the textured length of the spear tied to his saddle. The scarlet cloak of the Defender was bound there as well. They had left the high mountains behind, and through the pines that fringed the foothills they could see the Great Valley, veiled in brown haze.

"Or on foot—" She patted her pony's neck.

When the mists had swirled between them and the falls that guarded the gateway to Awahna four days before, they had found their horses, saddled and laden with provisions, awaiting them in the care of a white mare. The fact that Jo's stallion stood respectfully beside her was enough to suggest that this was no ordinary equine but one of the Guardians, even without the shimmer of light that streamed from her silvery mane. For the next two days the other two horses had been unnaturally well behaved. But this morning, the red stallion had taken a nip to bring the dun into line. How long, Luz wondered, before she and Jo began to fall into old habits as well?

"Now I know why the adepts don't say much about what happened to them in Awahna. How can you put it into words that those who haven't been there will understand?" Jo said at last.

"Even those who have been there might have trouble. I

think Master Granite's experience must have been quite different from what happened to me."

Jo looked at her and began to laugh with a freedom she had not heard since they were very young. *This is who you are,* she thought fiercely, *and I will fight to help you stay that way.*

"Luz, even in the annals of Awahna, if they have such a thing, I doubt anyone has experienced exactly what happened to you and me!" After a moment's thought, he laughed again. "And are you going to take a new name— 'Mistress of the Light'? Folk will think you've been hired to kindle the lamps in Laurelynn!"

"Thank you, 'Master Serpent'!" she replied, then shook her head. "People had barely gotten used to the names we took at our initiations. I see no need to change them, even though their meanings are different now."

Jo nodded. "Most people finish their initiations in three weeks. I think that ours have taken three years!"

"Just as long as it doesn't take us another three years to find the king. I heard General Marsh say they would head north for the summer's campaign as soon as the grasslands were dry. We can travel faster than an army. We'll head straight up the valley. If we overtake them in time, maybe we can stop the fighting. . . ." Her voice trailed off as she recalled the fanatical determination of the Children of the Sun.

"Stop it? Or join it?" The bronze spearhead glinted balefully as Jo touched the shaft.

From outside his window Tadeo Marsh heard the tramp of feet as yet another file marched past. Twelve hundred foot soldiers were marching out of Rivered. Too many of them were half-trained converts, but he had to leave the steadier men to garrison the conquered towns. Most of their light cavalry were converts as well. He was keeping some two hundred back to guard their march, but the vanguard of the army, with five hundred horse archers, was on its way. He would head out with the main body tomorrow morning. If he ever finished tallying the list of supplies, he corrected, turning back to the slate on which he had been figuring. He looked up again as the front door banged open.

"Tadeo, come! You must come quick! Our Mother has wakened!"

Tadeo looked up from his breakfast to see Sarina hovering in the doorway, her eyes alight, arms beckoning like the beating wings of some swift bird. As he got to his feet, he kept his features impassive, not quite certain whether his chief emotion was consternation or amazement.

The woman had lain without speaking for nearly six weeks, responding only enough to swallow a little gruel. That she had survived, much less recovered her senses, was a miracle. He should be pleased at any news that made Sarina so happy, but Mahaliel had been half-mad already. He suspected she might have been easier to deal with as a dead saint than as a living prophet.

Nor, he reflected as he picked his way among the bags and boxes set ready to load for the march tomorrow, did he think much of her timing. To launch a campaign was a complex operation, and to stop the process now would throw everything in disarray; but perhaps if his presence was needed, he could catch up with the army. Small groups could go much faster, but the columns, with their spear-wives and supplies, would do well to make twelve or fifteen miles a day.

As Sarina pulled him through the streets, Tadeo could see that the news had spread through the town. The grim resolve with which the Children of the Sun had faced the summer campaign was shifting to an omen-driven fervor. No doubt Mother Mahaliel's recovery would cause them to fight harder; whether they would fight better, he did not know.

A chattering crowd had gathered around the Mother's dwelling. The porch was heaped with early summer flowers. As he mounted the steps Tadeo waved aside the questions.

"Indeed, the Sun's been merciful, but be patient, lads—'til I've seen the Holy One I cannot tell you more."

In the house, the atmosphere had an excitement that reminded him of an army camp before a battle. Tadeo grimaced as he felt his own heartbeat speed, knowing he might need that added alertness here. He had seen soldiers awaken from such comas whole in body but out of their wits. On the other hand, with Mother Mahaliel, how could you tell?

Bett came out to greet them. Whatever had happened to her mistress, the woman had certainly recovered her old assurance. She ushered them into the main room with all the self-conscious ceremony of a factotum of the emperor in the old days before the war.

Tadeo paused as he entered the main room, blinking. All the windows had been thrown open, and for a moment all he could see were bright shapes moving there. Sarina hurried past him and cast herself down before the brightest, sobbing.

"Oh Mother, Mother! Sun's blessings, you're back!"

Tadeo followed, adjusting vision showing him a figure that must be Mother Mahaliel enthroned in the great chair by the hearth. She had always been a big woman with a certain massive power. She was still tall, but she had lost flesh. Now she was like a lantern, her bones a framework covered by stretched skin through which the light of her spirit glowed. As that lambent gaze turned toward him, he found himself going down on one knee.

"My Lady—" His knee hurt. He clung to that pain until he had the control to look at her once more.

"Oh, my child, I have seen such wonders!"

The voice was a little creaky, but Tadeo could feel her magic, like a tide of warm honey, easing the tensions in his soul. He had been priding himself on retaining an independent spirit, but he was just as vulnerable to her spell as the least of her worshipers. The only difference was that during those weeks when her eyes were closed he had realized that he would rather be free.

"Truly the Sun is with us! His radiance fills me 'til I can scarcely contain the power!" Her laugh sent a chill through Tadeo's skin. As he looked up, her aura brightened, and a spark blossomed at her fingertips. Still laughing, she gestured toward the hearth, and the logs from last night's fire burst into flame. A gasp of awe ran around the room.

Fools, thought the general. *Now she is* really *dangerous.*

Mother Mahaliel sank back into her chair. "While my body lay as if dead, I was taken into His kingdom. I saw the spirits of Light dancing in their files and companies . . . dancing. . . ." For a moment her voice faded as if the vision were taking her once more. "Up and down they moved, as if they climbed a great staircase, bearing the souls of the pure to bliss and returning again.

"And then it was given to me to foresee the future . . . ," she went on. "I watched as the Children of the Sun marched through a land all golden. The rivers ran with blood, but the Sun's radiance filled the land. I saw one sun in the sky, and one ruler over all these lands. Believe me, my son—we will go forth to victory!"

If that's a prophecy, I'll take it! thought Tadeo. He sank back on his heels and forced himself to meet that golden gaze.

"My lady, give me your blessing. Your army is already marshaled and ready to march upon the foe. My scouts report that the king of Westria is gathering men to the north of here. We have divided into three columns to make our way up the valley. When we have overcome their king, we will rejoin to attack the fortress called the Hold. I will leave a detachment to guard you here, and—"

"Here?" Mahaliel's laughter rang through the room. "But my strength is already coming back to me. I will travel with my people as I have always done—"

"But—" The general's protests died as cheering erupted outside. People must have been listening at the windows. And perhaps it was for the best, he thought as he bowed his head in acceptance. If Mother Mahaliel traveled with the army he would be able to keep an eye on her.

On the way home he started to say as much to Sarina, as soon as he could fit a word into her excited commentary.

"An eye? You mean you want me to join her household?"

Tadeo felt his heart sink at the new brightness in *her* eyes. For him, the most they had ever held was a gentle glow.

"No!" he replied, more sharply than he had intended. "If I am to do the Mother's work, I will need you," he added diplomatically. "But surely you may spend time with her, carry messages and the like, for on the march I'll sometimes be unable to visit before it's time for her to seek her bed."

"Oh, it's true—she must take care!" Sarina's eyes rounded with anxiety and she reached out to take his hand. Singing filled the street as files of white-clad soldiers went by.

> *Through plain and desert we march on,*
> *Our purpose still unyielding,*
> *No mortal power shall bar our way,*
> *For holy fire we're wielding!*

Tadeo shuddered, remembering how the fire had leaped from Mother Mahaliel's hand. He returned the automatic salutes as the soldiers strode past, but their eyes were fixed on some distant glory. The final verse drifted back as the last of the company marched past.

> *The Sun He is our Guide,*
> *His will we must abide,*
> *This single truth we know—*
> *Where He would have us go,*
> *We'll follow Him forever.*

Once, thought the general, they had sung about a promised land where they would find a home. Surely, whatever they might sing, that was still the goal. All he had to do was to catch the king in order to claim Westria.

"No, no—of course we don't want them to catch us—only to think that they can!" Julian grinned at Osleif's confusion.

A few miles away, a cloud of dust showed where the nearest of the Suns' columns was marching northward. Between them, blue water veined a maze of reeds and willow isles that lay in drowsy peace beneath the blue lid of the sky. To the east, the Dorada Buttes rose like a fortress from the flat valley floor. They drew the eye, but it was not yet time to seek their shelter. The morning had seen a brief, inconclusive skirmish between a party of scouts and the Westrian advance guard. The king had made sure that a few of the enemy got away. Now he waited with his guard in the shelter of a noble stand of valley oaks, resting through the heat of the day.

"I don't understand. Aren't we going to have a battle after all?" asked Osleif.

The boy had come back to him just after Beltane with a group that had slipped away under the noses of the Suns who garrisoned Laurelynn, bright-eyed and eager to earn a place in the tales of Julian's heroic resistance. The survivors of Las Costas were still fighting a guerilla war under Lady Carola, but the men of the Royal Domain had answered the king's call, and more companies were making their way across the coastal mountains from Seagate, following Eric and Orm. The people who lived here had turned out to serve as scouts and guides. The remainder of the army lay hidden now in other patches of woodland, waiting for the darkness to cover their own advance. From somewhere nearby came a soft snore.

"Oh, yes," the king said aloud, "there will be a battle— but not until we can fight on *my* terms! You were at Condor's Rest, Osleif—you saw what happened when we did not choose the ground!"

A little of the eagerness left the boy's face and he nodded soberly. "So what do you plan to do?"

"Normally, when you are threatened by an invasion, you should make attacking so difficult that the enemy will find it more profitable to go home. If you have ever trapped a rattlesnake, you know that a beast with no escape is more dangerous because he has nothing to lose. If you leave an escape route, a cornered force will take it."

Marcos and Lenart, who were nearest, suppressed smiles, having heard all this at staff meetings—many times. It had become Julian's prayer, his affirmation, his litany. A covey of ducks floated past, quacking softly as if there were no such thing as war.

"But the Suns have no homes to go to," objected the boy.

Julian nodded. "That's so, but the instinct to escape is still there. If we can let some through, then close the trap again, we can divide their forces into groups small enough to handle." *I hope*, he thought. *If we can deceive them. . . .*

"But isn't that what we have been doing since they arrived?"

"Not quite. This time we have allies on the way. If we lead the enemy through marsh and mire until the northerners arrive, we can whittle down the Suns' numbers and increase their frustration. Smashing their way through our army will look like an escape by then."

"We certainly have the marshes," muttered Lenart, waving at the reeds before them.

Julian nodded. His warriors were willing, but in the past year it had become increasingly clear to him that his most powerful ally must be his land. The upper reaches of the Dorada were fed by mighty rivers that came down from the Snowy Mountains. Though the heat of the approaching summer had turned the grass on the higher ground from green to gold, streams still swollen by snowmelt had overflowed into the marshes that covered much of the central plain. In a flood year, the whole valley could turn into an inland sea. But today the interweaving of woodland and water, marsh and meadow, made a lovely picture beneath the hot blue of the sky.

"When we do fight, it will be at a time and place of *my* choosing," said Julian. "Their general won't expect subtlety from me, and the Guardians know he has reason. If we can keep him from finding out about the men coming down from the Corona and Normontaine, he won't see the trap until it closes." His glance turned toward the Buttes once more.

Lenart slapped at a fly and laughed. "And now that you know our plans, young man, you had better keep close to the king. You'd have to kill yourself before you let the Suns capture you, to keep from revealing all to the enemy."

"I wouldn't tell!" Osleif said stoutly, and then, "Do they torture prisoners?"

"They don't need to," said Lenart, the laughter leaving him. "Their demon-priestess captures men's minds. . . ."

———⟫⟪———

Mother Mahaliel's uncovered hair blazed like living gold in the harsh light of noon. It made Tadeo sweat just to look at her, but the woman had rejected all attempts to provide her with a hat, veil, or sunshade. Perhaps her internal temperature was such that the June heat that had turned the upper valley to an oven caused her no discomfort. The men whispered that she fed on sunlight, and it might even be true. Certainly she ate little enough at their evening meals.

In one thing her vision had at least been truthful. They had left the formation the locals called the Dorada Buttes behind them. To the north a snowcapped peak floated mockingly above a blue horizon, but now that the grass had ripened, the meadows and foothills were all gold. The general rode near the head of the middle column on the old road, or in places the causeway, that more or less followed the course of the Dorada. To his right, dust marked the progress of his mounted troops; while on the left, the more agile infantry made their way along the edge of the marshes. A screen of scouts guarded them against surprise.

He felt another trickle of perspiration wind down his back and sighed. He would have preferred to travel by night as they had sometimes done in Aztlan, but the terrain here was too uncertain. At least in the daylight he could read reports while he rode.

Tadeo broke the seal on a missive from Elaya and unrolled it. Idomeneo Yans, whom he had left to command the garrison at Los Leones, was inquiring, rather wistfully, about the progress of the northern war. In the south, he reported, there had been some trouble with guerillas holed up in the mountains of Las Palisadas, but they were a small and scruffy band, and for the most part, the country had been quiet. Did the general need reinforcements? Yans asked hopefully.

The general repressed a smile. No dedicated soldier enjoyed garrison duty, and Yans had been one of his early recruits. But a large army could be a liability. He had foragers out, of course, to pick up what they could. The marshes were full of waterfowl, and the hills were rich in grass. But they were far too many to live completely off the land. To the four thousand trained soldiers were added a third again as many noncombatants—the spear-wives and drovers, armorers and farriers, and the others whose labor supported them. The pace of the baggage train slowed their progress, but it carried the supplies that would get them to the Hold.

There was no hope of taking the Corona by surprise, he reflected, but a fortress could not run away, and these Westrian towns all had community storehouses that might have been set up for the convenience of invading armies. Of course, a siege would pin down his own army too, and make them even more vulnerable to the kind of hit-and-run attack King Julian's irregulars were annoying them with. It would be better to find and destroy the Westrians now.

The thought was not a new one. He had almost taken their king in Elaya, and at Sanjos and Laurelynn. Since then, the man had been damnably elusive. But he was out there—Tadeo squinted across the marshes—he could feel the presence of the Westrian king.

I still owe you for the blood I shed in Sanjos, he thought as the scar on his leg gave a twinge. *Where are you, Julian?*

As if in answer, a tumult ahead resolved itself into the muddied form of one of their scouts, chivvying a bound native up the road with the enthusiastic help of a file of Suns.

"Found him in th' marshes, sir. He says he's just huntin', but I think he was tryin' to spy!"

"Why should he bother?" observed the general. "That dust cloud will tell everyone in this province where we are. But bring him along. It's not what he knows about us but what he might know about the Westrians that interests me. . . ."

The prisoner let out a squeak of terror. He really was a pitiful object, brown as the mud with which he was liberally spattered, and clad only in a pair of short breeches. One of the soldiers was carrying the bow and arrows with which he had been armed.

By the time they stopped for the night, the captive had been fully primed by soldiers' tales. A meadow near the river had offered them a good campsite. The white tents of the files were grouped according to their companies on the higher ground and the more valuable animals pastured nearer the river, where the grass was high. The rest of the beasts had been taken in small groups to graze until it was fully dark, when they would be brought in and picketed by the wagons.

The man was obviously relieved to find himself confronted by Mother Mahaliel and her women, but that, thought Tadeo as he followed the guards to the campfire, was because he didn't know Mother Mahaliel.

"My poor child—," she was saying. "Have they given you food or water?" She gestured and Cho-cho brought a waterskin and a flap of warm panbread. White-eyed, the prisoner devoured it, then settled back on his haunches, watching the priestess warily.

"Tell me who you are, my son. Do you have a family? A dwelling?" Mother Mahaliel leaned forward. In the half-light, the glow on her face could have come from the fire. "Don't be afraid to tell me—truly, the religion I preach is one of love. . . ."

Now, as the setting sun cast a gentle light across the encampment, it was easy to believe that. A rhythmic murmur rose and fell as the priests attached to each company led the men in evening prayers. Drifts of woodsmoke carried the scent of this evening's meal—the daily ration of rice and beans with whatever wildfowl the hunters had brought in, seasoned with herbs the women gathered on the march and the spices they had in store. Sarina had a gift for making the most unpromising ingredients into a tasty stew. He wished he was sitting in front of his pavilion now, watching her as she moved back and forth before the fire.

To his relief, Mother Mahaliel had not objected when Tadeo told her of his marriage. Since her recovery, she no longer seemed to care about a number of things. Whether this was good or not remained to be seen. Tonight, each spear-wife would sleep with one of the men of her file. But Sarina would be in the general's bed; his flesh quickened at the thought of her sweetness, and he wrenched his attention back to the prisoner. From the man's mumblings, they gathered that he was a bird-hunter who lived in the marshes. He'd had a wife, but she died of fever some years back.

"And you know the marshlands as a farmer knows his fields, isn't it so?" Mahaliel had moved closer. As the night grew darker, she shone more brightly, drawing from the prisoner the simple boasts of a hunter, and when his focus wandered, gently bringing him back to talk of paths and islands once more.

"And then the riders came, didn't they?" she said softly. "Men from outside, trampling the feed and scaring off the birds. But they don't know the paths as you do—where are they blundering now?"

She knelt beside the man, and her golden aura expanded to include him. Tadeo felt a little sick, watching the fear in the man's face give way to a wondering smile.

"Oh, they gotta bunch o' men an' horses up near where th' creek comes in. You look like my wife, y'know?"

"That's because I love you," she replied. "Are those men still there, or have they moved on?"

The bird-hunter was yearning toward her now like a plant that turns toward the sun. "When 'tis dark they move, but there's only one way they kin go. You want t' see my house? 'Tis right pretty in th' wetlands when ye know how t' see."

"First we must make the loud men go away," Mahaliel said firmly. "These are my sons—go with them, show them where the loud men are. And remember—" She set her hands on either side of his face and held his gaze. "You belong to me. . . . ."

———◦◦◦———

"Was it ethical, do you think, to use that poor man as a hunter sets a wooden decoy in a pool?" asked the queen. The sun had set, and as the sky dimmed, long shadows were reaching across the valley. Only the tips of the Dorada Buttes and the highest peaks of the Ramparts still retained a rosy glow. An evening stillness held the world, in which the thud of a hoof from among the waiting horses, the chink of harness, or a soft murmur of conversation were no more intrusive than the soft quackings of ducks in the reedbeds and the hollow croak of the bittern from across the marsh. Even the singing of the men who had gathered around the fire on the island before them seemed muted. Were the Suns close enough to hear them too?

Master Granite shrugged. "All we know of the enemy tells us that so long as the man cooperates, the Suns will do him no harm. But he refused to leave his home, and his neighbors say he's too simple to lie. So our choices were to imprison him ourselves or to let him make himself useful. Making sure he heard what we want him to pass on was the best we could do."

Both of them looked across the pool to the high ground where the decoy campfire made a cheerful point of light in the gathering dark.

A very practical attitude, thought Rana, if rather lacking in soul. "Is our goal in life to be useful?" she said aloud, touching the bag of medical supplies beside her. However the fighting went, they would be needed soon.

He looked at her a little oddly. "A few are called to the Great Work, while others seem to have no purpose at all. The rest may as well help each other on the way."

"And what about love?"

"Ask Mother Mahaliel," answered the adept. "According to her, you need no more. Simple minds find it an attractive theology. Her general knows better. Among the Suns, Love is only a means to Power."

"And if you chose one virtue to serve, what would it be?" she asked then.

He gave her that quizzical look again. "I suppose . . . Truth, in whose clear light all is known."

Rana frowned. Gods might be able to face such truth; she was not so sure about men. Or some gods—she had been trained by Coyote, after all, who if asked to consider two sides of a question would probably find three.

Remembering the bright spirit she had sensed in Luz, she wondered how the girl had dealt with this man, and then, how she was dealing with Johan. Garr had said the fugitives were heading into the mountains. The scouts who crept unseen each night to listen at the Suns' campsites would have heard if they had been captured. But where had they gone? The Wanderer's news had only left her with more questions.

But at least she could now keep an eye on Julian. Her bed might be a hard one, but it was not empty, and if this meant she also must listen to the king's nightmares, that was both her right and her duty. She could see his focus narrowing toward that moment when he would stake all on the battlefield, and though they never spoke of it, she knew that he would pour out his own blood if that was the price of victory. She treasured every hour she held her husband's hard-muscled body in her arms, knowing they might be numbered.

Julian was out there somewhere now, hiding in the marsh with the rest of his men. The last she had seen of him was a flash of white teeth in a mud-blackened face as they moved off through the reeds.

She had not told her husband what she had learned from Garr and the Wanderer. *I am like that queen from the Lady of Heronhall's tale who knew all but said nothing,* she thought, *and now I know why. Hope is a distraction that Julian cannot afford.*

But hope was all that Rana had.

Moment by moment, the heavens were altering from lemon green to a translucent turquoise that deepened to sapphire. The willows that screened the path lifted an exquisite tracery against the sky. A mosquito sang softly in the stillness, and the queen slathered more mint oil on her face and neck. If the wind changed, the enemy would be able to track them by scent alone. She pitied the men who waited in the marsh with only mud to protect them.

"Fly away little sister! Feed on those who've grown fat on the spoils of Westria." Rana smiled when the insect's humming faded. And then the night exploded in a tumult of shouting men and flashing swords.

She surged to her feet, striving to make sense of the shadows that leaped before the fire. The Westrians who had waited there had not been as heedless as they looked; they would be grabbing the weapons they had laid ready as their hidden allies drew their bows and let fly. Men screamed as the arrows bit. From farther down the road came the deep grunt of a bear, followed by a hysterical neighing as the horses that had brought the enemy here stampeded into the night. Rana grinned, knowing that Bera was near.

A pillar of glowing steam shot up through the trees as someone doused the fire. The Westrians who had waited there would be retreating to muddy their own faces while the rest continued the attack. Julian had ordered his men to fight in silence. The Suns were doing the shouting, and they were growing shrill with fear. The great danger to the Westrians had been in the first moments of the battle. Now, deprived of horses on which to flee and with no light to see their way, the enemy would find the marshes a maze of terror. The queen considered their plight with grim satisfaction. Once, she had been merciful. Perhaps she could learn compassion again when this war was done.

"Scream!" She sent the thought toward her enemies. *"You say all powers but your own are demons? Then as demons we will hunt you down!"*

Bared fangs gleam in darkness. A claw slashes the night and blood soaks the ground. Men are screaming. He feels their terror as he feels the feral rage of their foes. . . .

Jo fought free from the tangle of blankets, his own shriek echoing in his ears. The covers heaved again as Luz sat up and grabbed him, the grip of her small hands surprisingly hard. The blue oaks that sheltered their camp were masses of shadow, but the stars were fading into a gray pre-dawn sky.

"It's all right, it's all right," she murmured sleepily. "I'm here."

Jo shuddered, his inner ear still resonating with those screams. "Hold on to me for a minute—just hold me." He felt Luz stiffen. "What's wrong?"

"You sounded like Fix," she whispered.

"No, I'm not Fix, and I'm not the Dragon," he answered bitterly. "But I'm beginning to remember why I welcomed them. It's hard to be only Jo."

"You are not alone!" Luz said fiercely. Her shape was as dark as the oaks whose branches now showed black against the paling sky, but her spirit warmed him as if he sat next to a fire.

"I know." He put his arm around her, appreciating the wonderful contradiction of her strength and softness. By repeating their recollections of Awahna to each other as they rode, they had managed to fix the content in memory, though the feeling was beginning to fade. But the week and a half it had taken them to get up the valley had not weakened the spiritual connection they had developed there. "That's what's keeping me sane. But I was wrong about being alone in my head. I used to hide and let the others take over. There's another inside me that I never let out because I didn't know him—the prince of Westria. Now I am both of them all the time, and *he* feels everything that's happening in the land."

Carefully he extended that awareness, relieved to sense nothing more violent than the severing of spirit in the grass as their horses tore at the last green blades beneath the trees. That was less a death than a transformation, part of the natural cycle that included the slow growth of the oaks and the watchful hunger of the buzzard circling above.

Luz sighed. "Was it another dream?"

He looked down at her and saw her face grow bright as the first light filled the sky. "I hope that's all it was! I saw men with animal faces, blood everywhere, an orgy of killing. I could feel their fury. . . . But what made it so terrible was that they were Westrians!"

In the afternoon light, the peaks of the Dorada Buttes gleamed on the horizon as if carved from gold. At the sight, Luz felt her heart beat faster. More than three weeks had passed since they left Awahna—it was now nearly June. The last time she had seen those buttes, she had been a prisoner of the Suns. The memory might almost have belonged to someone else, so much had happened since that day. But since then her understanding of identity had become rather more flexible, so perhaps it was all the same.

Jo heard her laugh and turned in the saddle, one eyebrow quirking in inquiry.

"I feel like my own ghost," she said in explanation. "When I see my family, they will ask me what happened, and what will I say?"

He nodded understanding. As the sun sank toward the horizon, it burnished his hair to a deeper flame. It had grown out sufficiently for people to recognize him, but no one knew better than she how illusory any assumption that this was the same boy who had disappeared two and a half years ago would be.

"I'm afraid, too, but it isn't going to matter if we don't reach them before the battle," he said soberly. "The land trembles to the tread of marching feet. The armies are gathering. Tonight I think we should push on as far as we can."

Her gaze moved from his face to the long spear tied to his saddle. Was it the sun that lent it that extra glow? She reached out to clasp his hand, feeling the life in him running strong beneath the warm skin.

"We will be in time."

22

THE SONG OF THE SPEAR

In the tents below someone was singing. Even from the top of the slope Julian could hear the song. The army of Westria lay encamped in a motley gaggle of shelters nestled into the folds of the hill on the northern side of the Dorada Buttes. As the late early-summer dusk fell across the land, campfires blossomed among them like red flowers, and the rich scent of roasting meat drifted upward on the breeze.

"They sound so cheerful," said Lenart.

"It is often so before a battle," answered the king. "It was like this when we waited for Caolin's army on the Seagate Road. There's a relief at knowing the danger will be over soon." He sighed as a breath of wind stirred his hair.

"One way or the other," muttered the younger man.

"Yes," Julian said gently. "By tomorrow's battle we will stand or fall." *And I will stand victor upon that field or it will be my grave.* The two outcomes were not exclusive, but it seemed to him that his life would not be too high a price to pay. This war had gone on for too long, and he was tired.

His scouts reported that while the Suns' baggage train continued its slow progress up the valley, their army had turned back and was camped now at a dry meadow in the marshlands about five miles to the north. From here, Julian could see the smoke of their cookfires smudging the sunset sky.

"The envoys will be returning soon. Do you really think the Suns will accept our terms?" Lenart asked.

"No," said the king, "but we had to try. While the envoys are talking, our men will have time to finish the defensive ditches and build brush blinds to screen the archers. If they are never used, I do not think anyone will complain."

"Well, we will know soon. If we go down now," Lenart added hopefully, "we can eat before they arrive."

Julian sighed. Behind him, the foothills of the Snowy Mountains were fading from rose to gray. To the west, a few clouds still flew banners of flame above the dark masses of the coastal range. In the valley, the last light gleamed on the curves of the Dorada River and the marshland pools.

This place is like the top of the Red Mountain . . . , he thought then, *as if with one sweep of my arm I could gather in the whole of Westria.* "Give me a moment longer," he said aloud. "The land looks very lovely from up here. . . ."

"The land is rich," said Lord William. "Why should we fight when there is enough for all? My king has sent me here to see if we can come to terms." Night had fallen. The chirping of the frogs in the marshes seemed louder in the silence that followed his words.

The Westrian envoy was a nice-looking young man, thought Tadeo Marsh, with all the softness worn off him by a year in the field, although men said his sister was the fiercer fighter. The Westrian priest who had come with him surveyed his enemies with a disdainful glare.

The commanders and clan-fathers gathered beneath the broad awning were muttering, but Mother Mahaliel, enthroned between two of the torches, sat like an image in her white robes. The general sighed.

"Why should we negotiate for what we can take? We have beaten everyone who opposed us so far."

That was not completely true—against the guerilla tactics that had whittled away at the Sun forces during the march north there was little he could do. The frustration that had impelled him to turn back and pin King Julian against the Buttes was as much the army's as his own. Whatever had impelled the Westrian king to offer formal battle? He could only suppose that the Westrians must be as tired of hit-and-run warfare as the Suns were.

"Why? Because enough men have already died. We will ask the Guardians to grant room for your people," Lord William replied. "For a time we would need to settle some of the protected lands, but most of your men are unmarried, and in a generation—"

"We will breed sons on *your* women, puppy, and in a generation the people as well as the land will be ours!" snapped Loris Chiel. The four Westrians who had ridden as escorts to the envoys stiffened, but subsided as they remembered that they were unarmed in the midst of their enemies.

"They will be barren!" snapped the Westrian priest. "And your fields will not bear! Do not mock the Guardians!"

Master Granite, they had named him, of high rank in the Westrian religion, though one would not think it to look at his worn gray robe. But Tadeo recognized the fanatical gleam in his dark eyes. The men had made the sign against evil when he rode in, but if the Westrian had the demonic powers that the Suns ascribed to the enemy's priesthood, he had given no sign of it so far.

"Why not?" muttered someone behind him. "Seems t' me they haven't helped you much so far!"

"The king"—Master Granite's face darkened—"holds to the Covenant, and so far you have mostly stayed within its bounds. But I think you have already felt the displeasure of some of the minor powers. . . ."

If the looks this provoked had been daggers, the priest would lie bleeding on the ground, thought the general. The hysteria that swept the camp when they encountered some new pest had more than once threatened to end the campaign. Mother Mahaliel leaned forward, fixing the enemy priest with her golden gaze.

"Our soldiers will destroy your army, and your demons will bow to the power of the Sun. . . ."

Tadeo repressed a grin. He had wondered how long she would endure their defiance. If these had been real negotiations, her interference could not have been tolerated, but the outcome was not in doubt. When his battle-hardened squares faced the Westrian rabble, the Westrians would fall. And without King Julian's leadership, the two provinces the Suns had not yet conquered would surrender as well.

"We shall see—," began Master Granite.

"Indeed we shall!" Mother Mahaliel overrode him. "Together," she added, signaling to the women of her guard.

Before Tadeo could object, two of the more muscular guards had grabbed the Westrian priest. The man cast an outraged look at the general.

"We are envoys, sacred in our office!" cried Lord William.

"You cannot take hostages!" Tadeo exclaimed.

"Not hostages—witnesses." Mother Mahaliel smiled sweetly. "And I will have the princeling as well—"

As more guards reached for Lord William, Master Granite drew breath and began to intone a Word of Power. Tadeo was still clapping his hands to his ears when light flared, whipping around the prisoner with blinding force and cutting off the sound. If the general had not been so angry, the priest's look of disbelief would have made him laugh.

"They are mine," said Mother Mahaliel, but he could hear the steel beneath her sweetness. "Will you dispute me, General?"

Tadeo's officers looked shocked, but the clan-fathers and the men who had crowded forward when the shouting started were fairly dancing with glee. The eve of battle was not the moment for dissension in the high command.

"Go!" the general told the horrified Westrians who had formed the envoys' escort. "You have my word that no harm will come to them," he added with a glare at Mother Mahaliel. As the Westrians were hurried away, he stepped closer.

"I mean that, Mahaliel," he said in a furious whisper. "I have been a soldier for twenty years without dishonoring my sword. In honor I have served you—but if these men are not still safe when the battle ends, it is over. I will take my men and you may try to rule this country alone."

"Do you think they will follow you?" she asked, her voice just as low.

"They will follow the man who leads them to victory."

"Victory comes from the Sun," she answered with sublime authority.

———

"The sun has turned the woman's brain!" Rana exclaimed. Her brother Edwin, who had been sent by Julian to escort the envoys, nodded unhappily.

"Probably. She looks like a scarecrow in white robes, but Rana—she *glows*. She's the kind who doesn't look before sitting down because she knows a chair will always be waiting. And her guards are almost as bad. We didn't have weapons and there were hundreds of them. There was nothing I could *do!*"

"I know, Cub," she said absently, using his milk-name. "You had to stay alive to bring us the news."

Westria's lords and senior commanders were gathering in front of the royal pavilion, where Julian stood by the fire. William's loss was like an open wound, although no one, she noticed, was lamenting the capture of Master Granite. The only one who had been silent was Julian. His rage had gone cold, thought Rana, and that frightened her most of all. He had been like this, she remembered, when the sorcerer Caolin tortured Silverhair.

"The Suns are doing their damned Snake Dance," said Lucas Buzzardmoon. "When the wind shifts, you can hear the drumming."

"I hope the snakes bite them," muttered Edwin.

"If they don't, I will," Jeanne said viciously. "Behold my fang!" Steel hissed as she drew her sword.

"We all have swords," replied the king, his voice so low they had to be still to hear him. "Our task now is to make sure we have a chance to use them." He straightened, his dark gaze drawing them in. "So far, our plan has worked well. This time it is the Suns who must attack a position which we have prepared."

"But won't they suspect some trap?" asked Rana.

"I doubt General Marsh thinks enough of my intelligence to suspect me of much subtlety." Julian flashed her an ironic smile.

"But they have William—," whispered Lord Philip, "and he knows our plans. If they compel him to tell them—" His voice failed, but the thought of torture was in all their minds.

"They won't need to hurt him," said Lucas bitterly. "That damned woman magics the souls from her captives."

"I told them that if anything went wrong they should not offer resistance," the king said harshly. A sudden flare from the fire highlighted the strong lines of his brow and nose and shadowed his eyes. "But even if they talk, I do not think the general will believe them. Lenart, tell the commanders to put out a third of the watchfires. The Sun scouts will calculate a hearth for every twenty men. If they report our numbers as less than William has given, the general will think he was trying to impress them."

"They will *want* to underestimate us," said Lord Eric, but his voice was more confident than his eyes.

"For as long as possible, they must do so," agreed the king. "Two thirty-man squads of archers are already on their way to the southwest side of the Buttes to provide cover if we are pushed back that far. A hundred will take up position on the hillside and two squads will hide in the marshes. The Suns will not march until they have daylight. By then the rest of us will be waiting for them."

"And you say they've let their baggage train go on ahead?" asked Lord Philip.

He must be sick with fear for his son, thought Rana, but he was hiding it well. *And where,* she wondered, *is* my *son?* She had not been able to coax the Wanderer into another appearance, and of course Garr did not know.

Edwin nodded.

"Well, perhaps the men from the Corona will snap them up," said Eric.

"I am sure they will be delighted," murmured Lenart. "The Suns' supplies should be very welcome after the northerners have spent a few days eating biscuit and dried meat on the trail."

"So long as they don't delay to enjoy them. Have we had any word?" Eric asked.

"They were to set out a week ago," said the king. "They will be here in time."

We hope, thought Rana, but no one dared to say that aloud.

"Sharpen your weapons." Julian flashed a grim smile. *"And I'll ready my bandages,"* Rana silently replied. "Hearten your men," the king went on. "Get some sleep. We must be ready to march when the sun lifts above the hills."

Light rippled across the hillside like a running flame as a thousand points of steel cast back the morning sun. The great square rock on which the king stood commanded the hillside as if it had been set there by the Guardians to be his throne. Below it, the might of Westria was assembled, a sight that had not been seen for more than twenty years. If they lost this fight, it might never be seen again.

He banished the thought, focusing on the array before him. Even men whom he had last seen looking like muddy marsh sprites had found some bit of color to cheer them into battle. Westria could not match the Suns in infantry, but Julian had spent the winter drilling his three hundred pikemen in the use of their twelve-foot spears. Five hundred mounted lancers were drawn up beside them, green pennons fluttering from their shafts. Sunlight sparkled on their mail. On the other wing, some three hundred heavy cavalry from Seagate and the Ramparts stood waiting, the curves of vambrace and greave that showed beneath their surcoats sending back the light in spurts of flame. Julian's own guard stood ranked around the rock, their blue cloaks fastened with his silver star.

The king opened his arms and the air shook with the intensity of their cheers. He lowered his hands and the whole great crowd of them grew still.

"Children of Westria, the last great battle lies before us. We have readied our weapons and our spirits. We have drawn the enemy to the place prepared for him. It is time to take back our land!" He paused as another cheer rolled upward.

"The Suns are on their way. The foe will think they have us outnumbered, but that is what we have planned. There is not one soul here who has not some sorrow to avenge. Hidden allies will come to your aid, and the land will fight for you." He lifted the banner of Westria that had been planted behind him. The gold of the circled cross blazed upon its green field.

"You are fighting for the circle of life and the balance

that maintains it, for the Covenant that preserves us, for the souls of your ancestors and the future of your children. May the Lady of Westria uphold us, and may the Defender strengthen our arms. Fight for Westria!"

"For Westria!" The answer rolled back to him on a tide of energy that lifted every hair.

Lady Jeanne dipped her lance in salute and nudged her gray warhorse into a trot, leading the knights westward around the Buttes toward a fold in the hills that would hide them until the best moment for their charge. The ranks of pikemen wheeled sharply and marched after them, followed, in somewhat looser order, by the light cavalry.

"My lord, your horse is waiting," said Lenart.

Shadow stamped as the king mounted. Behind him Osleif jiggled with excitement on his nervous bay. Julian cast a final glance around him. The time for contemplation was over. He would have all the leisure he needed to appreciate the beauties of Westria if he survived this day.

Jo stares as the sun lifts over the eastern ridges, seeing its brightness overlaid by a crimson glow. He tries to protest as Luz puts food into his hand. But even in Awahna they had to eat. . . . Is that her thought or his own? The Buttes loom ahead, a half-day's ride away. For most of the night, they have traveled, stopping only to rest the horses. Consciousness has become a waking dream. He could not sleep, cannot rest now, gazing northward as if will could carry him where he must go.

If he were truly the Dragon, he could spread scarlet wings and stoop upon the battlefield. But he is something other, suspended between worlds. He feels Luz within as she rides beside him, her cool radiance balancing his flame. The earth trembles to the tread of marching feet. The shaft of the godspear quivers beneath his hand.

At moments like this, Tadeo Marsh remembered that battle could be beautiful, at least at the beginning, he corrected, when the opposing forces maneuvered into position to begin their deadly dance. The Westrians were moving down from their first position on the slopes, banners fluttering cheerfully in the sun. It was warm already. There would be hot work today in more senses than one.

He could make out three groups of pikemen—a pitiful number compared to his own infantry—with assorted horse-archers and lancers behind them. Where, he wondered, were their heavy cavalry? The battlefield the Westrians had chosen formed a rough crescent between the Buttes and the marshes, about six miles long and two wide. Room enough, he thought as his files began to form up, six squares in the front and five behind, with his own in the rear. The snake rattles around their ankles hissed in deadly unison as they came. There was space for his cavalry to either side, but none for an attack on their flanks.

It seemed almost too simple. You could learn a commander's mind from his strategies, and Tadeo had thought he understood Julian. *He's hiding something—this year we have taught him not to stake all on one throw.* He peered at the hillside, wondering what his scouts had missed. But he would find out soon enough, and deal with it when it came. He was glad, though, that he had sent Mother Mahaliel and her prisoners off on the road that led around the east side of the Buttes, escorted by a squadron of light cavalry. If any pursuit should get past them, it was best to keep her out of the way.

A horn-call echoed across the killing ground. The general stood in his stirrups and behind the pikemen glimpsed the blue of Julian's houseguard. Then, from both sides, the arrows came.

The enemy was shooting from behind screens of foliage in the marshes. A guard beside him fell with a gurgling cry as a shaft pierced his neck. From the squares ahead, he heard cries. As men fell, they were dragged to the hollow center and others stepped up to fill their places. More arrows zipped by, thrumming like maddened bees. Some banged against his shield and bounced away.

"Manuelo, get your men in there and clean out those vermin!" he cried, and a squadron of cavalry wheeled away.

He heard another horn-call. The Westrian pikes were widening their formation so that horsemen could dash between them, shooting from the saddle as they swooped past. But now the Sun horse-archers dashed forward to meet them. Cheering rose from the squares as Westrians began to fall.

Tadeo signaled to his own trumpeter, and with disciplined precision, the squares began to advance, raised shields locked against the arrow storm.

From the healer's camp on the hill Rana had all too clear a view of the arrows that flew in black clouds above the fray. Already, the wounded were being brought in. She stiffened as horsemen swirled toward the cluster of blue cloaks that surrounded Julian. Swords flashed as some of them broke through. For a moment she saw him clearly, trading blows with three of the enemy. Then two frantic men from his houseguard reached his side and took on the foe.

"The king is fighting well," said Lord Eric, who had reluctantly agreed to guard the healers after Julian ordered him to let his son Orm lead the Seagate men.

"Yes," said Rana. "Too well. Your grandson was with him on the hill last night. He told me that Julian kept looking at everything as if he would never see it again. I don't think he expects to survive."

"My dear, Julian is a fighter. If the battle is lost, we may begin to worry; but it's early yet, and he surely won't give up until all his tricks have been tried. His houseguard will have their work cut out for them though." The old man laughed.

Rana looked at him and shook her head. Julian might have forbidden Eric the battlefield, but nothing could stop him from following the fray in spirit and exulting at every blow.

Step by step the Sun squares were moving forward. They met the Westrian pikes with a crash of shields and spears. For endless minutes the two groups heaved back and forth, as the pikemen tried to hook enemy spears and the spearmen to thrust past them. Then Osleif trumpeted a few short notes and the Westrians gave ground, separating to let more horsemen dash out before the Suns could stiffen their line, using their lances to stab down over the shields. The pikemen took advantage of the respite to close up once more, and when the riders wheeled away, they were waiting.

"That's not a retreat, is it?" asked Rana when the sequence had been repeated for a third time. Now the enemy were coming into range for the archers stationed on the southwestern slope of the hill. Though the Suns were advancing, behind them white-clad bodies littered the ground.

"You've noticed." Eric grinned. "I wonder if their general has too. Maybe not—I think he's with the group at the back. He can't really see what our men are doing, and he won't expect such discipline."

Julian's hard work with the pikemen was paying off. Still, each time the two groups clashed, Westrians fell, and unlike the Suns, they could not afford to lose a man. Now the casualties had chest and gut wounds, and for most, there was little Rana could do but give them a shady place in which to die.

She was holding a flask of water to the lips of one wounded man when a flicker of light from the north caught her eye. She blinked as it came again.

"What's that?" she began, but Eric was on his feet, staring.

"Horses. . . ." He pointed to a cloud of dust on the horizon. "Coming fast." Grinning, he took a mirror from the pouch at his waist and signaled back, then turned and sent another flicker of light toward the boiling of blue cloaks that guarded the king.

"Elinor is coming with Alyce of Normontaine. Our reinforcements are on their way."

Rana felt some of the tension leave her in a long sigh, and realized that she had not really dared to hope until now. But would they arrive in time?

It was then just an hour past noon.

Habañero and the dun gelding labor upward, blowing with the stress of that last push over the shoulder of the South Butte. On the next ridge the figure of a sentry stands in silhouette against a blazing sky, but his attention is all on the battle on the other side of the hill. Light flickers from the mirror in his hand.

For Jo and Luz, urgency has become endurance. When the clamor of battle abruptly stills, for a moment they believe they've simply grown too exhausted to hear. The beasts slow as they crest the rim, and suddenly they see the armies arrayed below.

For Tadeo Marsh, it had been a very long morning, during which he had had more than enough time to reget accepting battle on terrain his enemy chose. He thought the Suns still had the advantage, though too many of his men had gone down. The worst of it was the lack of some safe place from which he could *see.* And so, when the enemy horn blew the call for parley, he signaled to his own trumpeter to reply.

The armies faced each other, sweating in the blazing sun. Above, buzzards circled. *Be patient,* thought the general; *your time will come.*

The Westrian king was sitting a tall roan horse that threw up its head, whinnying, as Tadeo pushed through his cavalry and reined in.

"Our forces seem well matched," said King Julian. "It seems a pity to destroy more good men."

Tadeo remembered the voice, though behind all the bright armor he would have had trouble identifying the man. But as Julian brought his horse forward, the general recognized the pride in the dark eyes beneath the helm.

"What do you propose?" he called.

"The last time we met, I marked you—" White teeth flashed in the brindled beard. "Would you like your revenge?"

For a moment, sheer astonishment held Tadeo speechless. This was not how one fought a war! But perhaps in Westria it was.

"Sir, you mustn't risk yourself," came Commander Anaya's voice behind him. But he could also hear the harsh breathing of men pushed hard. They could use a respite, and by all the gods, *he* could use the exercise! He had been held helpless in the rear for too long!

"And what will the victor win?" he asked then.

For a moment the king hesitated. "Let the victor take what he can. . . ."

The Westrians looked even more horrified by the prospect of a duel between the two leaders than the Suns. Julian's blue surcoat was slashed and splattered.

If he falls, the heart will go out of them. He's seen action already, and I am fresh, thought Tadeo, and gave a nod.

"Very well, but my mount is not battle-trained. We'll fight on foot, as we did before."

They dismounted and handed the reins to their men. The king settled into position, knees a little bent with the left foot forward, sheltered behind his shield. Tadeo grasped the hilt of the great two-handed blade sheathed across his back and tugged it free. King Julian brought up his own blade and Tadeo saluted in return. *Putting on a good show for the men,* he thought. In their first scrambling fight, there had been no time for such courtesies. He felt a reminiscent twinge in his calf at the memory, but he had used that leg hard enough in the past months to trust that it would not betray him.

Tadeo found his own balance, rising a little on the balls of his feet and then settling with sword angled before him as his opponent circled. He was distantly aware of whispers behind him. One man was even taking wagers, though Tadeo was pleased to hear it was on how long it would take the general to beat his foe, not on who would win.

Without conscious awareness, he knew the moment when Julian began his attack. Steel screamed as the blades scraped. Tadeo disengaged, feinted and struck, but Julian's shield blocked the blow. The pretty paint was scarred now, the general was pleased to see, and there was a nick in the rim.

Swords clashed once more as they met and parted. He got another blow in on the king's shield. The star in its center seemed to be exploding as paint and wood were stripped away.

Someone in the Westrian ranks shouted. Distracted, Tadeo almost let Julian's next blow get through.

He thrust from his mind all awareness of anything but his foe and sent his own blade whirling round. *Come to me . . . come to me . . .* , he thought, *I am learning you now.* A swift step brought his sword inside Julian's guard; the sharp tip sliced through the shield strap, and the king leaped awkwardly backward as it fell.

That woke you up, didn't it, my lad! Tadeo laughed as he had when he was a green recruit and the only skin he had to worry about was his own. Did this man realize what a gift he had given him? Did he find joy in their combat too?

Julian carried a hand-and-a-half-hilted blade, and now he was wielding his sword with both hands as well. As one, they stepped together. The blades kissed and slid apart; Tadeo felt a sting and realized that his foe's tip had slashed his arm. Blood began to drip from the wound.

The king paused, listening to something beyond their charmed circle. Tadeo's steady prowl became a rush, blade blurring around to knock the king's sword away, twisting downward. As it sliced diagonally across breast and belly, mail links sprang glittering away.

The shouting grew louder as the king of Westria swayed, his weapon dropping from his hands.

Have I killed him? Tadeo fell back, surprised to find that thought carried its own stab of pain as Westrians ran forward to catch their king. Someone called the general's name. Commander Anaya was running toward him, the bay horse in tow.

"Sir, get mounted. Riders are coming, Westrians. Holy Sun, you are bleeding—"

"It's a scratch!" The general was already reaching for

the reins. "Form up!" he roared. "Brace your lines! Rear squares reverse; prepare to receive the foe!"

———◦◦◦———

From the Westrians comes a cry of horror as the king goes down. Jo's shriek is silent, but it shatters the spell that has held him and Luz as they watched the king's duel. As the northern charge bears down on the Sun army, Luz pulls the pack from the stallion's saddle. They need no words. Jo shakes out his steel-studded brigandine. He lifts his arms as her clever fingers deal with the buckles, bends his head so that she can drape the scarlet cloak across his shoulders. She hands him the Spear.

But with the cloak comes a great stillness.

"Wait. . . ." The voice is within and around them.

Together, Jo and Luz brace the Spear. Earth and heaven are linked by the shaft; their hands' grip unites ice and fire. And the Other, invisible, stands with them, a mighty Presence whose implacable patience alone can leash their power.

"Wait for the summoning."

———◦◦◦———

"Father!" Julian heard his son's voice call.

Was he dying? He gasped as hard hands lifted him and the world spun crazily. He could feel the tremor in the earth, the disturbance in the air. The men of the north were here.

He saw Lenart's worried face above him, then closed his eyes, teeth clenched to keep from screaming as men carried him from the battlefield.

As they laid the king down, he heard Osleif's trumpet shrilling a greeting and a chorus of horns answering him. Hooves thundered as the northerners charged.

At least, he thought, *I bought them time.*

Hands that tried unsuccessfully to be gentle tugged off the remains of his surcoat and shirt of mail, and cut away the padded arming tunic and shirt beneath.

"Guardians, there's so much blood!" someone exclaimed.

That's good, the king thought muzzily. *My blood should feed the ground.*

"Give me soft cloths to soak it up," Rana snapped, "then wet swabs so I can see what we're dealing with here."

A belly wound, then. . . . He tried not to think about how painful his dying was going to be.

"This may hurt," Rana said more softly, bending over him.

"Never mind. Tell me what's happening." He opened his eyes and tried to smile.

Abused flesh screamed as things were done to him, but Julian fixed his mind on words that seemed to come from very far away.

"They've formed wedges, one for each square. The banner of the Corona is in the lead."

That was Eric's voice—good—he would understand what he was seeing down there.

"They're going to hit—no, the horses won't face those spears. They're sheering off to let their horse-archers through. Damn, those lads know their job! Snakes are falling; now the Normontainers are casting their javelins. Ha! They've made an opening in one square. Elinor, go! Get your horses in through that hole!"

"The blade sliced through the first two layers of muscle," came Rana's voice in counterpoint, still with that same unnatural calm.

"Are those his guts?" someone squeaked.

"I don't think the blade reached them. Leave the wound open now, but keep swabbing. I have to see. . . ."

So do I, thought Julian. "Eric," he whispered, "what now? What's going on?"

"Two of the squares are broken; the others are holding. But our pikes are making a nice spiked fence to keep them in. You were right about the extra length in the spears, Julian— the Snakes can't reach them without breaking formation."

"Good!" murmured the king, then yipped as Rana pulled apart the edges of his wound.

"Get out of my light, damn you! And hold this—," she said to someone. "We've got to get every last shred of padding out of there!"

Or I'll die of wound-fever, he thought with an odd detachment. He supposed that was better than a gut wound. . . .

"A square on the left is trying to pull away," said Eric. "They're breaking free—no, our cavalry are driving them into the marsh. Arrows are flying—the archers there will know how to welcome them."

"How many squares?" grunted Julian.

"Nine left standing," the old man replied, "but the attack is losing momentum."

"Get out the mirror. I think it's time . . . for Jeanne to join the party . . . don't you?"

Even through closed eyelids, Julian could sense the flicker of light as Eric angled the mirror toward the sun. He imagined the man they had posted on the next hill standing, turning, and calling to the knights who waited below.

"All right—" Rana's voice shook a little. "I think we've got it all." She touched Julian's cheek. "Brace yourself, my love, because this is going to hurt."

Hooves beat out a thunderous rhythm on the hard earth. He did not need Eric to tell him when the Suns sighted this new foe. Their own fighters had been told to get behind the enemy when this happened so that they and the northerners could force the Suns to stand still to receive the charge.

A river of fire washed through Julian's belly as Rana poured in spirits to disinfect the wound, but his scream was lost in the rending clamor as the Westrian heavy cavalry crashed into the Sun squares.

The melee had become general now. Intent on Eric's narration, Julian scarcely felt the pricks as Rana began to sew the slash closed. Would it be enough? The Suns were now outnumbered, but their discipline remained superb.

When Rana had bandaged Julian's belly, she let them prop up his stretcher so that he could see down the hill. But he would not take the infusion of poppies she offered him, though with every beat of his heart his belly pulsed red fire.

The sun was dropping toward the western hills, dyeing the bloody field with a deeper light. The Westrian alliance might not lose this battle, but could it win? If even a diminished Sun army escaped, the general would build them into a new force and it would be all to do again. And if Julian survived, it would be long before he could take the field.

Would it have been different if the Guardians had accepted his sacrifice?

Wild fancies of leaping down the hill to spit himself upon the lances played through his brain as he watched the struggle below, but Rana's hand was firm on his shoulder, and he knew he would not have gotten three steps before she tied him down. Now that the need for control was past, she was weeping, but he could not spare the attention to comfort her.

"Defender—," his spirit writhed in silent prayer, "help us! I have done everything I can. . . ."

As if he had heard, Piper began to sing.

> Oh God of Warriors, here below,
> We hear the horn of battle blow,
> To cleanse the land of every foe,
> We seek Thy aid, oh be not slow!
> Praise to the Lord of Hosts!
> In fear their ranks before us go,
> Beneath our blades, Thy power they know.

At the sound of that singing, power shocks through the Spear. As one, Red Dragon and White awaken, the Red to send his steed hurtling downward while the White Dragon rides with him in spirit. As the red stallion gathers speed, the swordsmen strike more swiftly. The Westrian pikes are thrusting in rhythm to the song.

> To Thy great rhythm, Lord, we dance:
> The music of the sword and lance,
> Resounds as partnered foes advance,
> And fall as weapons slice and glance,
> Praise to the Lord of Hosts!
> Nor shall one warrior fall by chance,
> Uplifted by the battle trance!

———◆———

"Who's that?" Eric pointed at the next hill.

In the light of the setting sun, the king saw a red horse plunging toward the battlefield. From the rider's shoulders a scarlet cloak flared. The stallion reared and light blazed from the tip of the great spear as the horseman swung it above the foe.

"Sing!" Julian cried, denying his own agony. "It is the Defender! Sing for him!"

Rana's fingers tightened painfully on his shoulder, but her voice rang out with Piper's as the red rider launched his steed down the hill, cloak flaming behind him. From hill and plain, Westrian voices took up the song.

> *We follow still the Spear of Light,*
> *That strikes with Thy relentless might!*
> *Before our foes it blazes bright,*
> *And sears the evil-doer's sight!*

Then from the Sun squares came a cry: "The Red Dragon! The Dragon rides to war!"

"Praise to the Lord. . . ." The Westrian singing faltered, for their enemies were greeting the rider as a deliverer.

Pain blurred Julian's vision; he saw the figure of the horseman expand and lengthen into that of the dragon they had named him. Or were there two dragons, red and white entwined? As the shining figure hurtled onward, men recoiled. Light flared from a fang of gold.

Cries of greeting changed to screams as the fang struck and struck again. Whether he was the Red Dragon or the Defender, he was fighting for Westria.

"Unwearied, we sustain the fight—," a little shakily, the Westrians sang, *"Undaunted, put the foe to flight!"*

———※◎※———

The Sun hordes are fleeing, casting down their weapons in panic and despair. Some recoil across the wreck of the field while others seek refuge in the marshes.

The Dragons settle around the figure of the red rider and fade from view. He reins in the stallion, the godspear dropping to rest at his side as the Westrian riders fall upon their routed foes. Triumphant, their singing resounds across the field.

We praise Thee by the blows we deal,
Our hymn the music of our steel:
Oh God of War, renew our zeal,
And so the foe Thy wrath shall feel.
Praise to the Lord of Hosts!
They flee, they fall, despairing reel,
Before Thy glory, Lord, they kneel.

⊶ 23 ⊷

TEST OF FIRE

Tadeo Marsh lay in the mud, fighting memories. The world had narrowed to a torment of muck and mosquitos and the sour taste of fear. He told himself that the air was too dry and the night too cool for this to be the bayou where the knights of the Iron Kingdom had hunted him after the fall of the Empire of the Sun. But it was little comfort to remember that the horsemen he could hear crashing through the reeds in search of fugitives were Westrians.

It seemed an eternity since Commander Anaya had dragged him from the field, though by the stars it was scarcely midnight. But that stunned moment when they had seen the red rider poised upon the hill still burned in his brain. Tadeo had recognized the horse, grinned as his men began to shout in welcome, and shared with them the panic when the flying figure became a dragon that swooped to savage them. Since then he had had far too much time to wonder what he had really seen. But whether the Dragon was a joint hallucination or some Westrian devilry, it had decided the battle. The Suns who survived had scattered or surrendered to their foes.

Someone hallooed and the hunters splashed away. Tadeo spared a moment's pity for whatever poor soldier they had spotted before continuing to creep along the muddy channel that led from the slough. The gash in his arm throbbed dully. If it did not go septic on him he would be lucky. But he could worry about that if he lived through the next few hours.

The ground grew harder and he dared to stand, alert for any movement in the darkness. He had wormed his way around the edge of the slough, and now the bulk of the Buttes were in front and to his left, looming against the sky. Reason told him to keep going. But somewhere on the southern slopes of that pile of stone, Sarina had been sent to wait with Mother Mahaliel and a troop of Sun cavalry. He hoped they had had the sense to flee when no one came to inform them of a victory, but to pick up their trail he must go and see.

His need to find Sarina was all that had kept him from giving himself up or lying down to die. Half-crouched and wary, he moved forward.

To the north the ground beyond the Buttes fell away into marsh and plain, but in this direction the slope dipped into a narrow pass bounded by another line of hills. As Tadeo approached, he saw men moving against the firelight. A rough breastwork of logs and brush had been built across the entrance to the pass. He had not ordered it, so it must be a Westrian construct, set to repel any attack on the Westrian rear. Certainly the victors held it now—he could hear laughter and a snatch of song.

Had they scoured the hills behind them, or were they sticking to orders and holding their line? Either way, the pass was closed to him. Carefully Tadeo squirmed backward through the dry grass, keeping his movements as random as the rustling of the wind.

He would have to make his way along the far side of the hills to the eastern end of the pass. It would take him all night, but Sarina was waiting. There was no power but death, he thought grimly, that would keep him from reaching her. And he knew that he feared her death more than his own.

How strange, thought Jo as he guided the red stallion through the confusion of the field where the men of Normontaine were pitching their tents to the Westrian encampment; he had returned to a triumph beyond all his hopes, and he wanted to run away. . . . At least he was not alone. As numbed as he by reaction, Luz brought her dun up beside him. It had been so easy when they were both Dragons, charging down that hill toward the Sun army. But now he had to face his family—and Westria.

The impromptu escort that had brought him from the battlefield was dispersing, shouting the news of his return. Jo turned, searching the gaggle of tents for the one where the king's banner flew. He saw yellow canvas, lit from within. On one side the green banner of Westria lifted in the wind. On the other rippled folds of blue. Torchlight glittered on its silver star as the stars blazed in the clear sky above. He reined the stallion forward, trying to barrier himself against the crowds' emotions—curiosity and amazement, and transcending all of them, the overwhelming joy of victory.

"It is the Defender . . . ," came the whispers as he passed.

"Nay, it's Prince Johan—'twas only the Defender's cloak he wore," someone replied.

"But the prince was lost—"

"He is the Phoenix indeed!"

"Has he returned from the dead?"

Yes, thought Jo as comments bombarded him from every side. *For surely the boy I was when last they saw me is no more.*

In the center of the camp a great bonfire was burning. The singing of the men who gathered around it echoed from the Buttes behind them. Inspired by the festive atmosphere, Habañero arched his neck and began to lift his knees in the rolling, nearly motionless trot of the circus ring.

Show-off! thought Jo, nudging him forward.

The people of Elder had brought food and drink—strong drink, by the look of some of the flushed faces. They stared at him as if one of the Guardians had come among them.

How do I convince them that I am just an ordinary man?

"Especially when you're nothing of the kind?" Luz's amused thought crossed his own. *"You had better settle for being a hero. . . ."*

As if in agreement, the stallion sank back on his haunches, rearing with neatly folded forelegs as if posing for a statue of a conqueror. "Baby, stop that!" Jo shifted his weight to bring the horse back down. Ears flicking, Habañero carefully placed his feet to display the muscles that rippled beneath the red hide. "You clown—," Jo muttered. "You're not making this any easier for me." But then he had never thought it would be easy to go home.

This kind of thing never happened to his father, and he was willing to bet that King Jehan's horses had obeyed him as well. Wondering, he searched within.

Red and Fix seemed content to remain memories; the Dragon was a daemon that he could hope had been permanently transformed. He missed Jehan's counsel. But he had better not even think about being someone else, except, perhaps, the self he had been in Awahna. The Jo who walked the Sacred Valley had been serene and secure. He had to hold on to that memory.

Thinking about Awahna inevitably brought Luz to mind. To his eyes she was as beautiful as she had been in the valley. *"Look at her,"* he wanted to cry to the people who were thronging around them. *"A goddess has come among you. Look at her, not at me!"*

The crowd rippled and he glimpsed a fair head bobbing above the rest. In another moment, Lenart pushed through. For a moment he stared from Luz to Jo, his face flushed with unaccustomed emotion.

"It *is* you," he said finally. "I saw you on the battlefield. I thought it was an apparition. And you—" He looked back at his sister. "I don't know whether to kiss or to spank you for frightening us so!"

"Oh, Lenart!" Luz scrambled off the dun pony and hugged him hard.

In Lenart's wake came a boy whom Jo dimly remembered having seen as a visitor to Misthall. Osleif. The child had a scratch on his cheek, and he was a foot taller now. He took in the situation with a quick glance and grabbed the dun's rein, then turned to Jo.

"Sir—sir, may I take your horse? He *is* beautiful!"

"He's a circus horse, and he thinks this is a show." Jo grinned. "If he tries any tricks, call him 'Baby' and swat him on the nose!"

Lenart had released his sister. Before Jo could speak, Lenart stepped forward and grabbed him. Jo could feel hard muscle in the arms that held him, but he was astonished to realize that he was also sensing exasperation, anxiety, and above all, love, not as strongly as he did with Luz, but in the same way. He had not expected that; but then, since they had left Awahna, Luz was almost the only other human being he had seen. When Lenart let him go, both their eyes were bright with tears.

"I should go to my parents," Jo said when he could breathe again.

Lenart nodded. "The queen has been told. She's waiting. The king—"

He stopped, and Jo's heart clenched in fear. But his father could not be dead or the people would be mourning, even after such a victory.

"No, no—" Lenart read his expression. "He'll be all right. But it's a bad wound."

Luz gripped his hand. He could feel her steady support as he felt Lenart's love. He let them guide him forward.

And then he was in the great gold tent with its border of green laurel leaves. The kindly light did not quite veil the marks of strain in the faces of those who turned as they entered—Lord Eric, solid as ever though his hair was completely white now; Master Frederic, eyes filling at the sight of his daughter; Lord Philip and cousin Jeanne. And his mother, new silver tempering the flame of her hair.

What could he do? What could he say? Rana solved the problem for him with a swift embrace and a confusion of images carried on a wave of love and fear. Instinctively he stiffened, and she let him go, gazing up into his face.

"It's not you," he said swiftly. "I'm . . . too open. . . ."

Rana blinked and shook her head. "And you're sending it all back to me. My fault. I should have been more careful. But you used to be—more contained."

That surprised a short laugh from him. "A lot of things have changed. . . ." Now, he thought with a sinking heart, they were all going to ask him where he had been, but once more his mother surprised him.

"Garr has told us something of what happened to you," she said. "We'll want to know more, but there's no need to go into that now. But he couldn't say where you went when you left the Suns. . . ." She paused hopefully.

Couldn't, or wouldn't? wondered Jo, swallowing his surprise. Why shouldn't Garr have joined the Westrians? Luz detached herself from her father's arms and came to his side.

"Sun patrols were pursuing us. We had to go somewhere they could not follow." She paused, and Jo realized that even she was finding it hard to choose the right words. "I took him to Awahna."

The stunned silence that followed was broken by Frederic's sigh. "I felt it," he said softly. "I saw the light of the Sacred Valley in your eyes. But what will Master Granite—" He stopped suddenly, the worry coming back into his face.

"What's happened to him?" Luz asked swiftly.

"Last night we sent him and William on an embassy to the Suns. Julian didn't think it would do much good, but it bought us some time." Rana shrugged. None of that mattered now. "The general seems to be an honorable man, but that woman seized them. We think she took them north to rejoin their baggage train. We've sent riders after them."

"Oh, Guardians!" whispered Luz. "Master Granite and Mother Mahaliel! He wanted to meet her. He said she hadn't yet faced a real adept here."

"We'll get them back safely," said Lord Eric reassuringly.

Jo shook his head. "Her powers are . . . different. He has no idea what she can do!"

"Well, there is nothing *we* can do about it until we know where they are," the queen said briskly. "In the meantime—"

"May I see my father?" Jo glanced toward the curtain that separated the public part of the pavilion from the private half. Better get it all over with quickly, he thought. Then he would know who he was.

"Yes . . . ," Rana said doubtfully, "though I don't know if he will be awake. He refused any painkiller until the battle was over. Then I forced some syrup of poppy down his stubborn throat to keep him quiet. I couldn't very well sit on him with a belly wound."

She was babbling, and as she met his gaze she realized he knew it and fell silent, allowing him to see her fear.

"How bad is it?" he asked.

She sighed, accepting his right to know.

"Not nearly as bad as it could have been. Through the muscle, but not into the gut. And he's always had the constitution of a horse."

I hope not, thought Jo, remembering what delicate creatures horses could be. But he understood what she was trying to say. His father's air of indestructability was one of the things he had always found overwhelming.

But there was nothing to awe him in the figure that lay on the cot, unless it was the idea that the king could lie so very still. Rana knelt beside the bed, smoothing back the sweated hair from his brow.

"Julian, love, wake up. Our Phoenix has come back to us. It was all true, Julian—our son is here!"

The king's eyelids flickered. He drew breath more strongly, winced, and opened his eyes. They seemed all pupil, wells of shadow into which Jo might fall. Rana sent him a beseeching glance, and he made himself go forward and kneel on the cot's other side.

Slowly the drugged gaze shifted. "Johan?"

"I am here, father," he whispered. "Can you see me?"

"I see. . . ." The dark eyes focused, but on what, Jo was not sure. "I see . . . a dragon. . . ." He smiled, and closed his eyes once more. His breathing deepened.

"Poppy dreams," murmured Rana. "He will be clearer tomorrow." She let Jo help her to stand.

Perhaps, he thought as she wept against his chest, or perhaps the drug had enabled his father to recognize something he would not otherwise have admitted he could see.

"My lady—we've seen Mother Mahaliel."

Tea splashed from the mug as Rana set it down, staring at the scout who knelt before her. With Julian incapacitated, she had taken command, but for a moment she could not even make her voice obey. Fortunately the man needed no encouragement to go on.

"She's on the south side of the Buttes with a few of their soldiers and a lot of women and old men. Under our noses all the time!"

From outside came shouting as the news spread. The sun had lifted above the Buttes, filling the pavilion with a golden glow. Even those who had gotten drunk the night before were waking, eager to be avenged on the enemy they had most feared.

And none, thought the queen, *is more eager than I.* There were volumes missing from what she had heard of her son's story, things he might never tell them. But she had seen how he looked when they spoke of Mother Mahaliel. *That woman has a great deal to answer for, and she will answer to me!*

As if her thought had summoned him, Jo himself appeared in the doorway, Luz at his side. Rana raised an eyebrow. Last night she had recognized the bond between them, though she was not sure of its nature. Lenart and his father and grandfather came crowding after them, and then Lord Philip and Jeanne. Good—she might as well inform the whole family at once.

"I heard the news," exclaimed Jeanne. "Give me a half hour to get my men ready and I'll go after the bitch."

"Excellent," Rana said blandly. "You can escort me."

"But you can't go," protested Philip.

"I am regent while Julian lies ill, and I say I can. He fought the general. Who has a better right to face the priestess than I?"

"I do—"

It took Rana a moment to recognize that harsh voice as her son's.

"And I," added Luz. "We were her captives."

"All the more reason for you to stay here," exclaimed the queen.

"We know her. We know her tricks, her powers," exclaimed the two young people. By this time the others were adding their arguments in a rising tide of controversy that ended only when the queen slapped the table.

In the surprised silence she beckoned to Osleif, who had apparently been hoping that if he sat quietly no one would notice he had joined the conclave. "I want you to find the man they call Garr. He tents with the riders. Bring him here."

"You speak as if you know him well!" said Luz as Osleif slipped out the door.

"I ran into him after he left Rivered," the queen replied. "He guided me to Elder."

"But why do you want him now?" Jo asked warily.

"Before I met Garr . . . I met someone else who spoke with Garr's voice. . . ." Rana caught the look that passed between her son and Luz. "I see that you know who I mean. It seems to me His counsel might be useful here."

"Yes, we know," the girl said with quiet authority. "Who do you think gave Jo that spear? But the Powers go where they will. They are not to be commanded even by the queen of Westria."

"Even a queen may *ask*. . . ."

"So long as that is what you are doing," responded Luz. "I was taught at the College that to call a Power into one who has not consented is not ethical."

Rana glared at her. Did the child think that because she had helped the prince of Westria, she had the right to correct the queen?

"Garr has done this before," she said repressively.

"That is between him and the Wanderer. I don't even know if Garr is aware of what happens to him at such times."

Remembering the confusion in which Garr had awakened at her campfire, Rana thought Luz might be right.

Lord Eric stepped into the gap with his own argument for going, while Frederic pointed out that as the only other adept available, the task of dealing with the sorceress should be his.

"You are not the only one who has been to Awahna," his daughter objected, then stopped as the old armsmaster appeared at the door.

At the sudden silence, the old man paused, eyeing them warily. But as he stood with the doorflap still lifted, they saw his posture shift. Rana pushed the chair back and got to her feet. She did not know if the prickle that ran up her spine was excitement or fear. The man who stood there now looked bigger; his single eye surveyed her with uncomfortable acuity.

"Hail, Queen of Westria! Do not fear to strain your ethics this morning—your need was enough to call me here." His voice, too, was deeper than Garr's rough burr.

"You are very welcome," she said, flushing.

"Thank you." He gave a mocking bow and stepped into the room. Luz controlled twitching lips and bent in a curtsey as Jo bowed.

"Do you want the Spear back?" the prince asked, straightening.

The Wanderer shook his head. "It may still be needed. But do not fear to keep it. When its work is done, it will become no more than—a spear. Think of it as a new heirloom for your house. You have done well, both of you. Our confidence was justified. But as for you—" He turned to Rana, and the queen recoiled. "Did I not tell you that there were choices before you? You have called me here to forbid your son to go after Mother Mahaliel. But that is not my choice to make—or yours." She forced herself to stand fast as he came closer. "He has returned, but you can still lose him . . . ," he said softly. "If you refuse to let him go."

"He has borne dangers enough while I stayed safe at home," she whispered. "Surely I'm the one who should face this woman now. Is it not a battle of queens?"

"And who here will have the authority to command your king back to his bed if you should go?"

"But I have been so *useless*!" All her frustration burst forth suddenly.

"Ah, my dear, I see why my brother so enjoys you." He reached out to lift her chin. "You are altogether magnificent!"

"Is that supposed to be an answer?" She felt her anger slipping away.

"*You* are the answer. Look at me—."

In his single gaze she saw understanding and irony, pain and compassion, and a focused will that made all her own complaints seem no more than the fretting of a child. *"We all do what we must,"* he spoke to her spirit, *"to maintain the balance, to preserve the world. And nothing is lost forever, my queen. . . ."*

They are right, she thought numbly, who say that one should not lightly meddle with the Powers.

"This is their test, Queen of Westria—" He nodded toward Luz and Jo. "Let them go. . . ."

The door of a pavilion could not slam, but Julian recognized the sound of departure and wondered what had required a meeting on this morning after their victory. After a few moments the curtain stirred and Rana came in.

"What is it?" said Julian. "I heard shouting." He tried to turn, winced, and lay back again, breathing carefully as his belly throbbed.

"Nothing to worry you, love," Rana answered, but in her voice he could hear the strain. "A disagreement on procedure."

"And you lost." He opened his awareness to the conflict of hope and fear in her emotions. It was easier than he had expected. His physical vulnerability seemed to have opened him psychically. Last night he had sensed—He frowned, wondering if what he remembered was delirium. "Was Johan here last night, or was that a dream?"

"He was here"—her voice trembled—"and if the Guardians are not torturers, he will be here again!"

My son is alive. . . . The certainty flowered within him in a complexity of emotions. They should be feeling only joy, but Rana was afraid.

"He has gone off into some danger." Experience supplied an explanation. Slowly his mind worked through the possibilities. "He has gone after Mother Mahaliel." But that conclusion only brought more questions. "Why should he be the one to go?" he asked, and then, "Where has he been all this time?"

Rana began to gather the materials to dress his wound. She kept her back to him as she replied. "A man called Garr came over to our side. He told us Johan had been captured by slavers and then somehow ended up a prisoner with the Suns."

"And how long have you known this?" he asked with detached curiosity.

"A month, two—" she half-sobbed. "Since I got here. But all Garr could say was that Johan and Luz had escaped them. I didn't want . . . to worry you." She eyed him warily.

It must be the remnants of the drug, he thought, that were keeping him so calm. Or else it was some instinct for self-preservation.

"Now we can worry together," he said reasonably.

"Good! It will be a distraction while I dress your wound." She banged her tray of surgical supplies down on the cabinet. "In body, Johan seems well, but he's changed. I can see that he has been through a great deal." She drew back the blanket and began to undo the king's shirt.

He has become a dragon . . . , thought Julian, certain now that what he had perceived was truth, though he could not say what it might mean. But surely the Guardians had not preserved the boy this long to let him be killed now. He yelped as the queen yanked loose a bit of bandage that had stuck to the wound. "Careful! I'm not the enemy!"

"Oh, Julian!" She sank suddenly to her knees beside

him, weeping. "All that time I could endure because I knew he was safe, but now I'm afraid!"

***

Perhaps, thought Luz as she turned her pony to follow the red stallion up the slope, *we should have left this task to the queen.* At the thought of facing Mother Mahaliel again her mouth went dry. As she had told Rana, she knew what the priestess could do.

Above them, the red stone of the Buttes glowed against the blue sky. The grass at their base shimmered gold. Where the hill folded inward into a truncated box canyon, she could see a scattering of white shapes moving—Sun soldiers, said the scout who was reporting to Lady Jeanne, and the priestess and her followers. From here they looked like a flock of sheep. But a shepherd needs a dog to enforce obedience, and Tadeo Marsh was either dead or fled. What would Mother Mahaliel do for a sheepdog now?

But perhaps that no longer mattered, thought Luz as they drew closer. By the side of the road below, a dozen wagons stood abandoned. The Suns who remained had nowhere to run to and no way to run.

Jeanne frowned as she scanned the terrain. "You've done well," she told the messenger. "The bitch should be ready to trade her hostages for some food and water by now." She reined her horse off the road and led them up the hill.

The Sun soldiers formed a close line across the hill. Behind them a wagon cover had been stretched on spears to provide some shade. Pottery jugs were ranked along one side of it—perhaps they were not out of water after all. To one side, a bonfire was burning, an odd sight on so warm a day. Luz shaded her eyes beneath her hand, trying to make out Master Granite's gray robe and William's fair hair.

"I don't fancy charging uphill against those lances," Jeanne added as the Westrian riders moved into position. "If you think you can talk sense into the woman, now's the time."

Luz exchanged a glance of bitter amusement with Jo. Inspiration, yes, or power, but sense was not a word they associated with Mother Mahaliel. Jo nudged his horse forward, holding the Spear, and Luz followed him. A whisper of consternation ran down their line as the Suns recognized first the red horse, and then its rider.

"I'll speak first," muttered Luz, sensing his distress. "Mother Mahaliel—" She pitched her voice to carry as Master Granite had taught her. "Your army has been destroyed. There is no escape from here. Tell your men to lay down their arms."

A figure in shining white came out from under the sunshade. Luz stared in shock to see how thin the woman had become. But the voice was the same, sweet and low, focused by some configuration of the rock so that it seemed to speak to each man's soul.

"Sombra, how could you betray me? I kept you safe. You ate at my table and slept beneath my roof. I loved you. . . ." At that, even some of the Westrians looked at Luz reproachfully.

"I never swore allegiance to you or to your god," she replied, but her words sounded weak and whining. She could not deny that she had gone like a spy into Mahaliel's household, that she had betrayed the Mother's trust in her.

"And you, Red—I took you from slavery and made you my son! I can protect you from your demons. Do you think these idolaters will still want you when they know what you have done?"

The red horse sidled suddenly as if to some incautious jerk of the heel. Luz glanced at Jo in alarm, seeing on his face a look that had not been there since before Awahna. Closing her eyes, she summoned the image of the towering cliffs that guarded the Sacred Valley, as if by invoking those walls she could shield their souls.

"But why are we shouting?" Mother Mahaliel said then. "Come—my men will not harm you."

"And give her another pair of hostages?" hissed Jeanne. "I don't think so."

The thought of getting any closer to Mother Mahaliel made Luz's skin crawl. But Master Granite and Lord William were still prisoners. She could see them clearly now.

"Offer a truce," she said reluctantly. "If she swears by the sun, she will keep her word."

Too quickly, it seemed, the Sun soldiers were withdrawn to one side of the slope and the Westrians to the other. Luz and Jo dismounted and made their way up the hill. Beneath the sunshade, Lord William anxiously watched them, guarded by old Loris Stef. Master Granite's eyes burned like coals, but he had been gagged as well as bound. Well, that would explain how the Suns had been able to keep him captive.

As they neared, Bett shepherded the others to one side, glaring over her shoulder. If looks could kill, thought Luz, she and Jo would be burnt to a crisp by now. These were the most devoted of the Mother's worshipers. Most of them had come with her from the Sea of Grass, but Luz was saddened to see among them the pretty dark Westrian girl who had lived with Tadeo Marsh.

Mahaliel stretched out her hands. "My sweet boy— when you disappeared, I was afraid for you! I am glad to see you so well!"

The same could not be said for Mahaliel, thought Luz. There was nothing motherly about her now. Her skin was like old leather, her tangled hair like straw. But her eyes still glowed. As the woman moved toward him, Jo groped for Luz's hand instead. For a moment, rage flickered in those golden eyes; then Mahaliel damped the flames.

"Stay with me, Red," she crooned, "and I will take care of you. . . . You are my dragon. Let the witch go, child— you belong with me. . . ." Her eyes grew brighter; the air around her began to glow.

Luz scarcely dared to breathe. Jo's grip tightened painfully.

"My name is not Red. I am Prince Johan Starbairn, and I belong to Westria. . . ."

At his words, Luz felt her fear borne away by a tide of joy. "And I am Luz of Bongarde." Her affirmation echoed his. "An adept of the College of the Wise!"

Master Granite frowned as he heard that claim. Then she felt his awareness brush hers and his wonder as he recognized the mark of Awahna. For a moment, his eyes blazed with joy.

Luz turned back to Mother Mahaliel. "We will grant you greater mercy than you have shown our priesthood. We offer you exile from the golden land in exchange for your prisoners."

"And if I refuse?" the priestess said, very softly.

"Then we will take both them, and you!" Jo replied, letting the point of his spear drift downward till sunlight flared from the bronze blade.

"You think you have learned power?" the woman said then. "Well, so have I—more than you can dream. You think I am conquered because you have defeated my army? I have walked in my Father's kingdom and returned alive. I live in the Light, and so do those who follow me!"

"You live in delusion," snapped Luz. She turned to the others. "Can't you see that it's over? Surrender yourselves and the king will have mercy. We will find a place for you."

"Live in the Light!" cried Bett defiantly, and a dozen voices responded.

"Destroy the Darkness!"

"Now comes the time to prove our power!" Mahaliel cried. "When we have passed the test, all men shall bow before us and our Father will be supreme on earth as He is in the sky!"

"The time has come!" Bett yanked the stopper from one of the clay pots and poured its contents over herself. For a moment Luz thought she was trying to cool off, but the liquid flowed too slowly to be water. As the others opened their own jugs, her heart chilled.

"Stop!" she cried, but Bett's shout was louder.

"Holy One, grant us the test of fire!"

"I grant your desire," Mahaliel replied. "Come purified from the flame!"

Bett stepped to the bonfire and pulled out a flaming brand. A woman knelt before her, glistening with oil, and Bett thrust the fire at her breast. In the next moment she was burning, mouth opening in silent agony. A hideous scent of roasting flesh diffused through the warm air.

Someone screamed, but another woman was stepping forward. In the next instant she too was afire.

"Run!" pleaded Jo. "You'll burn! You must get away!"

Some few heeded, but the others were running toward Bett, some catching fire from their fellows, others receiving the flame from her hand. Bett's face was fixed in mad ecstasy.

As Bett herself began to burn, Mahaliel turned, her eyes ablaze. "Now do you understand?" She pointed her finger toward William and Master Granite, and at its tip Luz saw a spark of flame. "Can *they* pass the test?"

Master Granite's eyes closed in concentration. The air around him throbbed. Even gagged, he was calling a wind.

A great gout of flame spurted from Mahaliel's hand, and the breeze rolled it back toward her. Her gown began to smoulder, but she paid no heed. Loris Stef splashed oil over the Westrians, then scuttled away. Once more the priestess raised her hands. The flame spurted toward them; Master Granite's concentration broke as he cast himself in front of the younger man. For a moment Luz hoped, but a trail of sparks caught in his sleeve. As the oil-soaked cloth flared, he brought it up to his face—no, to the gag.

They all stared as cloth and beard blazed together. Then the gag fell. Luz sensed power gathering as the master's lips opened, but flames from his robe billowed upward, and what he drew in was not breath but fire. And what came out was no spell, but something too terrible even to be called a scream.

As he collapsed, Mother Mahaliel turned on Luz and Jo.

"Your high priest cannot withstand me! Can *you*?" She began to whirl, sparks flaring.

Deep within, Luz felt her spirit keening, but there was no time for horror. She drew breath, summoning the White Dragon, her spirit linking with Jo's. The Spear moved in a swift circle, leaving behind it a shimmer of white fire against which Mahaliel's fires beat in vain. The woman scarcely seemed to notice. Her exultant laughter echoed from the rocks as the canvas of the sunshade burst into flame.

As William stumbled toward them, Jo grabbed him and pushed him down the hill. Luz tried to reach Master Granite. For a moment she saw his face through the billowing flames. *"I have not failed!"* His mind touched hers. *"You are my victory!"* Then his eyes closed and he was hidden by the fire. Jo grabbed Luz's hand, jerking her out from under the sunshade as the burning canvas fell.

And still Mahaliel was laughing, or was that the crackle of the flames? As they stumbled down the hill, Luz looked back. Across the slope wavered pillars of fire that had once been living women and men. Mahaliel herself had become a lantern, consumed from within. Eyes, mouth were all fire, and then even the shape of her body was lost in light.

Tadeo Marsh saw the smoke first, and then the fire. He forced his body over the rim of the hill and hung there, panting, as he tried to make out what was happening below. The canyon lay like a stage before him. Through the heat-shimmer, he could see Mother Mahaliel facing Red and the Westrian witch with whom he had run away. Bett and the other women had drawn off to one side.

It had taken him all night to get here, hiding in the ditch or among rocks when Westrian patrols came by, and most of the morning to make his way to this spot where he could see without being seen. He knew already that he was too late to get Sarina away. The Westrians had all escapes blocked by now. But if he could not rescue her, he could share her fate—once he knew what that fate was to be.

The noon sun beat down and he shaded his eyes, trying to make her out among the others. He saw them pass the clay jugs. Liquid gleamed in the sunlight as Bett poured.

"Live in the Light!" Her words floated up to him. And now he could see Sarina behind her, joining in the reply. Then Bett started toward the bonfire and he understood what was happening at last.

"Mahaliel, you bitch, you've betrayed them—you'll burn in hell." But words could not express what he was feeling now. The drop below him was sheer. He could not get down there in time. Mother Mahaliel was forgotten. His gaze fixed on the women as one after another, they set themselves afire.

"Sarina, *no!*" His cry was lost in the screaming. He could only cry out in wordless denial as she took the torch, and her beautiful dusky body became a form of flame.

That brightness seared his vision. The after-image was stark black, the rock around him a confusion of grays. With Sarina, all color, all love, all joy, had gone from his world.

Groaning, Tadeo scrambled backward and stumbled down the hill. He could not escape his grief, but he could escape from Westria, and when he had done so, he would find a way to make this land weep as he wept now.

❖ 24 ❖

MIDSUMMER

That June, Laurelynn was a city of roses. Red roses and yellow bloomed in the gardens. White roses lay like drifts of snow upon the ruddy brick of the walls and their scent hung heavy on the warm afternoon air. For Julian, to sit by the lake on such an afternoon was like living in a dream. Or perhaps it was the past three years that were the nightmare, from which they had only now awakened.

Frederic sat beside him with a sheaf of papers, the red seneschal's robe he had resumed as brilliant as the flowers. That, too, might have been a scene from any summer during the twenty-five years before the Suns came. But from time to time the healing wound across Julian's belly still twinged. If the war with the Suns had been a dream, he would have to find some other explanation for that livid scar.

"My brother reports that the city is now secure, and

everyone in the Sun garrison accounted for. He had most of them under guard before you even returned to Laurelynn, of course, but a few were hiding out in the city."

"Hiding with our people?" asked the king.

"Some of them," answered Frederic. "I know what you fear, Julian, but most of the time they do not seem to have taken refuge with converts. They are Sun soldiers who fell in love with local girls and are eager to embrace the ways of Westria."

"So they say—"

Frederic shrugged. "Time will tell, but I hope they are sincere. They can set an example. You do wish to integrate our prisoners into Westria, don't you, or was that embassy that cost Master Granite his life only a way to gain time?"

Julian held up his hand. "You strike shrewdly for a man who bears no sword!"

Frederic smiled, his fair hair silver-gilt in the sun. "I rested while you labored—I've had time to think about what would come after the war. Of course I cannot promise you accurate reports until we have heard from all the provinces and cleaned out any last resistance."

"Carola has dealt quite . . . vigorously . . . with the garrison in Sanjos, I hear," said Julian. In fact, there had been a bloodbath, as if the new lady of the province had tried to wash away her father's blood with that of his enemies.

From Frederic's expression, he had heard it too. "The land needs healing, Julian. Not just Las Costas—everywhere. This war has shaken all our certainties. . . ."

"Did you fear we could not win?"

"I will admit to a few nightmares in which I was the chief entertainment at one of Mother Mahaliel's autos-da-fé." Frederic's lips twitched. "It sounds like a painful way to die."

"Oh, I hope so!" said Julian, thinking of Mother Mahaliel's end. Jeanne said all that was left of her had been ashes, and even those had been blown away by the wind. They still did not know what had happened to the Iron General. "I used to think that Caolin was the epitome of evil, but in his own way he loved Westria. At least *he* never betrayed his followers."

"Was it a betrayal? From what Luz has told me, the woman was quite sincere. She sacrificed all to the service of her god."

"Then *He* is evil!" snapped the king.

"Is light evil? Is fire? Is the sun?" Frederic gestured upward. "Mother Mahaliel forgot that we must balance light and shadow. We must all become whole again." His measuring gaze returned to the king.

"If you are wondering whether I will be able to carry out the Midsummer ritual next week on the Red Mountain, the answer is yes," Julian said briskly, ignoring the ache in his middle.

His city bore scars as well. The roses on the walls could not entirely hide the spots where Sun slogans had been scoured away. The sounds of hammer and saw resounded above the peaceful hum of the bees. They had rebuilt and restored Laurelynn after Caolin's War, and they would do it again. He only wished that he could recover as quickly as he had when he was twenty years old.

"Then I will leave you," said Frederic, gathering his papers back into their folder. "I see that Johan is here—"

Julian winced as he tried to turn and see. Both he and his land would heal. But they would never be the same. One of the things that had changed, he thought as he glimpsed red hair among the roses, was his relationship with his son. Whether it had changed for the better remained to be seen. If he was to work with Johan as heir of Westria, they would have to get beyond the careful conversations of the sickroom.

He heard Frederic's cheerful greeting as he and Johan met on the path, and the murmur of his son's reply. Then Jo emerged from among the roses, for once without Luz, walking like a young god crowned with fire. For William and Jeanne, the war had been a tempering. Julian knew their abilities. But he did not yet know what the past three years had made of Jo.

Jo stopped as he saw his father waiting for him. "How are you, sir?"

"Quite well. I was just thinking how peaceful it is here,

as if the Suns had never come. Then I am reminded—" He indicated his belly. "We can't go back. We can only go on."

Jo's posture changed, like a man preparing to face an opponent in the ring—which was, apparently, one of the things he had done on his travels. Julian found it hard to imagine.

"Mother said you wanted to talk to me about being your heir," the boy said in a rush. "Before you decide . . . there are things you need to know."

The king lifted an eyebrow. This was not a swordsman's attack, but a berserker's desperation.

"You know I was taken by slavers," Jo hurried on.

"That's something else that needs to be dealt with," growled Julian. If he had taken Frederic's advice three years ago and launched an attack on Arena, they would all have been spared much pain. But the Suns would still have come, and without Jo's amazing intervention, they might have won.

"Yes, the syndics of Arena feared Westrian retaliation if it was known they had taken me," Jo replied with a feral grin. "So they sold me."

"To Marvel's Circus," the king said helpfully.

Jo stiffened. "That was . . . after. My first price was far too high, but in the end they practically paid Garr to take me away." He turned nervously, reaching out as if to pluck one of the roses and blinking when he felt the thorns. "I was just like this rose," he whispered, "pretty, but treacherous. They sold me for a bedslave, to a . . . man." He took a breath, and for a moment his father wondered if he would go on. Then the words came—"He tied me up and began to do things. . . . I couldn't endure it. I went berserk and killed him." He stopped, breathing hard.

Julian realized that he had been silent for too long when he looked up and saw the despair in his son's eyes.

"Forgive me," he said with difficulty. "I was lost in my own memories. You see, when Caolin used me so . . . I gave in."

Astonishment wiped all other expression from Jo's face. "I knew you had been tortured, but not—"

"It was not something I cared to advertise," Julian said dryly. "Rana knows. . . . So you see, I am the last man to judge you. You survived."

"My body survived," Jo said bitterly. "I said I went berserk—it wasn't just a mindless rage. It was as if I'd been replaced by another being that had always lived inside me. I called it the Dragon, and Garr tamed it. It was all right when the beast only came out in the arena. I didn't have to see the men I killed. But you see, it was all too easy for me to escape that way, and Mother Mahaliel learned how to wake the Dragon and sent him into battle against you at Condor's Rest." Once more his face stiffened in despair.

"You were the warrior in red," Julian said slowly. "Now I understand what was so strange about him. But that was not done by your will, nor will anyone who knows the truth blame you."

Jo sighed. "*I* blame me. When I came to, I tried to fall on my sword. When they wouldn't let me die, I became . . . someone else . . . several someones, depending on the need. 'Jo' was nowhere. There was only the Mother's jester."

Julian remembered reports of the strange young man who had been part of Mother Mahaliel's entourage in Laurelynn. Suddenly he sat upright, eyes narrowing.

"Would one of those 'selves' know anything about some messages that came wrapped around an arrow and signed with a star?"

For the first time, Jo grinned. "You got them? Then I am somewhat redeemed. The others had to let me out to shoot—none of them was that good at archery, but the messages were penned by King Jehan. He started talking to me at the Sacred Wood, at my initiation," Jo added in response to his father's stare. "I am sorry you never had a chance to know him," he added hesitantly. "He was a good man."

Julian blinked, trying to sort the complexities of cross-generational relationships, then gave up with a sigh. He saw that Jo's stiff stance had eased.

"Luz called me back to myself," the boy went on, "but it was Awahna that fixed me—or started the process, anyhow.

You can only be your true self there. When people whisper behind my back, I feel the temptation to escape into one of those other selves. I will strive to be whole, but I cannot be sure I'll succeed. That is what you must know."

Now at last Jo sat down on the other bench, head bowed as if he waited for sentencing.

"You survived," said Julian. "In an intolerable situation, you found an escape. You were like a flame that divides around the blade."

"You would not have done so," said Jo.

"No . . . ," sighed Julian. "I am the stone, not the flame. Afterward, I became stone indeed, for a time, and was nearly shattered by what I could not endure." He took a deep breath. "I know I have not been the father you needed, and I cannot even promise to do better. You have to understand that for a king, the land is like a part of your soul, and her need comes first," he added unhappily.

"Oh, I know that," said his son with surprising vigor. "I knew it when I was carried outside Westria's borders and the moment when I returned. There were voices in the soil, in the wind—and in the water, that called to me. That was the second time I tried to kill myself. But Sea-Mother cast me back again."

Julian felt a chill, hearing his son speak about suicide so calmly. He strove for equal control in his reply.

"Will there be a third time?"

"I have not died as many times as you did when you won the Jewels," Jo's lips quirked. "But it is like death to make the passage into Awahna."

"That's another thing I haven't done," Julian said softly.

"You are always yourself—you don't need to." Jo laughed.

Julian shrugged, not sure that was a compliment. "I will tell you this much—if Westria has claimed you, then the choice of my heir belongs neither to me nor to the Council of Westria. Or at least that's what I said when they were deciding whether or not to choose *me*," he added ironically. "If they had not made me king, I would still have been bound to serve the land and the other kindreds that dwell here."

"That's more or less what the Lady told me. I only hope I will not fail her, or you. . . ." Jo's gaze softened, and by the light in his eyes the king knew what he was remembering.

"All that either of us can do is to try." The king reached out, and after a moment of hesitation Jo gripped his hand.

"Jo has been gone so long," said Luz. "What is the king saying to him? He was so anxious about this meeting."

Rana looked up from the bowl into which she was grinding comfrey root. Through the vines that hung over the window, the sunlight cast a dappling of gold across workbench and floor.

"Hand me that jar on the shelf, dear," she said, seeking time to frame a reply. She had brought Luz to the stillroom to keep her occupied while Jo was talking to his father, but she needed the distraction as much as the girl.

"Julian will not eat him," she said tartly. "It's wonderful how cooperative a man who knows he is helpless can be."

"But the king is healing well, isn't he?" Luz asked quickly. "His color is good. I don't feel any—" She broke off, her golden skin warming to a dusky rose.

"Is reading people's energy something they taught you to do at the College of the Wise?" asked the queen.

"Not without permission," Luz said in a low voice. "I would not have done it, but Jo was so anxious. . . ."

And the two of you might as well be joined at the hip . . . , thought Rana, though she took care to keep the thought shielded. She had always been fond of Luz, but she was not yet accustomed to the way in which her son had become bound to the girl. She and Julian had shared a great deal, but except at moments when they were linked in ritual, there had always been a little healthy distance between them.

She wondered if the connection between Jo and Luz would last. This was clearly not the moment to question it, but perhaps she could use it. She sifted the chunks of comfrey through a sieve and tipped those that remained back into the mortar.

"But you are very nearly one of the family," said the queen, taking up the pestle and beginning to grind again. The Suns who had occupied the palace must have had an herbalist among them, for she had found her stillroom stripped nearly bare. It would take some hard work to stock her shelves once more.

"What do you mean?"

"Why, you and Jo—you plan to marry, do you not?"

"We have not spoken of it." If the girl's face had been rosy before, it was flaming now.

"But you do love him?" Rana probed. Abruptly, she remembered a day thirty years ago, when Lady Rosemary had stood where she stood now, advising a much younger Rana on how to deal with Julian. Had she seemed as naïve as this girl did now?

Luz straightened, pulling dignity around her as the flush faded.

"I have always loved him," she said simply. "And since Awahna, I think we have shared a soul. In the Sacred Valley we were nearly spirits ourselves. I know I have a body now, but Jo . . . was wounded by the slavers in ways we cannot see." She sought for words. "I think that physical love is connected in his mind with killing. If that conflict was forced upon him he might . . . retreat . . . once more."

"Do you mean he would run away?" Rana set down the pestle.

"Not in body. But he's learned to defend his spirit by letting another self come in."

Rana groped for a chair and sat down. "So that's it," she whispered, remembering how Jo had guarded himself from her maternal probings.

"Did he ever do anything like that when he was a child?"

"No!" exclaimed Rana, and then, "I don't know. There were so many times when the king and I had to leave him while we traveled." She paused, trying to remember.

"There was only one occasion that I can think of . . . ," she said slowly. "Phoenix was three, and when I came back to Laurelynn, I found that he had stopped talking and was acting like a much younger child. But it passed, and he was all right again. Or so I thought. I don't even remember who was taking care of him." She ran her fingers through her hair distractedly. *However unwittingly,* she thought, *I failed him.*

When the Lady of Heronhall told her the story about the queen who lost her son, Rana had understood her sorrow. But what would have happened if her son had been ransomed from Hell and returned? Rana had thought that if only she could have Jo back, everything would be as it had been before; but Julian, who approached this resurrected child of theirs with painful trepidation, might be wiser than she.

"Jo is trying so hard to be the person he learned he was in Awahna," Luz said softly. "I don't want to threaten that."

"I understand," said the queen. "But everyone assumes that you two are lovers already."

"I know," Luz said ruefully. "When we were alone together on the trail it was so easy. We had left Awahna, but we were not yet part of the human world. My father says that it is always hard to readjust when one returns from the Sacred Valley, but Jo has been away from himself as well."

Rana nodded. "There's no need to decide anything right now. Next week is the Midsummer festival. Perhaps by then we will see a way—"

⁂

Luz looked down from the top of the Red Mountain, wondering at the way that had brought her here, to the center of Westria, to stand once more with everyone she loved. From here she could see all the roads—she had trod more of them than she ever expected, and Jo had gone even farther. This morning's journey seemed a mere step in comparison.

As the sun sank, the mist-veiled slopes of the Lady Mountain across the bay were deepening to a luminous blue. She could feel the line of energy that connected the two mountains as other leys linked them to the rest of the land. Was she still linked to the girl who had been initiated there? She remembered vividly the moment she had realized that she loved Jo—and decided to let him go. Now, she did not need to look to know that he was behind her, his presence as palpable as the scent of rosemary in the wreath she wore. Westria had changed as much as she and Jo. Now they must all learn to live together once more.

Her brother Lenart, his hair bleached and his skin darkened by months in the field, touched her elbow. "Time to stop looking at the scenery, little one. The ritual is about to begin."

The faint anxiety that had always marred his expression was gone. Instinctively she extended other senses to touch *his* spirit, interested to find a connection between him and another man who stood with her father near the king and queen.

"Is that Marcos? He looks much better than he did last summer." As Lenart's brown skin reddened, she laughed suddenly. "You're in love! How wonderful! Why did no one tell me?"

"We haven't announced it," muttered Lenart. "Well, we've been too busy—and then I thought people might say we were being disloyal to Lord Robert."

When her brother brought his lover to a family party like this one, he hardly needed to make a proclamation, she thought sardonically, but forbore to say so.

"Robert would *want* Marcos to be happy!" she said aloud, remembering that big handsome man who had been like an uncle to them all. "And I can see that he is, so why should anyone care?"

"You're so wise, little sister—" Lenart laughed. "Better get your own affairs into order before you start counseling me."

Silenced, she turned, and found Jo already coming toward her. With an ironic grin, her brother released her and they followed the others up the short slope to the peak where the stacked logs for the Midsummer bonfire were waiting beside Caolin's mound.

"My friends—no, I will call you all my family," the king corrected as they formed a circle. "We are gathered here on this holy mountain, where I often feared we would never stand together again. We have suffered great loss—" Julian's dark gaze moved to Marcos. "But there is much for which we may be thankful." His gaze flickered toward Jo. "It is our task now to go forward, to heal the land." As he paused, the queen took his hand.

"Much has been lost; many ties have been broken," she echoed him. "We must create new ones. Master Frederic, our son and your daughter have shared many dangers—will you and your lady consent to a betrothal between them?"

Luz did not have a chance to see how her father reacted. Shock reverberated between her mind and Jo's, but his fingers were tightening convulsively on hers.

"Did you know your mother was planning this?"

"You spent so much time with her—didn't you?"

They seemed to be the only ones who were surprised. Grins were flashing all around them. The only person who looked a little anxious was the queen. And well she might, thought Luz, springing a betrothal on them this way.

"With all my heart," said Frederic, "if it is both their wills."

At least *her* parent was asking, thought Luz.

"Is it your will?" She turned to Jo.

"Yes," Jo said aloud, "but you cannot be a Mistress of the College if you marry me." His anxious gaze flicked to Frederic and back again.

Tremors were running through his body. Luz looked at him in alarm. In his aura she sensed a flicker of scarlet wings, then realized that white wings were shining in her own. Some of the others blinked as if they were seeing them too.

"Was *that* what was concerning you?" Suddenly Luz laughed. To find full healing might not be easy, but here, at the center of their world, the truth was clear. "We have already been to Awahna," she continued. "With you, I am something more." From around the circle the laughter of the others echoed her own.

"It looks to me as if the binding has taken place already," said Rosemary, smiling at Lord Eric.

"My mother has earned the right to make predictions about marriage, having put up with my father for so long!" Frederic waited for a second gust of laughter to pass. "But you, child, have to make a choice which is like my own, so I will tell you that it is the bond itself, not its form, that will hold you. The Guardians have already blessed you. I can only do the same."

Luz looked from him to the king and queen. They were smiling, their life-lights linked in a way that had not been true when she saw them outside the gate to the Initiation Grounds almost three years before. There was something to be learned from that relationship as well.

"So that's settled!" said her grandfather. "And I see that the sun is setting. Can we get on with the ceremony?"

Frederic laughed and took his place on the eastern side of the circle.

"On this day we honor the triumph of the sun," he said when all had settled again, "as we celebrate our triumph over the *Suns*—" There was a murmur of bitter laughter. "But the power of the sun, like all else, waxes and wanes. In the morning we hail the Divine Child, glowing with promise. At noon the sun is a Sovereign, soaring in splendor. But at sunset he passes into darkness to become the Hidden Light. And so it is with the year. Tomorrow will be a little shorter, and so it shall go until Midwinter, when from the heart of the cold the sun will be reborn. Let us not forget this lesson. Every power must wax and wane, lest one upset the balance that maintains the world."

Denying that truth had been Mother Mahaliel's mistake, thought Luz. For the first time, she could think of the woman who had led the Suns against them with pity rather than fascination or fear.

The sun slipped behind the Lady Mountain and cool shadows lengthened across the land. Her father opened the lantern they had brought from Laurelynn, where a lamp lit from the perpetual flame in the city shrine flickered determinedly. Throughout the months of occupation, Master Martin had kept it going, even when he feared that he himself would burn.

Frederic transferred the flame to a torch and carried it to the bonfire.

"Thus do we reclaim the holy fire! Receive our offerings!"

The kindling in the center caught, and then, of a sudden, the whole pyre was roaring. One by one, those standing around it took off their wreaths and cast them into the flames.

As the perfumes of burning bay and rosemary mingled with the crisp scents of oak and juniper, cedar and applewood and pine, Luz felt her awareness expand. She could feel the spirits of her family, their faces aglow in the light of the fire. But she had a sense that there were others in the circle, that her physical eyes could not see. Had Robert come to bless Marcos and Lenart? It seemed to her that she could feel the presence of King Jehan, no longer replacing that of Jo, but alongside him. She made a mental bow in that direction, knowing that without his counsel she and Jo would not have escaped from Mother Mahaliel.

She turned, aware of a very different energy, acute and glowing, with a kind of focus that reminded her of her own. Julian was kneeling beside Caolin's mound, drawing a wooden box from beneath one of the stones.

"I forgot," said Jo. "You've never been on the Red Mountain for this festival. This is where the king keeps the Four Jewels."

"So, grandfather—," thought Luz. *"You ended up with them after all."* And it seemed to her that from the mound a flicker of amusement answered her.

As the box was opened, she recognized the powers she had met in Awahna, focused in the Jewels. Was it the firelight that woke them to splendor or the touch of their master? Suddenly the mountaintop shimmered with all the colors of the world. From another box, the king took a belt onto which he slid the Earthstone. The Sea Star went onto a cord of silver, which Julian handed to his queen.

But instead of putting on the Jewels, the king and queen were coming toward Jo and Luz. In one hand Julian held the forest-green and russet glow of the Earthstone. In the other glittered something that looked like a fallen star. The queen's hands blazed with water and fire.

"Westria has claimed you both," he said softly. "The Guardians have blessed you. Help us to bless Westria." He held out the Wind Crystal to Luz.

Should she be feeling terror, she wondered, amazement, or simple gratitude that at least she had gotten as far as the element of Air at the College of the Wise? Then she slipped the chain from which the Jewel was suspended over her head, and heard the music of Awahna once more.

Rana was offering a coronet to Jo. The great opal in its center coruscated with red and green fire.

"The Phoenix has risen from the flames. Johan of Westria, carry the Fire!"

How fearfully the Guardians have forged us, thought Luz as she saw the apprehension in Jo's face transmute to ecstasy. Once more he was the eternal soul she had known in Awahna, and as he gazed at her, she knew herself the same. She looked at Julian and Rana and for the first time understood who they really were.

As they moved to their positions at the cardinal points of the circle, Luz looked westward, where the sun was only a fading memory. The coastal hills had become a black frame for the horizon, from which the heavens shaded from pale turquoise to a luminous sapphire sown with stars. From the bonfire, sparks swirled to add new constellations to those that were appearing above.

The silhouette of the Lady Mountain showed sharp and elegant against that sky. Light blazed suddenly from its summit. On the great half-dome above Awahna a fire would be burning as well. To the south and north, other peaks were blossoming with flame, from the Father of Mountains to the borders of Elaya, proclaiming the return of Westria's rightful lords.

King and queen, prince and princess, they balanced each other around the fire. As one, they lifted their hands, and as Earth and Water, Air and Fire found their equilibrium, their power rayed out along the pathways marked by those mortal flames and laid a blessing of peace upon the land.

THE COVENANT OF WESTRIA

I affirm
that I and all else that lives are children of the same
Mother,
created equal in value by the Maker of All Things.
Therefore, from this day forward I will
take no life without gratitude or without need.

———

I will uphold
the right of the other kindreds to life
and to the means of life,
if need be at the expense of my own.
So was Westria established, and so shall it endure.

———

I call to witness this oath
all Powers of Earth and Water, Air and Fire;
all that grows from the earth, all that lives within its
waters,
all creatures that go upon its surface,
all that ride the air.

———

And if I fail in this,
may the earth give way beneath me,
the air depart from my lungs,
food and water refuse to nourish me,
and may my spirit wander forever without a home.

PEOPLE AND PLACES

People in the Story

Brackets designate characters who are dead before the story begins. Capital letters denote major characters.

WESTRIANS

Alaric of the Hold   son and heir of Elinor of the Corona

Alexander of House Battle   lord commander of the province of Las Costas

Anders Thorgeirsson   jarl of the Danehold

Ardra of Las Palisadas   commander of the fleet; daughter of Aisha of Elaya and Caolin; consort of Frederic; mother of Lenart, Bera, and Luz

(Master) Badger   an instructor at the College of the Wise

(Mistress) Bera of Haven   older daughter of Frederic and Ardra, priestess

[Brian of Las Costas   lord commander killed at Battle of the Dragon Waste]

[Caolin   seneschal of Westria, sorcerer, father of Ardra]

Carola of Sanjos   heir to the province of Las Costas

Cordelia   a deputy seneschal

Edwin of Registhorpe   landholder and captain of Julian's guard, younger brother of Queen Rana (milk-name was Cub)

Elen of Rivered   wife of Philip of the Ramparts

Elinor of the Hold   lady commander of the province of the Corona, cousin to Julian

ERIC of the Horn   lord commander of the province of Seagate

(Master) FARIN Piper   a bard on walkabout

[Farin Silverhair   Master harper, uncle to Julian]

[Faris of Hawkrest Hold   queen of Westria, mother of Julian]

FREDERIC of Haven   Master of the Moonpath, seneschal of Westria

(Master) Granite   head of the College of the Wise

(Mistress) Iris   an instructor at the College of the Wise

Jeanne of Hightower   daughter of Philip of the Ramparts

[Jehan Starbairn   king of Westria, father of Julian]

Jessica Starbairn   dowager lady of the Ramparts, aunt of Julian

Joffrey   a student at the College of the Wise from Las Costas

JOHAN Starbairn ("Jo")   prince of Westria

JULIAN Starbairn   king of Westria

[Julian the Great   first Master of the Jewels and king of Westria]

[(Master of the) Junipers   mentor of King Julian]

Kamil   a student at the College of the Wise from near Santibar

Khelys of Midvale (and his son Turtle)   a landholder from Seagate

(Master) Kieran   head of the Goldsmiths' Guild, representative of the Free Cities to the Estates of Westria

(Mistress) Larissa   a priestess

LENART of Haven   son of Frederic, deputy seneschal

Loren Farwalker   a holder from the Ramparts, formerly in Julian's guard

Lucas Buzzardmoon   a scout and investigator of crimes against the Covenant

LUZ of Haven   second daughter of Frederic and Ardra

Marcos de Vega   Robert's lover

(Master) Martin   high priest of the community at Laurelynn

(Mistress) Melissa   herbmistress at the College of the Wise

Orm of Haven   second son of Eric and heir to Seagate

Osleif of Greyhaven   Julian's trumpeter and squire

Philip of Hightower   lord commander of the Ramparts, cousin to Julian

Phoenix   milk-name of Johan

Radha   Luz's friend at the College

RANA of Registhorpe   queen of Westria

Ragnhild   wife of Anders and new jarl of the Danehold

Red/ or the Red Dragon   Johan's name among the Children of the Sun

ROBERT of Hightower   younger brother of Philip, Julian's cousin, Champion of Westria

ROSEMARY of the Hold   lady of Seagate, wife of Eric, mother of Frederic, grandmother of Luz

[Sandremun of the Hold   commander of the Corona, Elinor's father]

Sarina of Oakhill   a Westrian girl taken captive by the Suns

Sombra   milk-name of Luz

Thorolf Andersson   son of the jarl of the Danehold

Veɾara a student at the College of the Wise from the Danehold

William oɾ Hightower son and heir of Philip of the Ramparts

OUTLANDERS

Alonᖙro a slave-trader of Arena

Alyce queen of Normontaine

(Commanᖙer) Anaya division leader in the Sun army

Bartolomé High King of Aztlan

Bett headwoman in Mother Mahaliel's household

Chigaio anᖙ Chiquita horse trainers in Master Marvel's circus

Cho-cho a maid in Mother Mahaliel's household

Ezequial a juggler in Master Marvel's circus

Garr armsmaster and trainer of gladiators for Master Marvel's circus

(Commanᖙer) Hallam commander of a square

Iᖙomeneo Yans Sun commander in charge of Los Leones

Prince Harun ruler of Elaya

MOTHER MAHALIEL leader of the Children of the Sun

Liza anᖙ Bon clowns in Master Marvel's circus

Loris Steɾ a senior clan-father of the Suns

Manoɾuerte a former gladiator now scouting for the Suns

Manuelo a convert from Aztlan, troop leader

"Master" Marvel owner of the circus

Milagra ᖙe Mirabal daughter of the Alcalde of Ogaponge

Nathaniel Akenson a Sun scout

Prince Roderi   ruler of Arena

Supervisor Lake   Jo's first master

TADEO MARSH ("the Iron General")   commander of
the armies of the Children of the Sun

Tam   animal trainer in Master Marvel's circus

Vincent Chiel   a senior clan-father of the Suns

PLACES IN THE STORY

Acoma   Acoma Pueblo, New Mexico

Amata River   Cosumnes River, California

Arena   trade center in the Barren Lands near the border
of Westria (Reno)

Awahna   home of the Guardians of Westria
(approximately Yosemite but not entirely in our
world)

Awhai   sacred valley on the borders of Elaya (Ohai),
Southern California

Awishi   Zuñi Pueblo, New Mexico

Aztlan   southwest Arizona, southern Colorado, and most
of New Mexico

The Barren Lands   Nevada, eastern Oregon, and
eastern Washington

Bongarde   capital of Seagate (Santa Rosa, California)

Cibola   seat of the high king of Aztlan, near
Albuquerque, New Mexico

City of the Firebird   Phoenix, Arizona

The Corona   northern province of Westria

Cottonwood   a town on the Platte River near the site of
Lincoln, Nebraska

The Danehold   Solvang, California

The Darkwater   river flowing up the Great Valley
(San Joaquin River, California)

Deseret   The Mormon theocracy—Utah

Dínétah   Navajo territory, the Southwest

The Dorada   river coming down from the Snowy Mountains (Sacramento River, California)

Dorada Buttes   Sutter Buttes, west of Marysville, California

The Eagle   Feather River, California

Dragon Waste   southern part of the San Joaquin Valley, California

Dragon's Tail   the Grapevine and pass to Southern California

Dragon Mountains   the Tehachapis, mountains between northern and southern California

Elaya   confederation to the south of Westria

Elder   Yuba City/Marysville, California

Elkhorn   Moss Landing, California

Empire of the Sun   southeastern North America

Father of Mountains   Mount Shasta, California

Flags' territory   Flagstaff, Arizona

Frog River   Mokolumne River, California

Gateway   near Hills Ferry, California

Gold River   Yuba River, California

Great Bay   gateway to Westria (San Francisco Bay, California)

Great River   Rio Grande

Great Valley   valley in center of Westria (San Joaquin Valley, California)

Hightower   Lord Philip's fortress above Rivered

Indé territories   Apache lands, Arizona

Iron Kingdom   Midwest/Great Lakes area of North America

Lady Mountain   sacred mountain at southern end of Seagate (Mt. Tamalpais, California)

Las Costas   southwestern province of Westria

Laurelynn   capital of Westria at the confluence of the
   Dorada and the Darkwater

Madona   San Luis Obispo, California

Mercy River   Merced River, California

Mother of Fire   Mount Lassen, California

Normontaine   kingdom to the north of Westria
   (Oregon and western Washington)

Ogaponge Adentro   border town of Aztlan, on the site
   of Santa Fé, New Mexico

Painted River   Colorado River

Pueblo of the Lake   Laguna Pueblo, New Mexico

Ramparts   eastern province of Westria

Red Mountain   Mount Diablo, California

Registhorpe   childhood home of Rana in Seagate

Rivered   principal city of the Ramparts, near the site of
   Sacramento, California

Salt River   Salinas, California

Sanjos   capital of Las Costas (San Jose, California)

Seagate   northwestern province of Westria

Seahold   fishing village and fortified manor in Seagate
   on the Great Bay (Sausalito, California)

The Sea of Grass   the Great Plains, from eastern New
   Mexico north to the Dakotas

The Silvershine   American River, California

Tamiston   a hamlet near Elder

Tewa territories   lands along the northern Rio Grande,
   New Mexico

Tohono O'odham territories   Papago lands, Arizona

Wildwater   Stanislaus River, California

Yavapai territories   mountains south of Flagstaff,
   Arizona

AFTERWORD

I was still writing the first chronicles of Westria when the idea for this book came to me. We had just heard how Jim Jones fed poisoned Kool-Aid to his followers in Guyana, and it seemed to me that for a spiritual leader to thus betray those who trusted him was far more evil than Caolin's love/hate relationship with Westria. At the same time, Clint Bigglestone asked me what might happen if invaders from outside attacked the golden land, and we began to plan the campaign. If the gap between the publication of *The Jewel of Fire* and the appearance of *The Golden Hills of Westria* has been shorter than the years between Caolin's War and the arrival of the Suns, it has still been long enough for many things to change.

We have now seen far too much of the suffering that results when fanatics of any religion try to impose their worldview on the world. Clint is gone, like my brother-in-law Paul Edwin Zimmer, who used to critique all my battle scenes. We still miss them. My first fans, like Julian, now reach for their reading glasses when a new book comes to hand. My son Ian, who was a child when I first began writing about Westria, now has children of his own. I have made many new friends and met the Wanderer on my own spiritual journey. One thing that has not changed is my editor, David Hartwell, who bought the first story about Westria, and who twenty years later believed me when I said that more tales remain to be told.

I would like to thank him, as I do all the friends who have enthusiastically supported me through the writing of this book. My gratitude goes especially to Jennifer Tifft and Loren Davidson, Companions of Westria since the beginning, to Lori Buschbaum and Buzz Nelson for advising me on military matters, and to those who shared their insights on multiple personality disorder. Thanks also to Leigh Ann Hussey for permission to use stanzas from her songs "Black Swan Rising," in Chapter 7, and the first verse of "To the West," in Chapter 11.

And then there's Lorrie Wood, who never ceased to cheer me on. She persuaded me that we really could drive all the way to Albuquerque so that I could do more than imagine Jo's journey, and to the Sutter Buttes and Mount Lassen and the top of Mount Shasta as well; let me take pictures of all these places with her digital camera; and created a Web site for Westria where, among other things, I can share them.

Look it up at www.westria.org and, once more, be "welcome to Westria!"

Feast of the First Flowers, 2005